Love Story Next Door!

REBECCA WINTERS
BARBARA WALLACE
SORAYA LANE

First Published in Great Britain 2016
By Mills & Boon, an imprint of HarperCollins*Publishers*
1 London Bridge Street, London, SE1 9GF

LOVE STORY NEXT DOOR! © 2016 Harlequin Books S. A.

Cinderella On His Doorstep, Mr Right, Next Door! and *Soldier On H*
Doorstep were first published in Great Britain by Harlequin (UK) Limite

Cinderella On His Doorstep © 2009 Rebecca Winters
Mr Right, Next Door! © 2012 Barbara Wallace
Soldier On Her Doorstep © 2011 Soraya Lane

ISBN: 978-0-263-92066-6

05-0516

Our policy is to use papers that are natural, renewable and recyclable
products and made from wood grown in sustainable forests. The loggi
manufacturing processes conform to the legal environmental regulatio
the country of origin.

Printed and bound in Spain
by CPI, Barcelona

CINDERELLA
ON HIS DOORSTEP

BY
REBECCA WINTERS

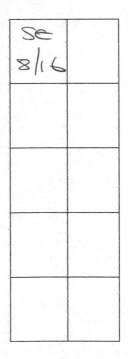

Rebecca Winters, whose family of four children has now swelled to include five beautiful grand-children, lives in Salt Lake City, Utah, in the land of the Rocky Mountains. With canyons and high Alpine meadows full of wildflowers, she never runs out of places to explore. They, plus her favourite vacation spots in Europe, often end up as backgrounds for her Mills & Boon Romance novels because writing is her passion, along with her family and church.

Rebecca loves to hear from her readers. If you wish to e-mail her, please visit her website at www.cleanromances.com.

To my son, Bill, whom I often call Guillaume, because he speaks French too and loved France and the vineyards as much as I did when we traveled there. I called upon him for some of the research for this book. Once again we had a marvelous time discussing one of France's greatest contributions to the world.

CHAPTER ONE

Sanur, Bali—June 2

"Martan?"

Through the shower of a light rain Alex Martin heard his name being called from clear down the street. He paused in the front doorway with his suitcases. The houseboy whose now-deceased mother had been hired by the Forsten Project years earlier to help clean the employees' houses, had attached himself to Alex. Without fail, he always called him by his last name, giving it a French pronunciation.

"Hey, Sapto—I didn't think I was going to see you again." He'd been waiting for the taxi that would drive him to the Sanur airport in Bali.

Before the accident that had killed William Martin, Alex's Australian-born father, William would turn on Sapto. "Our last name is *Martin*! Mar-TIN!"

Sapto had stubbornly refused to comply. In recent months he'd lost his mother in a flood and knew Alex had lost his French mother to an aggressive infection several years back. He felt they had a bond. Alex had been rather touched by the boy's sensitivity and never tried to correct him.

"Take me home with you." His dark eyes begged him. "I've never been to France."

Home? That was a strange thing for Sapto to say. Though Alex held dual citizenship and was bilingual, he'd never been to France, either. As for Sapto, he guessed the fifteen-year-old hadn't ventured farther than twenty miles from Sanur in the whole of his life.

Alex's family had moved wherever his father's work as a mechanical engineer had taken him, first in Australia, then Africa and eventually Indonesia. With his parents gone, he didn't consider anywhere home. After flying to Australia to bury his father next to his mother, he was aware of an emptiness that prevented him from feeling an emotional tie to any given spot.

"I wish I could, Sapto, but I don't know what my future's going to be from here on out."

"But you said your French grandfather left you a house when he died! I could live there and clean it for you."

Alex grimaced. "He didn't leave it to *me*, Sapto." The letter meant for his mother had come two years too late. It had finally caught up to Alex through the Forsten company where he worked.

The attorney who'd written it stated there was going to be a probate hearing for the Fleury property on June 5 in Angers, France. This was the last notice. If Genevieve Fleury, the only living member of the Fleury family didn't appear for it, the property located in the Loire Valley would be turned over to the French government.

After making a phone call to the attorney and identifying himself, Alex was told the estate had been neglected for forty odd years and had dwindled into an old relic beyond salvaging. The back taxes owing were prohibitive.

Be that as it may, Alex had the impression the attorney was downplaying its value for a reason. A piece of ground was always worth something. In fact, the other man hadn't been able to cover his shock when he'd learned it was Genevieve's son on the phone.

Something wasn't right.

At this point the one thing driving Alex was the need to visit the land of his mother's roots and get to the bottom of this mystery before moving on. With no family ties, he was free to set up his own company in the States.

By now the taxi had arrived. Sapto put his bags in the trunk for him. "You will write me, yes?" His eyes glistened with tears.

"I promise to send you a postcard." He slipped a cash bonus into the teen's hand. "Thank you for all your help. I won't forget. Take care."

"Goodbye," Sapto called back, running after the taxi until it rounded the corner.

Hollywood, California—August 2

"Lunch break! Meet back here at one o'clock. No excuses!"

With the strongly accented edict that had been awaited for over an hour, the actors and cameramen left the set in a stampede.

When Jan Lofgren's thick brows met together, Dana knew her genius father was in one of his moods. Most of the time the Swedish-born director was so caught up in the story he wanted to bring to life, he lived in another realm and lost patience with human weaknesses and imperfections of any kind, especially hers.

As his only offspring, she'd been a big disappointment. He'd wanted a brilliant son. Instead he got a mediocre daughter, whose average brain and looks would never make her fortune. When she was a little girl her mother had cautioned her, "Your father loves you, honey, but don't expect him to be like anyone else. With that ego of his, he's a difficult man to love. You have to take him the way he is, or suffer."

The truth was as hard to take today as it was then. Dana had been through a lot of grief since her mother's death five years ago, but had learned to keep it to herself. Especially lately while he was having problems with his present girlfriend, Saskia Brusse, a Dutch model turned aspiring actress who had a bit part in this film. She wasn't much older than Dana's twenty-six years, the antithesis of Dana's mother in every conceivable way.

Privately his love life pained and embarrassed Dana, but she would never have dared articulate her disapproval. The same couldn't be said of her father who'd been outspoken about her disastrous relationship with Neal Robeson, a young actor looking for an in with the famous director, rather than with her. She'd thought she'd found love. Her mistake. It was a lesson in humiliation she would never forget.

Granted she'd made a gross error in getting involved with anyone in the film industry, but for her father to explode over that when he never seemed to notice anything else she did for him had caused a serious rift between them. It would never heal if left up to him, not when his anger was over the top. Once again she found herself making overtures to breach the gap.

"I brought you some coffee and sandwiches."

Deep in thought he took the thermos from her and began drinking the hot liquid. After another long swallow he said, "I've decided to shoot the rest of this film on location. Then it will ripen into something worthy."

Her father needed atmosphere, that ethereal ingredient the studio set couldn't provide. He flicked her a speculative glance. "Everything's in place except for the most important segment of the film in France. I'm not happy with any of our old options and want something different."

Dana already knew that and was ready for him. Since her mother's funeral, finding the right locations had become Dana's main job besides being chief cook and general dogsbody to her irascible father. She had to concede he paid her well, but the sense that she was invisible to him inflicted a deep wound.

If he wasn't directing one of his award-winning films, he had his nose in a biography. She was a voracious reader, too, and had inherited his love of firsthand accounts of World War II in the European theatre. Over the years they'd traipsed from the coast of England to the continent, pinpointing the exact locales to bring his creations to life.

"I've come across something on the Internet that sounds promising, but I'll need to check it out first. Give me a couple of days." If she could solve this problem for him, maybe he'd remember he had a daughter who yearned for a little attention from him. When she was his own flesh and blood, it hurt to be a mere cipher.

"That's too long."

"I can only get to Paris in so many hours, but once I'm there, I'll make up for lost time. Expect to hear from me tomorrow evening."

"What's your final destination?"

"I'd rather not say." She could hope that if she found what he was looking for, it would ease some of the tension between them, but she doubted it because her mother had been the only one who knew how to soothe him. Now that she was gone, no one seemed to exist for him, especially not his only child.

Around the next bend of the Layon river, Dana crossed a stone bridge where she saw the sign for Rablay-sur-Layon. So much greenery made her feel as if she'd driven into a Monet painting done at Giverny and had become a part of it. The string of Anjou region villages nestled against this tributary of the Loire gave off an aura of timeless enchantment.

How shocking it must have been for the French people to see soldiers and tanks silhouetted against gentle slopes of sunflowers as they gouged their way through this peaceful, fertile river valley. Dana cringed to imagine the desecration of a landscape dotted with renaissance chateaux and vineyards of incomparable beauty.

A loud hunger pain resounded in the rental car. Between her empty stomach and the long shadows cast by a setting sun, it occurred to her she ought to have eaten dinner at the last village she'd passed and waited till morning to reach her destination. However, she wasn't her father's daughter for nothing and tended to ignore sensible restrictions in order to gratify certain impulses for which she often paid a price.

No matter. She wanted to see how the light played against the Château de Belles Fleurs as it faded into darkness. One look and she'd be able to tell if this place had that unique ambience her father demanded.

Following the map she'd printed off, Dana made a right at the second turn from the bridge and passed through an open grillwork gate. From there she proceeded to the bifurcation where she took the right fork. Suddenly she came upon the estate, but unlike the carefully groomed grounds of any number of chateaux she'd glimpsed en route, this was so overgrown she was put in mind of a *bois sauvage*. Without directions she would never have known of its existence, let alone stumbled on to it by accident.

A little farther now and a *tour* of the chateau's bastion with its pointed cone appeared as if it were playing hide-and-seek behind the heavy foliage. Clumps of plum-colored wild roses had run rampant throughout, merging with a tall hedge that had long since grown wild and lost its shape.

She pulled to a stop and got out of the car, compelled to explore this ungovernable wood filled with wild daisies hidden in clumps of brush. Once she'd penetrated deeper on foot, she peeked through the tree leaves, but was unable to glimpse more.

A lonely feeling stole through her. No one had lived here for years. The estate had an untouched quality. Secrets. She knew in her bones these intangible elements would appeal to her father. If she'd combed the entire Loire valley, she couldn't have found a more perfect spot. He demanded perfection.

"Puis-je vous aider, madame?" came the sound of a deep male voice.

Startled out of her wits, Dana spun around. "Oh—" she cried at the sight of the bronzed, dark-haired man who looked to be in his midthirties. "I didn't know anyone was here." Her tourist French was of no help in this situation, but judging by his next remark, she needn't have worried.

"Nor did I." His English sounded as authentic as his French, but she couldn't place the pronunciation. His tone came off borderline aggressive.

His hands were thrust in the back pockets of well-worn, thigh-molding jeans. With those long, powerful legs and cut physique visible beneath a soil-stained white T-shirt, she estimated he was six-three and spent most of his time in the sun.

"The place looks deserted. Are you the caretaker here?"

He flashed her a faintly mocking smile. "In a manner of speaking. Are you lost?" She had the impression he was impatient to get on with what he'd been doing before she'd trespassed unannounced. Twilight was deepening into night, obscuring the details of his striking features.

"No. I planned to come here in the morning, but my curiosity wouldn't let me wait that long to get a sneak preview."

His dark-fringed eyes studied her with toe-curling intensity. For once she wished she were a tall, lovely brunette like her mom instead of your average Swedish blonde with generic blue eyes, her legacy from the Lofgren gene pool.

"If you're a Realtor for an American client, I'm afraid the property isn't for sale."

She frowned. "I'm here for a different reason. This *is* the Château de Belles Fleurs, isn't it?"

He gave an almost imperceptible nod, drawing her attention to his head of overly long dark hair with just enough curl she wagered her balding father would kill for.

"I'm anxious to meet the present owner, Monsieur Alexandre Fleury Martin."

After an odd silence he said, "You're speaking to him."

"Oh—I'm sorry. I didn't realize."

He folded his strong arms, making her acutely aware of his stunning male aura. "How do you know my name?"

"I came across a French link to your advertisement on the Internet."

At her explanation his hard-muscled body seemed to tauten. "Unfortunately too many tourists have seen it and decided to include a drop-in visit on their 'see-France-in-seven-days' itinerary."

Uh-oh— Her uninvited presence had touched a nerve. She lifted her oval chin a trifle. "Perhaps you should get a guard dog, or lock the outer gate with a sign that says, No Trespassing."

"Believe me, I'm considering both."

She bit her lip. "Look—this has started off all wrong and it's my fault." When he didn't respond she said, "My name is Dana Lofgren. If you're a movie buff, you may have seen *The Belgian Connection*, one of the films my father directed."

He rubbed his chest without seeming to be conscious of it. "I didn't know Jan Lofgren had a daughter."

Most people didn't except for those in the industry who worked with her father. Of course if Dana had been born with a face and body to die for…

She smiled, long since resigned to being forgettable. "Why would you? I help my father behind the scenes. The moment I saw your ad, I flew from Los Angeles to check out your estate. He's working on the film right now, but isn't happy with the French locations available."

Dana heard him take a deep breath. "You should have e-mailed me you were coming so I could have met you in Angers. It's too late to see anything tonight."

"I didn't expect to meet you until tomorrow," she said, aware she'd angered him without meaning to. "Forgive me for scouting around without your permission. I wanted to get a feel for the place in the fading light."

"And did you?" he fired. It was no idle question.

"Yes."

The silly tremor in her voice must have conveyed her emotion over the find because he said, "We'll talk about it over dinner. I haven't had mine yet. Where are you staying tonight?"

Considering her major faux pas for intruding on his privacy, she was surprised there was going to be one. "I made a reservation at the Hermitage in Chanzeaux."

"Good. That's not far from here. I'll change my clothes and follow you there in my car. Wait for me in yours and lock the doors."

The enigmatic owner accompanied her to the rental car. As he opened the door for her, their arms brushed, sending a surprising curl of warmth through her body.

"I won't be long."

She watched his tall, well-honed physique disappear around the end of the hedge. Obviously there was a path, but she hadn't noticed. There'd been too much to take in.

Now an unexpected human element had been added.

It troubled her that she was still reacting to the contact. She thought she'd already learned her lesson about men.

Alex signaled the waiter. "Bring us your best house wine, *s'il vous plait.*"

"*Oui, monsieur.*"

When he'd come up with his idea to rent out the estate to film studios in order to make a lot of money fast, he hadn't expected a Hollywood company featuring a legendary director like Jan Lofgren to take an interest this soon, if ever.

He'd only been advertising the château for six weeks. Not every film company wanted a place this run-down. To make it habitable, he'd had new tubs, showers, toilets and sinks installed in both the bathroom off the second floor vestibule and behind the kitchen.

Alex needed close access to the outside for himself and any workmen he hired, not to mention the film crews and actors. The ancient plumbing in both bathrooms had to be pulled out. He'd spent several days replacing corroded pipes with new ones that met modern code.

Since then, three different studios from Paris had already done some sequence shots along the river using the château in the background, but they were on limited budgets.

It would take several years of that kind of continual traffic to fatten his bank account to the amount he needed. By then the deadline for the taxes owing would have passed and he would forfeit the estate.

So far, at least fifty would-be investors ranging from locals to foreigners were dying to get their hands on it so they could turn it into a hotel. One of them included the attorney who'd sent out the letter, but Alex had no intention of letting his mother's inheritance go if he could help it.

With the natural blonde beauty seated across from him, it was possible he could shorten the time span for that happening. There was hope yet. She hadn't been turned off by what she'd seen or she wouldn't be eating dinner with him now. Her father was a huge money-maker for the producers. His films guaranteed a big budget. Alex was prepared to go out on a limb for her.

Dana Lofgren didn't look older than twenty-two, twenty-three, yet age could be deceptive. She might be young, but being the director's only child she'd grown up with him and knew him as no one else did or could. If she thought the estate had promise, her opinion would carry a lot of weight with him. Hopefully word of mouth would spread to other studios.

After spending all day every day clearing away tons of brush and debris built up around the château over four decades, her unexplained presence no matter how feminine or attractive, hadn't helped his foul mood. That was before he realized she had a legitimate reason for looking around, even if she'd wandered in uninvited.

"How did you like your food?"

She lifted flame-blue eyes to him. With all that silky gold hair and a cupid mouth, she reminded him of a cherub, albeit a grown-up one radiating a sensuality of which she seemed totally unaware. "The chateaubriand was delicious."

"That's good. I've sampled all their entrées and can assure you the meals here will keep any film crew happy."

His dinner companion wiped the corner of her mouth

with her napkin. "I can believe it. One could put on a lot of weight staying here for any length of time. It's a good thing I'm not a film star."

An underweight actress might look good in front of the camera, but Alex preferred a woman who looked healthy, like this one whose cheeks glowed a soft pink in the candlelight.

"No ambition in that department?"

"None."

He believed her. "What *are* you, when you're not helping your father?"

The bleak expression in her eyes didn't match her low chuckle. "That's a good question."

"Let me rephrase it. What is it you do in your spare time?"

The waiter brought their crème brûlée to the table. She waited until he'd poured them more wine before answering Alex. "Nothing of report. I read and play around with cooking. Otherwise my father forgets to eat."

"You live with him?"

Instead of answering him, she sipped the wine experimentally. Mmm…it was so sweet. She took a bite of custard from the ramekin, then drank more. He could tell she loved it. "This could become addicting."

Alex enjoyed watching her savor her meal. "If I seemed to get too personal just now, it's because the widowed grandfather I never knew threw my mother out of the château when she was about your age. Both of them died without ever seeing each other again."

Her ringless fingers tightened around the stem of her wineglass. "Since my mother died of cancer five years ago, my father and I have gone the rounds many times, but it hasn't come to that yet." She took another sip. "The fact is, whether we're at home or on location, which is most of the time, he needs a keeper."

Amused by her last comment he said, "It's nice to hear of a father-daughter relationship that works. You're both fortunate."

A subtle change fell over her. "Your mother's story is very tragic. If you don't mind my asking, what caused such a terrible breach?"

Maybe it was his imagination but she sounded sincere in wanting to know.

"Gaston Fleury lost his only son in war, causing both my grandparents to wallow in grief. When my grandmother died, he gave up living, even though he had a daughter who would have done anything for him. The more she tried to love him, the colder he became.

"Obviously he'd experienced some kind of mental breakdown because he turned inward, unable to love anyone. He forgot his daughter existed and became a total recluse, letting everything go including his household staff. When my mother tried to work with him, he told her to get out. He didn't need anyone."

In the telling, his dinner companion's eyes developed a fine sheen. What was going on inside her?

"Horrified by the change in him, she made the decision to marry my father, who'd come to France on vacation. They moved to Queensland, Australia, where he was born."

"Is your father still there?"

"No. He died in a fatal car accident seven months ago."

She stirred restlessly. "You've been through a lot of grief."

"It's life, as you've found out."

"Yes," she murmured.

"My father's animosity toward my grandfather was so great, he didn't tell me the whole story until after mother died of an infection two years ago. Gaston never wrote or sent for her, so she never went back for a visit, not even after I was born. The pain would have been too great. It explained her lifelong sadness."

Earnest eyes searched his. "Growing up you must have wondered," she whispered.

He nodded. "To make a long story short, in May a letter meant for Mother fell into my hands. The attorney for the abandoned Belles Fleurs estate had been trying to find her. When I spoke with him personally he told me my grandfather had died in a government institution and was buried in an unmarked grave."

She shook her head. "That's awful."

"Agreed. If she didn't fly to France for a probate hearing, the property would be turned over to the government for years of back taxes owing. It consisted of a neglected château and grounds. I discovered very quickly the whole estate is half buried in vegetation like one of those Mayan temples in Central America."

The corners of her mouth lifted. "A perfect simile."

"However, something inside me couldn't let it go without a fight. That meant I needed to make money in a hurry. So I came up with the idea of renting out the property to film studios."

She eyed him frankly. "That was a brilliant move on your part for which my father will be ecstatic. You're a very resourceful man. I hope your ad continues to bring you all the business you need in order to hold on to it."

Dana Lofgren was a refreshing change from most women of his acquaintance who came on to him without provocation. While they'd eaten a meal together, she'd listened to him without giving away much about herself.

Alex couldn't tell if it was a defense mechanism or simply the way she'd been born, but the fact remained she'd come as a pleasant surprise on many levels. He found he didn't want the evening to end, but sensed she was ready to say good-night.

When he'd finished his wine, he put some bills on the table. "After your long flight and the drive from Paris, you have to be exhausted. What time would you like to come to the château tomorrow?"

"Early, if that's all right with you. Maybe 8:00 a.m.?"

An early bird. Alex liked doing business early. *"Bon."* He pushed himself away from the table and stood up. "I'll be waiting for you in the drive. *Bonuit, mademoiselle.*"

Monsieur Martin not only intrigued Dana, but he'd left her with a lot to think about. In fact, the tragedy he'd related had shaken her. His mother had become invisible to her own father, too. There were too many similarities to Dana's life she didn't want to contemplate.

She finished the last of her wine, upset with herself for letting Monsieur Martin's male charisma prompt her to get more personal with him and prod him for details about his family. That was how she'd gotten into trouble with Neal. He'd pretended to be flattered by all her interest. She'd thought they were headed toward something permanent until she realized it was her father who'd brought him around in the first place—that, and his ambition.

Of course there was a big difference here. Neal had used her in the hope of acting in one of her father's films. She on the other hand had flown to France because Monsieur Martin had advertised his property for a specific clientele. Dana wanted a service from *him*. The two situations weren't comparable.

Neither were the two men....

At her first sight of the striking owner, Dana was convinced she'd come upon the château of the sleeping prince, and *that* before the wine had put her in such a mellow mood. But their subsequent conversation soon jerked her out of that fantasy.

He was a tough, intelligent businessman of substance with an aura of authority she would imagine intimidated most men. Maybe even her own scary parent. That would be something to witness.

Disciplining herself not to eat the last few bites of custard, she left the dining room and went to her room. She could phone her father tonight with the good news. He'd be awake by now expecting her call, unless he'd spent the night with Saskia, which was a strong possibility.

All things considered, she decided to get in touch with him tomorrow after she'd met with Monsieur Martin again.

After getting ready for bed, she set her alarm for 7:00 a.m. She was afraid she'd sleep in otherwise, but to her surprise, Dana awoke before it went off because she was too excited for the day.

She took a shower and washed her hair. Her neck-length layered cut fell into place fast using her blow-dryer. Afterward she put on her favorite Italian blouse.

It was a dark blue cotton jersey with a high neck and three-quarter sleeves, casual yet professional.

She teamed it with beige voile pants and Italian bone-colored sandals. Since she was only five foot five, she hoped the straight-leg style gave the illusion of another inch of height. Dana was built curvy like her mother. Being around Monsieur Martin, she could have wished for a few more inches from her father who stood six-one. Barring that, all she could do was keep a straight carriage.

With her bag packed, she headed for the dining room where rolls and coffee were being served. She grabbed a quick breakfast, then walked out to talk to a woman at the front desk Dana hadn't seen yesterday. "*Bonjour*, madame."

"*Bonjour, madame*. How can I help you?"

"I'm checking out." After she'd handed her back the credit card, Dana said, "Last night I drank a wonderful white wine in the restaurant and would like to buy a bottle to take home with me." Her father would love it. "Could you tell me the name of it?"

"*Bien sur*. We only stock one kind. It's the Domaine Coteaux du Layon Percher made right here in the Anjou."

"It's one of the best wines I ever tasted."

"In my opinion, Percher is better than the other brands from this area. Sadly the most celebrated of them was the Domaine Belles Fleurs, but it stopped being produced eighty years ago."

Dana's body quickened. The woman did say Belles Fleurs. "Do you know why?"

She leaned closer. "Bad family blood." Dana had gathered as much already. There'd been a complete break between Monsieur Martin's mother and her father, but he hadn't mentioned anything else. "It's an ugly business fighting over who had the rights to what."

"I agree."

"The present owner has only lived in the vicinity a month or so," the woman confided. "The château has been deserted for many years."

So Monsieur Martin had told her. "It's very sad."

"C'est la vie, madame," she said with typical Gallic fatalism. "Would you like to buy a bottle of the Percher?"

"I-I've changed my mind," her voice faltered. It would seem a betrayal.

"Is there anything else I can do for you?"

"No, *merci.*"

Dana turned away and left the hotel. She was in a much more subdued frame of mind as she drove the five or so kilometers to the bridge where the trees cast more shadows across the road. The morning light coming from the opposite side of a pale blue sky created a totally different atmosphere from the night before.

This time as she reached the fork in the road, Monsieur Martin was there to greet her. It sent her pulse racing without her permission. She pulled to a stop.

He walked toward her, dressed in white cargo pants and a burgundy colored crewneck, but it didn't matter what he wore, she found him incredibly appealing. It wasn't just the attractive arrangement of his hard-boned features, or midnight-brown eyes framed by dark brows.

The man had an air of brooding detachment that added to her fascination. Combined with his sophistication, she imagined most women meeting him would have fantasies about him.

Under the influence of the wine, Dana had already

entertained a few of her own last night. However, because of her experience with Neal, plus the fact that she was clearheaded this morning, she was determined to conduct business without being distracted.

"*Bonjour*, Monsieur Martin."

When he put his tanned hands on the door frame, the scent of the soap he'd used in the shower infiltrated below her radar. "My name's Alex. You don't mind if I call you Dana?" His voice sounded lower this morning, adding to his male sensuality.

"I'd prefer it."

"*Bien.*" He walked around to the passenger side of her car and adjusted the seat to accommodate his long legs before climbing in. His proximity trapped the air in her lungs. "Take the left fork. It will wind around to the front of the château."

Old leaves built up over time covered the winding driveway. It was flanked on both sides by trees whose unruly tops met overhead like a Gothic arch. Dana followed until it led to a clearing where she got her first look at the small eighteenth-century château built in the classic French style.

Beyond the far end stood an outbuilding made of the same limestone and built in the same design, half camouflaged by more overgrown shrubs and foliage. No doubt it housed the winepress and vats.

She shut off the engine and climbed out to feast her eyes. He followed at a slower pace.

The signs of age and neglect showed up in full force. There were boards covering the grouped stacks of broken windows. Several steps leading to the elegant entry were chipped or cracked. Repairs needed to be done to the high-sloped slate roof. It was difficult to tell where the weed-filled gardens filled with tiny yellow lilies ended and the woods encroached.

Dana took it all in, seeing it through her father's eyes. She knew what the original script called for. This was so perfect she thought she must be dreaming.

"It's like seeing a woman of the night on the following morning when her charms are no longer in evidence," came his grating voice. Trust a man to come up with that analogy. "Not what you had in mind after all?"

Schooling herself not to react to his cynicism, she turned to her host, having sensed a certain tension emanating from him. "On the contrary. It will do better than you can imagine. Knowing how my father works, he'll need three weeks here. How soon can you give the studio that much time?"

CHAPTER TWO

FEW things had surprised Alex in life, but twice in the last eighteen hours Dana Lofgren had taken him unawares.

"I have nothing signed and sealed yet. Is the season of vital importance?"

Her nod caused her hair to gleam in the sun like fine gold mesh. "It has to be late summer. Right now if possible," she said, looking all around, "but maybe that's asking too much."

"Don't worry. It's available. My next tentative booking so far is with a Paris studio that won't be needing it until mid-September."

"Good," she murmured, almost as if she'd forgotten he was there.

"Are you ready to see the interior?"

"No." She sounded far away. "I'll leave that to my father. I've seen what's important to him. The estate possesses that intangible atmosphere he's striving for. I knew it as I drove in last night.

"Over the years of watching him work I've learned he doesn't like too much information. If I were to paint pictures, he'd see them in his mind. They would interfere with his own creative process." She suddenly turned and flashed him a quick smile. "His words, not mine."

Alex couldn't help smiling back. She had to be made of strong stuff to handle her father whose ego was probably bigger than his reputation. "Such trust in you implies a spiritual connection I think."

"I would say it has more to do with our mutual love of history. When I leave, I'll phone him and let him know what I've found. Before the day is out you'll hear from two people."

This fast she'd made her decision? Alex couldn't remember meeting anyone like her before. Did she always function on impulse, or just where her father was concerned? "I'll be waiting."

"Sol Arnevitz handles the financial arrangements. Paul Soleri is in charge of everything and everyone else when we're on location. Paul will go over the logistics and has the ability to smooth out any problem. You'll like *him*."

"As opposed to…"

She made a face. "Who else?"

Meaning her father of course. Dana Lofgren was a woman who didn't take herself too seriously. Despite what he assumed was a ten-year age difference between them, he feared she was growing on him at a time when he couldn't afford distractions.

"What more can I do for you this morning?"

"Not another thing." But her blue eyes burned with questions she didn't articulate, piquing his interest. "Thank you for dinner last night and your time this morning. It's been a real pleasure, Alex. Expect to hear from Sol right away. Here's his business card." She handed it to him. "He'll work out all the details with you."

To his shock she got in her car before he could help her.

"Where are you going in such a hurry?" He wasn't ready to let her go yet.

"A daughter's work is never done. I have to be in Paris this afternoon, then I'll fly back to L.A. Enjoy your solitude before everyone descends on you."

The next thing he knew she'd turned around and had driven off, leaving him strangely bereft and more curious than ever about her association with a father who was bigger than life in her eyes. Alex saw the signs. Ten, twenty, even thirty years from now he had a hunch Jan Lofgren's hold on her would still be powerful.

He stared blindly into space. Whether strongly present in Dana's life, or deliberately absent as Gaston Fluery had been in his daughter's life, both fathers wielded an enormous impact. The thought disturbed Alex in ways he'd rather not examine.

An hour later, after he'd changed clothes and had begun cutting down more overgrowth, his cell phone rang. It could be anyone, but in case it was Dana, he pulled it out of his pants pocket. The ID indicated a call from the States. He clicked on. "Alex Martin speaking."

"Mr. Martin? This is Pyramid Pictures Film Studio calling from Hollywood, California. If it's convenient Mr. Sol Arnevitz would like to set up a conference call with you and Mr. Paul Soleri before he goes to bed at eleven this evening. It's 7:00 p.m. now. Mr. Lofgren heard from his daughter and is anxious to move on this."

Alex was anxious, too, for several reasons. "Eight o'clock your time would work for me."

"Very good. Expect their call then."

After twenty more minutes loading the truck, Alex

went back to the château and entered through a side door leading into the kitchen. He washed his hands, then poured himself a cup of coffee before carrying it to the ornate salon off the foyer, which he'd turned into a temporary bedroom-cum-office. He liked living with the few furnishings of his parents he'd had shipped.

The salon's original furniture was still stored on the top floor. Once he'd made inroads on the outside of the château, he would concentrate on the house itself, that is if he made enough money in time. For now he'd supplied himself with the necessities for living here: electricity, cable and Internet, running water hot and cold, a new water heater, a stove, a fridge, washer and dryer and a new bed with a king size mattress and box springs.

He snagged the swivel chair with his foot and sat down at his desk. No sooner had he booted up his computer than his call came through. Once the other two men introduced themselves, they made short work of the negotiations. The company would be on location from August 8 through 31. Sol quoted a ballpark figure, but left it open because other expenses always accrued.

Alex didn't know if Dana had anything to do with the actual amount, but it was a far greater sum than he'd hoped for. Sol sent him a fax, making the contract official before he rang off.

Paul stayed on the line with him for another twenty minutes. They discussed logistics for the cameramen and staff. Alex e-mailed him a list of hotels, car rental agencies and other businesses in and around Angers such as Chanzeaux.

"Chanzeaux?" the other man said. "Dana mentioned she stayed at a hotel there last night. I believe it was the Hermitage. According to her it's the perfect place for her father."

It pleased Alex she'd given her seal of approval. "The food's exceptionally good there. Mr. Lofgren should be very comfortable."

"Since we're behind schedule as it is, we all want that," he admitted with a dry laugh that spoke volumes about Dana's father. "The crew will arrive day after tomorrow. Everyone else the day after. I look forward to meeting you, Alex."

"The feeling's mutual."

After clicking off, he headed outside again. Dana would be back in a few days, this time with her father. Over the years Alex had been involved in various relationships with women, but he'd never found himself thinking ahead to the next meeting with this kind of anticipation. He had no answer as to why this phenomenon was suddenly happening now.

During the taxi ride to the house, Dana phoned Sol whose secretary told him the contract with Mr. Martin had been signed. Relieved on that score she called Paul, wanting to touch base with him before she saw her father.

"Hey, Dana— Are you back already?"

"Yes, but only long enough to pack before I leave again. Sol says everything's ready to go."

"That's right. I've got us booked at three hotels fairly close together. Just so you know, the Hermitage didn't have any vacancies, but with a little monetary incentive I managed to arrange adjoining rooms for you and your father for the month."

She smiled. "You're indispensable, Paul."

"Tell your father that."

"I don't need to." Except that nobody told Jan Lofgren anything. Little did Paul know that even though he'd arranged a hotel room somewhere else for Saskia, she'd probably end up staying with Dana's father. "Listen, Paul—I'm almost at the house so I've got to go. Talk to you later."

"*Ciao*, Dana."

After she hung up, her mind focused on her own sleeping arrangements. Since the film studio had the run of the estate until the end of August, Dana decided she would stay in the deserted château away from everyone. When else in her life would she get a chance like this? She'd buy a sleeping bag. It would be a lark to camp out inside.

Her dad wouldn't need her except to do the odd job for him and bring him lunch. Once he settled in for work each day, he hated having to leave with the others to go eat. Maybe he used it as an excuse to be alone with his own thoughts for an hour. Who knew?

What mattered was that she'd have most of her time free to explore the countryside and only come back at dark to go to sleep. Her thoughts wandered to Alex. She wondered where he was staying. The concierge at the Hermitage indicated he lived in the vicinity. Considering the taxes he owed, she imagined he'd found a one-star hotel in order to keep his expenses down. It made her happy that the film company would be giving him a financial boost. He—

"Miss?"

Dana blinked. "Oh—yes! I'm sorry." They'd reached her family's modern rancho-styled home in Hollywood

Hills without her being aware he'd stopped the taxi. She paid him and got out.

Just in case her father had brought Saskia home, she rang the doorbell several times before letting herself in. After ascertaining she was alone, Dana took off her shoes and padded into the kitchen to sort through the mail and fix some lunch.

The clock in the hall chimed once, reminding her France was nine hours ahead of California time. She doubted Alex would be in bed yet. Was he out with a beautiful woman tonight? And what if he was?

For a man she'd barely met, Dana couldn't believe how he'd gotten under her skin so fast. It was that unexpected invitation to dinner with him. He didn't have to take the time, but the fact that he did made him different from the other men she'd known. She found him not only remarkable, but disturbingly attractive.

While she finished the last of her peanut butter and jelly sandwich, she reached for her mother's favorite French cookbook from the shelf. It wasn't a cookbook exactly. It was a very delightful true story about an American family living in France in 1937. Quite by accident they met a French woman who came to cook for them.

Everything you ever wanted to know about France was in it, including French phrases. It was full of recipes and little drawings, so much better than a Michelin guide. Both Dana and her mom had read it many times, marveling over a slice of history captured in the account. Dana would pack this with her.

In the act of opening the cover, warm memories of her mother assailed her. A lump stayed lodged in her throat all the way to the bedroom where she flung herself on the bed to thumb through it. Chanzeaux looked just like the adorable villages in the book with their open-air markets selling the most amazing items. She rolled over on her back, wondering about Alex. Having lived on the other side of the world, did he find France as charming as she did?

There were many questions she'd like to ask him, but she'd already probed too much. Anything more she learned *he* would have to volunteer when they happened to see each other. He could be slightly forbidding. It would be wise to stay out of his way. That went for her father, too, except to feed him.

Oh, yes, and remind him to go to the local hospital for his weekly blood test. No one would believe what a baby he was, which reminded her she'd better check the medicine cabinet and make sure he had enough blood thinner medication to be gone two months. After they left France, they'd finish up the filming in Germany where Dana had already checked out the locations ahead of time.

With a sigh she got up from the bed needing to do a dozen things, but a strong compulsion led her to the den first. Ever since she'd heard that the Fleury family had once produced wine, she wanted to learn what she could about it. The wine she'd had with Alex had left the taste of nectarines on her lips. As she'd told him that night, it could become addicting.

She typed in Anjou wine, France. Dozens of Web sites popped up. She clicked on the first one.

The Anjou is one of the subregions of the Loire Valley producing a variety of dry to sweet dessert wines. The two main regions for Chenin Blanc are found in Touraine and along the Layon river where the soil is rich in limestone and tuffeau. Long after you've tasted this wine, it will give up a stone-fruit flavor on the palate. The Dutch merchants in the sixteen hundreds traded for this wine.

That far back?

Fascinated by the information, Dana researched a little more.

Coteaux du Layon near the river is an area in Anjou where the vines are protected by the hills. It's best known for its sweet wines, some of the recipes going back fifteen centuries. By the late seventeen hundreds, several wine producers became dominant in the region including the Domaine du Rochefort, Domaine du Château Belles Fleurs and Domaine Percher.

There it was, part of Alex's family history. Dana's father would find the information riveting, as well, but for the meantime she'd keep it to herself. The owner was a private person. It would be best if she waited until he brought it up in the conversation, if he ever did.

A few minutes later she'd gone back to her room to do her packing. She had it down to a science, fitting everything into one suitcase. As she was about to leave and do some errands, her father came home and poked his head in the door. "There you are."

She looked up at him. "Hi."

"You just got back. How come you're packing again so soon?"

Dana had anticipated his question. "I'm going to fly to Paris with the camera guys in the morning."

"Why?"

"Because Saskia will be a lot happier if she has you to herself when you fly out the day after tomorrow."

"Saskia doesn't run my life," he declared.

No one ran his life. Dana certainly didn't figure in it except to fetch for him, but the actress didn't like her. "I know that, but it doesn't hurt to keep the troops happy, does it?" She flashed him a smile, hoping to ease the tension, maybe provoke a smile, but all she provoked was a frown.

"You really think you found the right place?" he asked morosely.

The film was on his mind, nothing or no one else. Until he saw the estate, he'd be impossible to live with. Good luck to Saskia. "If I haven't, Paul will switch us back to Plan B outside Paris without problem."

After staring into space for another minute he said, "Have you seen my reading glasses?"

"They're on the kitchen counter, next to the script. Have you eaten?"

"I don't remember."

"I'll fix you some eggs and toast."

"That's a good girl," he muttered, before leaving her alone.

He only said that if he needed something from her. Because he was a narcissist, it was all she would get. She knew that, yet because their natures were exact opposites, a part of her would always want more. Still, when she thought of Alex's mother being cut off by her father, Dana realized her relationship with her father hadn't degenerated to that extent. Not yet...

Alex was in his bedroom when the phone rang again. He'd just hung up from talking with another Realtor who hadn't heard the estate wasn't for sale and never had been. They never stopped hounding him. With each call he'd hoped it might be Dana.

"Monsieur Martin *ici*."

"*Bonjour*, Alex."

His lips twitched. Her accent needed help, but with a grown-up rosebud mouth like hers, no Frenchman would care. "*Bonjour*, Dana. How are things in Hollywood?"

"I wouldn't know. How are things in that jungle of yours?"

Laughter burst out of him. "Prickly."

"My condolences."

"Where are you exactly?"

"In front of the château."

He felt a burst of adrenaline kick in.

"I was hoping you would let me in, but considering your plight, I'll be happy to come back after you and your machete have emerged."

The chuckles kept on coming. "I'm closer than you think. Don't go away." He hung up and strode swiftly through the foyer.

As soon as he opened the front door of the chateau, she got out of the car. Today she was dressed in jeans and a white short-sleeved top. If the pale blue vest she wore over it was meant to hide the lovely mold of her body, it failed.

Though she gave the appearance of being calm and collected, he noticed a pulse throbbing too fast at her throat. He knew in his gut she was glad to see him.

"When did you fly into Paris?"

"At six-thirty this morning with the camera guys. When their rooms are ready, they'll crash until tomorrow, then probably show up around eight in the morning to start checking things out."

"What about your father?"

"Everyone else will arrive at different times tomorrow."

"I see. He didn't mind you coming on ahead?"

"Most of the time we do our own thing." She gave him a direct glance as if daring him to contradict her.

Alex had asked enough questions for now. It was almost noon. "Let's get you inside. In case you'd like to freshen up, there's a bathroom on the second floor at the head of the stairs."

"Thank you."

Dana followed him up the steps into the foyer dominated by the central stonework staircase. With no furniture, paintings, tapestries or rugs visible, the château was a mere skeleton, but she seemed mesmerized.

Taking advantage of her silence he said, "The place was denuded years ago. Everything is stored on the third level where the servants used to live."

He watched her eyes travel from the walls' decorative Italianate paneling to the inlaid wood floors. "There's a chandelier packed away that should hang over the staircase. Without it the château is dark at night. I told Paul that if night interiors are called for, he'll need to plan for extra lighting. Your father—"

"My father's very superstitious," she broke in on a different tack. "He gets that from his Swedish ancestry. When he stands where I'm standing, he'll be frightened at first."

"Frightened?"

"Yes." She turned to him. "It's always frightening for a figment of your imagination to come to life, don't you think? At first he won't know if it's a good or bad omen."

When her father saw the château, he would be speechless. His excitement wouldn't be obvious to the casual observer, but she'd see his eyes flicker and feel his positive energy radiate. For a while it would insulate him from his usual irritations. Even Saskia wouldn't grate on his nerves as much, at least not at first. But that was *his* problem. Dana had done her part.

"Would you mind being more explicit?" Everything she said intrigued Alex. Besides her shape and coloring that appealed strongly to his senses, she had an inquiring mind. It engendered an excitement inside him that was building in momentum.

"My father gave his favorite screen writer some ideas and they collaborated on the script for this wartime film. Your château and grounds could have been made for it. For some time I've had the feeling this is the most important project he's ever taken on."

He folded his arms. "Can you tell me about it, or is it a secret?"

"A secret? No." After a pause. "The film is filled with the kind of angst my father is best known for." He heard her breathe in deeply. "Does that explanation help?"

"About the setting, yes, but I'm curious about the story itself."

She gave a gentle shrug of her shoulders. "That's for my father to decide. I don't think he knows it all yet." As far as Alex was concerned, she was being evasive for a reason. "Dad's had a mind block lately. It's made him more irritable than usual. It will take settling into it here for those creative juices to flow again. But to give you a specific answer to your question, his films always leave the audience asking more questions."

That was the truth, but she was holding back from him and that made him more curious than ever. Evidently she knew better than to give too much away. Was that because her father wouldn't like it? "Why do you think he came up with this particular story?"

"How does any author come up with an idea? They see something, hear something that arouses their interest and a kernel of an idea starts to form."

She angled her head toward him. "Part of it could be the guilt he personally feels for his country's compliance with the enemy in the first days of World War II. Another part might be that deep down he still misses mother and wishes he'd had a son instead of '*moi*.'"

She'd said it with a smile, but Alex felt the words like a blow to the gut. He'd heard emptiness, sadness in that last remark. It made him want to comfort her. "Still, I have my uses. Thanks to you, I found *this* for him." She spread her hands, as if encompassing the entire château. "Heaven sent."

Alex swallowed hard. "For me, too."

"I'm happy if it helps you. I bet your mother is, too."

She kept surprising him. "You believe in heaven, Dana?"

"Yes. Don't you?"

"After this discussion, I want to."

A faint blush filled her cheeks. "I'm afraid I've rattled on too long and have kept you from your work. Please go ahead and do whatever you were doing. If it's all right, I'll just wander around here for a little while before I take a nap. I picked up a sleeping bag in Angers and brought it with me."

Why would she do that? "If you're that exhausted,

I'll call the Hermitage and tell them to get your room ready now."

"No doubt they'd make concessions for you, but I'm not staying there, so it's not necessary. Thank you anyway."

Alex rubbed the back of his neck in an unconscious gesture. "Paul told me he would arrange rooms there for you and your father."

"He already has, but while I'm in France I intend to be on my own most of the time. After everyone goes home at the end of the day's shoot, I plan to stay right here where I can have the whole château to myself."

An angry laugh escaped his throat. "I'm afraid that's impossible."

She flashed him an ingenuous smile. "Don't worry about me. I don't frighten easily and love being alone."

His eyes narrowed. Dana had seemed such an innocent she'd almost fooled him. "I'm afraid you don't understand," he ground out. "My ad didn't indicate the château could be used for anything but the filming."

A long silence ensued while she digested what he'd said. "I assumed that since the company had rented the estate for the filming, it wouldn't matter if I found myself a little spot in the château to sleep at night." Her supple body stiffened. "My mistake, Alex. I'm glad you cleared it up before any harm was done."

"Dana—"

She'd almost reached the front door before turning around. "Yes?"

He started toward her. "Where are you going?"

"To find me a place to stay."

"Wouldn't you be better off with your father?" he asked quietly.

"You want your pound of flesh, don't you." Her cheeks filled with angry color. "First of all, if I were seventeen I'd agree with you, but I'm going to be twenty-seven next week, slightly too long in the tooth to still be daddy's little girl."

His estimation of her age had been way off.

"Secondly, my father isn't in his dotage yet. In fact, his latest love interest is one of the actresses in the film and will be sleeping with him, which makes three a crowd. When you see Saskia, you'll understand a lot of things." She smiled. "If my dad ever found out your impression of him, he'd have a coronary."

Alex hadn't seen that one coming. It knocked him sideways.

"Thirdly, while I'm in this glorious region of France, I'd like to pretend I'm an independent woman who needs to spread her own wings for a change. It must have given you an uncomfortable moment thinking I'd made you my target. Again, I apologize."

He'd anticipated her flight and moved in time to prevent her from opening the door. Their hips brushed against each other in the process, increasing his awareness of her womanly attributes. The tension between them was palpable. She slowly backed away from him.

The last thing he'd wanted was to make an enemy of her, but that's what he'd done. One word to her father and he could kiss this deal goodbye. The hell of it was, he couldn't afford to lose this film studio's business, not when he needed the money so badly. A large portion of his life's savings combined with the modest inheritance from his father were all invested in this venture.

"Dana—it never occurred to me you might want to stay in the château."

She refused to look at him. "You're not a dreamer."

"You'd be surprised, but that's not the point." Trying to gauge what her reaction would be he said, "I live here."

Her gaze flew to his. By the stunned look in those blue depths, he knew instinctively his revelation had come as a surprise.

"The concierge at the Hermitage intimated you lived somewhere in the vicinity. To me that ruled out the château…" Her voice trailed.

Alex's first impression of the French woman in Chanzeaux had been right. She was a busybody. When Dana's father arrived and she learned of his importance, it would bring a flood of unwanted curiosity seekers to the estate. His mouth thinned in irritation. He would have to fit the gate with an electronic locking device to give the film company privacy while they were working. Today, if possible.

"I'm afraid there's been a lot of speculation about me since I flew in from Bali."

"Bali— What were you doing there?"

"My work. I'm an agricultural engineer."

She rubbed her palms against womanly hips, as if she didn't know what to do with them. "Are you taking a sabbatical of sorts then?"

"No. I resigned in order to settle mother's estate before leaving for the States."

Following his remark she said, "Then you're only in France temporarily."

"Very temporarily, even if my business venture should succeed—" he drawled.

"What is your plan exactly?"

"To restore the château and grounds to a point that the estate can be put on display alongside the others in the area. Millions of tourists pour into France each year willing to pay entry fees for a look around. With a couple of full-time caretakers, it could prove to be a smart business investment, leaving me free to pursue my career overseas."

Her expression had undergone a subtle change he couldn't decipher. "It's an ambitious undertaking, but with your work ethic I'm sure you'll make it happen." She glanced at her watch. "I need to go and let you get back to your work."

"Not so fast." He looked around before his gaze centered on her once more. "It does seem unconscionable not to let you live here when this was originally built to house several dozen people. Under the circumstances I *insist* you stay, but it means we share the château."

CHAPTER THREE

INSIST?

The provocative statement was backed by a steel tone, making her tremble. It seemed Alex Martin had changed his mind and was willing to let her stay here. Not willing, she amended. Determined all of a sudden.

Why?

Maybe like Neal he could see himself making a lot more money to save the château if he starred in a film. He was gorgeous enough to be a top box office draw, yet the mere idea that he saw Dana as a stepping stone to influence her father made her so ill, she shuddered.

If she was wrong about his motive, then for the life of her she couldn't think what the reason might be. The man could have any woman he wanted.

Alex's dark brows knit together. "Why so reticent now?"

The question coming from his compelling mouth was like a challenge wrapped up in a deceptively silky voice. It curled around Dana's insides down to her toes. If she didn't have to think about it, the idea of being under the same roof with Alex Martin for the next three weeks was so thrilling, she was ready to jump out of her skin.

But she *did* have to think about it for all the usual reasons of propriety, common sense and self-preservation—self-preservation especially because he could be moody and overbearing like her father, the very thing she'd wanted to get away from for a while.

And then there were the unusual reasons, like the fact that her father was coming here to direct the most important film of his career on her say-so alone. If she made a misstep with Alex now and he decided to renege on the contract, how would she explain it to her dad, let alone the rest of the company?

Money had changed hands. Too much was at stake on both men's parts for there to be trouble at this stage because of her.

When she'd declared that she wanted to be an independent woman and spread her own wings, she'd set herself up to be taken at her word and Alex had acted on it. He was probably laughing at her naïveté right now while he waited to hear that she'd changed her mind and didn't want to stay here after all.

The stakes were too high for her to turn this into a battle. An inner voice warned her there was wisdom in going along with him. Dana knew nothing like this would ever come her way again. Why not take him up on it? She wouldn't be human if she didn't avail herself of such an opportunity.

"Thank you, Alex. I'll do my best not to get underfoot." From now on she could fade into the shadows and be like Diane de Poitiers, Henri II's mistress at Chenonceau, who adored the château and oversaw the plantings of the flower and vegetable gardens.

Dana would glut herself on the history of Belles

Fleurs, but wherever she slept, she would make certain it wasn't anywhere near Alex. When she'd called his château small, she'd meant it hadn't been built on the scale of Chambord with its 440 rooms, but it was big enough for her to get lost in.

An odd gleam in his dark eyes was the only sign that her answer had surprised him. "With that settled, shall we go upstairs? You can have your pick of any room on the second floor."

By tacit agreement they both started toward the magnificent staircase. "How many are there?"

"Six."

While she was wondering where his room was located, he read her mind. "For the time being I've made the petit salon off the main foyer into a combined bedroom and office for me."

They'd be a floor apart. That was good. Of course when she wanted to go out for any reason, he'd be aware of her leaving through the front door, that is *if* and *when* he was around. After a few days of becoming aware of his routine, she'd make sure not to disturb him any more than she could help.

When they reached the long vestibule, she was overwhelmed by what she saw. "This is similar to the rib-vaulting at Chenonceau! It's utterly incredible!"

Alex nodded. "On a much smaller scale of course." She was conscious of his tall, hard-muscled frame as he continued walking to one end of the corridor on those long, powerful legs. "Let's start with the bedroom in the turret round."

"Oh—" she cried the second he opened the door and she took everything in. "This is the one I want!"

A smile broke the corner of his sensuous mouth. "You're sure? You haven't seen the others yet. The turret round on the other end has a fireplace."

"I'm positive. Look at these!" There were fleur-de-lis designs placed at random in the inlaid wood flooring. She got down on her knees to examine them.

"If the original designer of this château could see a modern-day woman like you studying his intricate workmanship this closely, he would be delighted by the sight."

"Go ahead and mock me," she said with a laugh before getting to her feet. For the next few minutes she threw her head back to study the cross-beamed ceiling. There were little white enamel ovals rimmed in gold placed every so often in the wood depicting flowers and various forest creatures. "How did they do that? How did they do any of this?"

She darted to the window that needed washing inside and out, but at least it wasn't broken. The entire room would require a good scrubbing to get rid of layers of accumulated dust. Even so there was a fabulous view of the countryside and a certain enchanted feel about the room. Eventually she turned to him. "Do you think this might have been your mother's?"

Her question seemed to make him more pensive and probably brought him pain. She wished she'd caught herself before blurting it out.

"My mother lived here until her early twenties. I have no idea which bedroom she occupied, but it wouldn't surprise me if it had been this one. The view of the Layon from the window at this angle is surreal."

"I noticed," Dana murmured. "I'm glad she met your father so she wasn't so lonely anymore."

Alex shifted his weight. "*Lonely* is an interesting choice of words."

"She would have been, wouldn't she? To know her father preferred her brother?"

"I'm sure you're right," he muttered. "Mother often seemed melancholy, at least that's what I called it, but you've hit on a better description. Even in a crowded room she sometimes gave off a feeling of loneliness that no doubt troubled my father, too."

"Forgive me for saying anything, Alex. It's none of my business. It must be the atmosphere here getting to me."

"You *are* your father's daughter after all, so it's understandable." She didn't detect anything more than slight amusement in his tone, thank heaven.

"If you'll tell me where to find some cleaning supplies, I'll get started in here before I bring up my sleeping bag."

He tilted his dark head. "I have a better idea. We'll drive into Angers in my truck and eat lunch. I need to pick up some items. While we're there, we'll get you a new mattress and box springs."

"You don't need to do that."

"I wouldn't allow you to stay here in a sleeping bag. After we come back, we'll clean the room together and I'll bring down a few pieces of furniture from storage. By sunset Rapunzel will be safely ensconced in her tower."

She chuckled to hide her excitement at spending the day with him, not to mention the rest of the month. "You're mixing up your fairy tales. I don't have long hair."

He gave an elegant shrug of his broad shoulders. "It's evident you haven't read the definitive version. Her father had her long golden tresses cut off so no prince could climb up to her."

A few succinct words dropped her dead in her tracks. In the tale Dana had grown up with, there'd been a wicked witch. Was he still teasing her, or had this tale suddenly taken on a life of its own. "Then how did the prince reach her?"

He paused in the doorway. "I guess you'll have to read the end of the story to find out."

His cryptic explanation was no help.

"I'll bring the truck around. When you've freshened up, meet me outside. I'll lock the door with my remote."

When she left the château a few minutes later, Alex was lounging against a blue pickup loaded with cut off branches and uprooted clumps of weeds. Dana marveled that he did this kind of backbreaking work without help. Pruning the grounds would be a Gargantuan task for half a dozen teams of gardeners, but he couldn't afford to hire help because the taxes were eating him alive.

She felt his dark fringed eyes wander over her as she came closer. They penetrated, causing her pulse to race. Still, everything would have been all right for the trip into town if their bodies hadn't brushed while he helped her inside the cab. Her breath caught and she feared he'd noticed. With nowhere to run, she had to sit there and behave like she didn't feel electrified.

"This won't take long," he said a few minutes later, jolting her out of her chaotic thoughts. They'd stopped at a landfill to dump the debris. Fortunately there was a man there ready to help him, making short work of it. Soon they were on their way again.

After driving this route several times already, Dana recognized some of the landmarks leading into Angers.

The massive castle dominating the town on the Maine came into view.

"Have you been through it?"

She shook her head. "Not yet, but I plan to. What about you?"

"One look at the condition of the estate and any thoughts I had of playing tourist flew out the broken windows."

Dana flicked him a sideward glance. "You know what that old proverb says about Jack working all the time."

He surprised her by meeting her gaze head-on. "Are you by any chance intimating I'm a dull boy?"

"Maybe not dull…" Dana said, before she wished she hadn't.

"You can't leave me hanging now—" It came out more like a growl, but he was smiling. When he did that, he was transformed into the most attractive man she'd ever seen or met. There was no sign of the boy he would have once been, one probably not as carefree with a mother whose heart had been broken.

"As you reminded me earlier, you'll have to read to the end of the story to find out."

"Touché."

Dana was glad when he turned onto a side street and pulled up near a sidewalk café full of locals and tourists. She slid out of the cab before he could come around to help her.

There was one empty bistro table partially sheltered from the sun by an umbrella. Alex escorted her to it before anyone else grabbed it. The temperature had been mild earlier, but now it was hot. A waiter came right over and took their orders for sandwiches.

Alex eyed her. "I could use a cup of coffee, but maybe you'd prefer something cold. The air's more humid than usual today."

"Coffee sounds fine." The waiter nodded and disappeared. She sat back in her chair. "I thought most French people preferred tea."

"I grew up on coffee."

"No billy tea?" she teased, referring to his Aussie roots.

He shook his head, drawing her attention to the hair brushing his shirt collar. In the light she picked out several shades ranging from dark brown to black. "I'm afraid tea doesn't do it for me."

"Nor me." She smiled. "You seem so completely French, I forgot."

"It's a good thing *my* father isn't around to hear that."

After a brief silence she said, "When you want to go home, that's a long flight."

"I have no home in the traditional sense. My father's work took us many places. We globe-trotted. Mother died in the Côte D'Ivoire and father on Bali where we were both working for the same company at the time. They're buried in Brisbane."

Dana took a deep breath. "Well, you have a home now."

One dark eyebrow lifted. "A liability you mean. I'm not certain it's worth it."

She wished she could lighten his mood. "That's right. You have other plans. Where in the States?"

"Louisiana. It's where my particular expertise, such as it is, can be fully utilized."

"Are you in such a hurry then?"

The waiter served them their order before Alex responded. "I wasn't aware of it, but I suppose I am."

While he made inroads on the ham and cheese melt, she took a sip of the hot liquid. "Sounds like your father's lifestyle rubbed off on you."

The gaze he flicked her was surprisingly intense. "From the little you've told me about yourself, I'd say you've been similarly afflicted."

"Afflicted?" An odd choice of word. She stopped munching on her first bite. Of course she understood what he meant. Years of traveling around Europe finding locations for her father prevented her from staying in one spot. But it didn't mean that under the right circumstances, she couldn't settle down quite happily.

"Some people never leave the place they were born," he murmured. "I'm not so sure they haven't figured out life's most important secret."

She chuckled. "You mean, while nomads like us wander to and fro in search of what we don't know exactly?"

An amused glint entered his dark eyes. "Something like that."

"Well, given a choice, I'm glad I'm the way I am. Otherwise I wouldn't be living this fantasy. My own little girl dreams of being a princess in a castle in a far-off land have come true. Never mind that it will all end in a month, I intend to enjoy every minute of it now, thanks to your generosity."

Aware she'd been talking too much, she ate the rest of her sandwich.

"You think that's what it is?" The question sent her pulse off the charts. "Little boys have their fantasies, too," came the wicked aside.

Fingers of warmth passed through her body. "My

mother taught me they're not for a little girl's ears."
After drinking the last of her coffee she dared a look
at him. "Just how young did you think I was when we
first met?"

"Too young," was all he was willing to reveal. He
put some money on the table and stood up. "If you're
ready we'll get some serious shopping done. Groceries
last, I think."

She would pay for her keep, she thought to herself.
He might be letting her sleep at the château, but she
didn't expect anything else.

After visiting a hardware store, he took her to the
third floor of the department store where the mattresses
were sold. Alex sought out the male clerk and they con-
versed in French. Their speech was so rapid she understood nothing. Within a few seconds the younger man
looked at her and broke out in a broad smile.

"I don't think I want a translation," she told Alex.

His lips curved upward. "You don't need to worry.
When he asked me what kind of a mattress we were
looking for, I simply asked him if he knew the story of the
Princess and the Pea. He said he had the ideal one for you."

She tried not to laugh. "I see."

The clerk spread his hands in typical French fashion.
"Would Mademoiselle like to try it?"

"She says yes," Alex spoke for her. They followed the
man across the floor to the sample mattresses on display.

"This one is the best. *S'il vous plaît*. Lie down."

"Don't be shy," Alex whispered. "He's not Figaro
measuring a space for your marriage bed."

An imp got into Dana. "Maybe he thinks he's measuring yours. Why don't you try it first and humor him?"

With enviable calm Alex stretched out on one side of it, putting his hands behind his handsome head. Through shuttered eyes he stared up at her, jump-starting her heart.

"Venez, mademoiselle." The clerk patted the other side. "He said you needed a double bed. See how you fit."

You said you wanted to spread your wings, Dana Lofgren. But she hadn't anticipated literally spreading out on a bed next to Alex for all creation to see. Several people on the floor had started watching with embarrassing interest. If she waited any longer, she'd turn this into a minor spectacle.

Once she'd settled herself full length against the mattress, she turned her head to Alex. "How does it feel against your sore back?"

He rolled on his side toward her, bringing him breathtakingly close. "You noticed." His voice sounded deep and seductive just then.

Afraid he knew that she noticed everything about him, she said, "I think we should take it. Look—even this close to me, the mattress doesn't dip."

"I noticed." This time when he spoke, she felt his voice reach right down inside to her core. The way his eyes had narrowed on her mouth, she slid off the bed in reaction and got to her feet on shaky legs.

"Eh bien, mademoiselle?"

She decided to make his day. "It's perfect"

He rubbed his hands together. "Excellent."

"Alex? I'll go to the linen department for the bedding. Meet you at the truck." Without looking at him, she made her way down to the next floor.

When the saleswoman asked what Dana had in mind, she described the beamed ceiling. "There's a mini print wallpaper of gold fleurs-de-lis on a cranberry field. I'd like to follow through with those colors."

"I have the exact thing for you."

Within minutes Dana left the store with a new pillow, pale cranberry sheets and bath towels with tiny gold fleurs-de-lis, a cranberry duvet and matching pillow sham.

Alex had reached the truck ahead of her. Together with two other men from the warehouse, he put the boxes with the mattress and box springs in the back. Upon her approach, he plucked the items right out of her arms with effortless male grace. While he stowed them, she climbed in the cab, eager to get back to the château and make up her new bed.

Without her having to say anything, he drove straight to a boulangerie where she salivated before loading up on nummy little quiches and ham-filled croissants. Alex bought three baguettes and several tranches of Gruyère and Camembert cheese.

"I already feel debauched and haven't even tasted a morsel yet," she moaned the words.

On the way back to the truck his eyes swerved to hers with a devilish glitter. "That's the whole idea. Earlier today I was accused of being a dull boy."

She quivered. If he got any duller, her heart wouldn't be able to take it. "I might have exaggerated a little."

"Careful, Mademoiselle Lofgren, or I'll get the impression you're trying to kill me with kindness." He turned on the engine and they took off.

She'd never had so much fun in her life and the day wasn't over yet.

* * *

"I'm coming down the hall, Dana. I hope you're ready."

He couldn't tell if she cried in fear or giggled. "Alex—please— It's almost ten o'clock. You've done enough! I don't need anything more." They'd cleaned every inch of the room until it gleamed. She was so genuinely appreciative of everything he did for her, it made him want to do more.

"I think you'll find this to be of comfort." Using his high-powered flashlight so he could see, he entered the turret round and put the heavy bronze floor candelabra near the head of the bed he'd brought down from storage. It was as tall as she was.

Dana held her own flashlight to guide him. She'd taken off her shoes and was in a kneeling position on top of her newly made bed. Using his automatic lighter, he lit the twelve candles in their sconces. Like the sun coming up over the horizon, the room slowly filled with flickering, mellow light.

"Oh—" she cried softly.

His sentiments exactly. The candles illuminated not only the inlaid woods of the Italian armoire and dresser, but the utterly enchanting female who'd worked hard right alongside him all afternoon and evening. Her peaches-and-cream complexion glowed, causing her blue eyes to dazzle him.

"The candles will burn down in an hour or so. Enough time to do some reading before jet lag takes over."

She shut off her flashlight. "I think I'm in a time warp."

"I feel that way every time I come inside the château." *Get out of her bedroom. Now.* "Before I go downstairs, we'd better discuss how you want to handle your father tomorrow."

Something in her eyes flickered that had nothing to do with the candlelight. "What do you mean handle?"

"I thought it was obvious. Sweet dreams, princess."

Dana had no agenda. No place she had to be.

After sleeping in until noon, she spent a long time in the modern bathtub, studying everything. She marveled at the superb job Alex had done of combining contemporary and eighteenth-century decor.

The tile work of the ancient looking floor had been laid in a stunning, stone-green and white checkerboard design. Her eyes followed the lines of the green border also carried out around the window and the door.

Delighted by every inch of work created by a master craftsman, she was loathe to leave her bath. However, the pads of her fingers resembled prunes. Without electricity to blowdry her hair up here, she needed to towel it some more, then brush it dry before she went downstairs.

An ornate, mural-size mirror with a rococo-style gilt frame hung on the wall opposite the tub, another sybaritic element of the château. A gasp escaped her lips when she stood up and saw herself reflected full-size. She had a mirror on the back of the door at home, but it was in her bedroom and seemed miniscule in comparison.

One more look at herself was a reminder that only a few days of enjoying the food they'd bought and she'd put on five pounds just like that!

Discipline, Dana. Self-control.

On the way back to the room in her robe, she repeated the motto that went for other things besides food. Like other people for instance. No, not other people. Just one person.

She clutched the lapels of her robe tighter. *A man like no one else.*

When she entered the room she could hear her phone vibrating on the dresser. Maybe it was Alex wondering if she was still alive. Suddenly breathless, she clicked on with a smile. *"Bonjour!"*

"Is that you, Dana?"

Her father's voice. What a surprise! "Hi, Dad. How was the flight?" He hated being closed in for long periods.

"Boring." That meant his girlfriend hadn't been able to keep him distracted.

"And Saskia?"

"She's at the Metropole in Angers."

"You sound tired. Where are you exactly?"

"I'm standing in my room at the Hermitage," he grumbled. "More to the point, where are you? The concierge said you never came in last night." He actually noticed?

"That's right. I've decided to stay at the château. It will save me a lot of coming and going."

Alex had the strange idea she was under her father's thumb. If he only knew the truth, that her father didn't think much about her at all. There was nothing to handle, but her host had insinuated something else and it rankled.

"I thought it was deserted."

"Not completely." She started brushing her hair. "The owner lives here. He's been very accommodating and made an allowance for me. After you've slept a few hours, drive over to the château in your rental car and I'll meet you at the gate."

There was a noticeable silence, then he said, "I'm coming now."

Clearly he couldn't wait to see if she'd pulled through for him. Everything hinged on her find.

"In that case let me go over the directions with you." Without Saskia in tow, he could walk around and think in peace. "See you shortly."

Once she'd pulled on jeans and a short-sleeved cotton top in an aqua color, she finished doing her hair and put on lipstick. Slipping her feet into her favorite leather sandals, she grabbed her phone and left the room. Later, after her father had gotten a feel for the estate, she would feed him a late lunch in the kitchen before he went back to the hotel.

Last evening she'd only had a brief glimpse of the salon. Today the door was closed. Alex could be inside at the computer, but in all probability he was out hacking away at his private jungle.

This was the way it should be. Out of sight, out of mind. Didn't she wish!

She stepped out into a day that seemed hotter than yesterday, but she hadn't noticed because the interior of the château was cooler. It felt like being in a cathedral to walk beneath the trees. Here and there sunlight dappled their branches.

As she continued on, the crunch of her feet on the leaves must have startled some squirrels. They chattered before she saw them scamper up a trunk and disappear. She was still laughing in pure pleasure when she came upon Alex at the gate.

He was down on his haunches in jeans and another thin white T-shirt, fastening something to the wrought iron. She could see the play of muscle across his shoulders. Her heart thudded so hard she was positive he could hear it.

"Sleeping Beauty at last," he murmured, scrutinizing her from head to toe with eyes so dark and alive this afternoon, it sent a delicious current of desire through her body.

"You're getting your princesses mixed up."

"No—" He went back to fastening a screw with his power drill. "You're a woman of many parts. I never know which one is going to emerge at any given moment."

His comment produced a smile from her. "You're full of it, Alex, but keep it up. By the time I leave here, I'll be taking a whole host of enchanting memories with me."

His hands stilled for a moment. "Where are you going next?"

"To a little town on the Rhine in Germany for a month where the last segment of the film will be made."

He dusted himself off and got to his feet. "Stand back and let's see if I've done this right." Pulling a remote from his pocket, he pressed the button. The gate took its time, but it clanged shut.

"*Bravo*. Too bad you didn't get to work on it sooner. It would have kept me out and forced me to phone you for an appointment."

Before she could take another breath, he shot her a laserlike glance. "As you've already surmised, I didn't mind the surprise or you wouldn't be living here." His comment filled her body with warmth. "But I've decided this was necessary to keep out trespassers while the studio is filming every day." He tossed her the remote. "It's yours. I have more in the office I'll give to Paul for anyone who needs one."

"Thank you."

She felt his gaze linger on her features. "Were you looking for me?"

Dana sucked in her breath. "No. My father's on his way over from the hotel. I told him I'd meet him here."

As if talking about him conjured him up, a red rental car appeared and came to a halt. Before Alex said anything that would remind her of his parting words last night, she pressed the button on the remote and the gate swung open.

"Hi, Dad. Drive on through."

He nodded his balding head and did her bidding. Once he'd passed through, he stopped the car and got out. Solid, yet lithe, he'd dressed in his favorite gray work slacks and matching crew neck shirt. His blue eyes, several shades darker than hers, gave them both a stare that others might consider fierce, but Dana was used to it.

"Dad, I'd like you to meet Monsieur Alexandre Martin, the owner of the estate."

"Monsieur." The two men shook hands.

"Call me Alex. I've seen several of your films which I found remarkable. It's a privilege to meet you."

"Thank you. Your English is excellent."

"He's part Australian, Dad."

"Ah. That explains the particular nuance I couldn't identify."

"Unlike your accent in English that no one could ever mistake for anything but Svenska," Dana quipped.

"Too true." His hooded gaze darted back and forth between her and Alex before he addressed him. "My daughter has convinced me I won't be disappointed with this location."

Alex eyed her father through veiled eyes. "Why don't you take a walk down this road alone. The left fork will bring you to the front of the château. The door's unlocked. Take all the time you want wandering around. I understand you'd rather do the discovering than be herded."

Dana's father looked stunned. That was because Alex had taken his cue from her. Among his many qualities, he'd just shown he was a master psychologist.

"Hand me the car keys, Dad. I'll drive it to the front courtyard and join you in a few minutes."

His surprised glance switched to her before he dropped them in her hand. After nodding to Alex, he turned and began jogging.

Once he'd disappeared around the curve in the driveway, she turned to Alex who'd started gathering up his tools. She could tell he was anxious to get back to his pruning. Considering he'd spent all day yesterday and last evening seeing to it she had a bedroom worthy of a princess to sleep in, she didn't want to be the reason he was kept from his work any longer.

As soon as she'd climbed in the car, she poked her head out the window. "You handled my father brilliantly, Alex. Congratulations on being one of the few." The last thing she saw was his dark, enigmatic glance as she started the engine.

Get going, Dana!

Afraid if she stayed any longer she'd end up blurting out something incriminating like, did he want help? she followed the driveway while studiously avoiding looking at him through the rearview mirror.

After pulling up next to her rental car parked in front, she gave her father a few more minutes lead before she got out. This was one time she was so confident of his positive reaction, it shocked her when he suddenly emerged from the château with a face devoid of animation. The look she'd expected to see in his eyes wasn't there.

"Follow me back to the Hermitage. We have to talk."

CHAPTER FOUR

ALEX was up in one of the tallest trees, cutting away dead branches, when he saw both cars leave the estate. Jan Lofgren couldn't have been on the premises more than ten minutes. That was quick, but Alex guessed he wasn't surprised. In less time, Dana had made the decision to rent the estate on behalf of the company.

His opinion of her father had been correct before meeting him. He personified conceit. Dana miraculously had none.

Two hours later, Alex was coming back from the landfill after another haul when his cell phone rang. Paul Soleri was calling to make sure he and the crew could get in. They were on their way to the estate.

The timing couldn't be better. Once Alex could welcome them and answer any questions, he'd resume his work. The knowledge that Dana would be coming back to sleep after dark never left his mind.

Before long a car and two minivans pulled up in the front courtyard. Alex stepped out of the château to meet Paul and the dozen light and camera technicians assembled. They all appeared delighted by what they saw. Their enthusiasm escalated as they entered the château.

After Alex introduced himself and pointed out the location of the bathroom facilities, he told them to look around and explore all they wanted. Except for the petit salon on the main floor and the west turret round on the first floor, everything else was available to them.

If they wanted to do any filming in the building housing the winepress or down in the wine cellar beneath the château, they were welcome. Already he could tell they were getting ideas as they left the foyer and darted from room to room checking things out.

Paul, who was probably in his midforties, took him aside. "Has Jan been here yet?"

"Yes. A few hours ago. He didn't stay long, then he left with his daughter."

The dark blond man pursed his lips. "I'm surprised I haven't heard from him yet."

"Perhaps he was tired from the long flight."

"That's not like him," he mused. "I assumed he'd be here."

"I have to admit I thought it strange he left in such a hurry," Alex commented.

"It doesn't matter." A pleasant smile broke out on his face. "We'll go ahead without him."

"Make yourself at home, Paul. As I told you over the phone, all the furniture is stored on the third floor. Nothing's locked. Use whatever you need."

He let out a long whistle. "When David gets here, he'll be floored."

"David?"

"The scriptwriter for this film. He'll be arriving any minute with the set designer and staff from costumes and makeup. They're all going to swoon."

"And that's good?"

"You have no idea. Since Jan wanted something unique for this segment of the film, we've been worried it didn't exist. Only Dana could pull this off. She's always had an instinct for picking the right places for him, but this time she outdid herself.

"Don't quote me, but she'll end up being a more brilliant director than her father."

That piece of information came totally unexpected. "Is directing one of her aspirations?"

"Yes, but the last person to know it is Jan, and that's another good thing."

Alex remembered her answer when he'd asked what she did in her spare time. *Nothing of report. I read and play around with cooking. Otherwise my father forgets to eat.*

"If you'll excuse me, Paul, I have to get back to my work outside. Phone if you need me."

"Will do."

Inexplicably disturbed by what he'd learned, he strode down the hallway leading to the side entrance of the château. Dana had been emphatic about not wanting to be an actress. Now it seemed Paul had supplied him with a viable reason.

Inherited talent happened on occasion, but he had the distinct feeling it would take uncommon courage for her to step out from Jan Lofgren's legendary shadow. When she did break out, she'd be caught up in her own career. The thought caused Alex to grind his teeth.

Dana found a parking space outside the Hermitage and followed her dad inside to his room. On the short drive from the château she'd prepared herself to hear that he wasn't pleased with her find.

She knew the place was perfect for the script, so it had to be something else he objected to. For the life of her she didn't know what it was. That meant his mood had already turned wretched and the whole company would pay for it. If she knew Paul, he'd already assembled the crew over there to get to work.

It would be bad enough if they had to pack up again and leave for the Paris location, but there was Alex to think about. The contract Sol had sent him was standard. There was a clause that said Alex would only receive a percentage of the money if for any reason they chose not to film there after all. That wasn't nearly enough compensation for him.

By the time she entered the hotel room, she was ready to fight her father. If he was going to pull out of this deal due to one of his mystical whims, then she would insist Alex be paid all the money agreed upon in good faith.

As usual his room was a mess, but for once she didn't start automatically straightening things. Instead she shut the door and propped her back against it. While she waited for him to speak first, she folded her arms.

He stood next to the dresser, eyeing her while he lit up a cigarette, almost as if he were daring her to protest. She couldn't remember the last time she'd seen him smoke. Her mother had begged him to stop. As a concession to her, he'd cut down a lot. Dana had hoped he would find the strength to quit altogether. Unfortunately Saskia smoked, too. Dana guessed it was asking too much.

"Tell me about Monsieur Martan." He pronounced Alex's last name the French way.

A red flag went up.

Months ago her father had started out another conversation in the same manner, only the subject in question had been Neal Robeson.

So… This was about Alex—not about the suitability of the château. Relief flooded her body.

No doubt when Alex had told her father to go ahead and explore on his own because of something Dana had confided, he hadn't liked it. She knew her dad enjoyed being a mystery to other people, so it had made him uncomfortable to be more transparent to Alex because of her. That irritation would pass, particularly since Alex wouldn't be around while her father worked.

"Martin is his Australian name," she corrected him.

With one long exhale, the room filled with smoke. "He must want to get into acting very badly to give me free rein to his entire estate."

She moved away from the door. "Have you forgotten I went to him, not the other way around? He wants money very badly to restore the château and make it a viable asset before he resumes his career as an agricultural engineer."

Her father gave her one of those condescending nods. "So that's what he's told you."

Dana refused to let him get to her. "In this case you're not dealing with another Neal type."

"No," he muttered, "Monsieur Martan is older and has far more worldly experience. Inside that supposedly deserted château with no electricity beyond the main floor, your bedchamber has been laid out so exquisitely, it even took *my* breath."

She scoffed. "Careful, Dad. You're beginning to

make this sound like Beauty and the Beast. When I told him I was planning to stay there at night in my new sleeping bag, he insisted I have a decent bedroom."

He stubbed out his cigarette. "I forbid it, Dana."

Forbid? "I think you've forgotten I passed eighteen a long time ago." As she turned to leave, she heard knocking on the door.

"Jan? It's Saskia. Let me in, *lieveling*."

The timing was perfect, but her father looked ready to throw something.

"I'll get it," Dana volunteered before opening it. "Hi, Saskia. Did you have a good flight?"

"So-so." The brunette actress kissed her on both cheeks, a pretense at civility.

Dana went along with to keep the peace.

"I was just leaving. See you later, Dad."

Without hesitation she rushed out of the hotel. It didn't take her long to reach the château.

By the time she'd pulled up next to the cars and minivans parked in front, Dana realized there'd be no peace for her if her father was angry enough to renege on the contract. Alex didn't deserve it, not to mention everyone else who would be put out. It looked like it was up to her if she didn't want this boat to sink.

When she found Alex and told him she wouldn't be staying at the château after all, he would assume it was what he'd thought from the first—that she still answered to her father in everything. But as humiliating as that would be, it wouldn't matter if it meant Alex received all his money.

"Dana?"

She got out of the car in time to see David hurrying

toward her from the woods. He was her father's age, a wonderful family man with a great gift for writing.

When he caught up to her, he hugged her hard. "Bless you, Dana. Bless you, bless you for this. Words can't describe."

"I know." She'd felt the same way after seeing the château for the first time. It was how she felt now, only more so. He finally let her go, still beaming.

David's reaction settled it. This film was of vital importance to him, too; therefore she had no choice but to pack up her things and drive to the Hermitage. She checked her watch. It was ten to six. Pretty soon everyone would leave for the night. That's when she'd go inside to get her things so she wouldn't draw attention to herself.

Until then she would walk around the back of the château to find Alex. After what he'd done for her, she owed him an explanation of why she wouldn't be staying here after all. He would never know that because of him, she'd experienced the most exciting day and night of her entire life. A man like him was too good for her, but at least this was a memory she'd hug to herself forever.

After telling David she'd see him later, she followed the path next to the hedge at the side of the château. It led around to the back where she hadn't been before. To her surprise the ground, covered by a mass of tangled vegetation divided by a path, sloped gently toward the river.

She wandered down it a few feet, marveling at the sight. Alex had meticulously cleaned out one half of it to reveal individual fruit trees. Who would have guessed what had been hidden there? In its day, the grounds would have been a showplace.

The other part still needed to be tackled, but he was making inroads. She saw his truck piled with cleared-out vegetation. Nearby were various tools including a power saw.

"Bonsoir, ma belle."

Her heart raced. "Alex?" She'd heard his deep, seductive voice, but couldn't see him anywhere.

"I'm in a tree!" He tossed something small and green at her feet.

She reached for it, then looked up. A long, tall ladder had been propped against the trunk. Hidden by masses of leaves, she only saw parts of his hard-muscled physique. He brushed a few aside, allowing her a glimpse of his disarming white smile. Dana could hardly breathe.

"Are these all apple trees?"

"Blanc d'Hiver apples," he asserted. "The kind that make the best *tartes aux pommes.* By late October I might be able to harvest a few. The trees behind you yield Anjou pears."

Dana shook her head. "No wonder this place is called Belles Fleurs. When their blossoms come out, the sight from the château windows will be glorious.

"That all depends if I live long enough to make it out of this primeval forest to prune another day."

She chuckled. "How old are you?" She'd been dying to know.

"Thirty-three."

"You've got years yet!"

"Years of what?"

"I'm sure I don't know." Dana didn't want to think about his life when he moved on to other places. Other women… It would take a very special woman to capture his heart. "Tell me something—"

"That covers a lot of territory."

Laughter escaped her lips. "Can you see the vineyard from that altitude?"

"So you noticed the building housing the winepress."

"Yes, but I also heard that the vineyard once produced the famed Domaine Belles Fleurs label."

She heard the leaves rustle. In seconds he'd negotiated the ladder with swift male agility before jumping to the ground, carrying his hand saw. "Someone's been gossiping." He gathered the branches he'd just cut and threw them in the truck bed. "Wait, let me guess— Madame Fournier at the Hermitage."

Nothing got past him. "Who else?" She smiled, but he didn't reciprocate.

"Since my arrival, word has leaked out that a long-lost Fleury is back in Les Coteaux du Layon. It sounds like she was talking out of school again."

Dana had irritated him again; the last thing she'd wanted to do. "Only because I wanted to buy a bottle of the dessert wine we drank the other evening. She told me it came from the Domaine Percher, but she added that the very best Anjou wine used to come from the Domaine Belles Fleurs."

Alex rubbed his thumb along his lower lip. "There hasn't been a bottle produced since 1930."

"That's what she said. Naturally I was curious."

"Naturally," he came back, but to her relief he sounded more playful than upset.

"When I flew back to California, I did a little research on the Internet."

His eyes narrowed on her features. "What did you find out?"

"For one thing, Dutch merchants used to favor the Belles Fleurs brand."

He expelled a breath. "I might as well hear the rest. Knowing Dana Lofgren, you didn't stop there."

Embarrassed to be rattling on, a wave of heat washed over her. "There isn't any more, though I will say this— I'm no connoisseur, but if the Belles Fleurs wine was as good as the kind we had at the Hermitage, then it's the world's loss."

She noticed him shift his weight. "My parents never breathed a word to me about a vineyard."

"You're kidding!"

"My father was so intent on protecting my mother from any more pain, we simply didn't talk about her past. When the letter from the attorney for my grandfather's estate showed up, there was no mention of a vineyard. In fact, he led me to believe the place was virtually unsalvageable."

"Sounds like he was hoping you would forfeit so he could buy it for a song."

He nodded. "I got the distinct impression he was hiding something, but didn't understand until I saw the winepress building and eventually discovered the vineyard. No doubt he'd been bombarded by vintners throughout the Anjou region who wanted to buy it and work it, even if they couldn't afford to purchase the château."

"So he thought he'd buy it first," she theorized, "recognizing the money it could bring in."

"Exactly."

"Is it supposed to be a secret then?"

He put his hands on his hips, unconsciously emanating a potent virility that made her tremble. "Not at all."

"But you wish I'd mind my own business."

"You misunderstand me, Dana. There's something you *don't* know. Come with me while I make this last haul and I'll explain."

His invitation made it possible for her to be with him a little longer. She couldn't ask for more than that, but he paused before his next comment ruined the moment. "Unless of course your assistance is required elsewhere." His brow had furrowed. "Naturally your father has first call on your time."

Between Alex and her dad, she felt like a football being tossed back and forth. Both of them treated her like she was a child who couldn't act for herself. She'd thought she and Alex had been communicating like two adults just now, but she'd thought wrong!

Bristling with the heat of anger she muttered, "If that were the case, I wouldn't have come out here, would I?"

Turning on her heel, she started to retrace her steps, but Alex moved faster. In the next breath his hands had closed around her upper arms, pulling her back against his chest. "Why *did* you come?" he asked in a silky voice.

With his warm breath against her neck, too many sensations bombarded her at once. The solid pounding of his heart changed the momentum of hers. Aware of his fingers making ever-increasing rotations against her skin through her top, she felt a weakness attack her body. Pleasure pains ran down her arms to her hands.

"I—I wanted to thank you." She could hardly get the words out.

"For what?" he demanded, turning her around, causing her head to loll back. His dark gaze pierced hers. "That sounded like you're leaving on a trip. Mind telling me where you're going?"

"The landfill? It may be a French one, but I can still think of more romantic places."

"Dana." His voice grated.

Of course he already knew the answer to his own question, but his male mouth was too close. Her ache for him had turned into painful desire. She needed to do something quick before she forgot what they were talking about.

"I should have taken your advice before you went to so much trouble for me." She tried to ease away from him, but he didn't relinquish his hold. "My only consolation is that it's one room less you'll have to clean and furnish once you get started on the inside of the château."

Those black eyes roved over her features with increasing intensity. "You knew your father wasn't going to approve. What's changed?"

Dana moistened her lips nervously. "Remember the old saying about picking your battles?" She noticed a small nerve throbbing at the corner of his mouth. In other circumstances she'd love to press her lips to it. "This one isn't important."

She kept trying for a little levity, hoping it would help. It didn't. Her comment had the opposite effect of producing a smile. Some kind of struggle was going on inside him before his hands dropped away with seeming reluctance.

This was the moment to make her exit. "See you around, Alex."

Needing to put distance between them, she went back

to the château to pack. It had emptied except for Paul and David. While they were talking in the grand salon, she hurried out to the car with her suitcase and headed for the hotel.

The same woman she'd talked to before smiled at her. "*Bonsoir*, Mademoiselle Lofgren."

"*Bonsoir, madame.* I need the key to room eleven, please."

Her arched brow lifted. "Eleven? But it is already occupied."

"I know. My father and I have adjoining rooms."

"*Non, non.* A Mademoiselle Brusse checked in a little while ago. I've already given her the key."

Something strange was going on.

"I see. Thank you for your help, *madame.*"

"Of course."

Dana grabbed her suitcase and opted for the stairs rather than the lift. Once she reached the next floor, she walked midway down the hall and knocked on her father's door several times, but he didn't answer. No doubt he was with Saskia, but this couldn't wait. She pulled out her cell phone and called him.

"Dana?" He'd picked up on the second ring.

"Hi, Dad. What's going on? I tried to check in my room, but the desk said Saskia had picked up the key."

He answered her question with another one. "Where are you?"

"Standing in front of your hotel room door."

"I'll be right out." The line went dead.

Within seconds he joined her in the hall and shut the door behind him. His famous scowl was more pronounced than earlier in the day. "Saskia and I have been having problems, but I can't afford to end things with her until after the picture's finished. She doesn't know my intentions of course."

Dana was glad her father was coming to his senses for his own sake.

"She begged me to let her stay in the adjoining room while we work out our differences."

Poor Saskia. "That sounds reasonable."

His eyes darted to her suitcase. "Saskia's room is free at the hotel in Angers. I called and told the concierge to have it waiting for you."

"Thank you," she muttered, "but I'll make my own arrangements."

There was a long silence before he said, "If you go back to the château, you do so at your own peril."

Their gazes clashed. "And Monsieur Martin's, too?"

His eyes flashed with temper. "How did that man get his tentacles into you so fast?" he countered.

Dana stood her ground. "Why won't you answer the question, Dad?"

It took him forever to respond.

"I still forbid you, but as you reminded me earlier with all the carelessness of your culture, you're not seventeen anymore."

He went back in the bedroom. As she turned away, she heard the door close. Despite his hurtful remark, she was confident he wouldn't penalize Alex. Not because he'd had a sudden attack of human decency, but because he knew he'd never find a spot this perfect for his film.

Her throat felt tight all the way back to the château where she discovered the gate had been closed. A symbolic dagger for the trespasser to beware?

She closed her eyes, afraid she was being as super-stitious as her father. After a minute, she reached for her purse and pulled out the remote. Once she'd driven on through, she shut it again, then continued on to the courtyard.

After getting out of the car, she tried to open the front door, but it was locked and Alex's truck was no-where in sight. He might still be around the back, working. Acting on that possibility, she drove to the other end of the château. It wound around to the orchard.

He wasn't there.

A hollow sensation crept through her. She checked her watch. It was already eight o'clock. Disturbed that he might have made plans with a woman and had gone into Angers for dinner, she drove to the front of the château once more.

Of course she could phone him, but he wouldn't ap-preciate a call if he was with someone else. Besides, he'd thought she'd gone back to the Hermitage for good. The only thing to do was drive to the next village in the opposite direction from Chanzeaux where she wouldn't run into her father by accident. After grabbing a bite to eat, she would come back and wait for Alex.

"*Bonsoir*, Monsieur Martan."

"*Bonsoir*, Madame Fournier. Has Mademoiselle Lofgren checked in yet?" He hadn't seen Dana's car outside.

She shook her head. "*Non, monsieur.* She doesn't have a reservation here."

"Then her father isn't staying here, either?"

"But of course he is! The person in the adjoining

room is Mademoiselle Brusse. She's an actress doing a film with *le fameux* Monsieur Lofgren."

His hands clenched in reaction. If Dana hadn't come here, then she'd probably driven into Angers to get herself a hotel room. The last trip to the landfill had cost him time before he'd showered and changed clothes, thus the reason he'd missed her.

"Merci, madame." Before she could detain him with more gossip, he went back outside to phone Dana from the truck. It rang seven times. He was about ready to hang up in frustration when he heard her voice.

"Alex?" She sounded out of breath.

"What's wrong?" he demanded without preamble.

"My left front tire is flat. I've been trying to work the jack, but I've been having problems. Pretty soon I'll figure it out."

The band constricting his lungs tightened. "Where are you exactly?"

"Somewhere on the road between Rablay and Beaulieu."

"I'm on my way." He started the engine and drove away from the hotel. "Stay in your car and lock the doors."

"Don't worry about me."

"What caused you to go in that direction?"

"When you weren't at the château, I decided to get dinner in the next village, but I never made it."

The blood hammered in his ears. "You came by the château?"

"Yes. Dad and Saskia have been quarreling. It's nothing new, but while they work things out she's going to stay in the adjoining room."

"Why did you come back?"

"In order to ask if I could rerent my bedroom so to speak, that is if you don't mind."

He muttered something unintelligible under his breath.

"What did you say, Alex? I'm not sure we have a good connection."

This had nothing to do with the connection. His hand tightened on the steering wheel. "And your father approves?"

There was a brief silence. "No. Does that mean there's no room at the inn?"

Ciel! "You know better than to ask that question." The fact was just beginning to sink in that she'd come to him whether her father liked it or not.

"You sound upset. In case I've ruined your plans for the evening, please forget about me. If I can't fix the tire, I'll walk to the château and wait until you come home later."

"No, you won't—" A woman who looked like her wasn't safe in daylight. Alex didn't even want to think about her being alone in the dark.

"I realize you think I'm too young to do anything on my own, but I'm not helpless."

"Age has nothing to do with it. I'm just being careful."

"Point taken," she admitted in a quiet voice.

His body relaxed. "Where would you like to eat tonight?"

"You mean you haven't had dinner, either?"

"As a matter of fact, I went to the Hermitage in the hope we could drive into Angers for a meal, but Madame Fournier informed me a certain actress had taken over your room."

"Saskia didn't waste any time announcing herself."

"Madame Fournier lives for such moments."

Her sigh came through the line, infiltrating his body. "I don't want to talk about either of them. I'm too hungry. To be honest my mouth has been watering for one of those quiches we bought in Angers. Are there any left?"

He smiled. "I've saved everything for us. There's more than plenty for several meals." Alex preferred dining in tonight where he didn't have to share her with anyone. While his thoughts were on their evening ahead, he saw her car at the side of the road and pulled off behind her. "Don't be alarmed. I've got your car in my headlights."

"I have to admit I'm glad it's you. I'll hang up."

Alex heard the slight quiver in her voice before the line went dead. Though he had no doubt she could handle herself in most situations, her relief was evident. So was his now that he'd caught up to her.

After shutting off the ignition, he reached in the glove box for his flashlight and got out of the truck. She rolled down the window and poked her beautiful golden head out the opening. He caught the flash of those startling blue eyes in the light.

"Did I do it wrong?"

For a second he was so concentrated on her, everything else went out of his mind. "Let me take a look," he murmured, before shining the light on the tire. It was flat, all right.

She climbed out of the car. "What can I do to help?"

Her flowery fragrance seduced him. "If you'll hold the flashlight right there, I'll have this changed in a minute."

Their fingers brushed in the transfer, increasing his awareness of the warm feminine body standing behind him. He hunkered down to work the jack and remove the tire. Several cars slowed down as they passed before moving on. "You must have picked up a nail."

"I'll get it fixed tomorrow." When he started to get up she asked, "Would you like the light to find the spare?"

"Thank you, but I don't need it."

He opened the car door to trip the trunk latch. Except for her sleeping bag, there was nothing else inside. That made it easy to retrieve the smaller tire and put it on. After he'd tightened the lug nuts, he lowered the car and put the flat in the trunk with the tools.

She walked toward him and handed him the flashlight. "You did that so fast I can't believe it."

"All it takes is practice. Over the years I've gotten a lot of it driving trucks out in areas where you have to do the repairs yourself or walk fifty miles."

"Thank you for coming to my rescue, even if you pretend it was nothing."

"It was my pleasure." Unable to help himself, he briefly kissed those lips that had been tantalizing him. They were soft and sweet beneath his. He wanted so much more, but not out here on the road in view of any passerby. "Now let's get back to the château. I'll follow you."

He helped her inside the car, then he jumped in the truck. She made a U-turn and headed for Rablay-Sur-Layon only a short distance off. Once they'd turned onto the private road, he pressed the remote so they could drive through the gate.

The noise it made clanking shut was the most satisfying sound he'd heard in a long time. It signaled that they'd left the world behind. For the rest of the night it was just the two of them.

CHAPTER FIVE

ALEX's unexpected kiss had done a good job of melting her insides. She'd been wanting it to happen, but he'd caught her off guard out there on the road where other people could see them. To make things even more frustrating, he'd ended it too soon for her to respond the way she ached to do.

Dana had almost suffered a heart attack when she'd seen him walk toward her car dressed in a charcoal shirt and gray trousers. His rugged male beauty electrified her senses.

By the time he parked next to her in front of the château, she was feeling feverish with longings she couldn't seem to control. If she didn't get a grip, he'd be convinced he was dealing with a schoolgirl instead of a mature woman.

As she started to get out, he opened the back door and reached for her suitcase.

Being on her own so much, she had to concede it was wonderful to be waited on and taken care of. When she looked back on the dilemma she'd been in before he'd phoned her, a shudder rocked her body. He'd spoken the truth. She wouldn't have been safe inside the car or walking back to the château alone.

Alex used his remote to open the front door. Once they were inside he put down her suitcase and turned on the lights. She felt his dark-eyed gaze rest on her. "Food before anything else, I think."

"I like the way you think."

By tacit agreement she followed him through the foyer past the staircase to a hallway leading to the west wing. He turned on another light. Dana hadn't been in this part of the château before. They passed a set of double doors.

"May I see inside?"

"Of course." Alex opened them for her. "This is a drawing room that opens into the grand dining room. As you can see, boards have been nailed over the broken windows. When they're repaired, they'll look out on the front courtyard."

The beauty of the interior caused her to cross her arms over her chest and rub her hands against them in reaction. "I've never seen anything so lovely. The ornate walls and ceilings make me feel like I'm in a palace. After this, you wonder how your mother adapted to life in a normal house."

"I'm sure my father did his share of worrying about it, but they had a good marriage which hopefully made up for a lot of things." Just then he sounded far away.

"Believe it or not, my parents had a solid marriage, too, albeit an unorthodox one. Mom had to make most of the concessions, but she must have wanted to, otherwise she would have left him because he's quite impossible."

Dana followed his low chuckle back out to the hall and down to a turn that opened up to the kitchen.

"How incredible!" It was massive with a vaulted ceiling and an open hearth fireplace that took up one wall. Modern appliances had been mixed in with the ancient. A long rectory-type table with benches sat in the middle of the room. She estimated sixteen people could be seated there comfortably.

"Through that far door on the right are the steps leading down to the wine cellar. The door at the other end of the kitchen leads to a pantry and an outside door. Another leads to a bathroom."

"You've reminded me I need to wash my hands after ineptly handling that jack. Excuse me for a moment."

She darted through the pantry stocked with supplies. A new washer and dryer had been installed in there. The pantry was big enough to be a master bedroom. Beyond it she found the bathroom Alex had upgraded. It wasn't quite as large as the one upstairs, but it had every accoutrement.

The tiles covering the walls and ceiling were the same as the ones lining the counters in the kitchen. Each was an original and had been hand-painted on a cream background to depict grapes, apples, pears, all the fruits probably grown on the estate.

Continually charmed by everything she saw, Dana was in a daze when she returned to the kitchen. She'd been gone so long, Alex had already put their meal on the table. He was standing next to one end with a bottle of wine in his hand.

"Sorry I got detained, but the tiles were so adorable I had to study them."

"Now that I'm getting to know you better, I find that entirely understandable. Sit down and I'll serve you."

As she took her place, he uncorked it and poured the pale gold liquid into their glasses.

Their eyes met. "Is this a special wine?"

"It is now." His deep voice sounded more like a purr. He sat down opposite her and lifted his glass. "To us. May our unexpected month together hold many more pleasant surprises."

He'd just laid down the ground rules. She wasn't to read more into that kiss than he'd intended. After the month was over, this season of enchantment would come to an end. She smiled through her distress at the thought and clinked her glass against his. "To you, *monsieur*. May you outlive any regrets for your magnanimity."

With her emotions in turmoil, she forgot and drank her wine like it was water. Too late she realized her mistake and tried to recover without him noticing, but it wasn't possible considering she was choking. His dark brown eyes smiled while he munched on a croissant. "When you're able to speak again, tell me how you find your wine."

Embarrassed, Dana cleared her throat. "It's sweet like the one we had the other night, but it's not the same domaine, is it? This time I tasted honey."

"That's very discerning of you. When you seemed to enjoy the one we had at the Hermitage, I bought this bottle for you to try. It's another Layon wine called Chaume from the Domaine des Forges. I'm told it's the sweetest of all."

She got this fluttery feeling in her chest. Anxious not to appear disturbed by him, she bit into the quiche he'd warmed for them. It wasn't just his words, but the way he said them. Here she'd promised herself not to get carried away, but being alone with him like this caused her to think many forbidden thoughts.

"You were very thoughtful to do that. Now that I've sampled both, it makes me wonder what the Belles Fleurs wine tasted like."

"We'll never know…" His voice trailed. "Every bottle has disappeared from the wine cellar. I suppose there are a few connoisseurs who bought them up. They might still have them stored in their wine cellars for a special occasion. Good dessert wines can last for decades."

"It seems so sad there's no more wine being made from the grapes grown on your property."

He stared at her, deep in concentration. "I'm afraid I'm not a vintner. It's a whole other world that requires the best oenologist you can hire. A wine expert doesn't come cheap, nor a vintner and crew."

"What do you suppose happened to the records kept by the vintners of this estate?"

"I have no idea. Possibly they're hiding in one of the tons of boxes holding the contents of the library. You haven't seen that room yet. It's in the right wing next to the music room."

After she finished off her quiche, she asked, "Are the books upstairs with the furniture?"

"They're in one of the third floor turret rounds."

She peeled an orange and ate several sections as she digested what he'd told her. "Alex—aren't you curious about them? About the history of this place?"

He ate some cheese before swallowing the rest of his wine. "Not particularly."

"Why?" When he didn't immediately answer her,

she felt terrible. It was clear he didn't want to talk about his family's past. "I'm sorry. I didn't mean to pry. It's none of my business."

Unable to sit there any longer, she jumped up and started clearing the table.

"Leave it, Dana."

Ignoring his edict, she took everything over to the sink. "I want to make myself useful before I go upstairs."

"You're tired then?"

"Yes." She seized on the opening he'd given her. "You must be, too, considering how early you get up and the exhausting labor you do every day." She found detergent to wash their plates and glasses.

Her heart skipped a beat when he joined her with a towel to dry them. Soon she had the table wiped off and the kitchen cleaned up. They were both standing at the counter.

"Since one of your jobs is to provide your father with his daily lunch, feel free to fix it here."

Surprised by the offer, she lifted her head to look at him. "I would never presume on your generosity like that. I've already made arrangements with the Hermitage to bring them here. When everyone else breaks for lunch, he likes to stay put and eat alone. I always bring him hotel food when we're on location."

He stared at her through veiled eyes. "When I have a perfectly functional kitchen, that's a lot of needless going back and forth."

Dana's attraction to him was eating her alive. "I couldn't."

"Not even if I asked you to make lunch for me at the same time?"

Her heart skidded all over the place. "You mean, and bring it out to you while you're working?"

Something flickered in the dark recesses of his eyes. "It would save me a lot of time and trouble."

Yes, she could see how a cook would make his life easier so he could get on with his business. In that regard he wasn't any different from her father.

"I have to admit doing something for you would make me feel a little better about staying on the premises."

"Good," he said in a voice of satisfaction. "I'm anxious to clear out the debris from the rest of the orchard as soon as possible."

"That's right," she murmured, trying to disguise her dismay. "You're in a hurry to leave for Louisiana." The thought of him not being on his property one day was anathema to her.

She rubbed her palms against her hips in a self-conscious gesture he took in with those dark, all-seeing eyes. "W-what do you like for lunch?" Her voice faltered.

He studied her for a moment. "I'm certain anything you make will be delicious."

His charm caused her breath to catch. "In the morning I'll do some grocery shopping when I go into Angers to get the tire repaired."

"As long as you're doing that, would you mind buying enough food to cover breakfast and dinner for a week, too? In the end it will save our energy for more important matters."

Except that her job of making sure her father had his lunch wasn't on the same scale of doing it for Alex. The thought was preposterous. "You trust me?"

"Let's just say I'm willing to go on faith."

Her lips curved upward. "That's very courageous of you."

Alex's eyes glimmered. "Just as long as you don't simmer pickled pigs feet in wine sauce and tell me it's chicken, we'll get along fine."

Her chuckle turned into laughter. She would love to freeze this moment with him. To be with a man like this, to be the recipient of his attention and enjoy his company in all the little private ways brought joy to her life she'd never experienced.

Early in the morning she'd take stock of his kitchen to find out what staples were on hand. While her mind was ticking off her plans, he pulled out his wallet and laid several large denominations of Eurodollars on the counter. Dana was too bemused by events to argue over who would pay.

"Merci, monsieur." After gathering them, she walked over to the bench where she'd been sitting and stashed them in her purse.

"De rien, mademoiselle." When he spoke French his whole demeanor changed, making her wholly aware of the sensual side of his nature. "Let me get some more candles and my flashlight from the pantry and I'll accompany you upstairs. You look sleepy."

As he walked off, she reflected on his words. A woman wanted to hear certain things from the man she found desirable, but *sleepy* relegated her to daddy's little girl status.

Since meeting him she had to concede he'd been protective of her. However, that didn't translate into a *grande passion* on his part. Though he'd brushed his lips against hers earlier, not by any stretch of the imagination would she have called it hunger unbridled or anything close.

Afraid she was already giving off needy vibes, she left the kitchen ahead of him and walked through the château to the foyer. Eyeing her suitcase, she grabbed it and started up the stairs. He caught up to her at the top where there was no more light and guided her down the corridor to her room.

It wasn't really her room, but it's the way she thought of it. When the flashlight illuminated the interior, she felt she'd come home. The sensation stayed with her while he lighted fresh candles in the floor candelabra.

Avoiding his eyes, she put her suitcase down. "You didn't have to do that. My flashlight is right here next to the bed."

"I wanted to," came the deep velvet voice that was starting to haunt her. "Candlelight brings out the pink and cream porcelain of your skin. I've never met a woman with a complexion like yours."

What was she supposed to say to that? "Lots of people have told me I look like a cherub and pat me on the head."

His gaze narrowed on her mouth. "Don't you know any flesh and blood man seeing you doesn't dare do anything else for fear a bolt of lightning will strike him? Get a good sleep."

After he disappeared, she stood there shaking like the ground under her feet during a California earthquake.

On her return from Angers the next day, Dana parked around the end of the château and carried the groceries and other purchases into the kitchen through the side entrance. She'd purposely unlocked it before leaving.

Her father liked to eat at twelve-thirty sharp. She checked her watch. It was almost that time now. She hurriedly put things away, then made both lunches and packed them in the two baskets with a thermos of hot coffee each.

As soon as everything was ready she went in search of her father. He was in the grand salon opposite Alex's office talking with the two leads. In no time at all the staff had brought down furniture and everything was starting to take shape. Under Paul's watchful eye the place had become a beehive of organized commotion.

Knowing better than to disturb her dad, she stepped inside the room and put the basket next to the door. He didn't even glance at her before she darted back to the kitchen. Now she was free to deliver the second basket to the unforgettable male responsible for last night's insomnia.

Once she entered the orchard, the sound of sawing reached her ears. Alex had put the ladder against a different tree this time. Slowly but surely he was making progress. She admired him so much for doing everything single-handedly, she wanted to shout to the world how remarkable he was.

It seemed a shame he had to come down out of the tree for his lunch. Adrenaline gushed through her veins at the idea of taking it up to him. Why not? There was so much foliage, he could find a spot to secure the basket while he ate.

Without hesitation she started up the rungs, excited to repay him any way she could for his generosity. Almost to the top she called to him. "Alex?"

The sawing stopped. "Dana?" He sounded shocked. Evidently he hadn't seen her. "Where are you?"

Two more steps and she poked her head through the leaves. "Right here. The mountain decided to come to Mohammed," she quipped, but she didn't get the reaction she'd hoped for. His eyes pierced hers in fury.

In an instant his expression had grown fierce. Lines deepened around his hard mouth, giving him a forbidding expression. "Whatever possessed you to climb all the way up here? If you fell from this height, you could break a great deal more than your lovely neck."

She'd been prepared for a lot of things, but not his anger. "You're right. It was foolish of me. I didn't stop to think how guilty you would feel if anything happened to me and you'd be forced to report it to my father. *My* mistake. Here's your lunch." She formed a nest of leaves and propped it as securely as she could in front of him. *"Bon appetit."*

"Dana—" he ground out, but she ignored him. Without any encumbrance she was able to go back down the ladder in record time. He called to her again, this time in frustration.

"Stop worrying, Alex. You had every right to be angry!" she shouted back before running around the side of the château.

Since the rest of her day was free, she would go sightseeing. After grabbing her purse from the pantry, she made sure the door was locked, then got in her car and backed around to the front.

Her heart didn't resume its normal beat until she'd driven a good fifty kilometers on the repaired tire. At the next village she pulled off the road into a park. In the distance she saw some swans on a lake. The serene scene mocked the turmoil going on inside of her.

After the experience with Neal she'd promised herself she wouldn't get close enough to a man again to expose her deepest feelings. But the pathetic little stunt she'd just pulled revealed holes in her best intentions, forcing her to come face-to-face with her own idiocy.

The need to channel her roiling emotions drove her from the car. She spent the rest of the afternoon walking around the lake, making plans that had nothing to do with Alex. On the way back to the château she stopped for a meal and didn't return to Rablay until five-thirty.

She was relieved no one had gone to their hotels yet. With everyone still around, Alex would make himself scarce. That gave her time to reach her room without him noticing. She'd hibernate there until tomorrow. New day, new beginning.

No sooner had she started down the upstairs hall than she saw Saskia coming out of her bedroom. The brown-haired model turned actress could turn any man's head, but she didn't have the same effect on Dana. The invasion of privacy infuriated her under any circumstances, but if she'd been snooping around on orders from Dana's father, she was ready to declare war.

"Hi!" Saskia was a cool customer. She didn't have the grace to blush or act embarrassed. Dana couldn't bring herself to reciprocate with a greeting. "What did you have to do for the owner of this fabulous estate to give you special privileges?"

"Why don't you ask him yourself?"

"I haven't met him yet, but the girls in makeup tell me he's beyond gorgeous."

That was one way of describing him. Saskia's jaw would drop when she saw Alex for the first time.

"Didn't Paul tell you the petit salon and this bedroom were off-limits?"

"I didn't think he meant me."

"Why not?"

Throwing back another question managed to unsettle her a little. "Actually I was looking for you in the hope we could talk."

"About what?"

"Now you're being obtuse. You know very well your father and I aren't getting along right now. I was hoping you'd be able to tell me what I'm doing wrong."

"I can't fault you for anything, Saskia. I wouldn't presume."

"That's no help."

Dana took a steadying breath. "That's because there is no answer. You're not my mother, but you've always known that, so the truth couldn't be a surprise to you. If it's any consolation, I can't do it right, either."

Saskia flashed her a shrewd regard. "Maybe if I stayed here at the château, Jan would worry about me sometimes? See me in a different light?"

You mean, as mistress of the manor with a real live Frenchman attached? Now things were beginning to make sense. She'd been looking for Alex…

"I'm sure I don't know."

"Do you think the owner of the château would let me stay here?"

"Haven't a clue."

She pursed her lips. "I suppose it helped that you're Jan's daughter. Maybe being his girlfriend would work for me."

"It's worth a try."

Her green eyes gleamed in anticipation of confronting Alex. "I agree. Thanks for the talk."

Dana watched her slender figure disappear before she went to her bedroom. Saskia had been fighting a losing battle when it came to Dana's father. No doubt seeing the eight-by-ten photograph of Dana's mother and a smaller photograph of her parents propped on the dresser underlined the futility of Saskia's relationship with him.

As for Dana, she had her own problem in the futility department where Alex was concerned. He couldn't leave for the States fast enough. How ironic that because she'd seen his ad on the Internet, she'd unwittingly made it possible for him to reach his goal sooner. Saskia could dream all she wanted, but she was in for a shock.

Alex worked in the orchard until twilight. One more trip to the landfill and he'd call it a night. The delicious, filling lunch Dana had delivered air express without consideration for her personal safety had kept him going through the dinner hour.

Much as he'd wanted to go after her, he hadn't wanted an audience that included her father, *grace a dieu*. Since no one knew what had transpired, he decided it would be better to apologize to her after hours when they were alone.

On the way back from his last haul, he locked the gate for the night and drove on to the front of the château. The sight of her rental car meant she was home. His pulse shot off the charts as he hurried inside and made a quick inspection of the ground floor in the hope he might bump into her.

To his chagrin all he found besides furniture in the grand salon was an empty basket and thermos placed at the foot of the paneled door. It was identical to the one she'd brought Alex. He carried it to the kitchen where he'd put his on the way in from the truck.

A few minutes later after a shower and change of clothes, he phoned her while he was warming some food for his dinner. Maybe she'd come down and join him.

"Alex?" She answered on the fourth ring. "Is there something wrong?"

"Yes," he blurted. At this point in their relationship, nothing but honesty would do.

"Did you lose your remote and can't get in the château?"

"I'm afraid my problem can't be fixed that easily."

He felt her hesitate before she said, "Did the studio from Paris cancel on you for mid-September?"

The strong hint of anxiety in her tone plus the fact that she remembered what he'd told her humbled him. He'd grovel if necessary to get back on the footing they'd had before she'd brought him his lunch.

Alex cleared his throat. "I appreciate your concern, but the truth is, I was rude to you earlier today. It takes a lot to frighten me, but when I saw you appear among the leaves like some impossibly adorable wood nymph and realized how far you were from the ground, I lost any perspective I should've had."

She let out a wry laugh. "The relegation from cherub to wood nymph is a subtle improvement I like, so I'll take it."

Dana…

"As for the rest, I've had all day to ponder my actions over that brainless stunt. Chalk it up to the enchantment of this place."

He had to clamp down hard on his emotions. "I can safely say it was the best meal I ever had in a tree."

"That's another distinction I'll treasure, but to save you from an early heart attack, I'll leave your lunch basket on the fender of your truck from now on."

"Why don't you come downstairs and we'll talk about it over a glass of wine." If he hadn't made the rule that he would never take advantage by going up to her room after dark unless invited, he'd be there now.

"Lovely as that sounds, I'm already half asleep. May I confess something to you?"

"By all means." He had to swallow his disappointment.

"You'll think me more superstitious than my father."

That particular word wasn't on the growing list of adjectives he found himself ascribing to her. The mention of her father in the same conversation didn't improve his mood. "Don't keep me in suspense."

"Somehow it seems sacrilegious to drink anyone else's wine on Belles Fleurs property. Does that make sense?"

His eyes closed tightly for a minute because deep in his core he'd had the same thought last night. Like the seed of the precious *chenin blanc* grape buried in the soil of the Anjou centuries ago, it seemed to have germinated out of nowhere, reminding him of his mother's roots.

"More than you know," he answered huskily.

Until last night he hadn't felt that emotional connection. Now, suddenly, it tugged at him and he realized it was all tied up with Dana, who had everything to do with this unexpected awakening.

"Alex? Are you still there?"

"Mais oui." He gripped the phone tighter. "Do you

remember asking if I could see the famous Belles Fleurs vineyard from the top of the tree?"

"Are we talking about the same question you didn't answer?"

"Meet me out in back in the morning at eight. There's something I want to show you."

"I thought I'd been warned off climbing trees."

Alex rubbed the back of his neck absently. "This requires some walking. Wear boots if you have them."

"I don't. Will trainers do?"

"Those will protect your feet better than your sandals."

"We're not going to be trekking through some snake-infested region are we? I have an irrational terror of them."

A low chuckle rumbled out of him. "Few of the snakes in France are venomous. Even then their bites aren't worse than wasp stings. So far I haven't come across any."

"That's not exactly reassuring, Alex."

"I've survived the snake worlds of Indonesia and Africa."

"But you're—"

"Yes?" he prodded after she broke off talking mid-sentence. She'd left him hanging, the perpetual state he'd been in since meeting her...and didn't like.

"I was just going to say you're invincible."

"Not quite." She'd been making inroads on his psyche from the moment they'd met, infiltrating his thoughts. No woman he'd known could claim that distinction. "For what it's worth, I promise to protect you."

"Thank you."

He wanted to be with her now. "Are you sure you're

too tired for Scrabble? I brought the game with me from Bali. My father and I often played."

"In how many languages?"

He couldn't suppress his laughter. "Why don't we find out?"

"Maybe another night when I'm not worn-out."

"What's your birthdate?" She'd be turning twenty-seven. That wasn't a day he was bound to forget, not after his assumption that she'd been much younger.

"The sixteenth."

"Next Monday. Don't make any plans. We'll celebrate and I'll let you beat me."

"I intend to."

He grinned. "Where did you go today?"

"I don't really know. I kept driving until I saw this park and a lake. There was a mother swan. She had three cygnets who followed her around, matching her exact movements like they had radar. I kept running around the lake, watching them. You've never seen anything so sweet or fascinating."

Yes, he had… The picture he had in his mind of her made his whole body ache.

"No wonder you're tired. If you'd rather make it nine o'clock—"

"I'll probably be out there by seven-thirty before any of the crew arrives. I don't like them knowing my business."

Did that include her father? Alex had the strong hunch there'd been little communication between them by phone since she'd chosen to sleep at the château against his wishes.

"That's understandable."

"To be honest, I don't see how you can stand to have your own privacy invaded by a ton of strangers wreaking havoc."

He drew in a sharp breath. "It's called money."

"I know. Let's hope word has spread throughout the film world and you're flooded with new requests. Nothing would make me happier for you. Good night." The definitive click cut off his lifeline.

While he locked up and turned out lights, it came to him Dana was a gift that might come along once in a millennium *if* you were lucky. Her father had to know that. Perhaps it was the reason he guarded his golden-haired offspring so jealously.

In a very short period of time Dana had brought out the possessive instinct in Alex. Evidently it had been lying dormant these many years just waiting to spring to life when or if the right person ever made an appearance.

For the rest of the night he was taunted by dreams of a certain blue-eyed wood nymph smiling at him through the foliage. If the handsaw and the basket hadn't been in the way, the two of them might still be up there in a bed of leaves while he made love to her over and over again.

CHAPTER SIX

"SALUT, ma belle!"

She waved to Alex, who stood by the truck, dressed in thigh-molding jeans and another white T-shirt that revealed the outline of his cut physique. The sun brought out the black-brown vibrancy of his overly long hair, a style that suited him to perfection.

He'd seen her coming around the back in her white-washed jeans and T-shirt in her favorite mocha color. His eyes followed her progress with disturbing intensity, making her feel exposed.

"It's such a beautiful morning I'm not going to ask if you're fine because you couldn't be anything else." He was freshly shaven and the faint scent of the soap he'd used in the shower permeated the air around them.

"You're right about that," he murmured. She watched him pick up a pair of long-handled pruning shears. "Shall we be off?" There was a slight curve to his lips she'd only tasted for a brief moment the other night. Unfortunately it had set up a permanent hunger nothing but a much longer repeat of the experience would satisfy.

Dana nodded before following him down the path

that bisected the orchard. Maybe she was crazy but she felt something crackling in the air between them, the kind of thing that sizzled during a lightning storm.

He kept walking until they reached the perimeter of the orchard. Juxtaposed was a forest of briars taller than they were. It reached to the river, filling the entire hillside and around the bend. She'd never seen the likes of such a thing before.

A gasp escaped her lips. "The only thing I can compare this to are the briars that overgrew Sleeping Beauty's castle, but that was in a storybook."

He slanted her a mysterious glance. "If you recall, it was a *French* fairy tale." He folded his arms. "Behold the Belles Fleurs vineyard."

"No—"

As she tried to take it all in, her eyes smarted. She turned her head so Alex wouldn't see how it had affected her. Now she understood why he hadn't wanted to talk about it.

"This is what happens after eighty years of neglect," came his gravelly voice.

She shook her head. "When you drive here from Paris and see the rows of gorgeous green vineyards…to think they can look like this…" It was impossible to articulate her horror.

"Oh, Alex—for your family to let all of this die— it's beyond my comprehension." She wheeled around to face him. "How did you bear it when you saw this desecration?"

He put down the shears. "Don't be too sad." Taking a step toward her he wiped one lone tear from her hot cheek with the pad of his thumb. As their gazes fused, his hands cupped the sides of her face. "Believe it or not this vineyard is alive."

"But it couldn't be!"

"I assure you it is. Deep in those trunks are the makings of *chenin blanc* grapes grown on Belles Fleurs *terroir*."

"I—I can't fathom it."

"Vines are unusual creatures. They want to climb. They climb and they climb while the birds eat the fruit and drop the seeds where they will. What you're looking at is a tangled mess of what is probably the best prepared soil along the Layon. Eighty years lying fallow has made it rich. All the vineyard needs is a little work."

"A little—" she cried.

Chuckling quietly, he removed his hands and reached for the shears again, leaving her dizzy with unassuaged longings. "It would take five years to turn this into a thriving business again. The first year all these trunks would have to be cut down to three feet, like this."

She watched him in wonder and fascination as he shaped it down to size like Michelangelo bringing a figure out of the marble. He threw the castoff briars to the side. Dana crouched down to examine one of them. She lifted her head. "Then what happens?"

"The next year new canes appear." He tossed out another vine. Painstaking work. "They have to be treated like newborn babies."

When she smiled, he smiled back, giving her a heart attack. "You said five years."

He nodded his dark head. "In the third year you'd see buds. In the fourth, the first new grapes would appear. By the fifth year they'd be worthy of making a good wine."

"Five years..." He wouldn't be here in five years. The thought sickened her and she jumped to her feet. "When I asked you why you weren't concerned about the vineyard, it's clear why you chose not to answer me until now. They say a picture is worth a thousand words. In this case it's more like a billion."

"Vineyards are a business and family concern. Without one, or one that can't pull together, it doesn't warrant the effort it takes to make wine." There was a residue element in his voice, maybe sadness. It brought a lump to her throat.

"No. I can see that..." Her voice trailed. "Does this mean you're considering leasing the vineyard or even selling it to a prospective vintner?"

"I'm not sure." They started walking back. She could tell he was eager to get busy in the orchard. It was time to change the subject.

"Alex? You know what a bookworm I am. Would you consider it a horrible invasion of your privacy if I went through some of the boxes in storage, just to see what was in the library? I don't speak French, but I can read enough to understand titles and that sort of thing."

"Be my guest."

Excitement welled inside her. Maybe she'd find some family records or scrapbooks he would enjoy looking at. "You mean it?"

His dark eyes seemed to be searching her very soul. "What do you think?"

"Thank you!" she cried. Without conscious thought she put her hands on his upper arms and raised up on the tips of her sneakers to kiss his jaw. What happened next happened so quickly, she never saw it coming.

Alex dropped the shears and crushed her against him, covering her mouth with his own.

She didn't know who was hungrier. All that mattered was that he was kissing her until she felt pleasure pains run through her body clear to her palms. Though she knew she couldn't die from rapture, she felt she was on the verge.

When she moaned, he whispered, "My sentiments exactly. Your mouth tastes sweeter than any Anjou wine in existence."

"Alex—" Her body shook with needs bursting out of control. She circled his neck with her arms in order to get closer and pressed little kisses along his jaw. While Dana couldn't get enough of him, his hands splayed across her back, drawing her up against his chest where she felt the thud of his heart resound.

"You're so incredibly beautiful, Dana. Help me stop before I can't." His breathing sounded shallow.

She hushed his lips with a kiss. "I don't want to stop."

He groaned. "Neither do I, but someone's coming."

Thinking that whoever it was was ruining the moment, she had to force herself to leave his arms. Still breathless from their passion, she turned in time to see Saskia in the distance. She walked toward them with purpose.

Of course. Who else.

"Well, hello," Saskia said on her approach, eyeing Alex in stunned surprise that any man could be that attractive. At thirty years of age, Saskia looked good herself and knew it. She eventually tore her eyes away to stare at Dana. They looked greener than usual. "Aren't you going to introduce us?"

"Saskia Brusse? Please meet Monsieur Alexandre

Martin, the owner of the estate. Alex, Saskia is my father's girlfriend. She also happens to be one of the actresses in the film."

"But my part doesn't come until we're in Germany which is lucky for me."

"And what part is that?" Alex asked.

She blinked before staring at Dana. "You mean you haven't told him?"

Dana refused to be put off by her. "We haven't discussed the script."

Alex shook hands with her. "I'm happy to make your acquaintance, Mademoiselle Brusse."

"Thank you. You know, I was hoping to talk to you this morning. That's why I drove over here with Jan this early."

"Why did you want to see me?"

"Didn't Dana tell you about that, either?"

"I'm afraid we've had other matters on our minds. Please enlighten me."

While Dana willed her heart to stop racing, little red spots tinged Saskia's cheeks. She didn't like the way this conversation was going. "Jan told me Dana was staying here at the château. I wondered if I might occupy one of the rooms for the rest of the month, too. While we're here in France I have a lot of time on my hands and this is such a beautiful place."

"I'm glad you think so," Alex said with a smile. "But I don't allow anyone to live here with me except my staff. Dana is helping me put Belles Fleurs' library in order. It's quite a task. Since you're acquainted with her, then you're aware she's an historian like her father. Both are brilliant."

He picked up the shears. "Now, if you ladies will

excuse me, I have to get to work. It was nice meeting you, Mademoiselle Brusse. When the film is out, I'll look forward to seeing it."

Dana had never seen anyone think on his feet that fast! Poor Saskia didn't know what had hit her. For that matter, neither did Dana... No man had ever shown her the respect or treated her the way Alex did. To defer to Dana and compliment her in front of Saskia was a new experience.

When another man might have let her sleep in the château using her sleeping bag, he'd gone out of his way to pamper her like a cherished guest. The night she'd had car trouble, he'd been there for her in an instant. He worried about her safety.

Alex was the antithesis of her father.

From the corner of her eye she noticed Saskia watching his hard-muscled body with a combination of anger at not having gotten her way and undisguised hunger. Suddenly she turned to Dana. "I saw you two before you saw me. Mixing business and pleasure can be risky."

"As you've found out with Dad," Dana drawled. "Given enough time we all live and learn. Talk to you later, Saskia." Without staying to listen to anything else, Dana hurried up the path and around to the side entrance of the château.

Alex was already up in a tree pretty much out of sight. Although he'd only claimed that Dana was working for him to checkmate Saskia, he'd given Dana permission to rummage through the boxes on the third floor. He was wonderful!

Because of his generosity, she was determined to find out anything she could about Belle Fleurs's history.

Surely there'd come a day when Alex would want to know more. After she'd fixed the lunches, she'd go up and make an initial foray.

In the meantime she needed to keep working on his dinner for tonight. She wanted to cook him something authentically French. Yesterday she'd bought all the ingredients for it and had already done some preparations. On her way into the kitchen, she plucked her mother's French cookbook from the pantry shelf where she'd left it. She opened it to the desired page.

Soak an oxtail, cut in joints, in cold water for several hours.

"I've already done that."

Wipe with a clean cloth, and brown in butter with four onions and three carrots, coarsely chopped. When the meat is brown add two crushed cloves of garlic. Cover for two minutes, then add five tablespoons of brandy. Light this and let it burn for a moment, then add one half bottle of dry white wine, and enough bouillon so that the meat bathes in the liquid. Add salt, pepper, a bouquet garni, and cook slowly for three hours with the cover on.

In a little while she had it cooking on the stove. Next task.

Saute in butter one half pound of mushrooms, a good handful of diced fat bacon and about one dozen small onions.

She'd do that after she made the lunches and delivered them.

Later on in the afternoon she checked the recipe for more instructions.

Add the meat to this and pour over all the liquid

which has been strained and from which the fat has been removed. Cover and cook for one hour more in a slow oven. The meat should be soft and the sauce unctuous without recourse to thickening with flour.

During the hour it was cooking, she hurried up the stairs. A few of the crew waved to her, but no one wanted to talk. Her dad was somewhere around, but they didn't bump into each other. That suited her just fine considering that Alex had put Saskia's ski jump nose out of joint. No doubt she'd already reported to Dana's father what she'd seen in the orchard and had distorted it further.

Eager to explore, Dana took one of the side staircases to the third floor and walked the length of the château to the turret round. When she opened the door, all she saw was a sea of boxes in the musty room. Dozens and dozens of them. None were marked. Whoever had packed things up hadn't bothered to take the time to label anything. What a shame.

She tried opening a few, but she would need a knife or scissors to do the job. Some markers to identify what was in the boxes wouldn't hurt, either. And she'd need a chair. And some rags to clean off the dust. Tomorrow when she came up, she'd be prepared.

Once she'd returned to her bedroom, she put a change of clothes and some nightwear in a large bag she'd bought yesterday. It could hold most anything and was a lot easier to carry than a suitcase. A few toiletries and the contents of her purse and she was ready to go.

Dana stood at the top of the staircase and waited until no one was in the foyer, then she descended quickly and darted to the kitchen. It smelled good in here if she said so herself. In fact, it smelled the way a proper French kitchen should.

Pleased with her efforts, she turned off the oven, took the pot out and set it on one of the burners of the stove. With everything in order, she went over to the table and pulled out her notepad.

Monsieur Martin— Better put that in case anyone came in here and read it. *Your dinner is on top of the stove. All you have to do is heat it for a few minutes. Just so you know, I'll be staying in Angers overnight, but I promise I'll be back in the morning.*

D.

She put the note on the counter by the sink where he always washed his hands. That way he'd be sure to see it. With that accomplished she slipped out through the pantry to the side entrance and walked around the front of the château to her car.

Some of the cast and crew were getting in their vehicles. They all said hello to each other before she drove off. If Alex could see her leaving from his high perch in a treetop, so much the better.

After the way she'd responded to him in the orchard, she didn't want him thinking what he was entitled to think. Heat poured into her cheeks remembering how she'd practically devoured him. At eight o'clock in the morning no less!

Last night she'd practiced painful self-control and hadn't joined him when he'd phoned her. Tonight she knew she'd cave if he so much as looked at her. The only wise thing to do was remove herself from temptation in the hope of gaining some perspective. Since meeting Alex, she had absolutely none.

* * *

Dana must have brought Alex his lunch while he'd been sawing and couldn't see her. When he came down the ladder, there was the basket sitting on top of his truck. Though disappointed she hadn't called to him, he found himself salivating for his meal.

Tonight he intended to take her out for dinner and dancing. She couldn't plead fatigue two nights in a row! He needed her in his arms and wasn't going to let anything stand in his way.

Making it an early night, he did his last haul at six and slipped into the side entrance of the château with his basket, eager to find her. When he walked through the pantry to the kitchen, something smelled wonderful. His gaze went to a covered pot on the stove.

He set the basket on the counter and drew a fork from the drawer. Dana had cooked something that smelled sensational. He lifted the cover, unable to resist putting one of the pieces of beef in his mouth. It was kind of fatty and mild, but the stock was rich. He needed a spoon for it.

As he reached for one he saw a piece of paper lying near the sink. The note was short and sweet. He let out a curse. *Dana Lofgren—What are you trying to do to me?*

Before he exploded, he needed to calm down. If she thought she was going to hide from him tonight, she could forget it. He'd find her at one of the hotels Paul had lined up for everyone. After her scare on the road the other night, she wouldn't dare go anywhere else.

His eyes flew to the pot. Alex wasn't about to eat the rest of it without her. Forget dinner and dancing! He made a place for the pot in the fridge and left the kitchen.

By the time he'd showered and changed, the château had emptied. He locked up and left for Angers, driving his truck over the speed limit. This time he wouldn't forewarn her with a phone call. No more of that.

He stopped first at the Beau Rivage, but they had no listing for her. His frustration grew when the Chatelet could tell him nothing. By the time he approached the concierge at the Metropole, he was beginning to wonder if she'd checked in at another hotel altogether.

"*Bonsoir, monsieur.* My name is Monsieur Martin from the Belles Fleurs estate in Rablay."

"Ah…it's a pleasure to meet you. I understand the members of the Pyramid Film Company staying with us are shooting a film at your château."

"That's right, *monsieur*. It's very important that I speak to Mademoiselle Brusse. I understand she's in room 140."

"*Non, non.* The beautiful actress was staying in room 122, but she's no longer with us. Mademoiselle Lofgren, the director's daughter, is occupying that room now."

"You have no idea where Mademoiselle Brusse went?"

He leaned forward. In a low voice he said, "I believe with the director."

It seemed he and Madame Fournier had a lot in common. "You've been very helpful. *Merci, monsieur.*"

"*Pas de quoi.*"

Now that Alex knew where his fetching cook would be spending the night, he left the hotel to do a few errands.

Heat from a hot sun still lifted off the cobblestones. A summer night like this was meant for lovers, but he'd never been affected to such a degree before. He was aware of wants and needs growing beneath the surface.

To feel emptiness and dissatisfaction with his life after a hard day's work was a new phenomenon for him.

His jaw hardened. After discovering Dana would be gone until tomorrow, the idea of spending the night alone at the château sounded insupportable. How was it she'd become so important to him in two weeks' time?

Before long she'd be off to Germany. And then what? Paul intimated she had plans to become a director.

Alex should never have insisted she stay. Knowing she was around day and night had him tied up in knots. Yet if he were honest with himself, he'd be just as nuts if she'd stayed at the Hermitage. No hiding place was too far for him to find her, and find her he would, father or no father.

He'd decided to give her until ten o'clock. It was five to now. After putting his purchases in the truck bed, he returned to the hotel. Mademoiselle Brusse's room was on the third floor at the end of the hall. This experience reminded him of musical chairs, a game he'd once played in elementary school. Tonight, however, the adults had decided to make it musical bedrooms minus the accompaniment.

"Dana?" he called to her as he knocked. "It's Alex. I know you're using this room, so it would be useless to pretend otherwise."

"Why would I do that?" came a familiar voice behind him. He swung around in surprise to see her coming toward him in the same clothes she'd had on that morning.

The humidity had brought a flush to her cheeks. Her hair had little golden curls with more spring when she walked. His fingers itched to play with them. She was clutching a carton in her arms. Her eyes questioned his without flickering. "If you wanted to talk to me, why didn't you phone?"

He sucked in his breath. "Would you have answered?"

"Of course."

Since he hadn't tried, he couldn't accuse her of lying. "Why didn't you tell me you planned to leave the estate tonight?"

"Didn't you get my note?" She could play the innocent better than anyone he knew. "I left it by the kitchen sink."

"I saw it," he clipped out. "I'm talking about this morning."

A tiny nerve throbbed at the base of her throat. "If you recall, we were…interrupted."

"My memory's perfect," he murmured, unable to look anywhere except her mouth. She'd started a fire with it at the vineyard. "What about at lunch when you came and went so fast I wasn't aware of it."

She averted her eyes. "I didn't make the decision to stay in town until later in the day."

He glanced at the carton. "What have you got there? You're holding it like it's a newborn baby."

The color in her cheeks intensified. "Actually it's something very old and priceless."

Alex couldn't imagine. "In that case let's take it home in my truck where it will be safe and we'll enjoy that delicious dinner you made. The aroma that filled the kitchen was mouthwatering."

Her startled gaze flew to his. "Then you haven't eaten it yet?" She sounded disappointed.

"I ate part of it, but when I realized you'd gone, I put the rest of it in the fridge for us. After the trouble you went to, I didn't want to eat all of it alone."

It frustrated him she still wasn't convinced. When he didn't seem to be getting anywhere with her, he tried a different tactic. "Why don't I hold the carton while you gather your things. Tomorrow I'll drive you back for your car. I have to come in town again anyway on business."

She bit the underside of her lip, increasing his desire for her. Hopefully it was a sign she was weakening. "All right," she finally sighed the words, "but please don't drop it. I couldn't replace it for a long time."

That sounded cryptic. At this point he was consumed by curiosity.

"I promise I'll guard it with my life."

It could *be* your life, Alex.

With her heart hammering, Dana handed him the carton. A few minutes later she'd packed everything in her bag and they left the hotel. In truth she hadn't wanted to stay here at all and had dreaded returning to the sterile room after accomplishing her objective. For him to have shown up tonight thrilled her to her tiniest corpuscle.

When they reached the truck, she lowered her bag behind the cab, then took the carton from him while he opened the doors with the remote. "Let me hold it again until you climb inside."

Alex could be so sweet. When she was settled, he gave the carton back and carefully shut the door. After they left Angers he flicked her a penetrating glance. "Did you discover anything of interest when you were opening boxes today?"

"Without tools I couldn't see inside one of them and none are marked. It was very frustrating, but tomorrow's another day. How's your orchard going?"

"Thanks to those lunches, I've accomplished two more hours of work this week. At this rate I should be finished by the end of the next one."

The days were going by too fast. Dana was starting to panic. "What's your next project?"

"To tackle the undergrowth between the château and the winepress building."

Before long everything on the outside would be done. That left the interior. With his work ethic, he'd have the place ready for tourists in no time.

She felt his eyes travel over her. "What are you thinking about so hard?"

"All the work you've been doing without any help."

"It's the kind I like."

Dana admired him more than she could say. "You obviously love the outdoors."

"I've always needed my freedom."

Oh—she knew *that*. Alex had already defined the boundaries of their relationship to the month of August. How else had he managed to elude marriage all these years? Deep in thought she didn't realize they'd entered the estate until she heard the gate clank behind them. He drove around to the side entrance and turned off the engine.

When he got out of the cab and opened her door, he flicked her what looked like a mysterious smile. "I've been looking forward to a midnight supper with you. It appears tonight's the night."

She'd dreamed of such a night. "Aren't you tired after slaving out in the heat all day?"

"On the contrary, I feel energized." On that exciting note he used his remote to let her in the château and turn on lights. While she hurried through the pantry, he followed with her bag and some purchases of his own.

"Where do you think you're going in such a rush?" He'd taken the pot out of the fridge and placed it on the stove to heat.

"I thought I'd put this away first."

He eyed the carton. "It's dark upstairs. You might fall and break whatever it is you're guarding so jealously."

Dana couldn't afford for that to happen. "You're right." She put it down on the counter.

"Why don't you sit on the bench while I wait on you. After slaving over our dinner, you deserve a rest."

"I'd rather help, but first I need to wash my hands." She walked to the sink where she saw the note she'd left. When she'd written it, she never dreamed Alex would have come looking for her to bring her back. Her pulse was off the charts.

His actions had to mean something, but she was a fool if she thought he wanted more than a few weeks pleasure with her under his roof. Like this morning when she'd succumbed so easily, she could do it again and that frightened her.

Dana had been the one to ask if she could stay at the château. If anything, she'd been the one to take advantage of Alex, not the other way around. Whatever happened from here on out, she would have to accept the consequences and live with them.

Soon the smell of the meat wafted past her nostrils. When she turned, she noticed he'd already set the table. Along with French bread and the bottle of the wine they'd enjoyed the other night, he'd added an old silver candelabra with new candles.

Once he'd lit them, he turned off the kitchen light, transforming the room into an incredibly intimate setting. His eyes beckoned her to come and sit. The gleam in those dark depths sent a tremor through her body.

She twisted her napkin nervously as he brought the contents of the pot to the table in a wonderful old round bowl with handles. After sitting down opposite her, he ladled a portion for both of them onto their plates. "Bon appetit."

Dana hoped it was good and took a first bite. To her surprise it didn't taste like anything she'd ever eaten before. She took another, but it needed something. Maybe a baguette would help.

Alex had already eaten most of his. "My compliments to the chef. Among your many talents you're a superb cook, Dana."

She put her spoon down. "No, I'm not."

He flashed her a curious glance. "Why do you say that?"

"Because it's awful. I—I wanted to make you something spectacular," she stammered. "It's not."

"What do you call it?"

"See?" Tears threatened. "Even *you* don't know what it is."

"Isn't it beef?"

"No."

"If you're trying to tell me this is pickled pigs feet, I'm surprised it's this delicious."

"Wrong animal."

One dark brow lifted, giving him a sardonic look. "Cow?"

"No."

"Horse?"

"No!"

"Frog's legs?"

She shook her head. "You'll never guess. I found the recipe in my mother's French cookbook I brought with me."

He cocked his head. "Then this could cover anything from brains to innards to tongues."

"This is more of an 'end' thing. The *marchand* at the *boucherie* told me it was a great delicacy," she confessed.

"An end thing…" She could hear his brilliant mind turning over the possibilities.

When nothing was forthcoming she said, "It's oxtail. How can the French eat it? I think it's disgusting!"

CHAPTER SEVEN

ALEX's explosion of laughter echoed off the limestone walls. It was the deep male kind, so infectious her tears turned to laughter, too.

He reached for her hand and squeezed it. His touch shot warmth through her system. "I'm touched that you went to so much trouble for me."

"I should have fixed you something *I* love. Because you're the kind of man you are, you would never say anything to hurt my feelings, but even I can tell this would have to be an acquired taste. It's too mild and fatty, a terrible thing to serve a hungry man."

"Terrible," he teased. His gaze slid to hers. It was alive with emotion. "Let's have some wine with it."

"No—wait—"

Her cry resounded in the room, wiping his sensual smile away. "Why? What's wrong now?"

"Nothing. It's just that I bought us a special surprise while I was in town. Since I didn't think I'd be seeing you before tomorrow evening, I hadn't planned on producing it yet, but under the circumstances I think now is the perfect time."

"Do I get to open it?" He looked and sounded like an excited schoolboy waiting to tear away the wrapping on his long-awaited birthday present.

She nodded. "But please be careful."

In a few swift strides he reached the counter. She got to her feet and moved closer to watch him. The carton encased an old green bottle of wine packed in straw. He drew it out to examine the magenta and cream label. She'd already had the privilege. In fact, she'd stared at it for a long time, hardly able to believe she'd been able to buy anything so precious.

His face paled. "Domaine Belles Fleurs Coteaux-du-Layon Cuvee D'Excellence, 1892, Anjou, France." As he spoke the words, he sounded like a man who'd gone into shock.

Suddenly his eyes shot to hers. They were on fire. "Where did you get this?" His voice trembled.

"I went to an impeccable source. Madame Fournier was able to put me in touch with Monsieur Honore Dumarre, a wealthy businessman and wine connoisseur living in Angers. He had three bottles of Domaine Belles Fleurs from different vintages in his wine cellar. When I explained why I wanted one, he was gracious enough to sell this to me."

She could see Alex's throat working. Even his hand was trembling. "A bottle like this can cost upward of five thousand dollars. Even meeting his full price, he'd have an almost impossible time parting with it."

Dana smiled. "Once in a while it helps that I'm Jan Lofgren's daughter. The fact that he's shooting his latest film on the Belles Fleurs estate went a long way to make up his mind for him. I threw in the fact that the new owner lived on the other side of the world until now and has never tasted his family's wine before."

Alex resembled a war victim suffering shell shock. "I have no words for what you've done," he whispered, "but you have to return it and get your money back."

She took a fortifying breath. "I knew you'd say that, but I did it for the pleasure it gave me. Do you know he wants to meet you? He'll be phoning you to make the arrangements."

Alex's face darkened with lines, revealing the remote quality she sometimes glimpsed, the quality that made her shiver. "Didn't you hear me, Dana? If you don't return it, I will." He'd already taken possession of the bottle and put it back in the carton. It sounded like he hadn't heard anything else she'd told him.

Her chin lifted defiantly. "That was *my* gift. It came from my own savings, not the studio's funds, in case you were worrying."

"If your father knew about this…"

At the mention of her dad, her anger was kindled. "Do you intend to tell him?" she fired. "Go ahead. But if you think blackmail will make me change my mind, then you don't know me at all."

"Dana," his voice grated. "This isn't the kind of thing you give someone."

"Well, pardon me, but I thought I just did. Some friends give cars—jewels—in the profession my father works in, I've seen it all. It pleased me to give you something of your mother's history, the only tangible evidence left of a thriving estate. Where's the romance in your soul?"

His hands knotted into fists. "We're talking about your hard-earned money."

She shrugged her shoulders. "There's money, and then there's money. I've never had anything I wanted to spend it on before. But I should have remembered that you're in dire straits and need to get the taxes paid, so I tell you what. You go to Monsieur Dumarre. When you get the money back, you use it to make another installment to the bank so you can get out of here sooner and pursue your career."

Blind with pain, she grabbed her bag and flew down the long corridor to the foyer. She didn't need a light upstairs. Dana knew the place blindfolded. The second she reached her room, she threw herself on the bed.

"Dana—"

She might have known he'd be right behind her. Now she couldn't sob into the pillow. "Come back downstairs so we can talk."

"I'd rather not."

"Then I'm coming in. Just remember I gave you a choice."

When she heard the door open, she sat up on the bed and turned on the flashlight next to her bed. At first glance he looked ashen-faced, but maybe it was the starkness of the light against the dark.

Alex pulled the chair away from the writing table he'd provided earlier and sat down. He leaned forward with his hands clasped between his legs and stared at her for several tension-filled moments. "Your gift has overwhelmed me."

She lowered her eyes, too full of conflicted emotions to speak.

"Dana—how can I make you understand I've never known generosity like yours. I'm touched beyond my ability to express what I'm feeling."

His sincerity caused the tightness in her chest to break up. "I guess I wanted us to know what it tasted like so much, I went overboard in your opinion. But honestly, Alex, it wasn't that much money."

"How much?" he demanded quietly. "The truth."

"He gave me a discount as a welcome-to-Anjou gift for you. It only cost three thousand dollars. You see? Not as much as you'd imagined. It's less than what I make a month."

A sound of exasperation came out of him. She wanted to reach him, but how?

"Can't you understand how happy it made me to find a bottle of wine that came from *your* vineyard? After seeing the condition it's in now, it's like—I don't know—it's like finding this amazing treasure."

The torment on his handsome face killed her. "There's only one way I'd accept it," his voice grated.

She jumped off the bed. "I won't let you pay me for it, so I'll keep it for my own souvenir from France. One day I'll open it for an important occasion a-and I'll remember," her voice faltered. "Now let's forget the whole thing, because I have." She started for the door.

"Where do you think you're going?" He was on his feet in an instant.

"Down to the kitchen to throw out the rest of that awful *Hochepot en boeuf*." Dana had to get out of there before she blurted what she really wanted to say—that she was in love with him, the gut-wrenching kind that went soul deep!

Her father would call it temporary madness, but he would have to be careful because this intensity of feeling had happened to her mother after meeting the enigmatic Swede. Her world had never been the same after that, either.

"The dishes will keep." Alex had caught up to her near the top of the stairs. He swept her in his strong arms like she was weightless and carried her back to the turret round.

"No, Alex—" she cried, trying to squirm out of his tight grasp. "Now you're feeling sorry for me like I'm a little girl who'll be all better with a peck on the cheek and a lollipop."

He laid her on the bed and followed her down so he half covered her with his hard-muscled body. She felt his fingers furrow into her hair, as if he loved the texture. "You don't have any comprehension of what I'm feeling. Would that you were a little girl I could send home to your daddy. But you're not," he muttered in what sounded like anguish.

"You're a big girl I'd like to keep locked up in this tower for my pleasure." His lips roved over her features, setting tiny fires. "Do you understand what I'm saying?"

Her heart leaped. "Then stop tormenting me and really kiss me. I've been in pain since this morning when Saskia interrupted us."

"I've been in pain much longer than that," he confessed.

The way his mouth closed over hers produced such ecstasy, she knew nothing except that this marvelous man was creating a vortex of desire deep within her. No other feeling in the world could compare. They gave kiss for kiss, savoring the taste and feel of each other. Divine sensations held her in thrall.

As time passed she needed to get closer and slid her hands around the back of his head, luxuriating in the freedom of touching and kissing him. He groaned against her tender throat. "You have no idea how much I want you."

The feel of their entwined bodies created heat, making her feverish. His caresses caused her breathing to grow shallow. "Alex—" she cried in a rapturous daze, clinging to him with helpless abandon.

"What's wrong?" he whispered against her swollen lips.

Wrong?

His hands stilled on her shoulders. "Am I frightening you? This is all too new to you, isn't it. Tell me the truth."

In that second while her mind was still capable of hearing him, she felt her heart plummet to her feet. Didn't Alex know she'd cried out his name in a state of euphoria?

The thought came to her that he would never have asked that question if he'd considered her his equal. That was because he didn't see her as a mature woman. It stunned her that his first impression of her still clung to him. In his eyes she was a girl disobeying her father's wishes—a girl so impulsive she thought nothing of sleeping in a château with a stranger and worse— spending $3,000 of her money on a whim.

Dana forgave him for that. Of course she did. She was also aware few men would have been as decent in this situation. But as long as he saw her in that light, it took away some of tonight's joy. Maybe no man would ever take her seriously if she continued to be associated with her father. Neal had been a case in point. Slowly she removed her arms from around his neck.

Tonight this unparalleled experience had given her a lot to think about. Though it killed her, she eased away from him. "You didn't frighten me, but I guess if we're being truthful, I am somewhat nervous that things have escalated so fast."

His handsome profile took on a chiseled cast before he got up off the bed. He stood at the end with his powerful legs slightly apart, away from the flashlight's beam. "I made a vow I'd never cross your threshold while you stayed here. Tonight I broke it, but I swear to you it will never happen again."

"Alex—there's no one to blame. We both lost our heads for a little while. It's human. I'd be lying if I didn't admit I enjoyed every minute of it, but as long as we're being honest, I wish you'd tell me something."

His shadowed eyes swept over her in intimate appraisal, waiting.

"Would you rather I left? Arrangements have already been made for me to stay in Saskia's room at the Metropole."

The way his mouth tightened into a thin line made her shiver. "That decision is entirely up to you. Meet me at the truck at seven-thirty in the morning and I'll drive you to Angers to get your car."

Her heart thudded till it hurt. By asking him that question, she'd proved she was the girl he'd called her, not a woman who acted on her own. Let it be the last mistake she made. "Thank you. Good night."

His dark eyes impaled hers before he disappeared out the door.

She sat on the bed for a long time pondering what to do. A girl would have a meltdown. A woman would brazen her way out of this.

He'd told Saskia that Dana was part of his staff; therefore she'd behave like an employee from here on out. She'd fix the lunches, but beyond that she'd leave him alone until she left the château. The man didn't have time for drama. He was in a hurry.

At six-thirty the next morning, Alex got up to fill the truck bed with debris. Might as well take another load to the landfill on the way to Angers. When he drove around the front of the château, his pulse sped up to find Dana waiting for him. She looked sensational in white pleated pants and a mini print top of blues and greens on a white background. He'd never known a woman so appealing, all golden and fresh as a piece of summer fruit.

"Good morning." She said it with such a friendly demeanor, last night's fireworks might never have happened. The minute she climbed in the cab, she brought the fragrance of strawberries with her, probably the result of her shampoo.

"You sound rested."

She opened her window. "I had a wonderful sleep."

His fingers tightened on the steering wheel as they headed for the gate. Throughout the endless night his desire for her had never cooled. He could still taste her mouth, feel the mold of her body. Though he'd told her it was her decision about staying or leaving, he hadn't meant it. The château wouldn't be the same without her in it. He'd made up his mind to do whatever was necessary to keep her sleeping on the premises.

"When I came down to the kitchen a few minutes ago, I couldn't find the wine bottle."

He flicked her a shuttered glance, feasting on her lovely profile. "I put it in the wine cellar for sakekeeping."

She flashed him an enticing smile. "That's where it should have been all along. Thank you."

Something was going on in that unpredictable brain of hers. Silence stretched between them. Before they left the landfill he said, "How would you like to tour Angers castle this morning? There won't be as many tourists this early. We'll escape the worst of the heat."

To his surprise she gave a caustic laugh that didn't settle well. "Do you know you're so much like my father at times, it's uncanny?"

His black brows met together in disbelief. "How did he get into this conversation?"

"When has he ever *not* been a part of it in some way or other? Last night you lit in to me. This morning you're trying to placate me. That has been his modus operandi since I was a child. Throw Dana a tidbit and she'll forget."

He gunned the engine and streaked out of there until they were beyond the view of any workers. Then he slammed on the brakes beneath the trees. Turning to her, he slid his arm along the back of the seat and encircled her warm nape with his hand. He could feel her pulse quicken beneath his fingers.

"I haven't forgotten one second of what happened last night and know in my gut you haven't, either." Unable to stop himself, he kissed her neck, knowing her skin smelled that sweet all over. "The fact is, I want you to stay at the château and was hoping to tell you that while we took a little time off to play. You were right about Jack being a dull boy."

"I wasn't planning to leave," she stated quietly, jolting him in that inimicable way of hers. "As for Jack, it's a well-known secret dull boys are usually the most successful because they never waiver from their goal."

Dana understood him so well, it hurt.

"Knowing how anxious you are to get the estate ready for the public, you won't be doing either of us a favor by taking me through that monster castle. I have my own plans for today. Thank you anyway."

The desire to drag her off to an undisclosed location and kiss her until she cried for mercy was trumped only by the knowledge that she wasn't going to run away from him yet. He bit her earlobe gently before separating himself from her so he could start up the engine.

Neither of them spoke for the rest of the drive into town. He didn't mind. For now it was enough to know she didn't want to leave the château. She loved everything about it including his damn grapes lying dormant inside those gnarled trunks.

It seemed the only drawback in the scenario was Alex.

"There's my car." Her voice jerked him from his torturous thoughts. He maneuvered his truck through the hectic morning traffic and pulled into a parking spot near hers.

She alighted before he could help her down. "You didn't need to get out," she told him as he followed her to the car.

"I'm the one who told you to leave it here overnight. Just looking to make sure everything works." He watched her get in, then shut the door for her. After checking the tires, he told her to pop the trunk. "Everything looks good."

She started the engine. "Thanks for driving me in. See you later." As she backed out and drove off, he waved until he couldn't see her golden head anymore. Turning sharply on his heel, he walked two blocks to the post office to collect his mail.

There were a few bills and letters from his colleagues in Bali, as well as his contacts in Louisiana. He would read them when he got back on the estate. As he finished cleaning out his mailbox, a postcard fell on the floor. He picked it up. The picture of Sanur gave away the name of the sender.

Martan—thank you for the postcard you sent with the big castle on it. One day I want to see it and the house your grandfather left you. I am working hard and am saving my money to come and visit. Maybe work for you one day in the States? Are the French women as hot as they say? How many have you had so far? Write soon, Sapto.

A smile broke out on Alex's face. He walked around the corner to a tourist shop where he bought a postcard with a photograph of the Château de Chenonceau, Dana's favorite. When he returned to the post office, he wrote a message on the back.

Hey, Sapto—I liked your card. It brought back many memories. I'm glad you're working so hard. It'll pay off. Maybe one day we'll see each other again. The French women are definitely hot, but they can't compare to the American woman staying at my château. I have plans for this one. Alex wrote the rest of his thoughts about her in Balinese and signed it, *A. Martin.*

After affixing a stamp, he mailed it, then left for home in his truck. Halfway to the estate it struck him that for the first time since being in France, he thought of it as home. Something was happening to him. Something profound.

Deep in thought about everything that had transpired

last night, he almost didn't hear his cell phone in time to answer it. Hoping it was Dana, he almost said her name when he clicked on.

"Monsieur Martin?" a man asked in French. Disappointment swamped him.

"Oui?"

"This is Honore Dumarre. Perhaps Mademoiselle Lofgren hasn't had a chance to tell you about our meeting yesterday."

Alex straightened in his seat. Dana had warned him the other man would be calling, but he hadn't expected it this soon. "As a matter of fact, she presented me with an 1892 bottle of Belles Fleurs wine from your cellar last night."

The man chuckled. "Technically it wasn't from my wine cellar. I was just the keeper of it. Now I know why I held on to this one. It's a great honor for me to know it is now in the hands of the rightful owner. *Soyez le bien venu, monsieur.* I am so pleased to know a Fleury is back among us after all these years."

Something in Monsieur Dumarre's nature caused Alex to warm to him. "Thank you, *monsieur.* I'm touched by your words. As you can imagine, it was such an incredible gift, I'm still overcome. I'd intended to phone you before the day was out and thank you for parting with it."

"Mademoiselle Lofgren was so excited to give it to you, I couldn't have done anything else. Once in a while life offers us something beyond price. I'm not only thinking about the wine, but the beautiful young woman herself. Her soul shines right out of those heavenly blue eyes, doesn't it? What a prize she is."

"Yes," was all Alex could say because emotion had caught up to him.

"To think she's Jan Lofgren's daughter. His films are sheer genius."

"I agree."

"Did she tell you I'd like to host a party?" That was news. Dana probably would have told him if he'd given her half the chance. "All your vintner neighbors will want to meet you. I plan to invite the Lofgrens, too, and hope they can come."

"Thank you, Monsieur Dumarre. I'm sure it will please them to be included."

"*Excellent.* Call me Honore. My wife, Denise, and I were thinking Saturday, the twenty-eighth? Say seven o'clock? Would that be convenient?"

"I'll look forward to it with great pleasure. And please, call me Alex."

"*Bon.* It will be an evening everyone will look forward to."

"You're very kind."

"Not at all. *À bientôt,* Alex."

"*À la prochaine,* Honore."

On Monday morning Dana left the château early to meet with her father. She'd called him ahead of time to let him know she was coming. When she knocked on the hotel room door, he answered in his robe still drinking a cup of coffee.

"Hi, Dad." She moved inside, taking a glance around his messy room. "I'm here to run you to the hospital in Angers for your blood check. While I'm waiting for you, I'll do your wash with mine." She'd brought a laundry bag with her and started gathering up his things.

"I thought you'd forgotten."

How did he dare say that to her? It just proved how unconscious he was where she was concerned. "Have I ever forgotten anything?"

He eyed her moodily. "I never see you." Oh, brother. "From what I understand you're too busy putting the library in order for Alex."

"I never see you, either." She turned it back on him. "You're so busy directing, the only way I know you've been at the château is to find the empty basket by the door to the grand salon every afternoon."

After a brief silence he said, "Your lunches are appreciated. You cook like your mother." He set the empty coffee cup on the table.

Dana almost dropped the load of clothes she was fitting in the bag. A compliment from him came around about as often as Halley's Comet. "She was the best."

"I miss her, too. Dana—will you sit down? I want to talk to you."

"Why?" She sensed a lecture coming on, his only reason for a talk these days.

"Because I want to give my daughter a birthday kiss. When you're in constant motion, I can't." He put his arms around her and hugged her hard. Emotion welled up inside her. She hugged him back.

"I thought you'd forgotten."

"I could hardly do that now, could I." With a kiss on her forehead, he let her go and pulled a familiar-looking bracelet out of his pocket. It was twisted like fine gold rope, very elegant, very chic. He fastened it around her wrist. "I gave this to your mother on her birthday before she died. Now I want you to have it."

For him to part with something of her mom's was unprecedented. "Thank you," she whispered. "Mother treasured this. I will, too."

"I know." He cleared his throat. "After the hospital, how would you like to spend the day with me? We'll do whatever you want to do and enjoy a meal at some unique restaurant."

Since she'd walked in the room, she'd sensed he had an agenda, but this offer was way too out of character for him. "What about Saskia?"

He frowned. "She's not invited."

"Can you leave your filming that long?"

"They'll get by without me for a day."

No, they won't! "I thought you were on such a rushed time schedule, you couldn't let anything inter- rupt the shooting of the film. Come on, Dad. Tell me the real reason."

His face clouded. "You need guidance."

"In other words you were going to spend my birthday giving me another lecture!"

"Is it true you purchased a bottle of Belles Fleurs wine for Alex from a Monsieur Honore Dumarre at a cost of $3,000?"

Dana felt like he'd just thrown a pickaxe at her heart. Had Alex betrayed her? She couldn't bear it.

"Yes."

"Yesterday I received a call from him. He invited me to attend a vintner party in honor of Monsieur Martin on the twenty-eighth and asked me to bring my lovely daughter, Mademoiselle Lofgren, with me. He was quick to remind me that true beauty and generosity like yours was rare in this world."

Relief that it wasn't Alex who'd told her father what

she'd done filled her with exquisite relief. "How did he get in touch with you?"

"Apparently Madame Fournier at the front desk put you in touch with him in the first place. When he rang the hotel, asking for me, she put him through to my room."

"I see."

"Dana—don't you know Alex Martin is using you?"

Her father would never understand a man like Alex. He was a breed apart from anyone else. "I'm sorry you see it that way."

"Saskia saw you with him in the orchard the other day. From what she told me, I have every reason to be worried about you."

Saskia was furious that Alex hadn't given her the time of day, but her father couldn't see through it. He really was lost without her mother.

"You know what, Dad? It isn't good for us to be working together anymore. I love you very much, but after we're through here in France, I'm going back to California. I want to get myself an apartment and look for a job that can turn into a career."

She picked up the laundry bag. "Shall I wait for you in my car?"

He shook his head. "I'll drive myself to the hospital."

"All right. I'll get a key from the front desk so I can put your clean clothes in the room later. Thank you again for the gift. It's priceless to me."

Two hours later she'd finished all her errands and drove through the gate of the château, anxious to prepare the lunches on time.

Over the last few days she'd been sifting through the

library books, labeling the boxes to be put in their proper sections at a later date. There'd been many interesting finds, but so far she hadn't found anything to do with the Fleury family history. Perhaps by the time she left France, she'd come across something valuable to Alex personally.

As for the gorgeous owner of the estate, she'd seen him coming and going, but he'd been more preoccupied than usual and was out in the orchard at all hours. Sensing his urgency to be finished with the outside work, she'd come up with a plan to help him whether he liked it or not.

CHAPTER EIGHT

DANA went upstairs to change into jeans and a T-shirt. After removing the bracelet and putting it away, she slipped on her sneakers and hurried back to the kitchen. As soon as the baskets were ready, Dana took her father's to the grand salon and left it for him, then she went outside the front door with Alex's basket.

While she'd been in town, she'd turned in her rental car on a rental truck. It was only a half-ton pickup, not as big as Alex's, but it could hold a lot. She'd bought some gloves and was ready to roll. After climbing inside the cab, she drove around the back of the château to deliver his lunch.

She saw him loading a huge pile of branches and debris into his truck, more than it could possibly hold. Pleased to have arrived at an opportune moment, she pulled up on the other side of the pile.

Too bad she didn't have her camera so she could capture the stunned look on his burnished face. He paused in his work. "Do I dare ask what this is all about?"

Pleased that he didn't seem angry she said, "I traded in the rental car on this rental. It's my birthday and I want to do something that will make me happy. If you'll just let me help you haul this stuff away, it'll make my day. I'm a California girl and we love the sun."

"I haven't had an offer like that in a long time."

"Good." She slipped on the gloves and climbed out of the cab with his basket. "I'll put this in your truck. You can eat it on the way to the landfill." Dana felt his piercing gaze travel over her body. If he was wondering how long she'd last, she would prove she wasn't afraid of hard work.

Some of the branches were too heavy for her, but for the most part she was able to fill up the back of her truck with hefty tosses. When she saw how fast the pile was disappearing, she wished she'd thought of doing this a week ago.

"You keep up that pace and you'll wear yourself out."

"I'll take a rest when I need to," she assured him. They both continued working until the pile had disappeared. "Let's go dump all this stuff. I'll follow you." She climbed in the cab and started the engine.

The last thing she saw was his dazzling white smile before he got in his truck and took off around the château. This was so much fun, she didn't want it to end. Being with Alex made her happy. It didn't matter what they were doing.

By the end of the day they'd made six more hauls, turning out double the work in half the time. When they returned and she parked the truck in front, he drew up next to her. In two seconds he walked over and pulled her out of the seat into his arms.

"You're hired," he murmured against her neck. His slight growth of beard tickled.

She tightened her arms around his broad chest. "I hope you mean that because I intend to help you until I leave."

His lips roved over her sunburned features before plundering hers. They drank from each other's mouths over and over. Their bodies clung. She relished his warmth that combined with his own male scent. Both were hot, thirsty and tired. Dana had never looked worse, but the way he was kissing her made her feel beautiful. She'd never felt beautiful before.

"You deserve a long soak in the tub, but make it a short one. Meet me in the foyer in a half hour. I've been looking forward to our Scrabble game and don't want you falling asleep on me after dinner."

"I can't give you beautiful in half an hour, but I'll be clean."

"Then you don't mind if I don't shave?"

She smiled up into his eyes. "I like it. With that five o'clock shadow, no one would ever mistake you for our dull boy Jack." She kissed the corner of his jaw one more time before tearing herself out of his arms.

Thirty minutes later she hurried down the staircase in sandals, wearing a khaki skirt toned with a summery tan-and-white striped blouse that tied at the side of the waist. Her hair was still damp from washing it. She'd brushed it into some semblance of order. With an application of tangerine lipstick, she was ready.

Dana's heart was pounding far too fast. She would never be this age again and she would never have a birthday like this again with a man who could thrill her inside and out the way Alex did.

As he stepped out of his office and beckoned her inside, her legs turned to mush because he was so dark and handsome. He'd put on a cream polo shirt and tan trousers. "We match," she quipped to cover her emotions at being invited in the room where he worked and slept.

"I thought we'd eat in here tonight."

The interior came as total surprise because he'd surrounded himself with modern furniture. Amazingly it was like the kind in her parents' home in Hollywood. She glanced at him. "I take it you had all this shipped here?"

He nodded. "From Bali. Pieces of mine and my parents'. When I come in this room, it helps remind me I'm not a seventeenth-century man."

"I see what you mean. The château's atmosphere can swallow you alive. Every time I go to bed upstairs, I feel caught between two worlds."

She wandered over to an end table next to the leather couch where a framed picture was displayed. Dana studied it for a minute. "You get your height and bone structure from your father, but your coloring is all Fleury like your mother. They're very attractive people, Alex."

"Thank you. I think so, too. Will the birthday girl join me?" He held out a chair for her at a round game table made of mahogany. On the top he'd set up the Scrabble board. Next to the table was a tea cart with plates of club sandwiches, fruit and sodas. She noticed there was a supply of chocolate cookies for dessert.

Once she was seated she said, "I'm so glad we're not having oxtail or pickled pigs feet tonight."

He sat across from her, leveling a devilish glance at her. "After the hours of work you put in today, I wouldn't have done that to you. Help yourself to the food and we'll get started on our game."

Alex had made this casual and easy. She loved him for it. "I'll confess I haven't played this in years."

He sent her a sly smile.

For the next two hours they laughed and ate and played and fought over words they both made up when all else failed. Alex won every round.

"You're too good."

"I had to be in order to keep up with my father."

"Do you know my dad and I never played a board game of any kind? He simply didn't have the patience." Since her mother died, he hadn't had the time.

Alex eyed her steadily. "Some minds are too lofty."

"I think he was just scared to lose," she lied.

He chuckled. "It takes all types."

She nodded, wishing she could fall asleep in his arms.

"You look ready to nod off. Before you do, I have a present for you." He reached under the tea cart and handed her a wrapped gift. She assumed it was a book.

"This is exciting. Thank you."

Though Alex lounged back in the rattan chair, she sensed an intensity emanating from him while he waited for her to undo it. At first she didn't know what to think. The book was about an inch thick and bound in a dull red cloth. No title. It reminded her of an old chemistry lab notebook.

Curious, she opened the cover. Inside the paper had a slight yellow tinge. The French writing and notations, many of them numerical, had been penned in bold black ink. If anything it looked like an account ledger of some kind. She lifted her head to stare at Alex. "What is this?"

"You were so anxious to find something from the wine cellar, I rummaged through a couple of boxes upstairs you haven't opened yet and came across this book kept by one of the Belles Fleurs vintners."

"Alex—" she cried with excitement. "So not everything was thrown out."

"Evidently not. If you'll look down the left side, you'll see the notations for 1902. I'm sure there are other books."

"I wish I could read French well enough to decipher this."

"Let me translate a little for you." He got up from the table and came around to stand behind her. With one arm encircling her left shoulder, he used his right index finger to show her each line as he explained in English. His chin was buried in her hair, sending little bursts of delight through her body.

"June—at the critical moment when the buds burst forth, the rain throughout the month produced irregular flowering. Bunches of grapes emerged stillborn.

"July—mildew has been a problem. The rain has continued causing the Layon to flood its banks. We removed the excess leaves from the west side of the plants to allow any sun to shine on the maturing fruit. We eliminated some bunches that flowered improperly in hope that the remaining clusters would ripen completely.

"'August—the hard labor is nearly done. The weather has turned hot and sunny. We have hopes some of the vintage will be saved. God grant us a few more dry weeks. By September we could have fruit. June makes the quantity. August makes the quality. We will see.'"

She shook her head. "I can't believe it. To think he's talking about the vineyard out there. *Your* vineyard! This is like a voice reaching out from the past. It gives me chills."

"Me, too," he murmured deep in his throat. It sent delicious vibrations through her nervous system. "Let's get more comfortable and we'll read a few more pages."

They gravitated to the comfy couch. He pulled her down on his lap, cocooning her so her head lay against his shoulder. Page by page he read to her, giving them insight into the struggles and joys of a vintner's work. The whole process was incredibly complicated. Much more so than she would ever have imagined.

His low masculine voice was so pleasant on her ear, she never wanted him to stop. Her eyelids started to feel heavy. She tried to stay awake, afraid to miss anything he told her.

"You're falling asleep."

"No, I'm not. Please don't make me move."

He pressed his mouth to hers. "I won't."

She yearned toward him. "I love it when you kiss me."

"I love to kiss you. The shape of your mouth is like the heart of a rose. It was made for me."

"Don't leave me." Her need for him had turned into an unbearable ache.

"I don't intend to."

Dana melted into him, trying to absorb his very essence until she knew no more.

The next time she became aware of her surroundings it was morning. She discovered herself on top of her bed in the same clothes she'd had on last night minus her sandals, covered by the duvet. She remembered nothing after she'd curled up against Alex.

It meant he'd carried her all the way up the stairs and down the hall to her room. And *that* after he'd put in ten hours of hard labor and prepared her birthday dinner.

As she sat up, she saw her present on the table next

to the bed. Alex intended her to keep it, otherwise he wouldn't have brought it upstairs with her. She was touched beyond words, but at the same time it meant the book didn't have the significance for him it had for her. He had no qualms about her taking it with her when the company left for Germany.

A psychiatrist probably had a term for her wanting Alex to care about his own property when it had nothing to do with her.

She rolled out of bed and changed into another pair of jeans and a jade top. As she put on her sneakers, a few new aches in her arms and back reminded she'd put in some hard physical work yesterday. There would be more today. She couldn't wait. It meant being with Alex.

After she'd freshened up in the bathroom, she went downstairs to get some breakfast. He was already in the kitchen. She felt his gaze staring at her over the rim of his orange juice glass. "Sleeping Beauty awake at last."

"I'm sorry I passed out on you last night. That last long walk carrying me must have been a backbreaker."

His dark eyes were smiling. "Not even love's first kiss could waken you, but I'm not complaining."

For an odd reason she felt shy around him all of a sudden. "Thank you for a wonderful birthday. I'll never forget it." She reached for an apple and bit into it.

"I won't, either. I've never seen a woman work as hard as you do."

"Mother said it's the Swede in me."

She would never know what he was going to say next because Paul came in the kitchen looking for Alex.

"I'm glad I caught you before you went outside to work. For the next two days we'll be shooting some scenes here in the kitchen. They'll be night takes. The set director will want to come in here around 7:00 p.m. each evening to get everything organized. Will that be a problem for you?"

Alex shook his head. "Not at all. It will give me an excuse to play." His probing gaze swerved to Dana. "Mademoiselle Lofgren has accused me of being a dull boy. Two nights should give me enough time to rectify her poor opinion."

Paul winked at her. "Just don't let your dad know."

"What shouldn't I know?"

Dana jerked around in time to see her father enter the kitchen looking like thunder. Paul was quick on the uptake. "It's a joke between your daughter and me. Lighten up, Jan. It's only eight-thirty and we've got a whole day and night to get through." He disappeared out the door.

Her father walked over to her. "I need to talk to you in private, Dana. This is crucial." He flicked Alex a glance. "If you'll excuse us."

"Of course."

Disappointment swamped Dana. She'd planned to help Alex outside until time to fix the lunches. The absolute last thing she wanted to do was damage control for her father. He must have rattled one of the actors. Unfortunately when her father lost his temper, the ground shook and he used Dana to placate injured feelings.

Her gaze darted briefly to Alex before she left the kitchen.

When she found out what her father wanted, she hurried to find Paul. "Do me a favor?"

"Anything if it will put your father in a better mood. He and David don't usually quarrel."

"It's Dad. When he decides he wants something at the last minute, there's no dealing with him on a rational basis. I'm going to be gone for the next few days. Until I'm back, will you arrange for lunches to be brought in for him and Alex? Ask someone to take his out back and put it on his truck where he'll see it?"

"Sure."

"Thanks, Paul. Just hope I come back with good news."

"Amen."

Three more trees and the orchard would be cleared out. Alex drove his truck around the back of the château and got started on the first one. While he worked, he listened for Dana's truck. When she'd come in the kitchen this morning, she'd been dressed for work and his anticipation was growing.

After yesterday's experience he was spoiled and wanted her around every minute of the day and night, but several hours went by with no sign of her. Being employed by her father, naturally he had first call on her time. Where she was concerned, Alex had no rights at all.

Over the last few weeks he'd been listening between the lines. To his chagrin it appeared she'd be ready to move on to Germany at the end of the month, which was coming up too fast.

Lines bracketed his mouth. Regardless of her wanting to be independent, he noticed how quickly she jumped when her father snapped his fingers. Keeping in mind what Paul had told him, it made sense she continued to work with her father in order to study his directing skills.

Suddenly his saw slipped because he wasn't paying attention. He let go with a curse when he realized a couple of teeth had nicked him on the left forearm. Nothing major, but he needed a cloth to staunch the bleeding.

"Hello, Alex."

He stepped off the ladder to see Saskia Brusse, of all people, waiting for him with a large sack in her hand. "*Bonjour*, Mademoiselle Brusse."

"I'd say this was perfect timing. Did you know you're bleeding?"

"That's why I came down from the tree."

"I think there are some napkins in here that will stop it." She opened the sack and produced several.

"Thank you. Just what I needed." He pressed the paper napkins against it. Just as he thought, the cuts were mere surface wounds.

"You're welcome. Paul asked me to bring you lunch from the Hermitage. Mind if I stay out here and talk to you while you eat?" The brunette flashed him a smile that said she knew she was a knockout. Alex agreed, but he had other plans. He intended to find out why Dana hadn't come.

"I'm sorry, but I'm headed to the landfill." He climbed in the truck and closed the door. "It's been a pleasure talking to you, *mademoiselle*. I thank you and Paul for remembering me. Now, if you'll excuse me, I need to get back to work."

"But you've hardly taken any time off—"

"I can't afford to. There's still the undergrowth around the sides and the front of the château to get rid of."

For the rest of the day he worked steadily until the last tree had been pruned. When he returned from his last haul, it was six-thirty. Dana had to be doing an errand for her father because her truck wasn't out in front.

Paul was just heading out with some others in the minivan. Alex slowed down so they could talk. "I appreciated the lunch."

"No problem. Dana will be back in a few days."

Back? He struggled to control his shock. "Where did she go?"

"Maille."

Alex had to reach back in his mind. "As in the Maille massacre?"

The other man nodded. "It's near Tours. At the last minute Jan decided he wants to film a small segment there. She's gone ahead to make the arrangements."

"Understood." Swallowing his bitter disappointment, he drove on around the back of the château.

Dana could have told him. She could have asked him to drive her there, but she wouldn't do that. It wasn't in her nature. If he asked her about it, she'd say that she knew he needed to finish his work.

Before he got out of the truck, he phoned her. With the orchard finished, he'd take the time off. He needed her... But with each attempt to reach her, he got the message "no service." She'd turned off her phone!

In his gut he got the disturbing sensation she was intentionally separating herself from him. Was this her way of letting him down? Cut him off at the ankles and chop away slowly until there was nothing left by the time the company moved on to Germany? Was it of her own free will because she had a career to pursue and didn't need a complication like Alex?

Another colorful expletive escaped his lips.

He could go after her and search until he found her, but that would mean asking Paul to be in charge of the estate until Alex returned. He couldn't do that. The man was under enough stress with Jan in one of his dark moods, but no mood could be as black as Alex's right now....

Thursday morning Dana got up early and left her hotel in Maille for Rablay. It had felt like months instead of three days since she'd seen Alex. By ten o'clock she could hardly breathe as she pulled around the side of the château and saw him making inroads on the vegetation between it and the winepress building. That meant he'd finished the orchard!

Panic set in. Whether he made enough money to pay the back taxes or not, she feared his days in France were numbered.

Trembling with excitement to see him again, she climbed out of the cab and hurried over to the area where he was working on the ladder. She stood at the base and looked up, feasting her eyes on his well-honed physique.

"Pardon, monsieur," she said in her best French, which she knew was terrible. "I'm looking for a man named Prince Charming. Could you tell me where he is?"

His hands stilled on the branch he was cutting before he looked down and slanted her a dark, piercing glance. "I'm afraid he only lives in a fairy tale."

She swallowed hard because that remote veneer he sometimes retreated behind was in evidence. "Spoilsport," she teased, hoping to inject a little levity into the conversation. "You're so grumpy I think you've been missing my lunches."

"Saskia has done her best to make up for them."

Not Mademoiselle Brusse any longer? Somehow Dana hadn't expected that salvo. "She loves to fuss for people who appreciate it. If you'll be nice to me, I have a little present for you. It only cost me ten Eurodollars."

"Is it something to eat?" She thought he might be thawing.

"No."

"To read?"

She smiled. "No."

"I give up. Why don't you bring it to me?"

Flame licked through her. "Am I talking to the same man who terrified me last time I tried it? For self-preservation I think you'll have to wait until you come down later. After I run inside for a few minutes, I'll be back out to help you."

She made it as far as the kitchen when she felt his hands on her arms. He spun her around. Their bodies locked, causing her to gasp. His expression looked borderline primitive. "Why did you turn off your phone?"

They were both out of breath. "So my father couldn't bark at me the whole time I was in Maille. I know when I shouldn't invade his space, but when I'm doing business for him, he doesn't recognize boundaries where I'm concerned."

There was a bluish-white ring around his lips. "You didn't say goodbye." He gave her a gentle shake. "Not one phone call to let me know you were all right."

His words came as a revelation. "I—I wanted to call you, but I hated to bother you."

"Bother me?" he blurted. "By *not* phoning you've caused me two sleepless nights!"

"I'm sorry. I—"

But nothing else came out because his mouth had descended, devouring her with a hunger she'd only dreamed about. He crushed her against him, filling her with a voluptuous warmth. She swayed, almost dizzy from too much passion.

"While you were gone I almost went out of my mind," he whispered against her mouth before plundering it again. His lips caressed her eyes, her nose, her throat. He left a trail of fire everywhere there was contact.

"Don't you know I missed you, too?" She'd been living to be in his arms again.

"I don't even want to think about what it will be like when you're not around here anymore."

Dana heard the words, but their significance took a little time to sink in. If she understood him correctly, no matter how much he was attracted to her no matter how much he wanted her and would miss her—when the time came, he was prepared to watch her disappear from his life.

His past relationships had never lasted, yet she wagered every woman who'd loved him still bore the scars of a broken heart. She'd known it would happen to her even before her father had warned her of the perils of staying at the château.

Calling on some inner strength, she cupped his arresting face in her hands. "Well, I'm back for now and I'm dying to give you your present."

Those dark eyes played over her features with relentless scrutiny. "Where is it?"

"In my purse."

"I don't see it."

"It dropped to the floor when you caught up to me."

He pressed another urgent kiss to her mouth before releasing her to pick it up.

"Can I look inside?"

"Go ahead."

His hand produced a sack. He held it up. "Is this it?"

She nodded. "I didn't have time to get it gift wrapped." Dana reached inside the sack and pulled out a hat. "Here—let me put it on you."

His brow quirked. "You bought me a beret?"

"Not any beret. This comes from Maille. I came across a shop that makes these in remembrance of the men of the Resistance in the early days of the war. The proceeds go to a memorial fund for the victims' families who were massacred."

She placed it on his head at a jaunty angle. "You're a handsome man, you know, and the beret adds a certain *je ne sais quoi.*" She stared at him for a moment, trying to recover from her near heart attack. "Every Frenchman should look as good."

He paraded in front of her like a French soldier. "You think?" His disarming smile brought her close to a faint.

"You should listen to Dana. She knows what she's talking about."

They both turned to see the renowned French film star standing inside the entrance to the kitchen. Who knew how long she'd been observing them?

Dana smiled at her. "Simone? Please meet Alexandre Fleury Martin, the owner of the estate who made this location possible for us to rent. Alex? This is Simone Laval."

"Enchante, mademoiselle. I saw one of your French films when my family lived in La Cote D'Ivoire. You're an excellent actress, very intense. My mother was a fan of yours. If she were alive today, she'd love to meet you."

As Dana digested that bit of information, the actress's warm, sherry-brown eyes played over him in genuine female interest. "Call me Simone, and the pleasure is all mine."

Simone was still in her 1940s clothes and makeup. Obviously Dana's father had given everyone a break to use the restrooms or go outside to smoke.

As she shook hands with Alex, their conversation switched to French. Dana could tell he was totally taken with the winning charm of the thirty-eight-year-old divorcée. What male wasn't attracted to her? With her dark auburn hair, she was a natural-born beauty. A real babe, as the guys on the crew referred to her.

The two of them looked good together. Some people meshed on a first meeting. Dana could tell there was a spark between them. Maybe it was their Gallic connection. Whatever, she saw it in the attitudes of both their bodies. They were so intent on each other, Dana slipped unnoticed from the kitchen.

Her father expected a report on the trip. Now that she was back, she might as well do it while he was waiting to resume the filming.

CHAPTER NINE

"SHALL we go?" Alex cupped Dana's elbow and ushered her out of the movie theater to his truck. After a hard day's work hauling more debris, it had been heavenly to drive into town with him for dinner and a film.

"How did you like the *Da Vinci Code*?" Though it had been out for four years, he hadn't seen it. Now that they were headed home from Angers, she was curious to know his reaction.

He flashed her a curious glance. "I found the mixture of fact and fiction riveting, but I'm much more interested to hear what you thought about it."

"Why?"

His hand squeezed hers a little harder. "Come on, Dana. We both know the answer to that."

She heard an edge in his tone and was stunned by it. "We do? Perhaps you better tell me because I've forgotten."

"A while back Paul confided that you have plans to be a director. Today Simone confirmed it."

Dana was surprised Paul had said anything. She was even more surprised the subject had come up in Alex's conversation with Simone. Disturbed in a strange way, she removed her hand from his warm grasp. "What exactly did she tell you?"

"So you don't deny it."

A heavy sigh escaped her lips. "Alex—what's this all about?" How could such a perfect night have turned into something that created so much tension in him?

"Simone said that your input during several of the scenes at the film studio were so insightful, your father didn't contradict you. I've been thinking about that. If he didn't trust your directing instincts, he wouldn't send you off to arrange film locations for him."

"Before Mother died, she and I did it together."

"But you're the one with the talent."

She lowered her head. "Why do I get the feeling you're accusing me of something?" Out of the corner of her eye she saw his hands tighten on the steering wheel.

"Because when we first met, you misrepresented yourself."

The heat of anger prickled. "In what way?"

"You intimated you were at your father's beck and call, nothing more. In reality you're being groomed by him because he accepts directing as your destiny."

What? "Surely you're joking—" she cried in astonishment.

"Not at all. At first I saw his possessiveness as a desperate attempt not to lose you after your mother passed away." She couldn't believe what she was hearing. "However, in light of what I've learned, I've had to rethink that supposition."

"And what conclusion have you arrived at exactly?" came her brittle question.

"He's hated my guts from day one because he

doesn't want anything to get in the way of a brilliant career for you. Your father sees me as a possible threat."

Her pain was escalating in quantum leaps. "But since you and I know that's not the case, there's no point to this conversation. I don't understand what you have against the art of film directing. To each his own, I guess."

He muttered something dampening in French.

"As long as it's question time, why didn't you ask Simone to dinner tonight instead of me? Before Paul left the château earlier this evening, he indicated she's more than a little interested in you. I would have thought you'd love to spend time with such a lovely compatriot."

By now they'd arrived at the front of the château. He slammed on the brakes and turned to her. In the semi-darkness his features took on an almost menacing cast. "You'd like that, wouldn't you?"

She jerked her head toward him. "It's not my place to like or dislike what you do. When you said I could stay at the château, it was understood we were both free agents, able to come and go with no strings. You made that emphatically clear when you refused to accept the bottle of wine I bought you out of friendship."

His sharp intake of breath sounded louder in the confines of the cab.

"Why you're coming at me with this inquisition is beyond me. I've had enough. If you don't mind, I'm tired and need to go to bed."

"But I do mind—" He leaned across her to lock the door so she couldn't get out.

"I want the truth." His lips were mere centimeters from hers, but instead of kissing them, he was being relentless with his questions. "Are you planning to direct films in the future?"

Being a director might have appealed to her once, but after the Neal fiasco she realized she didn't want to be associated with the film world in any sense. Too many narcissists to deal with, too many artistic temperaments, too much blind ambition. But if she told Alex that, he would continue to believe what he wanted, so it wasn't worth the effort.

"I guess when Dad thinks I'm ready." Not only was it the answer he seemed determined to hear, but it would send the message that she had other things on her mind besides him after she left France. "May I get out now?"

Lines had darkened his face. He studied her through narrowed lids as if he'd been gauging the veracity of her words. "Not yet. A few weeks ago I asked you about the plot of this film. You held back on me. Simone told me the film was really your inspiration. She said you know every line and verse of it, that in fact, you helped write part of the script with David."

"What if I did?"

He sucked in his breath. "Why couldn't you have shared that with me?"

If she told him the truth now, that she'd been trying to be a mystery woman to arouse his interest, he would know she was desperately in love with him.

Deep down he already knew it, but she wasn't about to give him the satisfaction of hearing the words. Not when he was prepared to see her drive away from the château next Monday, never to return.

"Most people don't really want to hear the answer to the questions they ask," she theorized.

He sat back with a grimace. "You put me in that category?"

"I didn't know you that well."

She saw his jaw harden. "You do now. I'd like to hear the story."

"Wouldn't you rather see the film when it comes out and be surprised?"

"No," he muttered. "I don't like surprises."

Dana averted her eyes. "I know."

"I wasn't referring to your gifts. I like my hat," he added in a gentler tone.

So did she. On *him*. "Let's go inside first." Their bodies were too close here in the cab.

Once he'd helped her down, she walked to the front door ahead of him. After he opened it and turned on lights, she made a beeline for the kitchen and took a soda out of the fridge. Small as it was, it provided the symbolic armor she needed to keep him at a distance. Or rather, keep her from him.

He made instant coffee, then lounged against the counter to sip it while he stared at her. "I'm waiting."

"Why are you so interested?"

"How could I not be when you picked my estate out of all the French possibilities?"

She supposed he had a point there. "The story calls for a setting where a German soldier, that would be Rolfe Meuller, refuses to be a part of the Maille massacre of August in 1944 in the Loire Valley. It happened on the day Paris was liberated from German occupation.

"His superior shoots him and he's left for dead. Later

on he's discovered barely alive, having dragged himself to the garden of a nearby château that has suffered through two world wars and has been raided for its wine. Perhaps now that I've given you a few details, you understand why I knew the moment I glimpsed the château for the first time that it was perfect. Uncannily so."

Alex nodded.

"A young, aristocratic French woman, the second wife of her military husband who's been stationed in Paris for months, comes across his body. That would be Simone.

"He's very attractive. She's never been able to have children and has been trapped in a loveless marriage. The handsome blond German is someone's son and that sentiment causes her to help him.

"As you might assume, when he starts to heal from his wounds, she wants him to become her lover. That places him in a difficult position because he has a wife he loves, yet this French woman could turn him over to the Vichy French or the Germans at any time. He must find a way to placate her until he can walk on his own and escape.

"To stall for time, he uses psychology to get her to talk to him. The film explores both their psyches, exposing their tortured souls. His agony over the senseless murders and killings in the French town is the focus of the story.

"When she agrees to let him go and not tell the authorities, he makes it back to his wife in Germany. That would be Saskia. Their reunion is tragic because she's had a baby and it isn't his. She's burdened by her own guilt. He's broken by man's inhumanity to man at Maille, torn up over her infidelity and mourning his wasted life in a hideous war.

"They can continue on together, bound by their individual Gethsemanes, or they can go their separate ways. The film forces you to decide what they might or might not do. The viewer will have to examine his or her own soul for the most palatable answer."

He drank the rest of his coffee. "It's going to be a powerful film. Where did the kernel of the idea come from?" Alex used her former words to frame his question.

She tossed her empty can in the wastebasket. "There was a picture of Sarkozy in the newspaper. He was in Maille to honor the victims. I showed it to Dad and we discussed the massacre. Before I knew it, he'd dreamed up a basic storyline. That's how it came into being."

"With all your contributions, will your name be listed in the credits?"

"No. Make no mistake. This is Dad's picture. He's getting a masterful performance out of Rolfe Mueller, an unknown. When the film's released, he'll be a star."

She moved to the doorway. "As for you, your estate will be immortalized. By the time you have it ready for the public to visit, the stream of tourists will be never ending and make you a rich man. Good night, Alex. Thank you for dinner and the movie."

He didn't try to detain her. His nonaction sent another jab of pain to her shattered heart.

Dana didn't sleep well. In the early morning, she went up to the third floor with the intention of opening more boxes and labeling them. However, there was still so many to do and Alex appeared so uninterested in her project, she decided there was no point in going on.

She put the chair she'd borrowed back in the other room and took all her tools back to the bedroom. Restless and dissatisfied, she showered and dressed in fresh jeans and a T-shirt.

For the next two hours she would help Alex haul debris before she had to make the lunches. But in that regard she was stymied because his truck wasn't there and he hadn't left any piles for her to work on. She was so used to knowing where he was at all times, it upset her to find him gone.

At noon she packed the baskets, but he still hadn't returned. She left her father's in its usual spot and Alex's in the kitchen. When one o'clock rolled around and he still hadn't appeared, she went back upstairs to scour the bathroom and leave it as spotless as she'd found it weeks ago.

Her bedding and the bathroom towels belonged to Alex. He wouldn't mind if she used his appliances to get them washed and dried. By three she'd housecleaned the bedroom and had packed up everything.

Dana hadn't intended to move out of the château until tomorrow morning, but it was better this way. No goodbye scene.

On her way out of the side entrance to the truck, she thought about the bottle of Belles Fleurs wine resting down in the wine cellar. Much as she wanted to take it home as a souvenir, she knew it belonged here. Alex had given her the vintner notebook. That would have to be enough.

One more day's filming on Monday and everyone would clear out. Alex would get his château back. Dana's part was done. Her father wouldn't be able to fault her for anything, that is if she even figured in the recesses of his mind.

She put her suitcase on the floor of the cab and took off. If by any chance she and Alex crossed paths, she would tell him she had an errand to do for her father. He wouldn't question it. If he wanted to make plans for the evening, she'd tell him she'd get back to him when she knew something more definite.

Part of her was praying she'd see him coming so she could feast her eyes on him one last time, but it didn't happen. She found herself en route to Paris, free as a bird and filled with the most incredible loneliness she'd ever known.

There was a flight leaving Orly airport tonight for St. Louis. From there she'd take another flight to Los Angeles. The trick was to return the truck to the car rental in time to get through the check-in line.

While she maneuvered in and out of heavy traffic, she phoned her father. He'd be through filming for the day. His phone rang several times. Finally, "Dana?"

"Hi, Dad."

"I'm glad it's you. I just received another call from Monsieur Dumarre. He wants to be sure you're coming to the vintner party tomorrow night he's giving for Alex. After the filming is over tomorrow, we'll drive back to the hotel while I get dressed, then we'll go to his home from there."

The vintner party…Alex hadn't brought it up in days. Another hurt.

"Dad—I'm afraid you'll have to take Saskia with you."

"It's over with her. I want to take my daughter."

He wanted her mother. Dana was the next best thing. Her eyes smarted. "You don't understand. I'm on my way back to California as we speak."

A long silence ensued. "What's going on?"

"I told you the other day. I've got to make my own life. It's time. But I'm hoping you'll do me one favor."

He didn't respond because for once she'd shocked him, but she knew he was listening.

"Please go to the party and take Saskia. Do it to support Alex. H-he's a good man. The best there is." Her voice trembled. "Be nice to him."

"Dana—"

She hung up. For the first time in her life she'd cut him off. It was the beginning of many firsts to find her life. One that would never include Alex Fleury Martin.

If you could die from loving someone too much, she was a prime candidate.

After being in meetings all day, Alex arrived back at the château at seven-thirty, anxious to talk to Dana. No vehicles were parked out front. He drove around the side, hoping to see her truck. It wasn't there.

He let himself in the side door. Only when he saw the basket with his lunch still sitting on the counter did he realize he should have called her and told her he'd gotten hung up on business.

She'd packed some plums. He sank his teeth into one while he waited for her to answer her phone. The caller ID indicated no service. Not to be daunted, he strode through the château to his office and looked up Paul's phone number. He'd know where to find her.

Unfortunately all he got was his voice mail. Alex imagined everyone was out having dinner since it was a Friday night. He left Paul the message to phone him ASAP.

There was a voice mail for Alex from Monsieur

Dumarre. The other man had called to remind him of tomorrow's party. He mentioned that Jan Lofgren was coming and would be bringing Dana.

Alex had his own ideas on that score. That was why he needed to talk to Dana. He was taking her to the party and had plans for them afterward. If she insisted she couldn't leave her father, then the three of them would go together and the hostile director would have to handle it!

After making the rounds of the château to lock doors and turn out lights, he returned to the kitchen. He'd had a big meal in Angers with his friend from Louisiana who'd flown in at Alex's request, but he was still craving something sweet, like her mouth. Where was she? Why hadn't she called him?

He poked around in the basket and found a *petit pain au chocolat*. A smile broke out on his face. She had as bad a sweet tooth as he did. In two bites he devoured the whole thing.

Finally desperate, he phoned the Hermitage and asked to be connected to Monsieur Lofgren's room. Again he was shut down when there was no answer and he was told to leave a message. Alex chose not to. If he didn't hear from Dana in another hour, he'd phone her father again.

Maybe the whole company was out celebrating tonight, including Dana. This would be their last weekend in the Anjou before they left for either Maille or the Rhine.

Another film company from Lyon would be arriving in a week for a four-day shoot, followed by the Paris outfit scheduled for mid-September and another for the first two weeks of October.

Every few days he was getting more feelers from his

ad. Business was starting to pick up. After talking with his banker today, the outlook was promising that he'd be able to pay the first increment of back taxes by the November deadline.

When he'd come up with this insane scheme, he hadn't really believed it would work, but he'd been out of any other ideas. Then Dana had come trespassing on his property like a mischievous, adorable angel. Her presence had turned his whole life around until he didn't know himself anymore.

The next two hours passed like two years. He was driven to watch TV. No one phoned. He called the Metropole and asked them to ring Dana's room. No answer. Her father wasn't back in his room.

Feeling borderline ferocious over the way his evening had turned out, he took a cold shower before going back to his room. Dana was an early bird. He planned to be up and waiting for her when she drove in from town with the others.

As he entered the bedroom his cell phone rang. It was Paul.

"Thanks for calling me back."

"It sounded important. I'm sorry I didn't check my phone sooner."

"No problem. I was looking for Dana."

"To my best knowledge she's in Paris, seeing about one of the locations there in case Jan decides to add a small scene. He always keeps his options open and nobody negotiates like Dana. She ought to be back some time tomorrow."

All this time she'd been in Paris and unavailable....

"Thanks for the information. Good night, Paul."

The last thing he noticed before turning off the lamp was the beret he'd put on the dresser. Alex comforted himself with the fact that a woman didn't buy a man something like that unless she meant it.

When he awakened the next morning, his first thought was to check his phone in case Dana had called, but there were no messages. Eager to find out if she was back, he got dressed and rushed outside. Still no sign of her truck, either, in front or around the side.

By noon he'd lost all interest in work and decided to quit for the day. On his way down the ladder he heard his name called.

"Paul?"

"Hi. I brought you lunch."

"Where's Dana?" he fired before he realized he'd been rude.

"In Paris. She told Jan she'd meet you at the vintner party tonight. He asked me to pass that along."

Alex took the sack from him. He had to tamp down the surge of negative emotions tearing him apart. "Thanks for the information and the food."

"You're welcome."

Eight hours later Alex found himself in deep conversation with an enthusiastic crowd of the Anjou's most renowned vintners. Their genuine interest in Alex and their questions concerning his future plans for the estate were heartwarming to say the least.

But by halfway through the evening, Dana still hadn't arrived. Even Monsieur Dumarre, their congenial host who'd brought this very elite fraternity together seemed disappointed. Not even the presence of the famous Jan

Lofgren made a difference. However, Dumarre's reaction couldn't match the black state Alex was in.

Dana would never have missed this without a compelling reason. She'd be in her element discussing the Fleury's former contribution to the wine world. Something was wrong. He'd sensed it in his gut since yesterday, but fool that he was, he'd been biding his time because he knew they'd have the rest of the night to themselves.

Being as polite as he could, he excused himself from the crowd and made his way across the room to Jan, who was holding court to a cluster of fascinated listeners. Saskia was circulating with her own following. Without hesitation Alex walked up to him "Jan? I have to talk to you now. Alone," he underlined.

The older man's frigid blue eyes met his head-on. He nodded and excused himself to everyone. They walked through some French doors to a veranda overlooking the back garden. For the moment no one else was out there.

Alex's hands formed fists. This confrontation had been coming on for a long time. "Where's Dana? I want the truth. So far both Paul and Mademoiselle Brusse have been lying for you so don't deny it."

Jan eyed him pensively. "In California."

Hearing it was like being dealt a body blow, rocking him on his heels. "On another errand for *you*?" His accusatory question hung in the air, sending out its own shock wave.

"No," came the quiet response. "She quit her job yesterday and plans to look for a new one."

"You mean, as an independent film director." No

more tiptoeing around the almighty film director. It was past time to lay out the bare bones and be done with it.

To his astonishment, a strange light filled her father's eyes. Alex didn't know they could look like that. "She's good, but that doesn't appear to be her destiny after all."

The words shook him to the core. "What do you mean?"

"I mean, she's got too much of her mother in her— in my opinion the best part of her parents. I hope that answers your question because Saskia's signaling me to rejoin the others."

While Alex stood there in a shocked daze, Jan extended his hand, forcing him to shake it. "If I don't see you again before the company pulls out on Tuesday, I'd like to thank you. Not only for the loan of your magnificent château, but the generosity that went with it."

He cocked his balding head. "My daughter knew a good thing when she saw it."

As he walked away, Alex felt the world tilt. He'd fallen into quicksand of his own making.

When he drove hell-bent through the gate of the château an hour later and saw her truck parked in front, he feared he was hallucinating.

Dana heard Alex's truck before she saw it emerge from the trees. She knew it was impossible, but from the scream of the engine he sounded as if he was going a hundred miles an hour. When he applied the brakes, the truck skidded in a half circle before coming to a stop.

Out of the dust that went flying, he emerged from the cab, looking sinfully handsome in a formal dark blue suit. She'd never seen in him a dress shirt and tie before.

He'd gotten a haircut. Not a lot had been removed, but enough to add to his sophistication.

Her mouth went dry because she loved him so much, but he looked terrifyingly angry. In seconds he'd stalked around her side of the truck and flung the door open. He braced his other hand against the frame so she couldn't get out. "I thought you were in California." His voice sounded as if it had come from a subterranean cavern.

Only one person knew her plans. That meant Alex and her father had crossed paths at the party. It would have been a fiery exchange. She shivered, moistening her lips nervously. "I changed my mind, but I got back from Paris too late to come to the party. H-how was it?" she stammered.

His dark eyes studied her with a veiled scrutiny that made the hairs stand on the back of her neck. "Most everyone seemed to have a good time with several exceptions, one of them being Monsieur Dumarre. You made a conquest of him. He was visibly disappointed when you didn't show up."

Dana's hand tightened on the steering wheel. "I'll make it up to him. What I want to know is if *you* had a good time."

"That's a hell of a question to ask since you provided the impetus for him to give the party at all!" he bit out. "Did I have a good time?" His question rent the air. "If you mean did I enjoy getting to meet the prominent vintners in the region and hear stories about the glory days of Belles Fleurs? Then yes, that part was satisfying."

She bit her lip. "Did you take Simone with you? She would have loved it."

Alex made a scathing sound in his throat. "The only

star there was Saskia. I had no idea she was such an excellent actress. She managed to convey that you were off doing vital studio business no one else could do. Her performance to cover for your absence did her great credit."

Dana's father had no doubt choreographed Saskia's contribution. He'd actually pulled through for Dana. That was something to be thankful for at least. Alex's rage was another matter altogether.

"Are you always going to be angry with me because of it?"

"I don't know," his voice grated. "You're the one who got me into the predicament in the first place."

His arresting face was so close, she only had to move her hands a few inches and she could be touching him. "I'm sorry," she whispered.

"No, you're not."

Her head flew back. "You're right. I'm not sorry that because he found out you were a Fleury, he wanted to celebrate your arrival in Rablay with his friends. It was a great honor for you. I wish I'd been there. It's very upsetting to me that I wasn't, but it couldn't be helped." She stirred in place. "I'll find a way to apologize to him, whatever it takes."

The little pulse she'd seen before hammered at the corner of his taut mouth. "Your father told me you quit on him."

With that news out in the open, there were no secrets left. The exchange between them couldn't have been anything but ugly. "True. I'm now jobless and looking for a new career."

"With all your contacts, the field should be wide-open for you in California. Why didn't you get on the plane?"

Dana's lungs constricted. Holding her heart in her hands, she said, "While I was standing in line waiting to check my suitcase, it came to me what I really wanted to do with my life."

"Just like that—" he rapped out, sounding exasperated.

"Yes."

"I guess I shouldn't be surprised," he muttered. "It took you all of ten seconds to decide you wanted to rent the château for your father."

"When something becomes clear, I've found it's better not to hesitate."

"You mean, like charging up a ladder with no regard for your safety?"

Her eyes flashed sparks. "You're never going to let me forget that, are you? I can't help it that I inherited that trait from my mother."

She saw something flicker in the dark recesses of his eyes. "You still haven't answered my question."

"I'm getting to that. After I made my decision not to board the plane, I left the airport terminal and rented the truck back. But by the time I reached Angers, it was midnight. I was so exhausted I stayed at the Metropole and slept in late."

"You've been there all day?" He sounded livid.

"Yes. I had phone calls to make."

"Except to me." His words came out like a hiss.

"I couldn't call you until I'd worked everything out."

He made another violent sound that caused her to quiver. "But it didn't all mesh until it was too late to attend the party. Is that what you're saying?"

She nodded, afraid to look at him. "Could we go inside first?"

"If you'd come to the party, you could have savored dozens of the region's finest wines."

"I could have, but the one I wanted to taste wouldn't have been available. Or was it?" she questioned.

His dark brows lifted. "No. I'm afraid our kind-hearted host wasn't willing to give up a second bottle of Belles Fleurs. But who's to say what he would have done if you'd been there…"

On that note he scooped her out of the seat and set her on the ground. In the moonlight she looked so frumpy standing next to him in her jeans and T-shirt, she could have wept. No words passed between them as he pulled her suitcase from the floor of the cab and followed her into the château.

CHAPTER TEN

DANA'S heart skipped a beat when Alex opened the door to the petit salon and turned on the light. "Wait for me in here. I'll be back with your drink."

In this mood, she didn't dare argue with him. Forcing herself not to look at the bedroom end of the room, she moved one of the rattan chairs over to the desk where he'd set up his computer.

Before long he was back. He strolled toward her and set the cola on the desk next to her. Still not saying anything, he shrugged out of his elegant suit jacket. Next came the tie. He tossed them over a nearby chair before undoing the top buttons of his shirt.

The dusting of black hair against his bronzed throat stood out in contrast to the dazzling white of the material. His male beauty caused her to gasp inwardly.

"You wouldn't rather sit on the couch where you'd be more comfortable?"

She'd been there and done that the other night, but everything had changed since then. "This is fine right here for the business I have in mind."

He removed his cuff links and pushed the sleeves up to the elbows, revealing more of his bronzed arms. She saw the gash on his arm. "You cut yourself! When did that happen?"

"Yesterday."

"With the saw?"

"It's nothing. Let's not get off topic. Are you telling me you came back to the château to talk business?"

"Yes. I've had a lot of time to think and—Alex? Will you please sit down? I can't think while you're looming over me like that."

"Is that what I'm doing?"

"Yes."

To her relief he sat down in his swivel chair, extending his long legs so his shoes touched her sneakers. She tucked her feet under her chair. "Is this better?"

"Much."

With one arm on the desk, he gazed at her through shuttered eyes. "How long are you going to keep me in suspense?"

"Not any longer, but you have to promise you won't interrupt until I'm through."

He folded his strong arms. "I'm waiting."

"This is serious now."

"I can see that."

She sat forward. "Please don't patronize me."

"I apologize if that's what it sounded like."

"Sorry. I'm a little touchy about that sort of thing." Dana had thought she could do this, but now that the moment had come, she was in agony. "I have to give you a little background first."

"You mean, there are things about you I still don't know?"

"Exactly. For instance my mother did most of the

gardening when I was young. I liked to help her and took pride in the flower beds I planted and weeded. If someone were to ask what was the happiest time of my life, I would have to say it was out gardening, watching things grow. Being in the sun. A lot of beautiful flowers grow in Southern California. It's like a garden of Eden."

So far she seemed to be holding Alex's interest. "But at the time, I didn't consider it important work. Sometimes when I took dad his lunch at the studio, he'd let me stay on the set to watch. What he did seemed very important and I thought, one day I'll grow up to do what he does.

"Over the years I've been studying his technique. One day Paul and I were talking and I expressed my hope to become a director. When I asked him what he thought about it, he was quiet for a while, then he said, 'You're a natural at it, Dana, but I would worry about you because it's not a happy profession.'

"I knew that. My father was living proof he experienced a lot of difficult moments, but directing gave him an outlet for his artistic talent and that seemed very important.

"Little by little, Dad gave me more responsibilities to learn the craft. We often came at an idea the same way. After mother died he trusted me to do more for him. Scouting for unique locations was one example. Editing a script, making changes was another.

"I thought it was what I was truly *meant* to do. Yet in the back of my mind, Paul's comment continued to nag at me. I've kept asking myself if directing was what I *wanted* to do.

"That question got answered for me last week when

I started helping you in the orchard. It has taken me back to those times when I helped Mother in the yard. There's nothing like hands-on experience working in the out-of-doors.

"Lately I've been looking at the overrun vegetable and flower gardens at the other end of the château. So many ideas of how to replant them and make the grounds beautiful is all I think about. When Dad sent me to Maille, I didn't want to go."

She paused to rub her eyes. "After this long, boring speech, what I'm trying to say is that I'd like to be the first person in line for the estate manager job."

He muttered a French imprecation she didn't need translated.

"Believe me, when word gets out you're looking for one before you leave for Louisiana, there'll be lines out to the street hoping for the privilege. I can't think of any career I'd love more than to be put in charge of this place after you've gone."

"It's a lot of hard work, Dana."

"I like hard work. Besides, it's one of the most beautiful spots in France. I'm in love with it. You could trust me to do a better job than anyone else."

Alex stared at her as if he'd never seen her before.

Taking advantage of the silence, she said, "Until that time, I'd like to apprentice for it. I'll do any jobs that need doing. I'll help you clean every room and bring down the furniture. I'd love to put the books in the library and catalog everything.

"I'll plant and weed. I'll pick fruit when the time comes. I realize there are dozens of things I don't know how to do, but I can watch and learn from you."

That remote look she hated crept over his face.

"Please don't close your mind to this, Alex—I know what you're going to say. That you don't have the money to pay me right now, but I don't want pay. One day when it's finally open to the public, we can talk about a salary. Don't you see there's nothing I'd like more than working here?"

He got to his feet.

Though it was nothing tangible, she realized she'd crossed a line with him that probably spelled disaster for her. Dana had known it would be a huge risk, but she'd been willing to take it.

She jumped out of her chair. "Just promise me you'll think about it and give me your answer in the morning. If it's no, I'll understand and leave."

Afraid he might tell her no right now, she grabbed her suitcase placed by the door and hurried out of the room toward the staircase. For the third time in three weeks she lugged it up the steps.

When she reached her room, she turned on the flashlight so she could see to get ready for bed. But she was too worked up to change yet and went over the window. Moonlight had turned the view of the Layon into a river of silver.

For a long time she stood there remembering the night they'd cleaned this fabulous room together, the fun they'd had buying her bed. Her mind was filled with memories of the nights he'd come in here to light the candles, bringing the kind of enchantment you could never find in a storybook.

Hot tears trickled out the corners of her eyes. As she turned away to open her suitcase, Alex appeared in the entry, looking so handsome she almost fainted. He was still wearing the same clothes and carried several things in his arms. Her heart almost leaped out of her chest.

"Don't be startled. I've come to give you your answer now."

It was darker on that side of the room. She moved toward him, but she still couldn't see what he'd put on the table. Maybe it was new candles, but when he walked toward her, carrying two half-full glasses of wine, anything she'd been thinking about left her mind.

The way he was staring at her, she honestly couldn't catch her breath. "As interviews for a job go, yours was extraordinary," he began. "I'm very impressed you would forego a salary in order to learn how to be my manager, therefore, you're hired."

"You mean it?" she cried, hardly daring to believe it.

A ghost of a smile hovered around his lips. "Let's drink to your success, shall we?"

Alex was being very mysterious. It sent chills of excitement through her body. With a trembling hand, she took one of the wineglasses from him. He touched her rim with his and took a drink. She sipped hers, but the second the liquid ran down her throat she realized they weren't drinking Percher, Chaume, or any wine she'd ever tasted before.

Her eyes widened. "What domaine is this?" She took another sip. "The texture is so velvety. How could anything be this incredible? Can you taste that smoky sweetness?"

He nodded. "At the party I was told 1892 was a great vintage year."

When the meaning of his words got through, Dana

almost dropped the glass. She stared at him in disbelief. "You opened the bottle!"

"You said you were waiting for an important occasion. I would think taking on a new career constitutes as one. Don't you agree?"

Dana was in shock and could only nod her head. She took another drink. "The wine is out of this world. There's a richness that tastes of the earth itself."

"A nuance from the minerals. That's what comes from a hundred years of aging," he murmured.

Emotion caused her eyes to moisten. "To think we're drinking from your grapes that have been growing on Belles Fleurs soil for hundreds of years." She drank a little more. "Don't you feel a tingling to realize this is a tangible connection to your ancestors?"

"I feel a great deal more than that." He finished his wine and put both their glasses on the table. "While we were downstairs I forgot to tell you I met with my colleague from Louisiana yesterday. He's been anxious to know when I'm going to join him."

How odd she could go cold so fast when the wine had warmed her body clear through. "Did you tell him it won't be long now?"

"No. I informed him he'd have to find another agricultural engineer because France is home to me, permanently. I'm getting married."

Maybe she was dreaming.

"My bride-to-be and I have a life to live and a vineyard to work. Both need love and tender nurturing on a full-time basis."

"Alex—"

Her cry reverberated throughout the tower.

"I'm in love with you, Dana Lofgren. I have been from the beginning, but I sensed a battle with your father and was forced to bide my time before I made my move."

She launched herself into his arms, sobbing for happiness. "Oh, darling, I love you so much, you can't possibly imagine."

He rocked her body back and forth, kissing her hair, her face. "I think you convinced me downstairs."

"I couldn't leave you. When I was standing in that line at the airport, I felt I'd come to the end of my life."

Alex buried his face in her hair. "Try hearing your father tell me you'd gone to California."

She hugged him harder. "I'm sorry. I asked him to be nice to you, but I should have known better."

"You don't understand." He pulled back so he could look at her. "In his way, he gave me his blessing."

"What do you mean?" Her heart had started to thud.

He kissed the tears off her cheeks. "I was ready for a showdown with him until he told me something that changed everything. He said you'd make a good director, but it wasn't your destiny because you were too much like your mother."

"Dad admitted it?"

He nodded.

Dana was delirious with joy.

"Once I heard that, I couldn't get home from the party fast enough to collect a few things and go after you. If I hadn't seen your truck out in front, poor Paul would have gotten a phone call telling him to take care of everything while I was gone."

Dana slid her hands up his chest to his shoulders,

relishing the right to touch him like this. "And I sat there terrified you'd drive in with Simone."

"Simone who?" he demanded fiercely, shaking her. "From the night you trespassed on my property, I haven't been the same. Sapto will tell you."

"Who's Sapto?"

"The house boy in Bali who got attached to me. You'll like him. He's saving his money to go to college. I'm planning to fly him over to help us prune the vineyard. That should give his earnings a boost.

"In my last postcard to him, I told him he can stop asking about all the women in my life because I've found the one I want."

Dana pressed a kiss to his lips, too euphoric to talk.

"When I stopped at the post office this afternoon, I discovered another postcard from him. He said that from my description of you, you would give me many beautiful children."

Alex's eyes narrowed on her mouth. "I knew it over dinner that night at the Hermitage. You sat there in the candlelight and your femininity reached out to me like a living thing. It came to me in a flash you were the one I was going to love for the rest of my life, to make babies with."

"I—I knew it before you did." Her voice caught. "From the first moment I laid eyes on you coming out of the shadows. This is going to sound silly, but it wasn't to me. Like Sleeping Beauty in reverse, I felt that I'd come upon the castle of the Sleeping Prince. Everything in me yearned toward you."

His smile turned her heart over. "So now we know the true story of Rapunzel."

She laughed softly, remembering their crazy talk. "She had no shame and moved in on her prince, sleeping bag and all."

"He liked her style." In the next breath Alex kissed her mouth hungrily. "How about taking a walk out to the vineyard with me? We have serious plans to make and fast, because I don't intend to make love to you until you're my wife. I promised your father."

"When?" she half groaned. "I didn't hear you."

"It wasn't anything verbal, but the commitment was just as binding the second you announced your plan to find a spot in the château to sleep."

Dana hid her face in his chest. "You must have thought I was out of my mind."

He tangled his fingers in her hair. "To be honest I thought heaven had dropped a present at my door by mistake, but I wasn't about to give it back and had to think fast."

She gazed up at him, her blue eyes glowing with desire. "So you do believe in it?"

"Since a golden haired woman with a cherub mouth came climbing up my apple tree and peeked at me through the leaves. It was a new sight for this mortal." His dark head lowered. "You are a heavenly sight, *mon amour*," he whispered before his mouth closed over hers, giving her a taste of their glorious future.

MR RIGHT, NEXT DOOR!

BY
BARBARA WALLACE

Barbara Wallace is a life-long romantic and daydreamer, so it's not surprising she decided to become a writer at the age of eight. However, it wasn't until a co-worker handed her a romance novel that she knew where her stories belonged. For years she limited her dreams to nights, weekends and commuter train trips, while working as a communications specialist, PR freelancer and full-time mum. At the urging of her family she finally chucked the day job and pursued writing full time—she couldn't be happier.

Barbara lives in Massachusetts, with her husband, their teenage son and two very spoiled, self-centred cats (as if there could be any other kind). Readers can visit her at www.barbarawallace.com and find her on Facebook. She'd love to hear from you.

For Pete, my own special contractor.
I can't imagine life without you.

CHAPTER ONE

HE WAS doing it again.

Since she'd moved in a month ago, Sophie Messina's neighbor had been banging, buzzing and doing Lord knows what in his upstairs apartment, making it completely impossible for her to concentrate.

Didn't he realize some people liked quiet on their weekends? That people had work to do?

Breathing out a determined sigh, she redoubled her efforts. Allen Breckinridge, one of her managing directors, had announced yesterday afternoon that he needed this merger model for a meeting on Tuesday, which meant she needed to review and correct the work her junior analyst sent over this morning before passing the figures along. And, since no report could ever be finalized without repeating the process at least four times, she needed to make her notes quickly. A lot of analysts would be tempted to make nitpicky comments, more to emphasize their involvement than anything, but Sophie preferred to work efficiently. Last thing she wanted was the managing directors thinking she was the kink in the bottleneck. Especially since she planned on being a managing director herself someday. Sooner rather than later too if all went according to plan.

Bam!

Oh, for crying out loud, what was he doing up there? Kickboxing holes in the wall? She whipped off her reading glasses and tossed them on the dining room table. This was ridiculous. She must have slipped a half-dozen notes under his door asking him to kindly cease and desist whatever it was he was doing. First politely, and then threatening to bring the issue to the co-op owners association, but he'd ignored all of them. Well, no more. This noise was going to stop. Today.

Smoothing back her sleek blond ponytail, she stepped outside into the building entryway and shivered as her bare feet met the wood flooring. Before being renovated into co-op apartments, the building had been a brownstone mansion. For one reason or another, the architects kept the public areas and her apartment as true to the original decor as possible which was why a large and very ornate crystal chandelier hung in the entranceway. Sophie had to admit, she loved everything about the nineteenth-century fixtures, from the dark wood molding to the sprawling central stairway with its spindled railings and balustrade. They gave the building an Old World kind of feeling, conjuring up words like *historic* in her head. Words that implied stability. She liked stability.

She liked tranquility, too. A quality that had been distinctly absent the past four weekends. As she climbed the stairs, she swore the banging grew louder with each step. Did he have to do whatever it was he was doing at the loudest possible volume?

This wasn't how she envisioned her first conversation with a neighbor. Actually, she hadn't planned on having a conversation at all. One of the reasons she moved to the city two decades ago was because you could go months, years even, without exchanging more than a nod and a hello with the people around you. Not that she was antisocial. She just preferred being able to choose who she socialized with. She had too much she needed to accomplish to waste time frivolously. The only reason she even remotely knew this particular neighbor's name was because his mailbox was located next to hers, and she'd needed to know who she should address her letters to. G. Templeton. She'd seen the same name on the side of a pickup truck parked outside. Some sort of contractor, she believed.

Was that what he was doing now? Contracting? Memories of half-finished DIY projects and drunken destruction popped into her brain before she could stop them. What the heck? Buying her own place was supposed to distance her from those days, not bring them racing back. At her age she should be over being plagued by the ghosts of the past. Yet no matter how much she accomplished or worked, they never seemed to completely recede. She could always feel them, lurking, keeping her on guard. In some ways, their insistence was a blessing; they kept her working and focused. Otherwise, she'd still be stuck in some banged-up, roach-infested apartment like the one she grew up in on Pond Street, instead of owning her own brownstone co-op. A co-op she'd thought would be quiet and tranquil.

By the time she reached the second floor landing, noise punctuating each step, Sophie was thoroughly aggravated. Every bang seemed to reverberate off the fleur-de-lis wallpaper and settle right between her shoulder blades fueling her irritability. Mr. Templeton was going to get an earful, that's for certain. Summoning up every inch of her authoritative demeanor, she knocked on his door. The response was another bang.

Fine. Two could play this game. She pounded back in kind.

"Mr. Templeton," she called sharply.

"Hold on, hold on, I'm coming!" a gruff voice called out. As if *he* were the one being bothered.

Folding her arms across her chest, Sophie prepared to remind Mr. Templeton about the existence of other residents and the need to respect people's personal solitude, not to mention their right to an undisturbed weekend.

The door opened.

Good God Almighty. Sophie's biting lecture died on her tongue. Standing on the other side of the threshold had to be, hands-down, the most incredible-looking man she'd ever seen. Not cover-model handsome—*handsome* was far too benign a word anyway—but rugged in a sensual way with smooth tanned skin and a square-cut jaw. A slightly too-long nose kept his face from being overly perfect and yet on him the feature fit. Strong men demanded strong features and this, Sophie could tell, was definitely a strong man. He had hair the color of dark honey and eyes that reminded her of caramel candy. Not to mention a chest custom-built for splaying your hands against.

He was also at least a decade younger than she was, and holding a sledgehammer, the obvious source of her disturbance. Both realizations quickly brought Sophie back to earth. She lifted her jaw, once again prepared to complain.

"Mr. Templeton?" she repeated. Just to be certain.

The caramel eyes made a slow sweep of her from head to toe. "Who wants to know?"

If he thought the open assessment would unnerve her, he was mistaken. She'd been fending off harassing looks since college graduation. None of them as blatant or as smoldering perhaps, but she'd fended them off nonetheless. "I'm Sophie Messina from downstairs."

He nodded in recognition. "The lady who writes the notes. What can I do for you, Mrs. Messina?"

"Miss," she corrected, although she wasn't quite sure why, or why she didn't say "Ms."

Biceps rippled as he propped the hammer against the frame and folded his arms, mimicking her stance. "Okay, what can I do for you, Miss Messina?"

Sophie was pretty certain he already knew. "You've been doing a lot of banging lately."

"Renovating," he replied. "I'm gutting the main bathroom, getting her ready to install a claw-foot tub."

"Interesting." The image momentarily distracted her. Rough and rugged didn't go with claw-footed baths.

She smoothed her hair, as much to rein in her thoughts as to keep the unruly strands in line. "Well, I'm trying to build a financial model for a potential acquisition."

He drew his lips together. They were nice-shaped lips, too. "Financial model, did you say?"

"Yes. I'm an investment analyst. For Twamley Greenwood," she added, figuring the prestigious name might emphasize the project's significance.

"Good for you." Clearly, her employer credentials didn't impress him. "What would you like me to do?"

Wasn't the request obvious? Stop making so much blasted noise. "I wonder if you wouldn't mind keeping it down. Your loud banging makes concentrating difficult."

"Little hard to bang any softer," he drawled in reply. "By nature banging is a loud activity. Even the word— *bang*—" he let the word burst loudly from his lips "—implies as much."

Sophie gritted her teeth. She knew that condescending tone. He wasn't taking her complaint seriously. "Look," she said, drawing herself up to her full five feet and five inches—a meaningless gesture since he still had at least a half a foot on her. "I've asked you several times if you could please keep the noise down."

"No, you've slid notes under my door commanding me to 'cease and desist.' You haven't *asked* me anything."

"Fine. I'm asking you now. Could you please keep the noise down?"

"Sorry." He shook his head. "No can do."

No? "No?" she repeated.

"Told you, I'm gutting the bathroom. Do you have any idea what that entails?"

"Yes," she replied. Visions of those biceps swinging a sledgehammer came to mind.

"You sure? Because if you don't—" a gleam entered his brown gaze "—you're welcome to come in for a demonstration. Maybe even do a little swinging yourself."

"I—I—" Was he *flirting* with her? The audacity had her speechless. The image of those muscular arms didn't help, either.

Taking a deep breath, more to regain her mental purchase than anything else, she tried again. Blunter this time. "Look, Mr. Templeton, I have a lot of work to do—"

"So do I," he interrupted. He shifted his weight again, biceps rippling a little more. Challenging her or trying to distract her, Sophie wasn't sure. He was succeeding in doing both. "It's Saturday afternoon, not the middle of the night, and last time I looked, renovating *my* home, on *my* weekend, was completely acceptable.

If the banging bothers you so much, I suggest you go build your model somewhere else."

That wasn't the point. Sure, she had a nice big office in the financial district where she could work, but Sophie didn't want to go into Manhattan. What good was owning your own home if you had to twist your life around others' wishes, and besides, she shelled out a lot of hard-earned money for this place. If she wanted to work at home, by God, she should be able to.

Which begged the question of how a guy his age managed to buy into this address in the first place. It had taken her twenty years of saving and paying off her education loans before she accumulated a sizable down payment. Maybe he didn't mind having debt the way she did. Or he was a closet millionaire. But then why would he be redoing his apartment by himself on weekends?

Never mind; she didn't really care. She just wanted to get back to work. "I would agree with you if we were talking about one afternoon, but we're talking every afternoon for a month. That's a lot of gutting."

"What can I say?" he answered with a shrug. "I've got a lot of renovation to do."

He was purposely ignoring her point. Sophie couldn't help noting her analysts would never get away with copping such an attitude. Maybe this confrontation would go better if she'd approached him when dressed more professionally. She'd be the first to admit her cotton skirt and Polo shirt didn't scream authority. Casual clothes tended to make her look girlish.

Still, she tried, jutting her chin and mustering her sternest voice. A take-no-excuses tone she'd perfected over the years. "What about the other tenants? How do they feel about all these renovations?"

He shrugged again. "No one's complained so far."

"Really?"

"You're the only one."

Sophie smoothed her ponytail. Time to make him take her complaints seriously; show him she meant business. "Perhaps when I bring this up to the building association you'll hear differently."

"Oh, right. I forgot your last note threatened to contact the association."

At last, maybe they were getting somewhere. "Glad to see you read them. I'm sure you'd prefer not to make this a big, official issue."

"I would, except for one thing." The gleam reappeared in his eye. "I'm the association president."

He had to be kidding.

"The other tenants didn't want to be bothered with building maintenance issues so they gladly let me handle everything," he continued. He unfolded his arms, jamming one hand in his back pocket and letting the other rest off the hammer handle. "Come to think of it, that's probably why they don't mind the banging."

"Unbelievable," Sophie muttered.

"Not really. Not when I'm the best person for the job. Now if you'll excuse me, I've got some tiles I need to take down." He reached for the door.

"Wait!" She shoved her bare foot forward to block the door. Thankfully he noticed. "What about the banging? What am I supposed to do until you're finished?"

"The store around the corner sells noise-canceling headphones. If I were you, I'd consider checking them out."

Sophie barely had time to slide her foot back before the door slammed in her face.

Five o'clock came early, and it came even earlier on Monday morning. Earlier still since Sophie had spent until almost 1:00 a.m. making sure the last round of revisions were done and in Breckinridge's in-box before going to bed. Much as she longed to sleep in and make up for the late hours, she couldn't. The overseas markets were already entering their volatile hours and she was expected to know what was going on. That is, she expected it of herself. She didn't want to risk the chance she'd get caught off guard. Being prepared was something she prided herself on, like being efficient and goal-oriented. Although all three would be a lot easier with more than four hours' sleep.

Then again, a lack of sleep came with the territory. If you wanted to get ahead, you put in the hours.

And, she intended to get ahead. So far ahead that eventually Pond Street and all the other ghosts from her past were nothing more than vague, faded images. Then once she'd made it, she'd retire early and sleep in all the mornings she wanted. She was already halfway along her timetable and if the rumors were true and Raymond Twamley was planning to step aside, she could be even closer. A full two years ahead of her schedule.

Until then, she'd always have coffee. She flipped off the plastic lid to see how much of the lifesaving liquid she had left. A quarter of caramel-colored liquid greeted her. Interesting, she thought. Her neighbor's eyes had been a similar color, especially when they'd taken on that flirtatious gleam. Not that she cared. The man had shut his door in her face, the hot-looking, rude...

"Reading tea leaves?"

She didn't have to look up to know who was asking. While normally she made a point of maintaining a professional distance from her colleagues, David Harrington was the one exception. A member of the firm's legal department, he had introduced himself at the company Christmas party a few years earlier, and she'd quickly discovered he made the perfect companion. "More like trying to see if I could absorb the caffeine through my eyeballs," she muttered.

A slight frown crossed his rangy features. "That's obviously not going to happen."

No kidding, Sophie almost said aloud, before quickly biting the words back. Normally she found David's tendency to be painstakingly literal easy to deal with, but lack of sleep had her tired and quick-tempered. It was going to take a lot of caffeine to keep her pleasant and reasonable all day.

Proving her point to herself, she took a long drink from her cup.

The silver-haired lawyer settled himself on the edge of the desk. Despite the early hour, he looked perfectly put together in his gray suit and aquamarine tie. But then, he always looked put together. He didn't have to try to look professional; he simply was.

"I stopped by to see how you were doing. You sounded pretty stressed when you cancelled our dinner date Saturday," he explained.

Sophie felt a little stab of guilt. "I am sorry about that," she replied. "Allen had the whole office running in circles all weekend. I barely had time to breathe."

He waved off her apology. "Forget it. I know all about Allen's demands. We'll try that particular restaurant another time."

"Thank you for understanding." One of the things she appreciated about David was that he *did* understand these things. He was also unflappable, professional and career-focused. *Uncomplicated.* That was the best word for him. True, he wasn't the most thrilling man in the world and the physical aspects of their relationship wouldn't inspire love songs, but he was exactly the kind of man she would choose if and when it came time to think about a long-term relationship.

"I would have been lousy company even without Allen's last-minute project," she told him. "I was having neighbor problems. Remember the banger?" Briefly she filled him in on her encounter with G. Templeton, starting with the banging and ending with their abrupt goodbye. For obvious reasons, she left out the part about his biceps and flirtatious grin.

As she expected, David was appropriately outraged. "He just shut the door in your face? Without saying goodbye?"

"Clearly he felt he'd said all there was to say."

"More like he wanted to avoid the discussion. I'm guessing you weren't the first neighbor to complain."

"He says I am."

"Nonsense. Bet you ten dollars when the tenant association meets, there are lots of complaints."

"Doubtful. Turns out he's the head of the association. The other residents didn't want the hassle," she added when David's eyes widened.

Picking up her discarded coffee lid, she twirled the plastic circle between her fingers. "Looks like I'm stuck listening to the banging until he finishes his project."

"What exactly is he doing anyway?"

She shrugged. "This week? Gutting his bathroom." To install a claw-foot tub. She couldn't get that particular image out of her head any more than she could erase the picture of his biceps flexing as he swung the sledgehammer.

Quickly she slapped the lid on her cup. "Whatever he was doing, the noise kept up the rest of the afternoon," she told David. "Then on Sunday, he spent the day hauling away the debris—" which sounded suspiciously like bags of cement blocks "—making sure he set them down as loudly as possible outside my door." Every time Sophie had heard the noise, she'd been jerked from her thoughts and swore he was doing so on purpose.

"Poor baby. No wonder you were aggravated. You should have said something when I called. You could have come to my place."

"I'll keep that in mind for next time," Sophie replied, knowing she wouldn't. Why was everyone so eager for her to go somewhere else? Why couldn't they understand that she wanted to spend her weekends in her own home? Besides, hers and David's relationship worked perfectly the way it was. She wasn't ready to complicate matters by spending weekends together.

"In the meantime," she said, raising her cup to her lips, "thanks to spending the weekend on Allen's project, I'm behind on everything else."

"Including this morning's status report?"

Ignoring the fact he was interrupting their conversation, Allen Breckinridge strolled into her office. Sophie swallowed her mouthful of coffee. Naturally the managing director would arrive at the exact moment she mentioned being behind. The man had an uncanny knack for arriving at exactly the wrong time. Made her forever jumpy.

"Good morning, Allen," David greeted brightly. He was never jumpy. "Did you have a good weekend?"

"Good enough. Jocelyn and I spent it at the Hamptons," Allen replied. "About that progress report…"

"Right here," Sophie replied, shuffling through her papers for a hard copy. No sense pointing out that she had emailed a version to his computer last night; *I'm not at my computer,* he would say.

"Thank you," he said. He took the report while shooting David a look.

"I was just on my way out." The lawyer rose to his feet. "If you need any more information regarding that due diligence research, Sophie, let me know."

"I will." Silently, she added a "thank you." Another point in David's favor: his discretion. When it came to their outside relationship, he understood her desire to maintain a low profile.

Meanwhile, Allen was skimming the figures Sophie just handed him. Irrationally—because she'd double- and triple-checked the numbers—Sophie held her breath. There was an edge to the man's demeanor that made her perpetually worry she'd screwed up. To compensate for her nervousness, she fished through her papers again. "I also have the revised model figures you asked for."

"Never mind that." He tossed the report on her desk as though it were a meaningless memo. "I have a new project for you. Franklin Technologies is planning an IPO. I need an analysis for my meeting in Boston tomorrow morning."

"Of course. No problem." She and her staff could pull together a couple days' worth of research in a few hours.

And so began another typical Monday. She was going to need a whole lot of coffee.

Turns out, coffee wasn't enough. From the second Allen walked out of her office, Sophie found herself rushing around like a headless chicken, without about as much sense of direction, too. Every time she turned around someone needed something else, and she was asked to be the go-to girl. She missed lunch and dinner. Come to think of it, she decided while wolfing down a pro-

tein bar and a couple aspirin, having her head cut off
might be preferable. At least then her neck might not
be so stiff.

Finally she broke away for her nightly run thinking
the endorphins might improve her mood. Wrong. All
the forty-minute treadmill simulation did was add hot
and sweaty to her already gigantic list of complaints.
What the heck happened to the air-conditioning in the
club anyway?

"Hey, where you heading?" someone hollered out as
she made her way through the locker room to the showers. "Didn't you see the sign? The showers are closed."

What? Sure enough, a sign hung next to the door
advising patrons that the club would be painting the
showers and therefore shutting down the facilities early
for one evening. "We apologize for the inconvenience,"
the note chirped at the bottom.

Her head sagged. Fat good an apology did her. She
was a sweaty, frizzy-haired mess who still had several
hours of work ahead of her when she got home.

And of course, since she was eager to get home,
the trains weren't running on schedule. Meaning the
crowd waiting just grew larger and larger so that when
a subway car finally did arrive, she was forced to stand
pressed into a horde of commuters as ripe and sweaty
as she was. Naturally, the air-conditioning didn't work
on the subway, either. And did the guy standing behind
her, the one with all the shopping bags, really need to
bump into her backside every time they lurched to a
stop? *Lurch, bump. Lurch, bump.* No way was that a
French baguette in his bag.

By the time she reached her front door, all Sophie
could think about was stripping off her clothes and
dousing herself with water. Maybe disinfectant, too,

she added, thinking about shopping-bag man with a shudder. The water didn't even need to be hot. So long as she got clean.

Sliding her key into the front door was a little like greeting a long lost friend. *Home*. David and others, they could never truly understand the pleasure the word gave her. Or why she was so stubborn about spending her weekend here. That's because they'd been coming "home" their entire lives. They'd grown up in homes with normal parents and permanent addresses. For her, the term was still a novelty. True, since graduating college, she'd had apartments, luxury apartments in fact. Some in far better neighborhoods. But none had been hers. The day she signed her name to the mortgage, she'd achieved a goal she'd had since she was a teenager. She owned her own home. No more checks to landlords, no more temporary locations she could decorate but never really lay claim to. She could paint the living room neon green and it wouldn't matter because the place was *hers*.

With a welcome sigh, she tossed her gym bag on the bed and made her way to the shower. White-and-green tile greeted her when she switched on the light. When she bought the co-op the Realtor told her the previous owner insisted on keeping the original fixtures so, like the entranceway, the apartment had a very Old World, nineteenth-century look. David, of course, thought she should completely modernize the place and give it a sleeker look, but Sophie wasn't so sure. She'd clipped out a few sample photos from design magazines but nothing had truly captured her eye yet. Part of her liked the Old World feel. Again, it was that feeling of permanency. Knowing the building withstood the test of time. Kind of like her.

Then again, if she were using herself as a metaphor, modernizing made sense, too. A statement to the world that Sophie Messina had finally and truly arrived and was in control of her own destiny. Either way, she wasn't in a rush. She much preferred to take her time and develop a plan.

Right now, she'd take a hose and spray handle if it meant getting a shower. She reached past her green plaid shower curtain and turned the faucet handle.

Nothing came out.

Frowning, she tried the other hand. Again, nothing.

No way. This couldn't be happening. She checked the other faucets, including the small guest bath next to her second bedroom. All dry. Someone had shut off the water supply.

No, no, no! This couldn't be happening. An overwhelming need to pout and stomp her feet bubbled up inside her. Where was her water? Had she missed a notice about work here, too? Just to be certain, she peeked outside to see if a note had been stuck to her front door. Nothing.

The pouting urge rose again. Of all the days to suffer her first home-owner problem. Why couldn't the water wait until tomorrow to fail? Or better yet, this past weekend.

Weekend. Of course! As the realization hit her, Sophie did stomp—all the way to her front door. She knew exactly what happened. And it involved a clawfoot bathtub.

CHAPTER TWO

"What do you mean you said no?"

Grant ignored the incredulous tone of his brother, Mike, opting instead for taking a swig of beer. On the wall, the latest edition of the Boston–New York baseball rivalry played out in high definition. That's where he focused his attention. As far as Mike was concerned, he knew what was coming next.

"What heinous sin did the potential client commit this time? Choose the wrong paint color?"

Predictable as ever. "He wanted to go modern."

"Oh, well that explains everything. God forbid someone might like contemporary design."

"It was an original Feldman. Do you have any idea how rare those buildings are?" Scratch that. His brother had no idea. "There's maybe a handful of them left and this guy wanted to gut the place and turn it into two-bedroom condos."

"Better have him rung up on charges then. He's obviously committing a crime against humanity." Neither of them mentioned the fact that not so long ago, Grant would have committed the exact same crime.

"I hate to remind you, little brother, but there are people in this world who actually like living in buildings designed for the twenty-first century."

Grant didn't need reminding. "Then let them move into one built in the last twenty or thirty years, not rip apart an Art Deco gemstone."

"Says the man ripping up his own apartment."

"I'm not ripping apart anything, I'm righting a wrong." In more ways than one. He raised the bottle to his lips. "Somewhere my historical architecture professor is pulling out his hair."

"Give him a call, you two can ride off into the sunset on your matching high horses."

Talk about the pot calling the kettle black. Mike had been born on a high horse. "Since when is having principles a bad thing?" So what if he developed them a little late? He had them now.

"There's principles and then there's cutting off your nose to spite your face. Sooner or later this attitude of yours is going to rear back and bite you in the ass."

Couldn't be worse than the injuries his old attitude caused. "Least then I'll be symmetrical."

Mike's sigh could be heard in New Jersey. "Seriously, you can't keep turning jobs down. Not if you want to build a successful business."

Ah yes, success. The Templeton family mantra. Settle for nothing less than the top. Grant knew it well. Hell, for the first twenty-seven years of his life he'd embodied it. Better than his older brother even.

"Maybe I'm not looking for my business to grow," he replied.

From the way his brother huffed, he might as well have suggested running naked through Central Park. "How about survive then? Did you miss the part of economics class where they explained you needed to have an income?"

"I didn't take economics." And he had income.

Investment income, anyway. Enough to survive a good long dry spell as his brother knew perfectly well. "Another job will turn up. One always does."

"You hope. One of these days there won't be a job floating around. Then what? You're not going to be able to rely on that boyish charm of yours forever."

"Why not? Served me well so far." Though he preferred to use it for more personal transactions these days. Seduction was so much more pleasant without business attached. Less weight on the conscience.

"You need to think about the future, Grant."

Meaning he should get back on the corporate ladder where he belonged.

On television, the Boston first baseman watched a ball bound in front of home plate. Grant took a sip of beer in disgust, though whether it was over the team's million-dollar-arm's lousy performance or Mike's lecture was up for debate. No matter how many times he tried to get his family to understand, they just kept pitching. They thought he was wasting his education. Drifting. *Wallowing.*

"Do you and Dad draw straws to see who gets this week's 'straighten Grant out' phone call?" Grant asked. "I haven't talked to Nicole in a while, maybe she'd like a shot, too, in between surgical rounds."

"We're concerned about you is all. You used to be so focused."

No, he'd been a tunnel-visioned tool. Why couldn't they see that he couldn't go back to being that man? Not and live with himself. Just thinking about those days made him sick to his stomach. He took another swig to wash away the bile.

"It's been two years," Mike said in a quiet voice.

"Two years, four months," Grant corrected. Did Mike

really think that because some time had gone by, Grant would simply spring back to form? Nate Silverman wasn't springing anywhere, and Grant wouldn't, either, thanks to his self-centeredness.

"Nate would want—"

"Don't," Grant snapped. "Just don't." They both knew what Nate would want, and it had nothing to do with Grant or his future.

This time the bile couldn't be washed away. It never would be completely.

You were his best friend, Grant. How could you not see something was wrong? He called you for God's sake.

And Grant didn't take the call.

He squeezed his eyes shut. "Can we change the subject? Please?" The accusation haunted him enough. He didn't want to go there right now.

To his credit, Mike relented. Even he knew when to back off. "Sure. For now."

"Thank you."

"But you can't avoid the subject forever."

No kidding. His family wouldn't let him. "Did I tell you I met my new neighbor the other day?" Speaking of workaholics.

"The one who's been slipping notes under your door."

"In the flesh."

"What's she like?" Mike's voice took on a wincing tone. "Or is it a guy?"

"No, she's a woman, and she's exactly what you'd expect from a woman who uses phrases like 'cease and desist.'"

"I use that phrase."

"Precisely." Both his neighbor and his brother were high-end and tightly wound, only the neighbor was better looking. Grant could still picture her, all blonde and bossy with her "I'm trying to work" attitude. As if work was the be-all and end-all. Tension crawled up one side of him and down the other.

"I'm guessing from your description," Mike said, "you two didn't hit things off."

"She threatened to report me to the building association. I told her I was the building association."

"Nice. Now you know why you can't rely on your charm forever."

"We agreed you were going to drop that subject," Grant muttered.

"Merely pointing out that not everyone finds you charming. Though I am surprised you failed with a female."

Grant wasn't so sure he completely failed. "Only because she wasn't my type." Personality-wise, that is. He had no problem with blondes, especially good-looking ones with slender lines and perfect breasts. Unless that is, she was so perfectly put together you could practically feel the hair trying to work free from her ponytail.

Problem was Sophie Messina had felt way too familiar. Dial back a couple years—twenty-eight months to be exact—and he was looking at the female version of his former self.

A sharp knocking sound pulled him from his reverie. Perfect timing. He had a feeling Mike was winding up for another lecture. "My dinner's here."

Soon as he said the words, his stomach began growling. When it came to pizza, he was worse than Pavlov's dog. Giving a silent thank-you to whoever buzzed the deliveryman in, he told Mike he'd call him later in the week.

The pizza man was impatient. He knocked again.

Grabbing his wallet, he strode to the front door, mouth already watering.

Except, he discovered upon opening the door, it wasn't the pizza man. Instead, he found a very hot and bothered Sophie Messina, her arms folded across the very chest he'd just been thinking about.

"You took my water," she charged, eyes flashing. "And I want it back."

It took Grant a full minute to comprehend what Sophie was saying, partially because he barely recognized her. In fact, if pressed, he'd be hard to say this was the same person. The woman he met over the weekend had been glossy and tightly wound.

This woman though… Everything about her looked soft, right down to the way the front of her ponytail hung in long lazy curls around her face. One particularly twirly strand drooped over her left eye and practically begged to be brushed aside. And her lips…. He couldn't believe he didn't notice those succulent bee-stung lips on Saturday. The very male parts of his body stirred with appreciation. What had he been thinking about her not being his type?

"Well?" she asked, tapping her foot. "Are you going to turn it back on?"

"Turn what on?" he asked, distracted by the way her eyes switched hues. From deep blue to turquoise and back. He hadn't noticed those before, either.

"There's no need to stare at me like I have three heads," she said. "There's no running water at my place. You obviously turned the water off when you installed your tub. Since you're finished—" her gaze flickered toward the beer in his hand "—I would like you to turn the water back on so I can shower. As you can see, I'm badly in need of one."

Not from where he stood. But, that was neither here nor there. "Impossible," he said, getting back to her accusation.

Her eyes narrowed. Her smudged mascara gave them a sultry, smoky look that managed to transcend her scowl. "Why not?"

"I didn't turn it off."

"Then who did?"

"Beats me," he replied. "Did you pay your water bill?"

She stiffened, pulling her ramrod spine a little tighter. "I always pay my bills."

"Whoa, take it easy," he said, holding up his hands. *Damn.* He figured she'd be unamused, but the way she spat the words you'd think he'd delivered a blow. "I'm sure you do. I was just making a joke."

"I'm afraid I don't have much of a sense of humor right now."

No kidding. He would have said as much, but at that moment her shoulders sagged a little. "It's been a really long day and I just want to take a shower."

She said it with such longing, so much like a little girl who missed out on getting a treat, Grant couldn't help but actually feel a little for her. Enough to give her a straight answer anyway. "Wish I could help you, but the only water I had anything to do with in this building is my own, and I turned that back on yesterday."

"Any chance you turned mine off by mistake?"

"If I did, how would you have taken a shower this morning?"

His question cut off that argument. "Besides, even if I did turn my water off today—which I didn't—every unit has its own meter. You have to turn off each one individually."

"Are you sure?"

She didn't give up easily did she? "Positive. You're either going to have to wait for a plumber or shower somewhere else."

"Terrific." Her shoulders sagged a little more, and Grant swore for a moment when he saw dampness well up in her eyes. "Guess I better start making some phone calls." She turned and headed down the hall only to stop halfway, as if remembering something. "Wait a moment. Isn't this your job?"

"Excuse me?"

"You said you were head of the building association. Isn't it your job to look into building problems?"

Oh, that was rich. First she spends a month slipping notes under his door, then she accuses him of water theft, and now she wanted him to fix her plumbing? "Only regarding common areas," he clarified.

"Plumbing's common."

"Nice try." But like her complaint to the so-called building association, it wasn't going to work. "You're on your own, sweetheart."

"What else is new?" At least that's what it sounded like she muttered. She resumed her retreat, although this time her walk looked suspiciously like trudging.

Damn. Did she have to look so defeated? As if she were about to break? Guilt began snaking its way into his stomach. No way could he ignore that kind of distress. "Hold on," he called out. "I suppose I could look in the basement. Maybe give you an idea of what to tell the plumber."

"Thank you. If you don't mind, I would appreciate it."

He minded, Grant said to himself. He just couldn't say no.

* * *

Sophie continued her way downstairs, trying to decide if she felt foolish or justified. On one hand, seeing as how Mr. Templeton had disturbed her past four
weekends, checking out her pipes was the least the man
could do. On the other, barging upstairs and accusing
him of water theft bordered on crazy lady behavior. For
someone who believed in being aloof and in control
she wasn't doing a very good job. Templeton started it
though, by shutting the door in her face and acting all
flirty. She'd been stirred up for the past two days, and
now, between the sweat and the work and the bumpy
subway guy, she wasn't thinking rationally. That was
her excuse.

It was also, no doubt, why his presence felt as though
it was looming behind her. The back of her nylon running shorts insisted on sticking to her thighs, so that
when she stepped down, the material would pull upward, and, Sophie was certain, reveal way too much
bare skin. Even though a man her neighbor's age probably wouldn't notice or care about her legs, she felt exposed. Which was interesting because she'd just ridden
on two subway cars in the same outfit without a second
thought. Then again, no one on the subway looked like
her neighbor, either.

Two steps from the bottom she made a decision.
They would have to pass her door on the way to the
basement. She could slip into her apartment and ditch
the shorts in favor of something more appropriate. That
way, when he reported back about the pipes, she'd be
rid of this weird self-consciousness.

Unfortunately, her front door was where her neighbor
chose to catch up. "Oh, no you don't," he said when he
saw her reach for the door handle. He caught her elbow
with his hand. "You're coming with me."

Her pulse picked up. This new position had him standing almost as close as her subway friend. Either that or her awareness of him had increased again because he sure *felt* close. "I beg your pardon?"

"You're coming downstairs with me so we can both learn what the problem is together."

"But I don't know anything about plumbing."

"Doesn't matter. I want you to see that I checked everything out thoroughly."

She supposed she deserved that. "Fine." Stepping sideways, she broke contact, silently advising him to take the lead. If she was going downstairs to the basement with him, she could at least avoid the skin on the back of her neck prickling.

Back when it was first built, part of the brownstone's basement had been the servants' kitchen. Thus, instead of being greeted by cold damp air, Sophie found herself stepping into a room that was warm and stifling. She instantly felt the air close in around her. The lack of adequate lighting didn't help matters, either. There were, she knew, a line of overhead lights, but her guide apparently didn't need to use them. Instead, he deftly navigated the space using the dim glow of the night-light. Sophie followed along. They walked past the storage cages and the skeleton of the building's dumbwaiter and through the opening that led to the rear portion of the room. Here the air was slightly cooler but not by much. Lack of windows or space erased any air circulation that might have existed.

A cobweb dangling from the ceiling beam tickled Sophie's face. She wiped it away, spitting imaginary strands from her lips.

Oblivious, her neighbor pointed toward the rear of the room where the heating units sat side by side.

Perpendicular to them was a series of pipes with levers, each connected to a pipe feeding upward. He stopped in front of the first one on the left and bent down to study the joint.

"I think I found your culprit," he announced. "Come here."

She tiptoed forward.

"This set of pipes feeds to your apartment. Though I can't tell for sure, I'd guess your gate valve is broken."

"My what?" Peering over his broad shoulder, all Sophie saw was a collection of copper tubing.

"When they laid the pipes, the plumbers must have used an old kind of valve. Sometimes, when debris breaks off from inside the pipe, it knocks down the gate inside, blocking the water flow. I'm betting that's what happened here. The water came in through the main pipe, and then got blocked at the base of your pipe." He turned and gave a smirk from over his shoulder. "You can feel free to apologize at any time."

Apparently, the blood flow to her cheeks wasn't blocked because her face flushed with chagrin. "Can you fix it?" she asked. He was a contractor, right? She'd gladly pay him to get her shower running.

True to the rest of her day, however, he answered with a shake of his head. "Not without ticking off most of the area's plumbers. Repairs like this are out of my jurisdiction, so to speak. You're going to have to call a professional."

And so, she was back to square one. Her skin began to prickle, a sure sign stress was raising her adrenaline. Just what she needed; more sweat. Where was she going to find a plumber that made late-night house calls? More likely she was going to have to waste a chunk of her day tomorrow waiting on one. Leaving her more behind than ever, because Lord knows Allen wouldn't care what she had to stay home for. *That's why we gave you a laptop and smart phone, Sophie.* She let out a decidedly unladylike oath.

"You're welcome," a deep voice replied.

Once again put in her place, Sophie cringed. "I'm sorry," she said, brushing hair and cobwebs from her eyes. "I don't mean to take my frustration out on you."

"You sure? Why stop now?"

The remark made her smile, albeit ruefully. "I have been acting difficult, haven't I? Sorry about that, too."

He shrugged. "As long as we're apologizing, I might have played a small part in your bad attitude."

"When you say 'small,' are you talking about the banging or slamming the door in my face?"

"I did not slam the door. I shut it." In the dim light, Sophie caught the gleam of bright white teeth. "The high ceilings made the noise sound louder."

"My mistake then."

"Apology accepted."

Sophie brushed the hair from her eyes again—stupid curls refused to stay in place—grateful the darkened atmosphere shrouded her appearance. With their business in the basement now finished, she should be heading back upstairs to start looking for a plumber. Her feet didn't feel like moving, though. Instead, she leaned against the chain-link cage behind her, hooking her fingers through the gaps in the pattern. "I think we both got off on the wrong foot," she heard herself say. "I'm not normally such a witch."

"Sure you want to use a *W*?"

"Very funny. And, I'm normally not that, either. Although my assistants might disagree."

"I see. You're one of *those* bosses."

She drew her brow. "Those bosses?"

"The kind that demand a lot from their employees."

"If you mean I have high expectations, then yes, I am."

She could almost imagine him analyzing her words, and out of habit jutted her chin at him in silent challenge. Work hard and work smart. What was wrong with that?

"There's only one problem with that statement." He strolled toward her, his figure casting a towering shadow on the wall. "I don't work for you."

"I know that," she replied.

"You sure?" He smiled again, his curvy grin curving crookedly across his face. "Because the last couple of days you seemed to have a different impression."

Sophie's cheeks flushed again. Good Lord, but she'd blushed more in the past couple of minutes than in the past year. This man definitely made her act out of character. "Is that your way of asking for another apology?"

"Just making sure you don't forget the true nature of our relationship."

"Which is?"

"At the moment, barely civil neighbors, although I suppose now that we've buried the hatchet, we could drop the *barely*."

He strode a little closer, until the space between them wasn't more than a few feet. Without thinking, her eyes dropped to the V of his shirt and the patch of smooth skin peering out of the gap. His skin smelled faintly of beer and peppermint. Its aroma lingered in the basement air like a masculine perfume. Wonder if his skin tasted as good as it smelled.

What on earth...? Since when did she think such

kinds of things, about relative strangers no less. For goodness' sake, she didn't even know the man's full...

"Name!"

In the quiet basement, the word came out louder than necessary, causing them both to jump. "I mean, I don't know your name," she quickly corrected. "Only your first initial. From the mailbox."

"Grant."

"Grant," she repeated. That was better. Knowing his name made it better. That is, made him less of a stranger. She still had no business thinking about his skin. Extending her hand, she pushed all inappropriate thoughts out of her head. "What do you say we start fresh? I'm Sophie Messina."

"Nice to meet you, Sophie Messina."

His handshake was firm and strong, not the soft grip so many men adapted when greeting a woman. Sophie could feel the calluses pressing rough against her palm. They were hardworking hands. The sensation conjured up images of work-hewn muscles rippling under exertion.

Lifting her eyes, she caught the spark of...something... as it passed across his caramel-colored eyes, bright enough to light them up despite the shadows, and briefly she insisted their gaze dropped to her lips. Sophie's mouth ran dry at the thought. He cleared his throat, alerting her to the fact she still held his hand. Quickly she released his grip, and they stood there, awkwardly looking at one another.

Somewhere in the distance, a bell rang.

No, not a bell. A buzzer. Once. Twice. Then nothing.

"Dammit, I forgot..."

She stumbled slightly as Grant rushed past her. "Forgot what? What's wrong?"

He didn't answer. He was too busy taking the steps two at a time.

"Wait!" she heard him call to someone from the top of the stairs. It took her a second to catch up, but when she did, she found him standing in the foyer, front door open, staring at the traffic passing in the street. A missed date?

He glared at her from over his shoulder. "You owe me a dinner."

For the second time that evening, Sophie heard herself saying, "I beg your pardon?"

"That," he said, nodding toward the front door, "was my dinner. I missed the delivery because I was downstairs showing you the broken meter."

In other unspoken words, he blamed her.

"I'm sure if you call, he'll turn right around."

Another glare, this one accompanied by him jamming his fingers through his hair and mussing it. If only disheveled looked that good on her. "It was pizza from Chezzerones."

"Oh." Sophie was beginning to understand. Chezzerones had the best pizza in the area, as well as a very strict delivery policy. Fail to answer the door and your number got put on the "bad" list. Something to do with drunken university students and too many wasted calls. Sophie made the mistake of inquiring and had gotten a very detailed explanation from Chezzerone himself one night. It looked like, by helping her, Grant had gotten himself stuck on the bad list.

Darn it all, she *did* owe him a dinner.

CHAPTER THREE

LAST thing Sophie wanted was to have a debt hanging over her head. "All right, come with me," she said.

This time Grant was the one who scowled. "Why?"

"For dinner. You said I owed you a dinner. I'm paying you back. Now come with me."

As she fished her keys from her pocket to unlock her door, she once again felt him standing close, his peppermint scent finding a way to tease her from behind. A flash of heat found its way to the base of her spine.

What was with her? Lord, you'd think she'd had never crossed paths with a good-looking man before.

She so needed a shower and good night's sleep.

Of all the co-op residences in the building, Sophie's was the largest. U-shaped, the apartment reached around the back stairway onto the other side, where the master bedroom was located. The main living area was really two rooms, a parlor turned living room and a dining area. Both rooms featured the same heavy black woodwork as the foyer and contained beautifully scrolled wood and marble fireplaces. The kitchen was located in the rear, on the other side of the dining room. Having let them in, Sophie headed in that direction only to find Grant hadn't followed. Turning, she found him studying the framework dividing the two spaces.

"You kept the doors," he noted, tracing a finger along the molding.

He meant the pocket doors, which could be drawn to divide the space. Obviously he'd been in the space before. "For now. I've only been here a month. I figured I should live with the place awhile before making any major changes."

He nodded, and without asking, gave the door a tug. There was a soft scraping sound as the heavy panel moved outward. "Did the Realtor tell you that these are original?" he asked, brushing the dusty wood.

"He mentioned something."

"Etta—Mrs. Feldman, the owner, insisted on keeping a lot of the original fixtures. Most of the other units are far more modernized."

"The Realtor told me that, too." Apologized, really, over the fact that Sophie's hadn't been one of the redesigned spaces.

"My…" She found herself stumbling for a word to describe David. *Companion* was most correct but the word felt awkward on her tongue. Then again, she was finding talking difficult in general watching Grant caress the paneled door with the tenderness of a long-lost lover. "My…friend suggested I remove them and paint all the woodwork white."

"God, I hope not." She swore he winced at the suggestion. Better not to tell him David's full suggestion—that she gut the place. "This is black walnut."

"So?"

"So—" his look was way too condescending for someone so young "—you paint soft wood, like pine. Hard wood like walnut is meant to be shown off."

"I didn't realize wood came with rules."

What she did know was watching him run his hands

up and down the woodwork was damn unnerving. The soft brushing sound of calluses against the wood's rough surface made her stomach knot.

"Did you know Mrs. Feldman well?" she asked, pushing the door back into place.

"We met when she turned the building into apartments. She filled me in on the building's history."

"The Realtor told me she was the original owner."

"Well, not the *original* original," he noted. "This building predates the Civil War. But, her husband's family was. The only reason she converted was because she was convinced a developer would gut the place after she died." Sophie swallowed a kernel of guilt on David's behalf. "She fought right to the end to make sure the building retained as much of its original look as possible. Especially her living space. 'You can push me into converting, but you won't make me change my living room,' she used to say."

"Sounds like you two were like-minded."

"Last couple years, I've come round to see her way of thinking." He gave the woodwork one parting swipe.

There was regret in his words that made him sound older than his years. Look older, too, as a melancholy shadow accompanied them, darkening his golden features. Odd.

"I have to confess," she said, trying to break the mood, "I like some of the old fixtures. The entranceway for example. It's nice how the place is both modern and antique at the same time."

"A brilliantly designed blend," he softly replied. Almost sounded as if he was reciting a quote. Again, the words came across as weighted and old.

She had little time to wonder because Grant had crossed the dining room and was already pushing the swinging door leading to her kitchen. After trying to move him along earlier, she now found herself scurrying to catch up. She did only to find he'd stopped short again. This time he was studying the kitchen cabinetry with the same sensual attentiveness. She had to catch herself from bumping square into his back.

"Then there's the kitchen."

Unlike the edge from before, this time she heard a note of amusement in his voice. Though she couldn't see his face—she was still stuck behind his broad back— Sophie could easily picture his expression, basing the image on the many amused looks he'd shot in her direction over the past two days. Interestingly, in hindsight, those looks weren't nearly as infuriating as they seemed at the time.

"You don't like this room?" she asked.

"Etta was stubborn. She insisted on keeping it as is. Right down to the hardware. Making a last stand, I suppose."

The last line was said as he knelt down to examine a lower cabinet door. Sophie took advantage of the movement to slip past, sucking in her breath to avoid brushing up against him. Her neighbor, attention on the cabinet, didn't appear to notice.

"Maybe she simply knew her mind."

"That she did. Your hinges need replacing," he added, opening the cabinet door.

"I wouldn't mind replacing the entire room." Although she spent little time in the kitchen, Sophie found the space narrow and cramped. She found the room even more cramped now thanks to the addition of Grant's large form. His broad shoulders—so broad they practically filled the expanse between the counters. "Unlike

your Mrs. Feldman, I don't need to keep this room exactly as is."

"Won't get an argument from me. Any idea what
you'd do?"

Not really. Oh, she had ideas, but they were nebulous
and atmospheric, based more on fantasy than any actual plan. "Brighter, definitely," she told him. "Sunnier.
With windows and gleaming wood cabinets."

"Sounds like another woman who knows what she
wants." Their eyes met, and he flashed her a smile that
implied far more than cabinetry. Or so it felt from the
way her insides reacted.

"Pizza," she announced abruptly. Goodness but the
kitchen was cramped. And really warm. There was absolutely no air circulation at all on these hot nights.
"What kind would you like?"

"I have a choice?"

"Of course. I might not match Chezzerones, but I
have a decent variety. Cheese, pepperoni, Hawaiian,
chicken, pepper and onion…"

"Holy cow!" His voice sounded from over her shoulder causing her to jump. The guy didn't believe in personal space, did he? "It's like looking at the frozen food
section at the mini-mart."

"I like to keep food on hand in case of an emergency is all."

"What kind of emergency? Armageddon?"

Ignoring the comment, Sophie reached into the
freezer. Gooseflesh had begun crawling in the wake
of his breath on her bare neck, putting her out of sorts
again. She'd feel better once she was alone again.

"Here," she said, pulling a box from the stack and
thrusting it into his hands. "Go Hawaiian."

He looked down at the box, then back up at her.

"Is there a problem?" she asked him.

"What about cooking?"

She pointed to the side of the box. "Directions are right here. I don't have my reading glasses, but I'm pretty sure you preheat the oven to four-twenty-five."

"Okay." He didn't budge. Clearly he expected her to cook for him.

Sophie let out a frustrated sigh. It had been way too long a day, and she still had to track down a plumber and finish her paperwork. She didn't have time to entertain her neighbor. Especially one that had her set off balance since their first meeting.

She opened her mouth to tell him exactly that when a sound interrupted the kitchen's silence.

It was her stomach growling.

"Fine," she said, snatching the box back. "I'll cook. But you're on your own for dinner company."

With the pizza safely in the oven, Sophie excused herself and escaped to her bedroom. Hopefully, by freshening up, she could regain the self-control that seemed to be eluding her these past couple days and become more herself. Arguing about pizza? Thinking about what his skin tasted like? Not exactly the most mature of behaviors.

Don't forget barging up to his apartment like a madwoman.

She meant what she told him in the kitchen. He better not expect company. She had way too much to do.

Case in point. Her smart phone told her she'd missed eleven messages since arriving home. Make that a dozen, she amended as her in-box buzzed again.

There was a box of moist wipes in the bottom drawer of her vanity. She grabbed a handful to give herself a makeshift sponge bath. Not as refreshing as a shower, but she felt a little cleaner. "Score one for being pre-pared," she said as she used one to dampen down her hair. She combed out her ponytail and exchanged her running clothes for a jersey-knit maxi dress.

In the middle of touching up her eyeliner, she paused. *What are you doing, Sophie? Freshening up or fixing up?* She stared at her reflection. Instantly her eyes went to the deepening lines around her eyes and mouth. Two decades of adulthood lay behind those lines. And yet here she was so frazzled by a…a…a boy she was put-ting on eyeliner to eat frozen pizza.

"Get a grip," she snapped at herself. For goodness' sake, she wasn't some cougar on the prowl. There was absolutely no reason to let her neighbor get to her like this. Setting down the eyeliner, she grabbed a brush in-stead and combed her hair into a sleek damp bun. Much better, she decided. She looked more like herself again.

During her absence, Grant had moved into the din-ing room. Soon as she walked in, he looked up, and she swore the corners of his mouth turned downward. "What?" she asked smoothing the sides of her hair.

"You changed."

Why did he sound as if he meant more than clothes? Really, she chided, she had to stop reading undercur-rents in everything. Whatever tone Grant had, real or imagined, was irrelevant. The guy was here because she owed him dinner. Soon as he ate, he would leave and most likely, their paths wouldn't cross again.

The rattle of plates pulled her from her thoughts. Suddenly she realized Grant wasn't merely in the din-ing room, he was moving around the dining room table.

"What are you doing?" she asked him.

"Isn't it obvious? I'm setting the table."

"So I see." He must have gone through her kitchen because there were plates and flatware on the table. The only thing missing were her linen napkins. Two folded paper towels took their place. "But why?"

"Food's got to go on something." He disappeared back into the kitchen. Sophie followed and found him looking in the fridge. "Only a half-dozen choices. What happened? You get tired by the time you reached the beverage department?"

"Sorry to disappoint you," she replied. She was caught between annoyance and her desire to stare at how his shirt pulled up when he was bent over, exposing the smooth skin beneath. It was the skin that was keeping her from being overly annoyed at his prowling in her kitchen.

"Relax, I was joking. It's actually a damn impressive selection. You even have my favorite brand of beer." He waved an amber-colored bottle. "Would you like one? Or are you more of a wine woman?"

"Actually I don't drink."

"At all?"

Sophie shook her head. "My mother had a drinking problem."

"I'm sorry."

"Don't be. She wasn't your mother." Usually she simply told people alcohol didn't appeal to her and left it at that, but for some reason tonight the response had felt too trite. Seeing the awkwardness passing across Grant's face, however, reminded her why she preferred not to share the truth. "Anyway, now I only keep liquor on hand for entertaining." Which, she reminded herself, she was decidedly *not* doing.

According to the timer, the pizza was almost ready so she grabbed an oven mitt from a nearby hook. "Don't forget," she said, as she removed the baking sheet, "you're on your own for dinner. I don't care if you use my table and plates, but don't expect conversation. I have work to do."

"You work an awful lot."

"Comes with the territory. Stock market never rests, so neither do I."

"Never? You don't even take time out to go to bed?"

Sophie's hand slipped, sending the cutter careening up and over the edge of the crust. From the corner of her eye, she caught Grant trying to hide his smirk.

"I manage to grab a few hours' sleep," she answered. Pretending she didn't catch the innuendo, even though they both knew otherwise. "Some nights more than others. Some nights, like last night and tonight, less. Depends on how many interruptions I have." He wasn't the only one who could shoot off a veiled comment.

Unfortunately, unlike her, he didn't suffer an embarrassing reaction. Instead, he played with the edge of his beer label. "Do you ever wonder if it's worth the effort?"

"Of course it is. How else is a person going to move up?" she asked just before pushing the swinging door. "The world doesn't hand you success. You want something, you have to go for it."

She set the pizza in the center of the table, then took a seat in her usual chair. Grant settled in the spot across from her. Even with a table in between, the setup managed to feel cozy and Sophie wondered if letting him stay was a good idea. How long had it been since she'd shared a dinner at home with someone? Never as far as this place was concerned. David preferred eating out and before him… Wow, she couldn't remember the last time.

A few inches from her right hand, her BlackBerry

blinked, telling her she had another email. The total from Allen was already up to fifteen. Meanwhile, across the table, Grant was smacking his lips in overly dramatic fashion. "Not bad," she heard him say. "Not Chezzerones quality, but for a frozen pizza, it's pretty good."

"Glad to know my mini-mart meets your high standards." She was busy typing an email to Allen before her in-box buzzed again.

"You should try a slice."

"I will."

"I mean before the pizza gets cold."

She looked up and he immediately held up a hand. "I know. You're working. Doesn't end, does it? The pressure. No matter how much you accomplish, there's always something more to be done."

"Clearly you've seen my to-do list."

There was a pause while he took another bite. "Do you mind if I ask a personal question?"

Sophie felt her heart skitter. "Personal how?" she asked, looking up.

"What goal are you trying to reach with all this work?"

Oh. That wasn't what she expected. "I told you in the kitchen. I want to get ahead."

"Just ahead."

With a sigh, she put aside her phone. Obviously her "guest" had no intention of letting her email until she answered him. "My plan is to be named managing director of my firm."

"Ambitious. Then what?"

"Then I'll be at the top of the food chain." She'll have climbed higher than anyone expected a member of the Messina family to climb—including members of the Messina family. "And then I'll be the one pestering people with emails."

"Sounds like you've got everything planned out."

"I do." Although she didn't owe him any further explanation, she decided to give him one anyway. Who knows, maybe he'd learn something from the advice. *Like you're interested in mentoring him.* "I came in as a junior investment analyst, worked my way up to senior and with time and effort, I'll move up to the next level. In fact, rumor has it one of our directors is retiring, putting me in a very good position to take his place."

"Then what?"

It was like answering a broken record. Then what. Then what. "Then I can focus on the other items on my list."

"Items?" Reaching over, he lay a slice of pizza on her plate. "Here. Eat or be eaten. What do you mean by 'items on your list'?"

Sophie sighed again. "I didn't realize dinner came with an inquisition."

"I'm curious."

"All right. If you must know, I have a Life To-do List. Goals I want to accomplish." Everything she needed to officially consider herself having succeeded in life. A college degree. An MBA. A house of her own. A high-powered job. A successful, mature companion. A summerhouse.

"Like a bucket list."

"More like a master life plan."

Grant was nodding as he raised his drink. "How very…rigid of you," he said.

Rigid? Maybe but rigidity had served her well so far. More than he'd ever know. That sexy smile probably never encountered a hurdle in its life. "Don't you believe in planning for the future?"

To her surprise, the question caused his jaw muscles to tense. His eyes grew distant and dark. Only for a second, though, then the darkness disappeared, replaced by a lopsided grin. "Where's the surprise in that?"

"I'm not big into surprises. I prefer forewarning and foundation. When you're older, you'll understand."

The lopsided grin slid into sexy territory. "Are you trying to sound like my mother on purpose?"

"Why not? I'm almost old enough to be."

"Hardly."

"All right, maybe not that old. But I am old enough. Older than you." And apparently felt the need to remind both of them of that fact.

He took a drink. "I wouldn't go filling out your nursing home application quite yet. And trust me, you look nothing like my mother." As if to prove his point, he let his gaze travel from the top of her head to her waist.

Feeling her self-consciousness threatening to rise again, she used her pizza as an excuse to look away. Didn't matter. As she tore her crust into tiny bites, she could still feel the warmth flooding her cheeks. Scrutiny, even flattering scrutiny, was never something she enjoyed. Reminded her too much of unwanted attention. Over the years she'd cultivated a tolerance for being looked at, but for some reason her neighbor's gaze penetrated deeper than most. Its imprint lingered on her nervous system, feeding her awareness long after the look had ended. It was most disturbing, particularly during moments like this.

The buzz of a cell phone interrupted the silence.

"Duty calls," she heard Grant say.

"Always does." Out of the corner of her eye, she saw

the blinking email indicator on her cell phone. Calling to her. She ran her fingers lightly across the face of the phone.

Grant picked up on the hint and pushed away from the table. "Guess I'll be on my way then," he said. "Wouldn't want to derail your trip up the corporate ladder."

"Thank you," she replied. There seemed an underscoring of sarcasm in that comment, but she chose to ignore it.

"Thank you for the pizza."

"Does this mean we're even now?"

"Even?"

"For costing you dinner. And accusing you of stealing my water," she added.

In Sophie's mind, the appropriate answer would have been "don't worry about it." At least that's the response she would give. Instead, he gave her another one of those long unnerving looks. One that wrapped itself tightly around her and squeezed. "We'll see."

We'll see? What kind of answer was that? Either they were even or they weren't. *We'll see* implied unfinished business. She hated unfinished business. Absolutely loathed it. Why on earth would he imply something like that?

And why did her insides do a little tumble at the prospect?

Grant let himself out. Sophie was already on her phone and didn't notice. Click, click, clicking her way on her climb to what was it? Managing director? Listening to her talk about her "master plan" made his blood chill. It all sounded so determined, so calculated. And oh so achingly familiar.

The night had started out so differently. Order pizza, kick back and watch the game. A simple enough plan. Who decided to add Reminders of Mistakes Past to the agenda? First Mike, then his sexy workaholic neighbor.

Heaving a sigh, he washed a hand across his features and headed toward the staircase. Seeing Etta's apartment in all its untouched splendor didn't help. Bad enough he got a stab of guilt every time he mounted the staircase.

He wrapped his hand around the banister. Days of use had already worn the gloss away, creating a dull but warm-looking patina. The way wood should be, he thought, stroking the grain. God, but this house had been magnificent in its original form. Time worn, but with all the previous grandeur still alive beneath the surface.

And you helped talk her into chopping up the place. Yet another example of how blind he'd been to the obvious back then.

At least he was doing his best to repair the damage now. His apartment was one of the few mistakes he could fix.

For some reason, his thoughts drifted back to the first floor apartment and the woman working away at her dining room table. Bet if he knocked on her door three hours from now, she'd still be sitting in the same place, BlackBerry in hand, pizza untouched. A complete waste of legs and beauty if you asked him.

She reminded him of someone. Other than himself, that is. He'd been racking his brain all evening trying to figure out who, and he couldn't. Definitely not his mother, that's for sure. Last time he checked, his mother didn't have lips as ripe as berries. Too bad Sophie was such a workaholic, or he'd have tried a little harder to taste them.

On the other hand, maybe he should try to taste them *because* she was a workaholic. Show her what she was missing. After all the woman could use some loosening up. If anyone knew the cost of tunnel vision it was him. Besides, he'd never met a blonde he didn't want to kiss, and those lips were far too delicious looking to pass up.

Yup, he thought as he reached his apartment door, he was definitely going to have to give this idea some thought.

CHAPTER FOUR

NEXT morning Sophie woke to the sound of someone knocking on her door. And she'd been right in the middle of a good dream, too. At least she assumed it was good. Only the sensation remained. Prying open one eye, she saw the time and groaned. After last night's impromptu dinner, she'd stayed up late catching up on the market activity she missed. Her reward to herself was to be sleeping in to six-thirty. That's when David would be picking her up so she could shower at his place. He'd originally suggested she come over last night, but she'd begged off, insisting she needed to work. In reality, she was reluctant to start a pattern.

Not to mention you felt a little awkward after spending part of the night flirting with your man-child neighbor.

The knocking started anew. She slipped on her robe, ran a comb through her hair—thank heaven for ponytails, bed head's best friend—and padded into the living room just in time to call off round three. "Coming!"

"Good morning," Grant greeted when she opened the door. He looked entirely too fresh and showered for so early in the morning. His bright blue shirt clung to his shoulders almost as obscenely as his jeans clung to his hips. The attraction she fought all last night came rolling back so strongly her knees almost buckled. "Do you have any idea what time it is?" she asked him, tightening the belt on her robe.

His expression was unapologetic. "Is that any way to greet the men who fixed your water?"

"You fixed my water?"

"Not me, him." Belatedly, Sophie realized Grant wasn't alone. An African-American man with salt-and-pepper hair stood next to him. He carried a toolbox and wore a blue-and-white-striped work shirt with a patch that read A Plus Plumbing.

"This—" Grant clapped the man on his shoulder "—this is Erik Alvareen. Only plumber you'll ever need."

Sophie was still a little fuzzy. Grant had called a plumber? For her? Why? She shook the man's hand. "Sorry for the abrupt greeting. I had no idea you would be by."

"Normally, I wouldn't show up this early," Erik explained, "but I've got another job midtown that's gonna take most of the day."

"Plus, he owes me," Grant added, giving the man's shoulder a squeeze.

"Not anymore I don't," Erik replied. "You dragging my rear end out of bed at four in the morning makes us even."

"Like you weren't going to be awake anyhow. Erik's already looked at the meter," Grant told Sophie, "but he wanted to check your faucets, too."

"Just to make sure. Best to cover all bases."

As if she could argue with that. Sophie stepped aside and let the two men in.

"Do you mind if I take a second to throw some clothes on?" she asked, tugging on her belt again. For the second day in a row, Grant managed to find her in her skimpy clothing. This morning's short robe was perfect for hot weather, but not for entertaining two men. Especially Grant, whose eyes immediately dropped to the hemline.

"Don't bother on our account," he said.

The remark did not help. Sophie could feel her skin turning red. What was he doing here, anyway? The plumber seemed to have everything well in hand.

"I'll only be a minute," she told them. "If you'd like, you can check out the kitchen first. Grant knows where it is."

When she returned five minutes later in a far more appropriate set of yoga pants and T-shirt, she found Grant alone. "Erik is looking at the guest bathroom," he said.

Much to her irritation, Grant had found both her collection of coffee and her coffee mugs and was operating her single-cup coffeemaker. "I don't recall offering you free rein to dig through my cupboards."

"I didn't dig anywhere. I saw the coffee last night when I was getting the plates." The mug finished brewing and he handed it to her. "Figured you might be looking for some caffeine since we dragged you out of bed so early."

All right, she'd forgive him the intrusion this time. "The plumber was a surprise," she said, scooting by him to get to the refrigerator. "You didn't have to do that."

"I didn't want to risk a complaint being filed with the building association. Besides, Erik is the one guy I know who will do the repair right."

"I have to admit, I do appreciate things being done right," Sophie conceded.

He popped another pod into the brewing chamber. "Why am I not surprised?"

Finished doctoring her coffee, Sophie offered him the nonfat creamer only to have him shake his head. "No thanks. I'm more a black and bold kind of guy."

"Bold, anyway," she murmured, thinking how he made himself at home. And at home was exactly how he looked, too. Propped against the countertop, his long legs crossed at the ankles, he looked custom built for the space. The hem of his T-shirt ghosted the top of his low-slung jeans, just short enough so that when he moved his arms it inched upward revealing a sliver of plaid, from his boxers. Sophie cursed the warmth that unfurled in her stomach. It was way too early in the morning for such overt virility.

She gripped her mug a little tighter and positioned herself across the aisle. "Are you always like this?" she asked him.

"Bold? Absolutely."

Ignoring the way his answer seemed to slide down her spine, she said, "I mean, do you always do favors for strangers? Especially ones who have been—"

"A pain in the butt?"

"I was going to say 'at odds.'"

"Tomato, tomahto. I thought we settled all that with last night's pizza."

Had they? She seemed to recall a sense of unfinished business. "Either way, it was still nice of you. I'm looking forward to taking a shower."

"Glad I could help. Although, if you ask me," he said with a slow smile, "you also look pretty damn good for a woman who's been denied bathing privileges."

"Benefits of bottled water."

"Very resourceful. Somewhere there's a Boy Scout

leader wishing you were in his troop. You'd be the queen of merit badges."

"Thank you."

"What makes you certain I'm giving you a compliment?"

"I'll take it as one." Cradling her mug, she fortified herself with a good long sip. She could already feel the caffeine in her bloodstream, kicking up her pulse and causing her insides to churn. At least she chose to blame the caffeine. She refused to acknowledge the voice in the back of her head suggesting her company was having the greater effect. "Same way I'll attribute your mocking to jealousy."

"Jealousy?"

"Sure. Because I'd carn more merit badges than you."

He laughed. "I'll have you know that no one earned more merit badges than I did back in Scouts. I mastered every skill. I can even rub two sticks together and make fire."

His feral smile was making Sophie's knees buckle. If she hadn't been holding her coffee, she'd have gripped the countertop.

Heat pooled at the base of her spine. At some point during their exchange, she'd leaned forward, bringing her into his physical space. Peppermint reached her nostrils. She was close enough now to see the faint lines near the corners of his eyes.

And, he was close enough to see the bags under hers.

She practically slammed her spine against the counter edge straightening her back. "So," she said, covering by taking another healthy gulp of coffee. "Four o'clock in the morning, huh? Your friend Erik must have owed you one heck of a favor. What did you do?"

"Nothing big. I helped his grandson out of a jam this past winter is all."

"More like he bailed the boy's sorry ass out of jail," Erik said, bursting through the swinging door. "You're all set," he said to Sophie. "I checked all the faucets, and they're working fine."

She suppressed the urge to hug him. "You have no idea how happy I am to hear you say so. You forget how much you depend on running water until you don't have it for a few hours. Thank you so much."

"Anything for a 'friend' of Grant's," the older man replied with a knowing grin. Sophie was so grateful for his assistance, she let the misunderstanding slide. "Besides, my wife would have killed me if she ever caught me making a lady wait for her shower."

"You're wife's a wise woman," she told him.

After having her coffee offer declined and promising she would call him for all her plumbing needs, Sophie walked Erik to the door. She assumed Grant would leave with his friend as well, but he surprised her, hanging back in her doorway.

"Still have half a cup of coffee," he pointed out when she shot him a frown.

Sophie tried to work up some indignation but couldn't. He did, after all, get her water back. "You really didn't have to make the man come by so early," she said, pushing open the kitchen door.

"You'd rather wait all day?"

"Absolutely not. I love the fact he stopped here first." It saved her from having to trek all her belongings to David's apartment, along with keeping her from wasting part of her morning on the phone.

She contemplated the liquid in her cup, thinking once again how the color resembled Grant's eyes. There was a question she'd wanted to ask since Erik spoke earlier. "Was he telling the truth? Did you bail his grandson out of jail?"

He waved off the incident as though he was chasing off a fly. "Kid was in the wrong place at the wrong time is all. Erik and I were working on a project together at the time, so when Bryant couldn't reach his grandfather, he called me."

And Grant rode to his rescue? She thought of other late-night phone calls. The shrill ringing of the phone shattering whatever temporary calm had settled in the apartment. The pleas for help. The promises that this time would be the last time. Didn't matter which parent made the promise because there never was a last time. There was only chaos and drama. So much drama it made you sick. Until you moved as far away as possible and hoped those phone calls would never find you again.

"He's lucky you took the call," she said quietly.

A dark look came over his bright features, so dark it made her forget her own shadows. "That time, anyway," he said over the rim of his coffee cup.

"Bryant gets into trouble often?"

"What?" He looked surprised she'd spoken. "No," he said, quickly shaking his head. "Not at all. That was a one-time, stupid kid mistake. He learned his lesson."

What then caused the shadow that crossed his face? The bleak, distant state that killed the sparkle in his eyes. Grant Templeton wasn't as laid-back and carefree as he would like the world to believe.

Conversation over, they stood and sipped their coffee in quiet. A strange kind of silence, it was, too. Unnerving and serene at the same time. For while she was far too aware of his presence—the way he breathed through his nose, the rustle of fabric when he raised his arm, the soft slurp when he sipped his coffee—she found the sounds strangely natural. They were the kinds of sounds she always imagined a home would be full of.

In the back of her mind she knew she should get to her much anticipated shower, but she didn't move. It was the need for more caffeine. Two nights with too little sleep had her needing extra fortification.

Keep telling yourself that, Sophie.

"Behind you." Grant's voice broke the silence. "That's where I'd put the window."

Sophie looked over her shoulder and straight into a cabinet door. "You think? What happened to not touching the original fixtures?"

"Guess old habits die harder than I thought." His attention returned to his cup, a little more somber than before. "It really is the perfect spot for a window, though."

Sophie studied the space, trying to picture a window instead of a wood door. She only saw cabinet.

"Would I get sunshine?"

"Enough."

Enough sounded good. "Tell me more." She was starting to get excited. A voice in the back of her head suggested part of her enthusiasm was to brighten his voice again. Even so, she wanted to hear what he had to say.

And boy did she hear. For the next several minutes he laid out suggestions, weaving a spell of mental images that left her captivated. Although to be honest, if asked, she didn't think she could repeat a single idea. What seized her attention was the authority with which he spoke. Clear, strong-voiced. There was no doubting his vision. And the way he demonstrated each idea with his hands—gesturing about the small space with grace and surety—she could easily imagine him making those suggestions reality.

Bet he could do a lot with those hands. She had to bite her lip at the thought.

"Sounds like you've given this a lot of thought," she said when he finished. A lot. Plus he spoke with a knowledge she was ashamed to admit she didn't expect from a young, live-in-the-moment contractor. Another layer to ponder. It was clear he had much more expertise than she gave him credit for.

"More than I should," he admitted. Was that a blush or a shadow on his cheeks?

"Regardless, your ideas are amazing. Too bad I don't know a good contractor."

"Too bad indeed."

The carousel of plastic coffee pods sat on the counter from when Grant first used them. Empty cup in hand, she moved across the room, selected one and popped it into the chamber, all the while trying not to feel Grant's eyes on her. There was a soft gurgling noise and the smell of dark roast coffee filled the air as the machine began brewing.

It was a bad idea. She knew less than nothing about him, even less about his work skills. Regardless, her next words came out before she could stop them. "I don't suppose you're interested."

"Don't sell yourself short, sweetheart."

Oh, but it was way too early in the morning for her stomach to be quivering. "I meant the kitchen. I was wondering if you'd be interested in the job."

"Oh, that."

Could his voice be any flatter? She'd heard him let out a long breath. "We'll see," he answered finally.

Again with the "we'll see." Only this time, instead

of being vague, it sounded resigned. "You don't want the job?" Why spend all this time waxing on with ideas then?

"I'm very selective about the jobs I take on," he replied.

"You don't say." She reached to take her mug from the coffeemaker. "I didn't realize contractors could afford to be picky in this economy."

"Historical renovator, and I can," he corrected, joining her on her side of the counter.

The arrogance in his voice was overwhelming, too much so if you asked Sophie. However, if he was trying to hook her interest, the tactic worked. "Tell me then," she asked, unable to help herself, a habit she seemed to have developed around him, "what kind of projects do you take on?"

"Ones that interest me, or that are special. A rare building, an interesting concept."

He was holding something back, but she couldn't tell what with all the cockiness wrapped around his answer.

"And my kitchen isn't interesting or special?" she had to ask.

"Unfortunately, you're both."

Sophie frowned. "What's that mean?"

"Means you could tempt a man into doing most anything."

Goose bumps ghosted across Sophie's skin. When had he moved so close? And for that matter, were they still talking about her kitchen, because she wasn't so sure.

Callused fingertips caught the edge of her jaw, forcing her face to turn right. His breath smelled of peppermint and coffee. Sophie struggled not to lick her lips.

"Anyone ever tell you that you're incorrigible?" she asked.

He lifted her face closer. Light as his touch was, Sophie could feel every bump and rough patch, every pinprick of pressure against her skin.

"All the time." His eyes dropped to her mouth.

This time Sophie did lick her lips. And held her breath. And leaned closer...

Whoa! Whoa! Whoa! Sophie slammed on the brakes, bringing the moment to a screeching halt by bolting toward the door.

"Will you look at the time?" she babbled, sounding like a complete idiot since, other than the digital display on the microwave behind her, there wasn't a clock in view. "I'm going to be late for work if I don't get into the shower."

"It's only six-thirty."

Figures he could see the clock.

"Exactly. I'm usually on my way to the office by seven." Some days. Never mind she planned on sleeping in today. Inside her stomach, her nerves were doing the triple jump. *Hop, skip, plunge.* What on earth had she been thinking?

She wasn't. That was the problem. Her brain—and body—developed a whole new set of behaviors around him. Ones she didn't recognize.

Like the way her insides shook just now. "I've going to go now," she announced. As if the flight weren't obvious. "Feel free to take your coffee with you. No sense wasting a freshly brewed cup."

"You're the one who brewed the second cup."

"Right. I forgot." Fortunately, she had her back to him so she was spared looking at his amused expression. "Do you mind letting yourself out, as well?"

"If that's what you want me to do."

Okay, he didn't just drop his voice a notch when asking the question, did he? "Yes, that's what I want. Thank you."

Her hand was on the door, and she was about to push when she regained a sliver of her senses. "And thank you again for bringing Erik by. I really appreciate it. Especially after I was so…" Oh, Lord, the word faded right out of her head.

"Anyway, I guess that means I—" inwardly she winced, realized what she was stupidly about to say "—owe you again."

Sophie gasped as his breath tickled the back of her neck. He was standing close again. Whether on purpose or by coincidence, she couldn't say, but from the spreading heat, her body obviously did. "No problem. We can negotiate how you can pay me back another time."

Her arm began to tingle as he leaned even closer, his arm tickling the hair on hers as he reached past her and laid his hand on the door next to hers. "Enjoy your shower." Dammit, but his voice dropped *again*.

"Oh, and by the way," he added, pushing the door open. "Erik said you might have to let the hot water run for a bit before it kicks in."

That's all right, thought Sophie, rubbing her tingling forearm. Cold water would do just fine.

That, Grant thought, watching the door swing back and forth, was…interesting. Definitely worth getting up early for. Though he wouldn't admit it to Erik, he owed the plumber now.

Calling his friend occurred to him last night during the ninth inning. Right after he pictured Sophie banging on his door because the plumber she hired didn't do a good enough job. And while Sophie on his doorstep wasn't an unpleasant idea, he figured why not cut short the inevitable glares by getting the one man he knew would fix the problem right the first time? Rousting Sophie from bed had been the added bonus. Gave him a chance to sneak another peek at the Sophie he met last night. The clean-scrubbed, mussed-hair Sophie.

Oh, yeah, he definitely owed Erik.

Things did get a little unnerving when he slipped into his old role rattling off design ideas. Scary how easily that happened. Again, it was Sophie. Something about her description last night triggered his inspiration. He found himself wanting to give her the kitchen she envisioned.

In a way, his desire to do so rattled him as much as the slip. Women didn't inspire him for the most part, at least not so far as wanting to please them. Designwise that is. Sophie was the first. His disdain for Etta's kitchen must have gotten to be too much for him to control.

Or it was Sophie. He rubbed his fingers together, reliving the feel of her skin. His neighbor wore flushed well. Real well. Damn shame she backed away before things could get even more interesting.

Next time, he decided. Smiling to himself, he poured Sophie's untouched coffee into his cup. Next time.

"Everything all right?" David asked when she called. "You sound distracted."

Distracted was an understatement. Try horrified, disturbed, off balance. "Everything's fine." *I almost kissed my upstairs neighbor in the middle of an impromptu job interview is all.* "Late night."

"Figured as much. I caught the early morning financial report. Looks like you'll have an equally busy day."

"I've already heard from Allen." His voice mail had been waiting for her when she retreated from the kitchen. An electronic reminder to keep her head on straight. "We have a meeting first thing."

"Sounds like you've become his regular go-to person in a crisis."

"I think so." You'd get no complaints from her— Allen's favor bode well for when the company decided to name a new manager.

In the distance, she heard the click of her front door; the sound of Grant leaving. After his comment about the water, she'd pushed past him and gone to her bedroom so quickly she hadn't realized he'd lingered. Must have decided to have that coffee after all. Was it her imagination or did the apartment suddenly feel emptier? Had to be her imagination.

"…water back."

"What?" She hadn't realized David spoke.

"I said you must be glad you got your water back."

"Very. You don't know how much you appreciate running water till it's gone." She'd said the same thing to Erik and Grant. "Plus, I don't have to put you out now."

"You weren't putting me out. We could have had coffee."

"True. We'll have to wait till this weekend now." Sophie looked to the floor, a guilty knot in her stomach. Another reason she should be ashamed of her behavior back in the kitchen. She and David had an *understanding*.

"Which reminds me," David said. On the other end of the line, there was the rustle of paper. "This Friday, the Bar's Business Law Division is hosting an event at the Natural History Museum. Networking-wise it makes sense to attend with a guest."

"Sure," she accepted, swallowing her reluctance. After her behavior, she felt too guilty to say no, even if going out on Friday did go against their usual routine.

"Wonderful. The event will be good for you, too. You'll meet some great contacts for when you make managing director."

"Sounds great." Sophie smiled a guilty smile. That was another thing. David understood her priorities. He looked out for her career. He was good for her.

She finished the call by promising to talk with David later in the day. Then, hanging up, she looked at her reflection. The woman in the mirror had a grim expression.

"You should be ashamed of yourself, flirting with Grant like that," Sophie told her. "The man's not even your type for crying out loud."

David was. In fact, he was exactly the kind of man she should be wanting. Stable. Mature. *Age-appropriate*. He wouldn't show up on her doorstep by surprise or turn a discussion about kitchen renovations into some kind of seductive game. Nope. With David, what you saw was what you got. The man he was this Friday night would be the same man she would see next weekend, and all the weekends after that. Consistent. No surprises. No hints of unfinished business. Just the way she preferred.

Simply put, David fitted in to her plans. Her neighbor, with his T-shirts and peppermint aura, did not. End of story.

CHAPTER FIVE

Sophie and Grant didn't cross paths for the rest of the week. Sophie told herself the feeling in her stomach was relief, especially on Thursday when she thought she saw him at the mailbox only to discover it was someone from the fourth floor.

Friday afternoon, however, she came home to find a large white bathtub on the sidewalk. On any normal day, the sight in itself would have startled her, but she was too distracted by the sandy-haired man standing next to the tub.

Hands planted on his narrow hips, Grant didn't notice her approach. Good thing since she needed a moment to recover from the wave of attraction that crashed over her the second she saw him. It was as though the man released pheromones that made her body react as if it had a mind of its own.

Catching her breath, she put on her best nonchalant voice. "Interesting place to install a bathroom."

Caught off guard, Grant looked up quickly, his brown eyes catching the light and looking so close to golden it made Sophie's head swim. "I'm waiting for the delivery guy to park the truck so we can carry her upstairs. Apparently he has a thing about leaving the truck double-parked and unattended."

The tub was large and white with four clawed feet. The kind built for taking a long relaxing soak. Sophie started to picture Grant doing just that then thought better of it. The less she thought of Grant in anything other than a work capacity, the better.

She ran a hand along the smooth white rim. "Shouldn't it be in a box or something?"

"I bought it salvage."

Which, apparently, explained everything. "What now?"

"Soon as Eddie, the driver, gets back, we carry it upstairs. Want to help?"

She shook her head. "No thanks. I'll stick with my nice light briefcase."

"Wimp."

"Maybe so, but at least I won't be complaining about a bad back tomorrow morning."

"But if my back hurts, I'll have this nice big tub to sink into." Leaning over, he knocked on the side, causing a deep clanking noise. "Hear that? Exactly like the kind the original building had."

Though she couldn't care less about antique bathtubs, Sophie nonetheless found herself caught up by the enthusiasm in his voice. The sparkle in his eyes didn't hurt, either. "You certainly take your building history seriously."

"I've learned to." He looked to their building facade. "Do you ever think about how blind we can be to what's right in front of us? We think we're seeing everything, but we miss so much. With old buildings it's like, I don't know, seeing an oyster and not noticing the pearl."

"Unless the oyster didn't have a pearl to begin with," Sophie replied. In her opinion, some pasts were better distanced from, or erased altogether. Take her own past, for example. She doubted there was very much worth polishing there.

"There's always a pearl."

Maybe with buildings, but in the larger scheme, she knew better. Things like lives were best built by looking toward the future. "For someone so young, you are way too romantic."

"For someone not that much older, you aren't nearly enough."

He moved into her space, eyes heavy-lidded as though focused on her mouth. A mouth that had suddenly run dry. Breaking eye contact, she looked instead to the tub. Rubbing her hand along the cool white surface, she said, "I will admit, the tub does look comfortable."

"Want to try her on for size?"

"I beg your pardon?" She laughed. "You want me to get in the tub?"

"Sure, why not?"

"How about the fact it's sitting on the sidewalk?"

"So? Come on, give her a try." Sophie started to protest, but Grant refused to take no for an answer. Instead, he took her hand and the electricity passing up her arm distracted her into silence.

"Go ahead, sit," he urged after he'd led her one leg at a time into the depth. "Stretch out your legs. I want to figure out the maximum height requirements."

"You can't figure it out on your own?"

"I already know I'm too tall. Besides, you owe me a favor, remember?"

Did he have to bring that up? Or say the words in the same maddening murmur? "Couldn't I make you another frozen pizza?"

She hauled one leg over the side. "If my pantsuit gets dirty, you're paying the dry cleaning bill."

"You won't get dirty. Sit."

Sophie sat. The sides of the tub came up to her shoulders and neck. She felt like an idiot. "I mean really sit. Lean back and close your eyes."

She leaned back. She refused to close her eyes however. There were limits.

Grant squatted next to her and rested his chin on the rim. "Can't you picture yourself coming home after a hard day and relaxing in this baby? A candle, some bubble bath, your trusty rubber duck."

The last made her give a rather unladylike snort. "Somehow I don't picture you as being the wine and bubble bath type."

His eyes grew to a deep dark brown. "I'm into all sorts of things with the right company," he drawled.

Sophie had to press her thighs together to keep her legs from tingling. All of a sudden, her position felt way too intimate in spite of their open surroundings. With Grant behind her, his face hovering next to her ear. The way it might be if they were actually lounging in the bathtub. Why did he have to make everything sound so sexual?

"Can I get out now?" she asked, bolting upright. "The deliverymen are probably on their way back and I'm sure they'd prefer not to have to carry the extra weight." Plus, she'd prefer not to have them arrive while she was stretched out on the sidewalk.

"Sure, but for the record," Grant said, steadying the tub as she scrambled back to her feet, "it wouldn't be that much extra weight."

"Don't you mean, by comparison?" She lifted a

leg over the side, wobbling slightly on her heel as she stepped down onto the sidewalk.

Grant caught her by the elbow. "Careful now," he said, "I've got you."

"Thank you."

"Pleasure's all mine."

There he went again; drawling the simplest of words and making her body want to melt. "I wish you wouldn't do that," she said, righting herself.

Grant cocked his head. "Do what?"

"Say things in that voice."

"What voice?"

"You know darn well what voice I mean." He was acting obtuse on purpose. "You sound like you're flirting with me."

Understanding crested across his features along with a slow, sexy smile. "Oh, you mean this voice," he said, automatically dropping to the texture of rough honey.

"Yes, that voice," she snapped. "Please stop."

"Why?"

"Because it's not proper. I'm—"

"A beautiful woman?"

He thought her beautiful?

Stay on point, Sophie. "A prospective customer," she countered. "For that reason alone we should keep things professional."

He looked down into her face. "You make an interesting point."

A point that might hold more weight if she'd thought to break free of his touch. Her elbow was still nestled in his hand; the contact with her skin palpable despite the linen of her blazer.

"I wasn't aware my tone of voice had that much effect."

"It doesn't."

Reluctantly she lifted her arm free. "But given I'm considering hiring you, I figure it's important to be upfront with one another. After all, we've only known each other a couple days. I'd hate for either of us to misunderstand the other's intentions. Or for anyone else to get the wrong impression, for that matter."

"Okay, now you've lost me." He folded his arms. "Why would others get the wrong impression?"

"You know...older woman, younger contractor." He was so not going to make her say it aloud, was he?

"You're afraid people might think you're some cougar taking advantage of a poor innocent boy."

"Hardly." She may not have known Grant Templeton long, but *innocent* was definitely not a word she would use.

"Oh, then you're afraid they'll think I'm taking advantage of the lonely spinster."

"I am not a spinster." And he was pushing her buttons on purpose. She smacked his shoulder. "Be nice to your elders."

"Yes, ma'am," he said, chuckling. "Seriously, though, is it that important to you what people think?"

"Yes." Sophie replied without hesitation. He'd better believe it was important. After how hard she worked to become the woman she was? She wouldn't apologize, either.

Grant sat on the edge of the tub and regarded her. "Why?"

"Long story."

"One of those." He stretched out his legs and crossed them at the ankle. "Maybe one day you'll share it."

Doubtful. Suffice to say not every oyster had a pearl; some were man-made—or woman-made in this instance. As long as they weren't scrutinized too carefully, no one would know the difference.

"Are you sure your delivery people are coming back?" she asked, changing the subject. The tree-lined street had a number of people, but none looked dressed for moving a bathtub.

"Good question. They better or you won't be the only one who used this tub on the sidewalk. Only I won't be dressed in a linen pantsuit."

That image would be seared into her brain for the night. "Hope you have bail money set," she said, swallowing hard.

Grant grinned. "Worried about answering late-night calls?"

"Depends. If I answer, will I get a price break on my new window?"

Their smiles connected and Sophie found herself getting lost in a dazzle of caramel warmth. Why was it again that she thought maintaining distance was a good idea?

"Sophie?"

David. In a flash the connection fell apart.

Talking with Grant, she completely lost track, and naturally David was right on time. He wore a pale gray suit and his white shirt was crisp and wrinkle free as usual. His silver hair shined in the early evening sky.

"I thought that was you standing out here." Sophie resisted the urge to duck her head as he leaned in to kiss her cheek. Since when was she shy about David kissing her in public?

Although the public didn't usually involve a pair of caramel eyes watching her.

A frown creased the lines of David's high forehead. "Why is there a bathtub on your sidewalk?"

"Grant's waiting for the deliverymen to park their truck."

"And Sophie was graciously warning me about the dangers of bathing in public," Grant added, causing Sophie to blush again.

"A wise warning," David replied. He stuck out his hand and introduced himself.

Sophie had to give him credit for remaining unflappable about the whole situation. But then David was always unflappable. It was one of his best qualities. Watching the two men shake hands, she couldn't help but be struck by their contrasting appearances. David with his smoothly combed silver hair and sharp patrician features; Grant, rugged and handsome, wearing jeans and an obscenely tight collared jersey. One looked the perfect lawyer, which of course he was. The other looked...

Dangerous. With his pheromones and the way he demanded attention even in the most crowded and open of spaces. There was no better other word. He made David, whose long, lean frame stood the exact same height, look small.

To her embarrassment, she'd missed what David had said.

"Sophie?"

"What?"

"I asked if you wanted to bring your briefcase inside. We have a little while before we need to leave for the fundraiser. I thought I could beg a cocktail off you."

"Certainly easier than going out for one. I'm sure she has a fully stocked bar," Grant remarked drily.

Sophie felt another flush of warmth, this time exacerbated by David's perplexed expression. Bending, she retrieved her briefcase from where she dropped it when climbing into the tub. Thankfully David hadn't seen her doing that. "I wouldn't mind a few moments to freshen up," she said, changing the topic.

"If you'd like, but you look fine to me."

"I have to agree," Grant chimed in. He turned to David. "If you'd like, while you're waiting you can help me with the tub. The extra set of hands could come in handy."

"I would, but I'm not really dressed for the job," David replied.

"That's all right. If the deliverymen don't show up, Sophie's already said she'll take my phone call. Isn't that right, Sophie?"

He'd dropped his voice on purpose. Sophie narrowed her eyes.

Meanwhile, David was frowning again. "I'm afraid I don't understand."

"Never mind. I'll explain it to you inside." Turning her back on the grinning contractor, she hooked her arm in David's, leading him up the steps. "Right after I turn off my phone."

"I'm confused," David repeated once Sophie closed her front door. "I thought you said your neighbor shut the door in your face."

"He did. We've buried the hatchet, so to speak." Although if he kept it up, the hatchet might not stay buried for long. Bad enough Grant seemed to enjoy pushing her buttons so much, but did she have to react so easily? Every comment, every look, every touch. Her body was still overheated from their conversation earlier. "In fact, he's the one who fixed my water problem."

"I thought you said it was a plumber," David said, still frowning and watching Grant through the front windows. Sophie tapped him on the shoulder and motioned for him to follow her to the kitchen.

"It was, but Grant was the one who called him. He's a contractor—historical renovator, really," she corrected automatically, "and the plumber was one of his contacts."

"Oh, I see. But why was he making jokes about you having a well-stocked bar?"

"He's been making fun of that since he had dinner here the other night. Pizza," she added for David's scowl's benefit. "After he looked at the pipes."

She poured him a glass of Pinot Grigio. "It's a long and complicated story. I could have sworn I told you all this."

"Must have slipped your mind with all the work," David offered, accepting the glass.

"Must have," she agreed, putting the bottle on the counter with a guilty thud. The memory of how she almost kissed Grant in this very room weighed heavily on her.

"Turns out Grant worked on this building when it was being converted into co-ops," she said. "I'm thinking of having him do some work on my kitchen."

There. Couldn't say she didn't disclose that piece of information.

"You sure that's a good idea?" David asked.

After the tub business a few minutes ago, no. Somehow, though, she didn't think that's what David meant. "Why wouldn't it be?"

"What do you know about him? I mean the man's got a bathtub on your sidewalk. How do you know if he's even reliable?"

"Just because the man bought a tub from a junk dealer doesn't make him a bad contractor." One thing for her to have doubts; she didn't think David needed to get all high-and-mighty or insult her decision making process.

"It's hardly the first time I've hired someone," she added. "I think I'm capable of discerning whether or not the man can add a window properly."

"I'm sorry," David replied. "You're absolutely right. He threw me with all that nonsense about late-night phone calls. If I didn't know better, I'd say he was flirting with you."

"No," Sophie said. "That's just his way. I think he thinks it's charming." Not to mention as sexy as hell.

"Well, I know you'll make a careful decision. You're nothing if not levelheaded."

"Thank you." After how easily her resolve melted on the sidewalk, she wondered. Still she offered David her warmest smile. She had enough talking—and thinking—about her hot man-child neighbor for the day. Time to focus on the man she should be focused on. The one standing across from her.

The one who didn't make her kitchen feel tight and narrow.

"The delivery guys showed up right after they went inside," Grant relayed later that evening. "Good thing. I would have felt like a moron sitting on the edge of my tub waving goodbye. Probably would have said some smart-mouthed comment, too, just to see her reaction." He'd developed a thing for the way her cheeks flooded with color. Better looking than any cosmetic.

Next to him, Nate Silverman sat propped in his hospital bed, eyes aimed at the game playing out on his TV. On the screen, a ball passed the diving shortstop's glove.

"Tampa's been hot lately. Bet they make a run in September. Your Sox better watch out."

He sat back in the green leather chair and fiddled with the stitching along the arm. "The guy Sophie was going out with? Complete corporate shill. You remember the type. Designer suit, three-hundred-dollar shoes." The way they used to dress, only with silver hair. Wonder if he made Sophie blush deeply, too?

An odd, angry tightness gripped his chest at the thought. "Bet he's dull," he said aloud to Nate. "He looked it."

No, he looked exactly the way he expected a guy Sophie would date to look. She no doubt had a whole checklist of predetermined qualities. Wasn't that something someone with a master plan would do?

"I really don't know why I'm so fascinated with her. Besides the fact she's gorgeous. I think it's because…" His gaze grew distant. "You know the idea that people cross your path for a reason?" Something drew him to her. The answer lay right in front of him, too, only he couldn't see it. What else was new. He was good at being blind to what stood right before his eyes. "Maybe I'm supposed to show her how to loosen up." Or maybe she was here to remind him. To keep him from screwing up again.

"Did I tell you I started designing her kitchen? Dragged out the old CADD program and everything." Because she wanted a new room. "Scary how easy it is to get lost in the work again. Remember the buzz you could get when a design idea clicked? I forgot how addictive that feeling could be."

His choice of words made him wince. "Sorry, pal. Didn't mean to bring up a sore topic." The feeling he described was from a long time ago. Before Nate started chasing a different kind of buzz, one that he, lost in a chase of his own, failed to notice.

A petite woman with short brown hair appeared in the doorway. "It's getting late, Mr. Templeton. Nate needs to get ready for bed."

"Sure thing. We were just wrapping up." Grant rose to his feet. He stretched his arms high over his head and stretched. The soft crack of his vertebrae coming back into line echoed in the quiet. "Sorry to spend the whole visit gnawing your ear off about Sophie. Next time I'll focus more on the game. Promise."

Guilt rising in his throat, the way it did every visit, Grant reached down and patted the dark-haired man's shoulders. Nate didn't respond. But then he never did. The Nate he knew departed this world two years ago, leaving only the shell behind. A bedridden reminder of what was and what could have been.

And would never be again, thanks to Grant.

CHAPTER SIX

SINCE the day she left home twenty-two years earlier, Sophie dedicated Saturday mornings to doing three tasks: doing her laundry, cleaning her apartment and paying her bills. She was halfway through the third chore when the clanging started.

"You've got to be kidding," she said, tossing her ballpoint down. Grant's tub had been delivered. What on earth was he doing now? Images of him bent over, smacking on pipes with a wrench came to mind. The hem of his shirt would be pulled up ever so slightly, the way it did whenever he bent down, showing that sliver of tanned back. Or, perhaps the heat made him skip the T-shirt altogether and his muscular arms glistened slick with perspiration.

Nice, Sophie. Objectify the guy like one of the dirty old executives you read about in the tabloids. Though if her mind did insist on going down the objectifying road—again—Grant shared part of the blame. He was the one who talked about bathing on the sidewalk.

Still, she might as well see how long the racket would last. After all, if Grant intended on disrupting another one of her Saturday afternoons, she wanted to know.

That was the only reason she headed upstairs. It

had nothing to do with curiosity regarding his attire. Absolutely nothing.

Grant opened the door on the second round of knocking. He was, to her disappointment, wearing a regular old T-shirt. "Let me guess," he greeted, folding his arms, "you're here about the clanging, right? I'm disturbing you and your friend?"

She took a moment to understand his implication. "David isn't here."

"Sorry to hear that," Grant replied.

"No need. We, that is, I…" She didn't have to explain anything to the man. "I came upstairs to find out if you planned on making noise all day like last time."

"Interrupting work again am I?"

The sarcasm wasn't any more entertaining today than it was last weekend, despite their truce. "I'm trying to pay my bills at the moment, but yes, later I have to work."

"Stock market's not in session."

A throwback to the other night when she told him she worked when the markets were open. "Maybe not, but I still am."

"No rest for the weary, eh?"

Weary was what she felt. Thanks to him. "You haven't answered my question. Are you going to be making noise all weekend?"

"Actually, you'll be happy to know I'm almost finished. In fact, I'm about to hook up the final piece. Want to come in and see the finished product?"

"I…" Remembering all the sordid images having taken residence in her head, she should decline. "I don't think so."

"Why not?"

Because I got cozy with you on a public sidewalk and

spent way too much time focusing on what your skin tastes like. Lord knows what I'll do inside your apartment. "I have to get back to my bills."

"The bills will wait. Come on in. You know you're curious."

"No, I'm not," she started to lie, only to have him take her hand and pull her through the threshold. "Okay, maybe just a moment."

Grant's apartment was like the man himself: original, masculine and gorgeous. The narrow living room/dining area had many of the same features as her apartment. The fireplace had the same intricately carved woodwork for example. But despite the similarities, the room managed to have a personality all of its own. A granite island let light into the kitchen. She looked through with envy at the cabinets and stainless steel appliances.

"Do all the other apartments look like this?" she asked, thinking Etta should have been a little less stubborn.

"No, they're far more modern. In fact, you go to the top floors and you won't believe you're in the same building.

"The place was designed for selling," he added in a jaded-sounding voice. The tone didn't suit him.

"I've been trying to bring back as much of the original as possible. Can't completely turn back the hands of time, but I do what I can."

From the looks, he'd done a lot. The windows, the woodwork, all looked original, only in better condition. Decorating-wise, Grant apparently leaned toward bachelor sparseness. He was obviously more interested in structural details than curtains. There was a built-in bookcase actually filled with books, a plasma TV and a comfortable-looking leather sofa. A drafting table piled high with papers and reference books sat next to the doorway. There was also a large coffee table, which, from the looks of things, served double duty as a dining room table. Sophie noticed a coffee cup and two empty beer bottles holding down the newspaper. The entire room had been painted beige and brown adding to the masculine feel.

Sophie eyed the front windows with their beige trim. "Painted woodwork?" She arched a brow. "Aren't you breaking your own rule?"

"It's pine."

"Oh."

"Nice to know you paid attention, though."

Actually she hadn't. If she recalled, she'd been busy watching his hands. However, the lesson appeared to have made its way through to her brain nonetheless.

She strolled over to study the print hanging on his back wall. A black-and-white photo of Manhattan's Flatiron Building. Man liked his buildings, didn't he? "I imagine if your old neighbor saw all this work, she'd be impressed."

"Maybe. I'm not renovating to impress anyone, though."

"Why are you?"

"Because the house shouldn't have been torn up in the first place." His answer was uncharacteristically clipped. So much so, Sophie actually stepped back.

Seeing the reaction, his voice softened a little. Only a little, though. "Etta was pushed into the conversion," he explained.

"I thought you said she was afraid the place would get gutted after she died."

"Someone had to put the thought in her head, didn't

they?" And from the sound of his voice, he didn't like that person very much, either. "Since I moved in twenty-eight months ago, I've been working to put the place back the way it was."

Twenty-eight months. According to the Realtor, the co-ops didn't go on the market that much before, meaning he'd been renovating almost since the building was converted. A lot of effort for a man who worked on the original construction. Clearly he felt quite strongly about Etta being wronged.

"Want some coffee?" Grant asked her. "I was about to pour myself a cup when you knocked."

"Sure." After all, to say no would be rude, right?

She followed him to his kitchen, only to stop in front of an interesting wood cabinet tucked in the corner. Narrow and chipped, it had a small, carved door halfway down and what looked like a drop-down cabinet on the bottom.

"An antique phone cabinet," Grant told her when she asked. "I found it at the flea market on Thirty-fifth Street this past winter and decided it was too cool to resist. Guess you can say I'm a sucker for older, beautiful things."

His gaze, while he spoke, pinned her straight to the spot. All of a sudden the narrow hall got very warm and cramped. "You wouldn't have water instead, would you?" Sophie asked, rubbing down the prickles on the back of her neck.

Grant arched a brow, but didn't comment. "I'll see if I can rustle something up."

While he went to the fridge, she hovered in the door frame, preferring the distance. When he bent over, she forced her eyes not to search for the sliver of skin.

"Did you and your 'friend' have a good evening?" she heard him ask.

"His name is David, and yes, we did."

"Where'd you go? Fundraiser, right?"

"Yes." She shifted from one foot to another. "Are you really interested?" Talking about David with him made her nervous.

"No," Grant replied, back in her space. "I'm trying to be polite. So you went to a fundraiser," he prompted as he handed her a water bottle.

"At the Natural History Museum. It was a networking event. One hundred and fifty lawyers and their spouses mingling under the T. rex bones."

"Sounds scintillating. The networking I mean."

"David found it useful."

"Did you?"

"Not really. It was David's event," she murmured, only to bite her lip when she realized she'd admitted it aloud. "I mean our main purpose in going was to help David's career."

"Aren't you a good girlfriend."

Sophie's head shot up. "I'm not—"

"Not what?" he asked, brown eyes probing. "Good or his girlfriend?"

The doorknob pressed into the small of her back. She'd pressed herself so tightly against the door she expected to see the facet pattern imprinted on her skin. The correct response would be to tell him David was her boyfriend. They were dating, after all, and by admitting it, she could put an end to Grant's continual flirting.

Instead, she propelled herself away from the door and back into the main room. "Where is this infamous bathroom? That's what I came to see."

"Come with me." He motioned for her to join him in

a doorway a few feet way. Sophie found a bold graphic gray, black and white tile. The tub sat invitingly along the back wall, beneath a small built-in shelf. "It's gorgeous," Sophie said. "Though, aren't you going to miss having a real shower?" The tub had a handheld attachment.

"I still have a real shower, in the master bathroom," he replied, his voice coming from over her shoulder. "You didn't think I planned to bathe in this every night, did you?"

"I did have my questions." The image he suggested of him bathing naked on the sidewalk still hadn't left her brain yet.

"I suppose I can see how I might have given you the impression. But trust me, this baby is strictly for show." He paused what he was doing to look up at her. "Or company."

Sophie looked to her shoes. Company was not a good replacement image. It conjured up too many pictures of wet skin and strong arms wrapped around her waist. Particularly with his breath tickling her ear.

"So, do you like it?"

She started, mainly because his breath tickled her earlobe just as she got to a particularly steamy image. "Like what?"

"My apartment."

Right, his apartment. "Told you, the room is gorgeous. You definitely have..." At that moment, he leaned over and adjusted the towel that was hanging on a nearby towel ring. Peppermint and coffee teased her nostrils. "...skills," she managed to squeak out.

"Interesting choice of words."

Sophie shook her head. Damn if his arrogance wasn't appealing. And damn if his big broad chest wasn't brushing against her back. Took a second, but she managed to make her feet move and break their bodies' connection. "You need to work on your self-confidence," she told him.

Having delivered her comment, Sophie waited for the man to move so she could pass. Their various configurations of entering and exiting rooms were almost like a dance, weren't they? Draw close, separate. Professional and mature one moment, blushing and covered with goose bumps the next.

Distracted as she was with her thoughts, Sophie didn't see the drafting table until her thigh connected with its corner. The collision jostled the table, sending the mile-high pile of books and papers onto the floor.

"Are you all right?" Grant asked.

"Fine." She was more embarrassed about making a mess. "Let me help you pick this up."

"That's all right. You don't have to…"

Sophie's eyes widened at the titles strewn about her feet. *The Synthesis of Form. Traditional Details for Renovation and Rehabilitation. Form, Space and Order.* She glanced up. "Little light reading?"

"I was looking something up."

"You've got some hardcore resource materials." No wonder he knew so much about historical buildings. He obviously studied them. "Are you taking a class?"

"Did." He yanked the book she was holding from her hand. "Long time ago."

Couldn't have been that long ago. He wasn't old enough. "In college?"

"Why does it matter where I took the class?"

"I was just curious. I apologize." She of all people should respect a person's desire for privacy about even the most benign of subjects.

Unless said subjects involved her. A sketch that had fallen on the floor caught her eye. It was a computer drawing of a kitchen. A very familiar kitchen.

"Is this my place?" she asked, reaching for the paper. Sure enough, there was her kitchen, complete with the changes Grant described the other day. "Did you draw these?"

"Just something I was fooling around with."

"Your fooling around looks pretty impressive. Professional."

"Four years of Columbia architecture school will do that for you." He snatched the drawing from her hand, causing it to tear in two.

Sophie barely noticed. "You're an architect?" An Ivy League educated one at that.

"Was." Grant's face had grown so dark and grim you'd think she'd accused him of a crime. Same with the sour way he spoke. "Not anymore. I quit twenty-eight months ago."

Around the same time he moved in. After the building had been converted. But he said he'd met Etta during the time the conversion took place.

Suddenly it dawned on her. "When you said you met the owner…"

"I designed the building."

The man who turned the place modern even though it should never have been "cut up," to use Grant's words. The man that twenty minutes earlier she'd have sworn he held in contempt.

"What happened?" she asked in a soft voice. "Were you the one who convinced her to break up the building?"

Grant didn't answer. Dropping the drawing on his desk, he walked to his windows. In the bright summer light, his figure became a black silhouette. Large and brooding. Seeing him was enough of an answer. He had been the man he described so angrily earlier.

Sophie moved to join him. Yes, she should honor his privacy, but he looked so pained she couldn't help wanting to reach out. Why was he converting the place back again?

She was two steps from his shoulder when he spoke. "I have to see a vendor at the flea market about some lighting fixtures," he said, face still focused outside.

"Okay," Sophie replied. He didn't want to talk. She would take the hint. Respect it. "I'll get back to my—"

"Come with me."

He spun around so quickly she nearly stumbled. "What?"

"It's too beautiful a day to spend stuck inside. Come with me."

"I can't. I have to work."

There was an energy behind his invitation that she couldn't name. What did it matter if she accompanied him or not? Sophie was having trouble keeping her balance from the mood swings. She wished she could name the energy she sensed coming off him. Not for the first time she wondered if his enthusiasm was stronger than necessary. What are you trying to avoid, Grant Templeton?

"The work will be there when you get back."

Sure, along with a whole lot more, knowing Allen. "I really can't."

"Yes, you can," he insisted, closing the last couple of steps between them and tucking a finger underneath her chin. "You know you want to."

"So, you're a mind reader now?" The response might

have worked better if her jaw wasn't quivering from his touch.

"Not a mind reader," he returned. "Eye reader. And yours are saying an awful lot."

Forced enthusiasm or not, his touch was making her insides quiver. She wanted desperately to look away and refuse to make eye contact with him, but pride wouldn't let her. Instead, she forced herself to keep her features as bland as possible so he wouldn't see that a part of her—the very female part—did want to go with him. It also wanted to feel more of his touch, too, and the common sense part of her was having a hard time forming an opposing argument.

"If so, then no doubt you know they're saying, 'remove your hand.'"

He chuckled. Soft and low. *A bedroom laugh.* "Did you know they flash when you're being stubborn?"

Rather than argue, Sophie swallowed her pride and looked to his feet. That only earned her another maddening chuckle. "You so don't want me to move my hand, either."

"You're incorrigible. You know that, right?"

"Thank you."

"I still want you to move your hand."

"If you insist…." Suddenly his hands were cupping her cheeks, drawing her parted lips under his. Sophie's gasp was lost in her throat. As she expected, he tasted of peppermint and coffee and…and…

And oh, Lord, could he kiss!

It ended and her eyelids fluttered open. Grant's face hovered a breath from hers. Gently, he traced the slope of her nose and smiled.

"Your eyes told me you wanted that, too."

If she had an ounce of working brain matter, Sophie

would have turned and stormed out of his apartment then and there. Problem was one, she was trembling, and two, the fact she'd kissed him back probably wiped out any outrage she'd be trying to convey.

So she did the next best thing. She folded her arms across her chest and presented him with a somewhat flushed but indignant expression. "Do not do that again."

"Do what? Kiss you?"

"Yes, kiss me," she snapped back. His smug smile upped her indignity. "I don't care what you *think* you saw in my eyes, it's not appropriate, and I'm not interested."

He didn't even have the dignity to look chagrined. "I don't know about inappropriate," he drawled, "but you and I both know you're lying about not being interested."

Arrogant, overconfident, caramel-eyed… Before she could finish the thought, he'd wrapped his hand in hers and was leading her toward the door. "Come on," he said, pausing only to pick up his wallet from off the coffee table. "You can lock your door on the way out."

And that was how Sophie came to be mutely escorted down her front steps and across the street.

"Loosen up, Sophie. You look like you're being held prisoner."

Wasn't she? Sophie looked at the hand that had clasped hers since Grant led her from the apartment. His large fingers entwined with hers, gently and loosely. She could pull away anytime she wanted. The one holding on was her.

"Ever been to the flea market before?" Grant asked,

ignoring when she let go and stuffed her fist in her shorts pocket.

"No."

"You're in for an experience."

She wasn't sure she wanted another experience. Her fingers were tingling and her insides had become a big ball of confusion from the last one. Only yesterday she'd given herself a long lecture about decorum and professionalism and what have you, and what did she do? Let Grant kiss her. Kiss him back. Then, instead of doing the sensible thing and refusing to go with him, here she was strolling along as if they were on a date!

Her briefcase at home was filled with pressing work. With the day ticking by, she had absolutely no business traipsing about the city under any circumstances, let alone traipsing about with a man a decade younger than she was. No matter how romantic and enigmatic he seemed to be. And, since when did she use words like *romantic* and *enigmatic,* anyway?

To make matters truly bad, her lips could still feel Grant's kiss, and her body really, really wanted another.

Beside her, Grant nudged her shoulder with his. "I promise, the world won't stop because you took a few hours off."

"Easy for you to say. You weren't kidnapped and forced to go against your will."

"Forced to spend a beautiful summer's day outside. How horrible!" He clutched his chest in mock horror. "There's no need to be dramatic. You had plenty of opportunities to reject any or all of my advances. If I recall, you didn't put up much of a fight."

No, she hadn't, unfortunately. Hard to when you're dazed and dizzy. "Why did you kiss me?" she asked him.

"I told you, because your eyes said to." He grinned. "Along with certain parts of my body."

Sophie was not amused. "I'm serious, Grant. You've been flirting with me for days now and I want to know why."

"All right." His expression sobered. "Because you're a beautiful woman, and I'm attracted to you. Satisfied?"

No. "I'm a decade older than you are."

"Big deal. I don't give a rat's behind about age. You could be two decades older and I'd still find you attractive. And," he continued, preempting her by wagging a finger, "before you go talking about how it's unprofessional, it was one kiss. If you don't want me to kiss you again, say so and I won't."

"I don't want you to kiss me again."

"Liar."

Oh, for crying out loud! "This is a bad idea. I'm going back." She started to turn only to feel him grip her at the elbow.

"Relax. You have my word I'll be on my best behavior. No more kissing."

"Promise?"

"Absolutely. Unless you ask me to, of course," he added in the slow-honeyed drawl she'd come to love and despise.

Sophie wanted to kill him. "Grant…"

"Scout's honor."

Freeing her arm from his grip, she scowled, her displeasure aimed at the actual manhandling than the part of her that regretted making the deal. "You better be as good a Boy Scout as you claimed you were," she muttered.

The flea market entrance ended the conversation. Seeing the crowds, Sophie had to blink. She'd known bargain hunting was popular, but she'd had no idea how much so. This place was filled with shoppers, hundreds of them, all jammed around a collection of vendors and tables. From what she could tell, a person could find almost anything if they were patient and looked hard enough. She saw pottery, clothes, tools. There was even a row of vendors selling fresh food.

"I can't believe you've never been here," Grant said.

"Not much of a secondhand person," she replied. At least not now that she could afford firsthand.

"You've been missing out." Reaching into his back pocket, he took out a folded vendor map. "My guy is at table W-64. Over here."

They wound the row of tents of vintage clothes, antiques, crafts and other items. Grant, of course, insisted on guiding her with his hand splayed annoyingly close to the small of her back. He might as well have been touching her, for the warmth it caused.

Making matters worse was the fact it took forever for them to reach their destination. Even amidst the throng, vendors recognized Grant and would call him over to their table. Each time Sophie would find herself watching while Grant chatted them up, about items they wanted to show him, about items he might have purchased previously, or simply about innocuous topics like sports.

"You've got quite the network," she commented.

"Have to. Half the challenge of historical renovation is finding the exact right piece for a job."

"Is that why you got into the business? For the challenge?"

"Sort of" was his reply. A variation on "we'll see."

"Might as well bring back to life what I can. There's my guy."

Grant's vendor was in the corner, between a vintage clothing dealer and a man selling personalized street signs. Soon as he saw them, he limped to the back of the tent and dragged out a large box of what looked like, to Sophie, a pile of lamp shades and wires. Grant knew what they were, though. He immediately knelt down and began sorting through the items. Leaning against a rack of fur coats, she watched as he examined each piece, ultimately returning or discarding based on results. Occasionally the vendor would pipe up with information, but it was obvious the show was all Grant's.

He was an enigma, that's for certain. It would be so easy to write him off as a flirtatious stud, but the title didn't completely fit. Behind the sexy smile and perfect-looking features lived a layer of deep emotion. A bleakness that held her interest in a far stronger grip than his looks. Something happened twenty-eight months ago that clearly affected him deeply. What?

"Hard to resist, huh?"

Sophie found a chic, perfumed woman in a strapless sundress standing next to her.

"Nineteen-fifties. Very Audrey Hepburn." She reached into the rack to remove the fur and blue brocade coat whose sleeve Sophie had absentmindedly grabbed hold of while watching Grant. "You want to try it on?"

"No, thanks. I don't do vintage clothing. I'm merely killing time waiting for my..." Oh, goodness, she was tripping over the word *friend* again.

She shouldn't. Friend is what Grant was.

"But the color would look great on you," the vendor persisted. Before Sophie could protest, the woman had the coat off the rack and was thrusting it in her direction. "Go on. If you like it I'll give you a good price."

"No, I don't think—" Sophie was about to press the

coat back in the woman's arms when the sun caught the gold-green thread on the brocade, making the cloth look almost metallic. She didn't know about Audrey Hepburn, but it was pretty....

"Okay," she acquiesced. She might as well. If Grant heard the discussion he'd only come over and badger her until she did.

She slipped her arms into the sleeves. The cloth smelled like mothballs and the thick extra layer made the summer heat more oppressive than ever.

"Nice," the woman said with a smile. A few feet away a vanity mirror rested against an old coat tree. She angled the glass so Sophie could see her reflection.

Well, what do you know? She didn't look as foolish as she thought. In fact, the coat actually did look... nice. More than nice. It looked good. The cape style coat swung around her knees and, when she pulled the front plackets closed, the fur collar framed her chin perfectly.

"Wow! Sexy," a male voice said from behind her.

The open appreciation ran along her spine, warming her even more than the coat. "Thank you," she said, giving her reflection another admire before slipping the coat off. She placed it back on the rack.

Grant stepped into view. "You're not getting it?"

"Vintage clothing doesn't exactly fit with my lifestyle. I can only imagine the looks I'd get walking down Wall Street."

"Too bad. Could have been a new you."

"I'll stick to the old me, if you don't mind."

"If you say so," Grant replied. It was an innocuous enough comment. So why did Sophie suddenly feel as though she failed a test?

Changing the subject, she asked, "Are you finished with your business already?" She noticed he held only a small plastic shopping bag. "Your bag doesn't look big enough to hold light figures. Didn't he have what you were looking for?"

"Most of the stuff needed too much fixing to be worth my while. A couple of brass fixtures. Oh, and a few hinges to replace the one I saw was coming loose in your kitchen."

"Wait a minute. Back up. You bought a hinge for my cabinet?"

"A couple actually. Remember I mentioned yours needed replacing."

"Thank you."

"No big deal. I saw them and realized they matched your kitchen, so I grabbed them."

Perhaps he didn't see it as a big deal, but to Sophie it was an unexpected, odd, kind gesture. An inexplicable warmth spread through her. "Does this mean I owe you again?"

"We'll see." He cocked his head. "You ready for lunch?"

Sophie nodded. She gave the coat another last look and felt the queerest pull. A kind of longing or feeling of desperate want.

Don't be silly, she told herself. *It's just an old coat.*

CHAPTER SEVEN

REMNANTS of that strange sensation dogged Sophie long after they left the flea market and resumed walking. She simply couldn't shake the feeling she was missing out on something. It was a nagging uneasiness at the back of her brain, much like the feeling you got when you left the iron plugged in. Which was probably why she barely noticed until they sat down that the restaurant Grant had steered her toward was several blocks in the opposite direction of their apartment building. A small sidewalk bistro near Grand Army Plaza with tables shaded by linden trees.

Grant leaned back in his chair, sunlight and shadows dappling his hair. "Isn't this better than spending the afternoon inside doing paperwork?" he asked as a waitress served them tall glasses of iced tea she didn't remember ordering.

"I guess." Now that they were seated, the briefcase full of work had resumed nagging her. How much time had she wasted? She took out her BlackBerry to check.

Unfortunately, she couldn't tell, because no sooner did she find her phone then Grant's hand reached across and closed over hers, preventing her from looking at its face.

"Put it away," he told her. "This is a cell phone free lunch."

"I'm only checking the time."

"Why? Got hot plans for tonight? With your friend David maybe?" He blew the paper from his straw, aiming it like a missile in her direction.

"No, I don't have plans with David," she replied, batting away the paper with her free hand. "He's on his way to Chicago for a business trip." Actually, he had suggested last night they meet today for an early dinner, but she'd begged off claiming work. Work she hadn't got done because her neighbor had kidnapped her.

"If you don't have plans, you don't need your phone."

"I—" Did his grip have to be so...so solid?

"No arguments. It's a beautiful afternoon. Put your phone away and enjoy yourself. That's an order."

"I didn't realize you were in command," she muttered, angry with herself over how easily she capitulated. He had this uncanny ability to get her to do what he wanted. "Do you boss all your lunch companions around like this?"

"Only the pretty workaholics."

"You do realize that all you've succeeded in doing is making me work twice as late when we get home. Instead of being stuck inside Saturday afternoon, I'll be working Saturday night."

"Unless I distract you tonight, too."

He could, too. Quite easily. That was the problem. "You mean to tell me a man like you doesn't have plans on a Saturday night?" She sat back in her seat. "And you tease me about not having a life."

"What makes you think I don't have plans?"

"You just said you'd distract me."

"So you do want me to distract you."

"I didn't say that." Even though the thought sent shivers down her spine. She repeated her question. "Do you have plans?" If he did, perhaps she could shake the spell he seemed to have over her.

"The only plans I have involve enjoying the company of a very attractive woman." He raised his glass. "I'm curious, though. What did you mean by 'a man like me'?"

Sophie blushed deep from both the compliment and the question. So much for breaking the spell. Keep this up and she'd have to start telling people she had a sunburn.

"Have you seen our waitress?" she asked, ignoring the question. "I'd like to order so we can get back. I've been 'distracted' enough for one day."

"Honey, we've barely started." With a shake of his head, he handed her a copy of the one page menu for her to review. "Someone's got to teach you how to stop and smell the roses."

A job for which he clearly appeared to have volunteered. Question was why? "Why do you care?"

He was sipping his iced tea. "What can I say? I believe in rescuing damsels in distress. I hate to see a woman spend her days locked in her office toiling away at financial figures when she could be out enjoying herself in the sunshine."

"I appreciate the concern." But she didn't fully buy the explanation. She'd caught the way his smile faltered slightly when she asked. "Is that the only reason?" she pressed.

"You think there's more?"

"Uh-huh." Definitely. The more she thought about it, the more she became convinced his flirting and continual interest in distracting her *had* to have a catch. She simply wasn't that fascinating.

Sipping her drink, she watched and waited. With the tables turned, her young companion had lost a bit of his swagger. A part of her found pleasure in that. He was cute when he squirmed. The way he fiddled with the edge of the menu. How his brow furrowed as he tried to think of a smart answer. Definitely cute. If cute came in a big, sexy, virile package.

At last, he stopped his fiddling. "If you must know," he said, "you remind me of someone."

"Who?" She held up her hand. "Let me guess—your father."

He laughed. "Why on earth would you suggest him?"

"You already told me I don't remind you of your mother. Figured I'd try the other side of the family tree."

"You don't remind me of either of my parents," he told her.

"Good to know. Though I'm certainly old enough to be one of them," she added over the edge of her straw.

"Why do you do that?"

"Do what?"

"Keep referring to how you're older than me."

"How about because I am." One of them had to remember.

"So what? I happen to like old, remember?"

Old and beautiful. She remembered. "I thought that only applied to building materials."

"It applies to a lot of things."

"Oh." She took a long sip of her tea to quell the jumble in her stomach. Unlike a lot of his answers, this one hadn't come with any suggestive tone or innuendo, though you'd think from her sudden bout of shy uncertainty that it had. Feeling the unsettledness from before rising upward, she scrambled to regain control of herself and the conversation. "If I don't remind you of your parents, who do I remind you of?"

His face crinkled in thought. "That's just it. I'm not entirely sure. But you definitely remind me of someone.

"Besides myself, that is," he added in a lower voice. He'd raised the menu as he spoke so she couldn't see his features to know if the comment was meant to be flirtatious. His tone suggested otherwise.

"I remind you of you? How?" They couldn't be more different.

For the first time, the tables were truly turned and color tinged his cheeks. "Did I say that aloud?"

"Very much so. And now I'm dying to know how we're alike."

"Let's say I used to have a cell phone glued to my hands, too."

An incomplete answer and an intriguing one for when he spoke, the sadness returned to his eyes. He tried to hide the expression behind his menu, but Sophie caught it nonetheless.

"And you consider that habit a bad one."

"In my experience, tunnel vision of any kind is a bad habit."

Moving her drink and menu aside, Sophie leaned forward and prodded. "What experience?"

"Are you ready to order?"

Damn the waitstaff in the place. Efficient and invisible. Their waitress reappeared like a specter, her notepad in hand. Sophie could feel Grant's relief. Whatever experience, she could tell it hadn't been pleasant. She didn't like how the memory distressed him. She much preferred his smile. His warm, sexy smile.

The waitress took their orders and disappeared as

quickly and efficiently as she arrived. Without a menu to fiddle with, Grant quickly turned to his silverware for distraction, making a large production out of aligning his salad and dinner forks.

"Did you know our building has a secret passage?" he asked suddenly.

His attempt to dodge the subject at hand worked. Sophie was distracted. "Like a tunnel? Are you sure?"

"I know the building inside and out. Of course I'm sure. And we're talking a stairway, not tunnel."

Still fascinating. "Why build a secret anything? Were they bootleggers or part of the Underground Railroad?" The house was old enough to have seen both Prohibition and the Civil War.

"Nothing so romantic," he replied. The waitress materialized and wordlessly set down their salads. "A lot of houses built during the era had back staircases so the servants could travel between floors without being seen."

"Shoot. Here I thought I'd bought into a historic landmark. Where are these stairs? I never noticed any place that would hide them."

"Behind your pantry wall. The original kitchen is now our basement. There was a set of steps running from the ground floor to the roof. The top flights came down during renovation, but since the two flights from garden level to the second floor were already boarded up, we left them. Another one of Etta's insistences."

Good for her. Sophie picked up her fork and dug into her salad. "Are they usable? That is, if you knocked the wall down?" She thought of all the times as a kid she could have used a hidden passage. A place to disappear when real life got too crazy.

"Why? You interested in making a midnight visit to my bedroom?"

Cheeks hotter than Hades—because the notion put some way too appealing images in her head—Sophie stabbed at her salad. Figures the waitress couldn't materialize now when an interruption would be useful.

"Don't get any ideas," she warned.

"Too late," he replied, spearing his own tomato. "The idea has already been firmly planted in my brain. First thing tomorrow I'm getting out the sledgehammer and knocking down the walls. And you won't be able to complain about the banging because you suggested the idea."

"Then I'll install an alarm in the pantry."

"You mean those surplus boxes and cans stored in there won't be alarm enough?"

She tossed him a smirk. "They're to toss at unwanted visitors."

"Well, since you only throw them at unwanted visitors, I'm safe. What do you say, should I clear a path so I can come down and tuck you in?"

Sophie didn't think it was possible to flush more. "Must you turn every conversation sexual?"

"Can't help myself. You make me think sexual thoughts."

"Hardly." She rolled her eyes.

"I'm serious. Why do you find it so hard to believe that I'm attracted to you? You are a stunningly beautiful woman."

"Who is…"

"A decade older," he supplied. "As you've mentioned a decade worth of times. And since you feel the need to constantly put that out, it's only fair that I constantly remind you how desirable you are."

If it were only that simple, thought Sophie. But he was trying too hard, and she was beginning to see a pattern.

"Know what I think?" she asked, setting her fork down.

His reply was delayed by the well-timed arrival of their entrées. Sophie swore the restaurant was timing their efficiency for exactly those moments when she didn't want an interruption. She waited impatiently for the young woman to set each plate down.

"What I think," she continued when finally alone, "is that you're trying to distract me."

Grant swallowed the sweet potato fry he was chewing. "Distract you from what?"

Nice try. Repeating the question was a classic avoidance tactic. "My asking questions." Discussing the topic he so obviously wanted to avoid.

"You make it sound like I'm keeping secrets." His chuckle was low and nervous. She'd touched on a nerve.

"Are you?"

"Don't be ridiculous. I don't have any secrets to keep. What you see is what you get."

What Sophie saw was a man avoiding a painful memory. "All right then," she said, "if you don't have secrets, answer me this. Why did you quit architecture? Does it have something to do with Etta, the woman who used to own our building?"

He didn't answer. Instead he fiddled with his tableware, becoming inordinately interested in the clanking noise his knife made against the tiny pot of ketchup on his plate.

"Grant?"

"Not really," he replied, only to shrug and add, "Peripherally. I'm not proud of what happened with

Etta, but it was only a symptom of a far bigger problem."

This time it was Sophie's hand reaching across and covering his. Her need to know had moved beyond curiosity. The reproach she heard him struggling to keep from his voice called out for comfort.

"What happened?" she asked him.

For a moment, from the way he stared mutely at their hands, she wondered if he'd dodge the topic again. When he did speak, the words are soft and laced with sorrow.

"I nearly killed my best friend."

Sophie's soft gasp told Grant he'd succeeded in shocking her.

"You're being dramatic, right?"

Maybe, a little. Mike would certainly say so. The hole in his gut argued differently. Of course, now that he'd made the admission, he would have to explain what happened. Why'd he say anything? He bit back a groan. Flirting was so much easier.

Pulling his hand free, he kept his fingers busy by plucking sesame seeds from the top of his burger bun. Where to start?

With the damn award. "Every year the Architect Association honors the city's top young architect. Winning can cement your career. Coming out of Columbia, my goal was to win. I had it all planned out. I'd score a job with a top firm, win the award, be proclaimed the city's next star-architect and become a millionaire before I turned thirty."

He offered her a wan smile. "My family believes in setting big goals."

"Nothing wrong with aiming high," Sophie replied.

Naturally the woman with a master plan would agree.

"Anyway," he continued with a sigh, "everything was falling into line. I had the job. I was making great money. All I needed was to blow the socks off the partners and the Architect Association."

"So far this all sounds quite admirable," Sophie remarked. "What does it have to do with your best friend?"

"I'm getting to that." Man, was he getting to it. His mouth had run dry so Grant reached for his iced tea. Why was telling this story so hard? He'd been telling himself he wanted Sophie to loosen up. To open her eyes to the dangers of closing yourself off to everything but work. This was his chance.

"Nate and I went to college together. We were roommates. More than roommates. Best friends. Competitive ones at that, not that there was much competition. He beat me at everything. Awards, grades. We spent four years with him being number one, and me being right behind at number two. He even scored his job first. With Kimeout, Hannah and Miller, the city's top firm."

Memories of Nate doing his job offer dance popped into his head, making him smile. *They want me; they want me.*

"Sounds like he was born under a lucky star," Sophie said.

"Like you wouldn't believe. Too bad the luck faded after graduation."

"What do you mean?"

He shrugged. "Design in theory and design in practice are two different things. Maybe he simply had bad chemistry with the partners, but Nate just couldn't seem to catch a break. Meanwhile I was determined to best him at something. I had to be number one."

"You mean winning the award."

The damn award. His holy grail. Grabbing his iced tea again, he drank down the knot in his throat. Guilt never tasted good. "I put everything I had into becoming the best, fastest rising architect this city had ever seen. I worked round the clock, did whatever it took. Even if that meant convincing an old woman her building would go co-op."

"Our building."

"Bingo. Our senior partner wanted the developer's business. I knew if I could score Etta's building, I'd earn major points." It was the beginning of his downward slide.

"That's why you're renovating? To make amends."

He nodded. It wasn't much, but it was something.

"And what about Nate? What happened there?"

"I told you, he was competitive and used to being the star. The more I pushed, the more he pushed, too. Except…"

"Except what?" Her hand was back, soft and comforting on his wrist.

"He couldn't keep up. I was so caught up in the competition—in winning—I didn't see the signs." This is where the story turned its bleakest. "He was edgy all the time. Moody. Unpredictable. His work was erratic. One day he'd be flying all over the office, next he'd zone out during an important meeting."

"He was using."

"Cocaine. He'd snorted the stupid stuff in college once or twice. Said it boosted his creativity. I had no idea things had gotten so out of hand." In hindsight, the evidence was so overwhelming. Making him feel even worse.

"You were focused on your own work. You didn't know."

Grant expected her to say as much. But, his focus had been the problem. "We had this huge blowout one afternoon. Nate accused me of trying to poach his project after he caught me talking to his client. The guy called me because he couldn't reach Nate."

"Reasonable enough."

So the lie Grant tried to sell himself said, as well. Only his heart knew he hadn't exactly discouraged the man from calling, either, and that he would have taken the project, if asked. That's how low he'd gone.

"The argument got pretty heated and the partners told him to take the rest of the day off. I should have known then." But he was too angry and caught up in getting Bob Kimeout's approval.

"I'm sorry," he heard Sophie say. Her thumb rubbed soft circles on the skin between his thumb and forefinger. The touch was soothing. More soothing than he deserved, but he didn't shake her off. "He called me that night. Nate. I was out for drinks with the partners, discussing my future. I let the phone go to voice mail. Figured we'd hash everything out in the morning."

He could see Nate's name on the call screen clear as day. Just one flick of his thumb and the ringer turned silent. One flick. He pictured the image until it grew blurry in his brain. "He collapsed that night. The coke stopped his heart."

Sophie gasped again. "Oh, my."

Grant stared at his plate. "I saw his name and I ignored him. My best friend." Remembering made him sick to his stomach. Now she knew. His eyes stayed on his plate, too afraid to look up and see the judgment in

Sophie's eyes. She'd never look at him the same way again.

"It's not your fault," she said.

Why did people keep saying that to him? He'd become a man who turned off the phone when his best friend was in trouble. A man who didn't blink twice regarding anything, so long as it helped him get closer to his prize.

Might as well share the coup de grâce to his shame. "Want to know the kicker? I won the award. For my 'brilliantly designed blend of modern and historic.' Sound familiar? Congratulations to me." He raised his glass. "I quit the next day."

"Wow," Sophie said finally. "That's horrible." Sophie didn't know what more to say. What terrible regret for anyone to carry around. She was amazed the sadness in his eyes wasn't deeper, a testimony to how strong spirited he was. "I'm sorry for your loss."

"Wasn't my loss. It was Nate's."

No, it was both of theirs. Her chest ached. Like someone had sucker punched her breastbone. His story hit her in ways she hadn't expected. Yes, she felt his guilt and regret, yes, she empathized. Underneath the sympathy, however, she recognized a great realization. She felt as if she was truly seeing Grant for the very first time. The real Grant. Not her sexy younger neighbor, but a man. A flesh and blood man with a heavy soul and ghosts that could rival her own. A man a woman could easily fall for if she let herself.

A man who, like the flea market coat she put back on the rack, was all wrong for her.

Those thoughts dogged her the entire way home. Or rather they braided themselves with the sensation from the flea market leaving her insides all twisted. Since Grant wasn't doing a whole lot of talking, she had time to try and unravel them on the walk home. Unfortunately, all she could think of was how wrong the man was for her. There were so many reasons why, too. His age. The way he kept her off balance. His age.

The biggest issue, though, was the fact he simply did not fit into her plans. She wasn't looking for a fling; affairs weren't her style. And face it, what more could she do with Grant beyond a fling?

Plus, there was David, who was a far better fit for her lifestyle. Grant was simply some hot guy she'd known for a few days. Her feelings toward him were still mostly physical. The increased awareness, or whatever you want to call it, she was currently experiencing, meant nothing.

Glancing over, she saw that Grant remained lost in his own world. Regretting telling his story? Possibly. The muscle twitching in his jaw suggested as much.

"Thank you for lunch," she said, hoping to pull him from his reverie. "Or maybe I should say dinner. It's certainly late enough." Between the flea market and the restaurant, they managed to eat away a good portion of the day.

"Suppose this means you'll be up half the night working."

Sophie thought of the paperwork she left behind. "I did leave a lot unfinished. I hate unfinished business," she added softly. It reminded her too much of chaos. Of waiting for the next shoe to drop. She'd spent enough time waiting—and getting pegged by falling shoes—as a kid.

"My boss, Allen Breckinridge, tends to call at odd hours asking for information. Unfinished business means I have to scramble for a reason why I don't have the information he wants. Trust me, you never want to have to scramble in front of Allen Breckinridge."

"Breckinridge is the guy who kept calling the other night, right?"

"The one and the same. He's pretty sure the firm and the universe revolve around him. And, he expects perfection."

"I bet you give him perfection, too."

His tone didn't sound complimentary. Fallout from his confession no doubt. "I try." She didn't tell him about her fear of him waiting for her to make a mistake.

They'd reached their front door. Sophie fished out her keys, surprised to discover she was actually disappointed to be home. "I have to admit," she said, turning it in the lock, "as kidnappings go, this wasn't half bad."

"Careful, people might think Stockholm syndrome is setting in," Grant teased.

Falling for her kidnapper? Sophie smiled but didn't laugh. This was the Grant she'd come to expect, flirty and full of innuendo. Nonetheless, the joke hit a little too close to home. Her insides jumped at the thought. "Don't hold your breath."

"Tsk-tsk, such protest." Several strands of hair had worked their way loose from her ponytail. He smoothed them back from her cheek. Suddenly it was Sophie holding a breath. She held it while the fingertips traced her hairline, past her temple, over the shell of her ear and along her jaw. When he skimmed the curve of her neck, she had to choke back a sigh.

"What are you doing tomorrow?" he asked in that rough honey voice of his.

Sophie blinked. "Um, groceries." Took a moment,

but she finally wracked her brain and remembered. "Sunday is grocery day. Why?"

"I thought I'd come by and fix those hinges."

"Hinges?" He was tracing the collar of her tank top now making it hard to concentrate. What was he up to? She'd told him not to kiss her again.

"Among other things. If you'd like, I could show you the secret passage."

Oh, but the suggestion sounded so wicked. "I'd like that."

"I'll see you tomorrow then." He leaned in just as his fingers reached her bare shoulder. "Good night, Sophie."

He was going to kiss her again. She held her breath again and waited....

The other shoe never dropped.

Instead, with one last brush of his fingers across her cheek, Grant headed upstairs, leaving Sophie breathless, quivering and contemplating calling him back. Only the fact she lacked a working voice stopped her.

Dear Lord, she was in trouble.

CHAPTER EIGHT

NEXT morning found Sophie rescrubbing her kitchen with nervous energy. She'd already tackled the bathroom, not to mention reviewed the emails and reports she'd worked on until the middle of the night. Anything to keep her mind off yesterday's roller coaster ride with Grant.

Thing was, she didn't know what caused her insides to jumble more. That morning's kiss, the lack of a second kiss, or the emotional upheaval left by Grant's confession. It didn't matter. All three left her on edge.

The knock on the door made her stomach jump. "Coming!"

Quickly, she checked her appearance. She was wearing what she called her Saturday cleaning outfit: camisole, knee-length sweats and no makeup. Saturday's outfit on Sunday. Exactly what you'd expect a woman who wasn't in control to wear. At least her hair was combed. She readjusted the clip at the base of her neck, hoping she caught all the front strands and reached for the door.

It figured. With his hair mussed and morning stubble, Grant yet again looked as though he rolled off the pages of *Morning Sexy* magazine. In fact, the only flaw in his appearance was the circles under his eyes and even they looked good on him.

"Morning," Grant said. "I don't suppose you have coffee ready."

"Good morning to you, too," she greeted. "Late night?"

"Had trouble sleeping."

Join the club, she thought, closing the door behind him. Was he kicking himself for yesterday, too? She wasn't sure if she should be relieved or disappointed at the idea.

He was already in the kitchen when she pushed open the door. "Smells clean," he remarked to her. "Someone's been busy."

"I was up early with nothing to do." *Thanks to you.* "I figured I might as well start fall cleaning a few months early."

"I'm surprised you aren't nose deep in paperwork."

"That's because I finished my paperwork last night. Didn't really have a choice. Seems someone kept me tied up most of the day."

He scratched the back of his neck. "Yeah, about that." *Here we go,* thought Sophie. He'd come to his senses. "I shouldn't have dropped all my Nate baggage on you like that. The point of the day was for you to relax and let go. Not listen to the long sad tale of my mistakes."

That's what he was apologizing for? Not kissing her, but for sharing a painful memory? True, hearing it altered something inside her; her chest felt incredibly full every time she thought of him trusting her with his tale. But he shouldn't apologize. Ever.

She took the coffee cup he'd helped himself to with a smile. "You told a long, sad tale? I hadn't noticed."

The tease was enough for him to get the message, and he smiled back. "Thanks."

"For what?" She continued to play clueless.

"Just thanks." He touched her shoulder ever so lightly, and Sophie felt the roller coaster cranking anew.

To cover, she reached for the coffeemaker. "Bold, right?"

"Bold and black. By the way, I brought my tape measure." With the apology out of the way, his voice sounded lighter. More like the Grant she'd grown used to. "If you'd like, I can measure for a window."

When she realized what he was offering, she felt a ridiculous shiver of pleasure. The roller coaster ratcheted up another hill. "Does that mean I pass muster?"

His eyes raked her up and down with an approving glint. "You're getting there."

And down went her insides. Tumbling end over end. Forget the roller coaster. She was on one of those free-falling rides where they drop you from the sky.

"Do you miss it?" she asked a little while later. She was perched on her countertop drinking coffee and doing her best to stay out of Grant's way.

"Miss what?" Grant asked in a muffled voice. He lay on his back, head in a lower cabinet.

"Architecture. Being an architect." It was a nosy, pushy question, but after spending the better part of ten minutes trying not to stare at Grant's washboard stomach, she figured nosy and pushy weren't so horrible. "Do you ever regret quitting?"

She got her answer when his screwdriver froze in the air. "No," he replied flatly.

"Not even a little?"

"Sometimes," he corrected with a sigh. "When a client shows me a plan that I know I could do better or if a project doesn't require anything more creative than changing doorknobs and installing light fixtures."

"Like my kitchen," she teased. She thought of the drawings she'd spied on his drafting table. A simple window must not be much of a challenge.

"Your kitchen's different—it comes with coffee. Along with other benefits," he added.

Sophie was grateful his head was in the cabinet so he couldn't see her reaction.

"Doesn't matter," he continued. "I can't go back."

Can't? Sounded awfully final. Grant pushed himself out and sat up. "After Nate's heart attack, I swore to myself I would never be the kind of man I'd become again. I intend to keep that promise."

Through avoidance? Sure sounded that way. "I can understand wanting to bury the past," she began. Heck, she believed wholeheartedly in the practice.

But Grant shook his head. "I'm not burying anything. I'm honoring the past."

Really? Didn't seem that way to her. Sounded more like avoiding, but who was she to judge? She'd been "honoring" for twenty-two years.

Grant changed the subject. "Your hinge is fixed. Should hold you till you decide how much work you want to do in the kitchen."

"I already know how much. I believe you've got the drawings."

"Those were me fooling around. They aren't real designs."

They looked pretty real to her. "You captured exactly what I was describing. Right down to the color of wood I wanted. Those designs are perfect."

"I told you, they aren't real designs. They aren't even to scale."

"But they could be, right?" she asked him. "I know you said you didn't want to go back to architecture, but one set of plans wouldn't be going back, would it?"

"Was that why you wanted to know if I missed it?"

"No, I was honestly interested." Though now that the subject had come up, she wasn't above taking advantage of the situation. "You've already offered to put in the window. Why not take the project all the way? This could be your chance to finally redo Etta's kitchen. What do you say?"

Grant rolled his eyes, but not before she caught a flash in their depths. His passion wasn't completely extinguished. He wouldn't have started fooling around with those drawings in the first place if it was.

"We'll see," he said finally.

His favorite phrase again. Still, "we'll see" was better than no. In fact, she was pretty sure "we'll see" was closer to yes.

Scrambling to his feet, Grant joined her at the counter, naturally choosing to stand as close as possible. He had his elbow propped on the countertop edge. Sophie could feel the joint abutting her leg. Heat pulsed right through her clothes to her skin.

"You want to see the secret passage?" Grant asked.

Did she! Anything to break the contact. "Sure." She hopped down and headed toward the pantry. It wasn't until she reached up to turn on the light that she realized her error. Her "pantry" was little more than a narrow closet with shelves lined with boxes and canned goods. Grant took up most of the space standing by himself. Adding a second person turned the quarters intimate.

"Here I thought the fridge was well-stocked," he remarked, making his way around her. "You put most supermarkets to shame." Every item had been lined up in a row, with the labels pointing outward. That way, she could find what she needed or didn't need quickly.

"Doesn't that joke get old?" she asked him.

"Hasn't yet." He pushed a stack of cans aside. "Look right here," he said, urging her to move closer. "If you pay close attention, the walls are made of different materials. The side walls are made of horsehair plaster, consistent with materials used in the 1850s. The back wall, however, is drywall, which wasn't used until the twentieth-century. What's more…" He rapped first on the side wall, then on the back. The acoustics were different. "Hollow. That's because there's stairs back there."

"So once upon a time someone would bring the food up from downstairs into my kitchen so it could be served."

"And then bring the dirty dishes back down so the lady of the house never had to see them."

"I could use a service like that myself," Sophie mused.

"My offer still stands."

"I meant having someone whisking the dishes away. Your offer had more to do with the bedroom and tucking me in."

"Now who's the one turning the conversation into something sexual?"

The question was whispered in the dimly lit, tight quarters, and it was hard not to melt right into him. A very bad idea, Sophie decided. A better idea would be to stack the cans Grant disrupted. She could feel his eyes on her as she meticulously straightened each row, going so far as to make sure the labels of the soup cans faced outward. "You want a level?" he quipped.

"There's nothing wrong with being neat and organized. This way I know exactly what I have and won't be caught—"

"Unprepared." He did his part and straightened a box of pasta. "I bet you were one of those kids who kept all their crayons in nice neat rows and got mad if anyone colored out of the lines."

"Let me guess, you weren't?"

"Oh, no, I always kept my pens and drawing materials nice and neat. In fact, I won 'neatest desk' champion five years running. Would have been six but Jimmy Pierson sabotaged me. My locker on the other hand." He leaned back against the shelves, disrupting another set of cans in the process.

"My mother would forget to buy groceries," Sophie explained, straightening the cans around him. Whether because she felt a kinship with him following his confession or the words simply popped out, Sophie couldn't say. What she did know was that once out, the confession hung in the narrow space.

"She *forgot* to feed you?" Grant asked.

"Not all the time. Just once in a while."

Stiffly, she walked to the sink. His wide-eyed incredulity made her wish she'd never said anything in the first place. Personal issues were best kept quiet and internal.

Grant watched the woman rinsing out their empty coffee cups, shocked at what he heard. No wonder she stocked her pantry like a grocery store. She was afraid of running out of food. The notion confounded him. As busy as his parents were with their careers, he never went without food or warmth or any basics. What else had she gone without? The question broke his heart.

"Where did you grow up?" he asked her. "Was it around here?" He wanted to know more. Everything.

"Upstate New York. Nowhere that matters."

Again, she'd stiffened. Embarrassed. *Don't be,* he wanted to tell her. *It doesn't matter where you came from. Not to me.* "Your family still there?"

She shook her head. "My parents died a few years back and last I knew my brother was living in Ossining."

There was only one place in Ossining that Grant knew of and that was the prison. And, the catch in Sophie's voice when she answered was enough for him to believe that's where her brother was.

She'd obviously had to overcome a lot. Realizing so, the strangest sensation took hold of his chest. It felt fuller than full, like someone pumped his heart full of air. The desire to kiss her, to hold her close and pepper her face with kisses overwhelmed him. He had the sudden urge to tell her the past wouldn't hurt her anymore. That he would make sure her past demons never touched her again.

Since he couldn't, he settled for tracing his thumb down her cheek. "Impressive," he said.

"Hardly" was her response.

Oh, but it was. She'd shown him a glimpse of herself he knew she didn't show others. A side she kept covered with master plans and designer clothes.

Suddenly it hit him. Who she reminded him of.

When he was a kid, his sister, Nicole, had a blonde china doll with curly hair and a frilly blue dress. It sat on her bed. Few but his family knew that underneath the frills lay a scrollwork of black lines, courtesy of a Magic Marker and a toddler-size Grant.

Sophie was a real-life version of the doll. Beneath the gloss and polish, there existed lines, and she had just shown him a glimpse. Knowing so made his chest grow even fuller. He wasn't going to let this moment slide. "Are you doing anything today besides grocery shopping?" he asked her.

"Work, obviously. Why?"

From the glaze in her eyes, he could tell she was confused. Grant wasn't sure he had a true grasp on what he was about to suggest himself. He only knew he wanted to offer.

"I was wondering," he said, brushing her cheek, "if you'd like to meet Nate."

They drove to a long-term care facility in Long Island. A beautiful stately location with a big lawn and tall pine trees.

"Nate lives here?" When Grant first issued his invitation, she assumed they were going to visit him at his apartment. "I thought you said he had a heart attack?"

"He did. A massive one."

"Then why are we…?"

"By the time they got his heart started again, too much time had gone by."

Her stomach got a sick feeling. "He had brain damage."

"The correct term is 'persistent vegetative state.'"

"I'm so sorry." She seemed to say that a lot, but what else could she say? She was sorry, for both of them.

A television was playing in Nate's room when they arrived. A baseball game. "Nate's a big Boston fan," he told her, "but since he can't get those games, we make him watch the New York teams. Serves him right for being a traitor."

Sophie studied the man propped in the bed. He was Grant's age and had jet-black hair. Once upon a time, he'd been handsome. Maybe not in Grant's league, but good looking enough to turn heads. The drugs and hospitalization had taken their toll, though, and his face was thin and slack jawed. Blue eyes, which must have been piercing in their day, stared dully into space.

"Hey, buddy," Grant greeted. "I brought someone to meet you. Remember Sophie? The woman I told you about?"

Sophie was surprised. "You talked about me?" Hopefully he said good things.

"Nate and I talk about everything. Well, I talk and he listens which makes the conversation very Templeton-oriented. He loves that, don't you, pal?"

Sophie stood at the side of the bed, watching Grant interact with his friend. His monologue was overflowing with enthusiasm, an energy-level that had to be draining to maintain. You could tell the chatter was routine, too. There was a natural rhythm to it that told her what she was witnessing wasn't a performance. If Nate did comprehend, he had to be touched by the effort. She was. As she watched, her eyes grew moist.

"I told Sophie all about you, too," he was saying, as he adjusted the bedsheet, "and we figured it was time she got to meet your ugly face."

"Don't listen to him, Nate." Taking a cue from Grant, she moved closer to the bed. "He's just jealous. And don't worry, everything Grant told me was good."

"Most of it anyhow," Grant chimed in. From across the bed, he looked at Sophie and smiled a sad smile.

They stayed for well over an hour. Grant was drained. Visits with Nate always tapped him out, and this visit hit him harder than usual. Watching Sophie from the other side of Nate's bed, it struck him hard that what happened to Nate could have happened to any one of them. Perhaps not an overdose; that blanket of blame still lay at Grant's feet as far as he was concerned. But the determination to get ahead? That was the same.

Sophie had been amazing. Smiling and chatting with Nate as though he were actually responding. Did she, too, recognize the similarities? Or had she gone the extra mile for him? The thought, which had nagged the back of his brain since leaving the nursing home, squeezed at his chest and cut his breath short. It was an uncomfortable feeling, strange and exhilarating. He'd never experienced anything like it before. On top of the fatigue, it left Grant feeling raw and unsettled.

"Should have known you'd take a detour," Sophie remarked.

Distracted, Grant missed his turn. "Sorry," he replied. "Seeing Nate leaves me a little burned-out."

"Do you see him often?"

"Every week. I made a promise I'd keep him a priority."

He felt her hand brush his knee. "You're a good friend."

Oh, yeah, he was a real peach. "There's a diner up ahead," he said, spotting the sign. "Want to stop?"

"Um…I don't know. It's getting late and…"

Man, she was thinking of her freaking to-do list, wasn't she? "Never mind. I forgot you had work to do." The very idea she was thinking about work irritated him. Seeing Nate hadn't shifted a damn thing in her head. He thought… He didn't know what he thought. Angrily, he slapped at the stick shift, turning on his right directional.

"I know what you're thinking," Sophie said, watching him, "and it's not the same. My work ethic and Nate. The situations aren't the same."

"Never said they were," he replied.

"You're thinking it, though. You're not very subtle."

She sat stiff and straight as she stared out the windshield, her gaze focused on someplace far off. "I'm not looking to be number one. I'm just looking to move up as far as I can go. As far away from…"

"What?" Grant wanted to know. He had a pretty decent idea. The empty pantry. The brother in prison. She wanted to get away from the bad memories.

Sophie swiveled in her seat so she could face him. "I'm not like you, Grant. I didn't have an Ivy League education. I've had to work damn hard for everything I've got. Hell, most of the time people expected me to fail. My own family expected me to fail."

"At least you had nowhere to go but up." Her defense only irritated him more. Life on the other side of the fence wasn't all that easy, either. "Try living with success being the only option. In my house, it wasn't good enough to simply be a Boy Scout. You had to be the best damn Boy Scout in the troop, and earn more merit badges than anyone. The Templeton way. Number one or bust." He glanced over, not surprised when he saw Sophie's wide-eyed expression. "You think that sounds better?"

Didn't matter what she thought; he already knew. Knew what lengths the "Templeton way" had led him to. "Things were hard for you, but at least you can look yourself in the mirror with pride for all you've achieved. Maybe if I'd been on your side of the fence, Nate wouldn't be in that hospital bed."

"You don't know that."

"Don't I?"

"No, you don't," she told him. "What happened to Nate wasn't your fault."

"God, I wish people would stop saying it wasn't my fault!" The guilt and all his other feelings reached their tipping point. Yanking the wheel to the right, he steered the truck off the road and slammed to a stop. "Don't you get it?" he asked her. Practically *yelled* at her. "I ignored his phone calls. Five minutes. Five lousy minutes and I couldn't be bothered. I was too busy backstabbing him and scamming old ladies out of buildings to notice my best friend was killing himself!"

His words echoed in the truck, mocking him. He remembered it all clear as day. Nate's mother's anguished expression when she'd told him. His own reflection in the emergency room window. A man in a designer suit he barely recognized. *I don't know who you are,* Nate had screamed at him that afternoon. *Who are you?* The emotions, locked up for the past twenty-eight months finally boiled over, and all the anger and self-loathing he kept buried inside poured out as he smacked the steering wheel over and over. If only he'd tried. If only he'd taken the phone call.

"Stop it," Sophie ordered. She grabbed his arm before he could slap the steering wheel again, fighting with him to hold it back. "Stop beating yourself up. You didn't make Nate take those drugs!"

"I didn't stop him, either."

"No, you didn't. But were you the only person there? What about his family? Your coworkers? Was his well-being your sole responsibility?

"Yes!" In his guilt, the word came out as a shout. "Yes," he repeated, softer. "I knew something was off. I *knew*. That makes it my responsibility."

"If that's true, then am I responsible because my brother dealt drugs?"

"What?" Grant didn't know what she was talking about.

Sophie's eyes glistened with moisture of unwanted memories. "When I was in high school my brother got arrested for dealing pot. I'd known he was up to something for months but never told my family. So was it my fault he became a career criminal to pay for his own habit? Is it my fault my parents couldn't stop drinking or smoking pot?"

"No, of course not. They were addicts." Despite his self-loathing, his chest squeezed. "They wouldn't have listened to you."

"But Nate would have listened to *you?*"

"It's not the same." Grant washed a hand over his face. He appreciated the effort, he really did. All the consolation in the world wouldn't quiet his guilt. Nate's addiction wasn't the real demon here. The demon was the man that Grant feared still existed, waiting for a moment when he could return. "I hate that man," he said, not caring if Sophie understood who he meant or not. He understood. "I hate who he was. A backstabbing, tunnel-visioned…"

Sophie pressed her lips to his, cutting short the rant. She didn't know why she chose kissing to quiet him. She only knew she couldn't stand the self-recrimination any longer. Twice now she listened to him beat himself up. Twice she heard him describe a man that far as she could tell, didn't exist anymore. And so, she shut him up the first way that came to mind. With her kiss, she told him she understood. Understood the need to bury the past. To be so loathing of the past you wanted to keep it and the memories from ever returning. Her kiss was to tell him he wasn't alone. That she was right here with him.

What she miscalculated was the fire that would ignite when they touched. It took less than a second for Grant to kiss her back, and then all coherent thought left her brain. It wasn't long before she found herself sprawled across his lap as she made small mewling noises deep in her throat. She'd never been kissed like this in her life. Not by David, not by anyone. And while she knew it went against everything she'd resolved, she wanted more.

Much to her satisfaction, when the kiss ended, Grant looked as shell-shocked as she felt. Sophie held her breath.

"What was that?" he asked, forehead pressed to hers.

"I don't know." She'd never acted so spontaneously in her life. Words failed her.

Grant's fingers inched their way into her hair, tangling in the strands that worked loose from her ponytail. His breath was hot and minty against her lips. "Let's go home," he wished.

As she seemed to always do where Grant was concerned, Sophie allowed him to lead her away.

CHAPTER NINE

GRANT's tub was nothing short of amazing. And perfectly sized for two. Sophie knew because she took a nice long soak at Grant's insistence. This time, when she stretched out and felt his breath against her ear, it was because his face was nestled in the crook of her neck. She had to admit, lying there in his arms, she'd never had a better bathing experience.

Later, though, as she dried off and slipped into Grant's blue terry cloth robe, the spell that had begun weaving in the truck had begun to shimmer unstably. What was she doing? The guy was twenty-nine years old. He'd been in elementary school when she started college for crying out loud.

Grant was sitting on the sofa in nothing more than sweatpants when she padded into the room. The minute she saw him, desire stirred again. *I am a dirty old woman,* she thought to herself.

He had been reading something on his phone. Soon as he saw her, he set the phone down. "Feeling relaxed?" he asked her.

"Shouldn't I be asking you that question?" He was the one who had needed comforting, before things turned intimate.

"I feel terrific." He patted the sofa next to her. "Come

sit down and stop thinking so hard. I can hear your thoughts."

She wasn't surprised. They sounded pretty loud in her head. "It's just that I never…"

"Shh." He brushed her cheek with her thumb. "I know."

It was so easy to forget her doubts and mistakes when she looked into those eyes. Tucking her legs beneath her, she curled up against him, reveling in the warmth of his bare skin. "Isn't checking emails my job?" she teased.

"It's from a guy I met with a couple weeks ago. He keeps trying to schedule a second meeting even though I already passed on the job. Guy's persistent, I'll give you that."

"What was the job?"

Grant shrugged. "Renovating a high-rise. Turning the place into modern luxury apartments. He wanted me to head up the project."

"And you turned it down? It sounds like an amazing opportunity."

"I didn't like the design he had in mind. It went completely against the original intent."

Wow, he was the purist, wasn't he? She wondered if he turned down a lot of jobs for that reason.

Or was the reason simply an excuse? After today's meltdown, she wondered if he were simply punishing himself.

"So you're not going to meet with him?"

"I told you, I'm not interested in the job. Besides, I've already promised to do your kitchen."

Had he? She rememberd his answer being a little more noncommittal.

"My kitchen could wait."

"Nothing about you can wait. Although—" he glanced down at his phone screen "—if the guy doesn't stop calling, I'm going to have to meet with him just to make him go away. Obviously, he figures since he's a multimillionaire he can have whatever he wants."

"Must be nice," Sophie murmured, getting up from the sofa.

"Getting whatever you want?"

That, and turning down jobs out of principle. They were both such foreign concepts to her. "All I've ever known was hard work." Climbing up the ladder rung by rung until you got to the top.

Sophie stared out Grant's front windows. Outside, the sky had gone dark, leaving the light to the buildings and the stars. In the distance, she could see the gold dome of the bank building towering over the rest of the borough. "I should probably go downstairs and check my own emails," she remarked. She hadn't looked all day. There were probably dozens of messages from Allen alone.

A pair of warm, strong arms found their way around her waist. "Don't," Grant whispered in her ear. "Stay." Two simple words and they managed to freeze her on the spot.

"Why?"

"Because I like your company. And because you want to."

Sophie smiled. "Says you. Are we going to really repeat this argument?"

"No." In Grant's robe that smelled of peppermint soap and with the warmth of his chest pressed against her, it was difficult to argue the point.

Grant rested his chin on her shoulder. "Was your brother really a dealer in high school?"

"'Fraid so." Another Pond Street family secret. Grant was the first person she'd ever admitted it to. "First of many offenses. I've lost track. My family wasn't exactly Norman Rockwell material."

"You turned out all right."

"Only because I busted my behind to make sure I did."

Peppermint drifted in her direction as he planted a kiss on her neck. "I like that you're showing me the lines," he murmured.

"Lines? I don't understand."

"The stuff underneath all the polish and gloss. I like it."

Now she knew he wasn't making sense. The Sophie she showed him was nothing more than white trash who'd got a scholarship to the local college. She'd done everything in her power to eliminate that person in favor of a better, more sophisticated model. A pearl.

Still, wrapped in his arms, it was nice to pretend for a little while that the old Sophie wasn't so bad.

She returned her attention to the view. Funny, but she always felt small with regards to the world. An insignificant speck dressed up larger than she was, hoping no one found her out. Tonight, however, looking out at Brooklyn, with Grant's arms wrapped around her, she felt bigger. More significant than she'd felt in a long time.

"When I was a little girl, I used to wish I could fly. I'd imagine soaring out my bedroom window and flying all above our town. Everyone would look up and say 'Hey, there's Sophie Messina, the girl who can fly.' I imagine this is what the view would have looked like."

She let her head fall back against his shoulder. "I never told anyone that story before."

Grant smoothed the hair from her face. "What made you choose flying?"

"I was a little girl. I wanted to be special. I wanted—"
She didn't finish. She'd wanted to fly away from her
life. It'd been the beginning of her master plan. The
promise to herself that she would become someone different, live a life as different from her family's as possible. A perfect life with no fights, no crazy drama, no
one gossiping behind her back.

A life she controlled.

She didn't say any of it, however. She couldn't because Grant's hands had begun gliding down her shoulders and arms, causing her breathing to catch. His lips
delivered butterfly kisses along her temple, her cheek-
bone. "I know another way to make you feel like you're
flying," he murmured as his fingers skimmed her rib
cage.

She bet he could. She bet he could take her to heights
she never knew possible. Taking hold of his hand, she
wrapped her fingers in his. "Show me," she whispered
back.

He gladly obliged.

Later that night, Grant stood in front of the window by
himself, reliving the weekend. Not at all what he expected when he woke Saturday morning. But then he
hadn't expected Sophie, had he?

Sophie. He smiled, his insides warming from thinking her name. She'd surprised the hell out of him this
afternoon. Once you scraped off the designer clothes
and "I'm a professional" attitude you found a whole
cache load of unexpected surprises. Good ones and sad
ones. Pretty impressive how she pulled herself out of
what sounded like a hellish childhood. Her work ethic
started to make more sense.

Wonder if she'd ever stop?

The question disturbed him as much as always. Maybe more. Where did someone like him fit into her master plan, he wondered. Did he even? And if so, for how long?

A noise from behind saved him from his thoughts. Turning, he found the object of his questions in the hallway door. In her hand she held her BlackBerry, obviously purloined from her bag.

"What are you doing?"

"European markets," she answered. Checking the opening numbers.

Grant strolled toward her. She wore his gray T-shirt and her hair was loose and curly. The lips he found so enticing were red and ripe against her pale face. Desire stirred fresh at the sight.

"The numbers can wait," he said, reaching for the phone.

"But…" Though she started to complain, she didn't put up much of a fight; the phone slipped easily from her fingers.

"Later." Dropping the phone to the ground, he wrapped his other arm tightly around her waist and drew her close, until they stood chest to toe.

"Later," she repeated.

Good, they were on the same page. Lowering his lips to hers, he walked her backward to the master bedroom.

Anderson St. Pierre was a pest. No matter how many times Grant said no, the guy wouldn't give up. So here he was, up at dawn to meet him for a breakfast meeting. He'd much rather be in bed with Sophie, trying to coax her into not spending the wee hours of the morning checking the Asian stock market the way she had most of the week.

St. Pierre was already in the diner having breakfast when Grant arrived. "One of the things I love about New York City," he said as Grant took a seat, "is how you can get whatever you want any time of the day. You want fried chicken at the crack of dawn, you got it." He took a bite of a deep fried wing. "You want some?"

"Coffee's fine."

"Suit yourself. This chicken's amazing, though." His host waved a hand and a waitress dutifully hustled over to fill Grant's cup. Ten to one the drink didn't taste nearly as good as the stuff he drank in Sophie's kitchen.

"I'm glad you finally agreed to hear me out," St. Pierre continued.

"Hard to say no when someone calls a half-dozen times. Though I've got to be honest I don't see the point. I already told you I wasn't interested in the job last week."

"Renovating my building. I know." St. Pierre pointed a crinkle fry in his direction. "But what if I doubled your labor costs?"

"What?" Grant choked on his coffee.

"All right, tripled."

The guy was kidding, right? Triple his labor was a boatload of money. "Why?" The offer made zero sense, even if this guy was a billionaire. "There are plenty of contractors around who can do a perfectly good job."

"But none as good as you. I did my research, Templeton. You're good. More than good, and honest, I like to hire the best."

Grant had to chuckle. The man's brazenness rivaled his. "I'm good," he agreed, "at *historical* renovation. Accent on *historical*. What you want to do anybody can do. In fact, I'll even give you some names."

"I want you."

"Yeah, well, if you hire me, I'm going to turn around and ask them to declare your building a historic landmark."

"You should. That building is an original Feldman."

Stunned, Grant stared at the man. "I thought you wanted to gut the place."

"Nah. I just wanted to see how you'd answer." He bit off a bite of chicken. "When you turned me down, I knew I found my man. See, lots of contractors say they do historical renovations—I wanted a man who shared my level of vision. Someone who understood design as well as construction. An award winner."

At the last phrase Grant's blood chilled slightly. He had done his research. "That was a few years ago. I'm not with Kimeout anymore. I'm not even in architecture."

"I know. You're your own man. Exactly what I want."

"So," Grant said, still trying to figure out what was going on, "all this talk about tripling my labor costs was a test?"

"One you passed with flying colors." Pushing his plate aside, St. Pierre rested his elbows on the table and leaned forward. "Now, how about we discuss a real business proposition."

"That has to be the most unorthodox way of doing business I've ever heard of," Mike said when Grant called him. His first call had been to Sophie, but the call had gone straight to voice mail so he'd turned, reluctantly, to his older brother.

"I know. And get this, he's developing a housing complex out of an old block of row houses. He wants someone to head the project who has the same mind-set as he does. The person would be in charge of everything from the ground up. Design, construction, personnel. We spent the past two hours talking about the project."

"I owe you an apology, little brother. Turns out being a pain in the butt actually paid off. When do you start?"

"I haven't said yes yet," Grant said, smiling at the waitress topping up his coffee. St. Pierre had provided such an extravagant tip when he left, Grant imagined she'd be happy to pour him coffee all day long if he wanted.

On the other end of the line, he heard silence. Mike, busy rolling his eyes, no doubt. "Why not?" he asked finally.

"For one thing, the job's in Philadelphia."

"So?"

"So, my apartment's here." His life was here. The people he cared about. Mike. Nate.

Sophie. Her name gave him a heavy feeling in his stomach. What would she say about his job offer? She'd probably understand. In fact, she'd understand all too well.

"Philly's not far away," Mike reminded him. "You can drive back and forth in a couple hours. Come back on weekends."

"True, but…"

"But what? What's got you dragging your feet this time?"

Grant didn't know. Yes, he did. They were talking opportunity of a lifetime. Working with Anderson St. Pierre would bring a lot of notoriety. National notoriety. Success. The kind not even Young Architect of the Year could buy. His pulse kicked up a notch, and not in a good way. Would the man—the face from the hospital window—would he return?

"What about Nate?" he asked his brother. The question just came out.

"You come home weekends. Do your penance then."

"My visits aren't penance. Besides his mother, I'm the only visitor Nate has." For how long would he keep the visits going before work and his schedule became an excuse to stay away?

His thoughts returned, unbidden, to Sophie. What about her? Would moving away mean the end of what they began this week? He'd managed to distract her this week, but if he were gone, what then? Would she become so busy she no longer had time for him? How long before their affair fizzled out?

Dread washed over him. He didn't want that to happen. He wanted Sophie. Not for a few days or a few weeks. The realization scared the hell out of him. When did he start thinking of any woman in terms of a relationship? But with Sophie he did. He wanted this thing they had going on for as long as it lasted, maybe even forever.

He needed to see her. Right now. Needed to talk with her and see the reaction in her eyes when he shared his news. To know if this feeling that kept filling his chest was returned.

He needed her.

"I've got to go, Mike." Tossing a second tip on the table, he took off for Wall Street.

CHAPTER TEN

SOPHIE was having a long, lousy Thursday. It began when she slept through her alarm. A week of Grant coaxing her back beneath the covers had started a new habit, which to be honest she enjoyed. A lot.

Unfortunately, her new habit resulted in Allen calling to bark at her. Had she seen the European numbers? Why wasn't she at the office correcting the morning status report? He needed to see her *right away.*

Naturally, his call led to her calling both junior analysts, only to discover they were already in the office. In fact, everyone was in the office already except for her. That mistake she was certain Allen was waiting for her to make? Today was it.

She showered and dressed on the fly, opting to do her makeup during her commute—a decision that even on the best days, didn't turn out well—and arrived at the office a little before eight-thirty, coffee-deprived and underprepared. The only saving grace was the fact that Grant left early for a meeting because if he had been around, then she, in her mad dash to get ready, would have bitten his head off. If Carla, one of her junior assistants, didn't stop smirking at her still-damp hair, she might still bite someone's head off.

"Have you finished revising those figures Allen

needed?" she asked, delivering a silent warning to the young woman from over the rims of her reading glasses.

"Put them on your desk fifteen minutes ago," Carla replied.

Sophie thanked her, feeling foolish. She hadn't been this off her game ever. Earlier she even sent an email to Allen and forgot to include the attachment. Her coveted managing director's job felt as if it was slipping from her fingers.

This is karma for having too good a week. You know that, right? She did have a terrific week. Best she could remember in a long time. Best nights, that is, she thought with a smile. Work had been tedious at best. She'd spent the past five days waiting for them to end so she could return to Grant's arms. Scary how much she enjoyed his company. How much she wanted it. Surely the hold he had on her wasn't healthy. Theirs was, at best, a short-term relationship.

Their relationship certainly wasn't healthy for her career right now. Ignoring work for five days had her playing serious catch-up.

"Allen called," Carla piped up over her cubicle wall. "He's looking for the report on Harrington Pharmaceuticals."

"I'll email him a copy right now." Why hadn't Allen called her directly?

Her BlackBerry blinked, indicating a missed call. Allen, she told herself. He must have called when she walked out to Carla's desk. Of course he could have called her office. She was still his go-to person, right? She hadn't lost that title while enjoying the week, had she?

There wasn't time to dwell on the question. The market was going haywire. Up one minute, down three hundred points the next. Clients were bombarding the brokers with questions. Should they sell? Should they buy? It had the entire analysis department scrambling to provide answers.

When noontime rolled around, Sophie didn't notice. She barely had time to breathe let alone eat or grab a cup of coffee. She'd kill for some caffeine!

David called at twelve-thirty. Soon as she heard his bland, unflappable greeting, she got sick to her stomach. She'd been having such a wonderful week, she'd forgotten all about him.

"Thought I'd check the office temperature," he said. "I caught the market scroll on one of the terminal televisions. How are things?"

"Exactly what you'd expect. Wish I had time to clone myself so one of me could run to the bathroom."

"Except you don't know how to harvest DNA."

"I was making a joke."

"I know," he replied, then paused. "Everything all right? Your voice sounds off."

Because she *was* off. "Crazy day is all."

"I understand."

Naturally he did, she thought guiltily. Until she had a chance to talk to David about Grant, she supposed she was stuck with the stabbing sensation in her stomach. She wished she could tell him now, but after so much time together, she owed the man better.

As it stood, having the conversation face-to-face wouldn't be much easier. What was she supposed to say? *I know we've had an arrangement, David, but it seems I've developed an unhealthy obsession regarding my neighbor.* Wouldn't that go over well. All her plans would go flying out the window.

On the other hand, she couldn't very well keep David

in the dark while she waited for this thing she had for Grant to burn out.

No, she was going to have to let David know she was seeing Grant.

Seeing Grant. Such a bland term to describe the week. Was there a word that did? She'd spent the past five days simultaneously excited and scared. Reluctant yet unable to control her behavior. The minute he entered her orbit, her brain ceased working. She felt breathy, giddy. Girlish. Nothing at all like herself.

On his phone at the airport, David seemingly failed to notice she'd drifted off and continued talking in her ear. "With luck," he was saying, "the market will have rebounded by Saturday so we can enjoy a nice quiet dinner. I was hoping to try Troika. I read a review of the place on the plane. Sounds fabulous."

"Sounds good." Wonder if Troika had secluded tables reserved for awkward conversation. She swiped away a few errant strands of hair that had worked their way out of her ponytail. The two of them really needed to talk.

But like everything else today, that would have to wait. No sooner did she hang up with David then she received a call from one of the brokers on the buy side of the company looking for information on health care market projections. A snippy new hire who mistook bossiness for authority, he demanded Sophie have the figures he needed as soon as possible. "Dial it down a notch, Bud," she wanted to say. Moments like this made her seriously consider throwing professionalism to the wind. She was tired, and she didn't need the attitude. If the guy wanted people to treat him with respect, he should try acting like he deserved it. Take Grant, for example. He conveyed authority simply walking into a room.

Grant. She groaned. When did all her thoughts start revolving around him? She woke up thinking about him, she went to bed thinking of him. In between, she wondered what he was doing and if he was thinking about her. When did he become the nexus of her universe?

She had a real problem.

"Allen's still looking for the Harrington report," Carla called.

Give the email a chance to be delivered. "Should be in his in-box in a second," she called back. Carla needn't sound so self-satisfied about her new gopher status.

A knock sounded on her door. "For crying out loud, I said I sent the report," she snapped. "No need to scurry in here to double-check."

"Please don't tell me you're comparing me to a rat."

What? Now she was hearing Grant in her head?

Looking up from her computer screen, her heart stopped. Unless she'd gone completely round the bend, which was possible given her obsession, Grant stood in the doorway.

"Grant?" she asked. Just to make sure.

"I take that as a yes." He strolled in wearing faded jeans and a summer wool blazer. Suave meets sexy. From behind his shoulder Sophie saw the head of every female employee, along with a couple males, peering over their cubicle walls. The man literally caused work to stop. This is how you command authority.

"Bad time?" he asked in his slow-honeyed voice. Her body immediately reacted. She definitely had it bad. Very bad.

Clearing her throat, she pulled herself back to reality. "What are you doing here?"

"I, um…" There was uncharacteristic hesitation in

his voice, along with an emotion in the back of his eyes she couldn't quite define. "Coffee?" He held a green-and-white cup in her direction.

Talk about reading her mind. "I was just dreaming of a cup."

"Must have been sharing a psychic moment."

Their fingers brushed as he handed her the cup, sending sparks up her arm. He dipped his head slightly and leaned toward her cheek. Sophie felt her body sway, drawn as always by his inexplicable pull. If they weren't in her office...

But they were in her office, and people were watching. Abruptly, she pulled back, leaving him leaning into air. Surprise and something more—hurt?—flashed across his face.

"Thank you. For the coffee." Hoping the heat coming off the cup would burn away the feelings rippling through her body, she curled her fingers tightly around the cup.

"Well, I know how much you appreciate your caffeine."

The air in the office felt thick and awkward. She could see the junior analysts still stealing glances. Sophie's nerves started rising. Tomorrow she'd be topic number one on the office grapevine; if it took that long. She could already see Carla's devious little gleam. Might as well take out an ad in the company newsletter—Senior Analyst Caught Mooning Over Boy Toy.

Grant was watching her, too, with an inscrutable expression that made her insides even more self-conscious. "Was coffee the only reason you came by?" she asked, smoothing her hair. Even if her insides were trembling, she could at least give the appearance of professionalism.

"Do I need more of a reason?"

No. That is, *yes.* That is, "Things are really crazy here at the moment. Unless you have something important…"

Another flash of that emotion. "I did, but I've decided it can wait."

"Are you sure?" She was getting an uneasy feeling about the emotion she saw.

"Sophie, about this Harrington report. Do you have the figures broken down by month?"

Terrific. Exactly the person she didn't want popping in.

"Hello, Allen," she greeted, pretending as though having a stranger in her office was perfectly routine. "I'll pull those figures up right now."

"If it's no problem." His critical stare moved from her to Grant and back. Her already jumpy stomach plummeted. *Hop. Skip. Drop.*

"I was on my way out, anyway," Grant said. "I'll talk to you later."

"Don't rush on my account," Allen said. Naturally he didn't mean a word. Sophie could feel his impatience burning a hole in her profile. Outside, Carla and the others were watching, waiting, too.

"Grant just stopped by to deliver an estimate."

The lie flew out before she could stop herself. Allen looked as though he expected an explanation and delivering an estimate sounded so much more appropriate. Silently, she looked to Grant for help, only to realize too late, the mistake she'd made. The shutters had slammed down over Grant's eyes and what were once warm and expressive stared at her cold and hard.

"Delivering an estimate in person? Don't see that kind of personal service much anymore."

"What can I say," Grant replied with an edge only

Sophie would recognize. "I'm very hands-on. And Ms. Messina was a special case."

Was? She didn't think it possible for her stomach to drop further, but it did.

Grant's eyes burned hotter than any stare of Allen's. "Now that our business is over, I'll get out of your hair. I know how important Ms. Messina considers her work to be."

"Grant…" She wanted to grab his arm, ask him to stay so she could apologize. Explain herself. With Allen standing there, however, she could do little more than offer silent regret. "I'll talk with you tonight," she told him, "so we can sort everything out."

"No rush. I think everything's crystal clear." After offering up a handshake to Allen, he tossed one last crisp nod in her direction and left. Sophie was forced to watch his back as he marched away.

"Now about those figures," Allen said, voice clipped.

"Pulling them up on the screen now." Sophie returned to business. She'd apologize to Grant tonight.

Hopefully, he'd listen.

CHAPTER ELEVEN

THE best laid plans will go wrong. Wasn't that Murphy's Law? If not, Murphy said something awfully close, and Sophie was pretty sure he'd been talking about her day. Management's demands kept her at the office until well after ten.

Getting out of her taxi, she looked to the second floor and found Grant's windows dark. Disappointment washed over her. The past few days, he'd kept them on for her. Then again, she'd come home much earlier. Chances are he was watching his game in the bedroom and simply turned out the front lights to look like he was asleep, but in case he did go to bed early, she'd wait and apologize in the morning. Dragging the man out of bed didn't seem like the best way to mend fences. She'd apologize tomorrow morning when they got together for morning coffee. A good night's sleep and he'd have cooled off, putting him in a better position to accept her apology. After all, surely once he thought things through he'd realize she didn't mean to insult him.

Problem was, he didn't show up. Sophie heard his boots on the stairs, but the steps continued straight out the front door, leaving her with two cups of coffee and a kernel of uneasiness rolling around in the pit of her stomach.

Fine. They'd talk when she got home. Just to be certain, she scribbled a quick note and slipped it under his door.

Grant was seated on the stairs when she arrived home, thirty minutes after the time she wrote on her note. Seeing him, her throat thickened and her chest grew tight. The door clicked thunderously behind her. "Hi." The ache in her chest made the words a whisper. "You got my note."

Grant looked up. Cool brown eyes threatened to bore straight through her, and the longing she felt seconds early turned to unease. "You're late. You said five-thirty."

So much for a good night's sleep helping him cool off. "Allen dumped a project on us last minute. Took more time than I expected."

"Of course it did."

Doing her best to ignore the sarcasm, she smoothed her skirts and took a seat next to him. His peppermint soap teased her nostrils and it was all she could do not to close her eyes and inhale. Lord, but she'd missed him. She didn't realize how much until she saw him again. Hopefully they could put this incident behind them soon so things could go back to the way they were.

"If you want to talk about your quote, you're going to have to be quick. I've got to get to Long Island."

Sophie flinched. "You're still angry."

"You think?" Up close his eyes were even colder, like winter in August. "You told your boss I was your contractor."

"Well, you are doing my kitchen…."

"Really? Tell me then, what do you call what we've been doing the past few nights? Negotiating?"

"It was a joke."

"I didn't find it very funny."

Obviously. Her dreams of a quick resolution faded away. "Look, I'm sorry I told Allen you were my contractor. It was a mistake."

"No kidding."

But she'd apologized. Surely that should be enough. "It's just that Allen caught me off guard. Both of you did. What were you doing there anyway?"

He shook his head. "Doesn't matter now."

No, she supposed not. "Point is, had I known you were coming by I would have been better prepared. I could have—"

"Come up with a better cover story?"

"Stop putting words in my mouth." He wasn't being fair. "I admit I was wrong, but think about it for a second, Grant. What exactly was I supposed to say?"

"Gee, let me think." He leaned his back against the railing, increasing the distance between them. "I know! How about the truth?"

Which was what? *Hey, Allen, here's the guy I'm sleeping with?* Oh, yeah, that would have worked out really well.

Her thoughts must have played out on her face, because Grant suddenly sighed and shook his head. "You know, I really thought we were over this age difference thing."

"What are you talking about?"

"You're obviously embarrassed to be seen robbing the cradle."

"Don't be absurd. Just because I don't want the office to know my business doesn't mean I'm embarrassed."

"Really? Sure could have fooled me."

"Why, because I won't shout our affair to the world?

Excuse me for wanting to keep my professional life and my private life separate."

"But you're not embarrassed," he muttered under his breath.

Dear God. If her hair wasn't in a ponytail, she'd pull her hair out. Why was he being so difficult? She said she was sorry, for crying out loud. Besides, he should understand the circumstances. "For God's sake, Grant, it's not like we're talking about some random coworker. This was Allen Breckinridge, the most senior managing director. The man literally holds my future in the palm of his hand."

An undecipherable look clouded his eyes. "Allen holds your future," he repeated flatly.

"Yes." They'd discussed this. "He's in charge of naming the new managing directors. I screw up with him, and I've screwed up my career. You know how important becoming managing director is to me."

"Oh, I know. Do me a favor, and remind me not to stand in the way if you're ever in the line for chairman of the board. Instead of throwing me under the bus, you might actually push me in front of one."

"Stop being childish."

"Childish?" He blinked. "*I'm* being childish? No way. I'm not the one too immature to realize there's more to life than a freaking promotion."

"Like what, burying your head in the sand? Excuse me, but not all of us have the luxury of hiding out because we're afraid of the future. Some of us need to keep working to make something of ourselves."

It was a low blow. Grant's eyes narrowed. "What's that supposed to mean?"

"Nothing." She wasn't in the mood to psychoanalyze his guilty conscience right now.

But Grant didn't want to let go. "I'm not burying my head anywhere. You know damn well why I stepped off the fast track, Sophie."

"Yeah, I know why. I also know you've been hell-bent on trying to convince me to jump off with you."

"Excuse me for not wanting you to repeat my mistakes."

"And excuse me for not wanting to throw away twenty years of hard work on a fling!"

She whipped the words at him so hard he visibly flinched. His shoulders dropped slightly, and the look from before, that unreadable, disturbing look, returned to his eyes. "That how you see this? As a fling?"

"How else am I supposed to see 'this'?" she asked, her own voice dropping. "For all I know, we could fizzle out next week."

"Maybe, maybe not. Isn't that part of the risk in a relationship?"

Maybe. "I don't take risks, remember?"

"I know. I've seen your pantry."

"Then you should understand."

"But what if I asked you to?" he asked suddenly, looking her straight in the eyes. "What if I asked you to tell Allen and your entire office that we are together?"

The hairs on the back of her neck stood on edge. Tell Allen? It wasn't that simple. Allen demanded his employees give their whole lives to the job.

She took too long to answer. Grant immediately shoved himself to his feet. "Forget I asked. You've obviously made your choice."

"Grant—" There wasn't a choice to be made. She'd worked too long and too hard to become the Sophie Messina the world knew. To ruin that reputation for a fling…

It was a fling, right? A relationship with no future? Because she hadn't planned on... The hairs on her neck began to rise.

"Where are you going?" she called, seeing Grant heading for the front door.

"To Long Island. Nate's waiting."

"What about our conversation?"

He gave a soft, bitter laugh. "What about it? I asked you to tell Allen about us and you said no. There isn't much more to say, is there?"

"Except, I didn't say no."

"No, you hesitated. For the second time," he added.

"Because what you're asking is complicated. After I'm promoted I'll be glad to tell people."

He shook his head. "You still don't get it, do you?"

No, she got it. He was the one who didn't understand. How hard she worked. How much she needed this promotion. "Do you have any idea how hard it was for me to get to where I am? The demons I had to outrun?" He wasn't the only one with a past they wanted to erase. "There's a lot more at stake here than just your ego."

Ego? Grant blinked. She thought this was about ego? Grant stared at the woman sitting on the stairs. Took every ounce of self-control not to grab her by the shoulders and shake sense into her. "You're right," he said, his jaw squeezed so tightly it hurt. "There was a lot more at stake." And she blew it.

If he stayed in the foyer another second, he would lose his temper and do something stupid, so he spun on his heel and walked out the door, leaving Sophie sitting on the stairs. Alone. The way she apparently wanted it.

Allen holds my future in the palm of his hand. Allen.

Her freaking boss! He wanted to punch something. He settled for punching the steering wheel.

God, but he was such a fool. He slammed the door of his truck so hard the glass rattled. Dammit all! He should have known better. Her past hurts ran too deep. She was too afraid of, he didn't know what, being left without, that she made her choice.

And she called him afraid? Ha!

An emptiness like he hadn't felt in years engulfed him, extinguishing his anger and replacing it with a giant hole. He'd thought she... That they... The emotion danced on the tip of his brain, too hesitant to reveal itself by name.

What did he do now? Go back to Sophie's bed and settle for being second best? Pride wouldn't let him. Then again, the idea of passing by her door every day, of being so close and yet not close enough held even less appeal.

There was, he realized, a third option. Absent-mindedly, his fingers curled around his cell phone.

The opportunity of a lifetime.

Nate would want him to.

Sophie wouldn't care.

Afraid, huh? He'd show her afraid. Opening the contacts folder, he scrolled down to *S* and dialed.

On Saturday, Sophie attacked her usual chores. They didn't take nearly as long as usual. Probably because there was no banging to distract her. The building was quiet as a church.

Too quiet.

For what felt like the thousandth time, she replayed last night's conversation with Grant. Her actions back at her office were wrong; she admitted as much. Why then couldn't he accept her apology and move on? What did it matter when or if she told the world they were involved?

Was their relationship that important to him? She thought about the dark expression in his eyes when she referred to what they had going on as a fling. Thinking back, it had looked awful close to hurt or disappointment. An unreadable emotion of her own took flight in her stomach.

No, she thought, calming the flutters. They were just having a fling. A wonderful, intoxicating fling.

Or least they had been. The way Grant walked off last night felt a lot more final than what she wanted. She missed him. Fling or not, she wasn't ready to give him up. Soon as she talked with David she'd head upstairs. See if she couldn't smooth things over.

Spurred on by her plan, she called David and asked if he could come by earlier than scheduled. Sooner they talked, the sooner she could go see Grant. The lawyer's amiable agreement made her conscience cringe. David had been the man she expected to spend her future with. When had her plans gotten so turned around?

An hour later, she heard the front doorbell ring. Immediately her nerves went into overdrive. "Relax," she told herself. David was a reasonable man. He'd understand what happened even if she didn't. After all, wasn't that his best quality? His ability to understand.

David's blue eyes widened when she opened the door. "Shorts?" he asked. "A little casual for Troika, don't you think? Never mind, you look lovely anyway." He leaned in to kiss her hello. Sophie tilted her head so his lips caught her cheek instead. "I missed you while I was in Chicago," he said.

A noise sounded in the entranceway behind them.

Anxiety gripped her. Sophie closed her eyes. Grant. His body was stiff, his expression cold. "Don't let me interrupt the reunion."

Sophie's heart sank. She knew what he was thinking. Just knew. Catching his eye, she tried to let him know he was mistaken.

The message was ignored.

"Hello." Oblivious to Sophie and Grant's silent conversation, David extended a hand. "Sophie's neighbor, right? The man with the bathtub. Got it inside I see."

"Yes." Though he shook David's hand, Grant's eyes stayed locked on hers. Narrow slits that burned into her skin. "Everything is right in place. Isn't that so, Sophie?"

"I don't know," she replied. Two could play the cryptic game. "Is it?"

"From my view, anyway." He turned to David. "The two of you on your way out?"

"Yes, we're having dinner at Troika, soon as Sophie changes."

"Troika. Sounds special. I hope you don't have to wait long. For Sophie to change, that is."

"Oh, I don't mind waiting. After all our months together, I'm used to being patient. Isn't that right, Sophie?"

Sophie didn't reply. She wasn't sure who was annoying her more at the moment. Grant with his veiled remarks, or David who had suddenly decided to act possessive and drape his arm around her shoulder. As delicately as possible, she slipped out of his grasp. "We should probably go inside. I'll fix you a drink while you wait."

"Sounds great. You can tell me about your plans for

renovating your kitchen. You're going to be doing the work, aren't you?" he asked Grant.

Was he trying to bury her?

"Hopefully you'll be able to talk her into modernizing. Maybe if she hears from a contractor, she'll listen. I've been telling her to gut the whole place and start from scratch, but she keeps dragging her feet."

"Well, you know Sophie. She doesn't do anything without a master plan." The words, delivered with cool cordiality, sliced through her. But then he'd meant them to.

"Yes, she does tend to stick to her plans," David agreed.

"Not necessarily," Sophie replied. She looked at both of them, hoping they each got the intended message. "In fact, I hoped to talk with Grant later this evening about my plans."

"Unfortunately, I won't be able to be part of any plans," Grant replied. "I'm leaving town. I've decided to take a job in Philadelphia."

"You have?" His comment cut her at the knees. Philadelphia? "I didn't know…" She had no clue there was a job to be taken.

"I only recently decided. I'm taking a job with St. Pierre Development."

"Oh." Grant was leaving. Going to Philadelphia. No more nights wrapped in his arms. No more early morning cajoling to stay under the covers. No more coffee in her homely, cramped kitchen.

She swallowed the lump stuck in her throat. "I didn't think you wanted the job."

"Originally, no, but when we met Thursday morning, he made me an offer that was hard to turn down."

Thursday. Same day he'd showed up at her office.

She knew he'd had something on his mind. And she'd chased him off. This was her fault. Her doing.

"Congratulations," she heard David say. "Working for a man like Anderson St. Pierre will open a lot of doors for you careerwise."

"So I'm told. And since there's nothing holding me here…"

Sophie's stomach dropped another notch. "Are you sure there's nothing?"

"Positive." His gaze was harsh and pointed, challenging even. "Unless you know a reason why I should stick around?"

Yes, she wanted to say. *Me. Stick around with me.* But David was standing there, and besides, hadn't she determined they were only having a fling? He was finally moving forward, making plans to do something with his life. Who was she to stop him?

"When do you leave?" It took some effort, but she managed to ask without her voice cracking.

Although the glimmer of pain she caught passing behind his eyes was almost her undoing. "Soon. Anderson wants to start the project as soon as possible."

Meaning this might be the very last time they saw each other. The lump in Sophie's throat spread to her chest, the ache so strong it threatened to choke her.

The trio stood in awkward silence. There were things Sophie wanted to say. Things like "Don't go." But, the words wouldn't come. *Let him go, Sophie. It's over.*

David cleared his throat. "We should let your neighbor get going," he said. "We," as if they were a united force. "I'm sure he has a busy evening."

"As a matter of fact, I do," Grant agreed. He gave her one last look before heading toward the stairs. "Goodbye, Sophie."

"Wait!"

Grant turned around. "Yes?"

Let him go, Sophie. Let him go. "Good luck," she finally managed to choke out. It wasn't what she wanted to say, but it was the best thing to say.

He nodded. "You, too, Sophie."

To his credit, David waited until Grant's apartment door shut before speaking up again. "Philadelphia, huh? Thank goodness. Now maybe you can get over this construction worker fantasy of yours and things can get back to normal."

Whipping her head around, Sophie stared at him. His blue gaze was as dispassionate as ever.

And to think, she'd thought him oblivious. In reality, he was merely indifferent. That calmness and understanding she thought so wonderful was apathy. "Actually, David, I don't think so," she said. "I think you should leave."

He blinked. "But we have reservations at Troika."

Unbelievable. Missing their reservations. That's what finally managed to upset him.

"Sorry," she said, no longer caring about his feelings. Hard to hurt something that barely registered. "I'm too busy nursing my 'construction worker fantasy' to feel like eating. You'll just have to head to Troika by yourself."

She left him standing in the foyer, mouth slightly ajar. It was, perhaps, the most emotional she'd seen him the entire time they'd been together.

Soon as she closed the door, however, her satisfaction drained away and her heart began to ache once more.

Thank goodness for work. It kept her mind occupied all Saturday night and all day Sunday. There was a sort of fitting irony to the situation; the very thing Grant accused her of being obsessed with keeping her from obsessing over Grant. After parting ways with David, she thought of running upstairs and banging on Grant's door, but what purpose would that serve?

How about keeping him in your life?

No. Grant was not part of her life. He had been a momentary detour. A wonderful, unplanned weeklong fling that was now over. It was time to refocus her energies.

Monday morning she took extra care getting ready for work, applying her makeup so her sleeplessness wasn't visible. Her lack of sleep was solely due to staying up late working, not because she was ruminating over Grant. She had a lot of ground to make up after her recent "distraction." To sustain her efforts, she pulled out her favorite power suit, a black sheath dress and red-cropped jacket that made her look sophisticated and intimidating. She dug out her black patent leather stilettos, too. Surveying her reflection, she decided with satisfaction, the world would see a woman who had her act together. Certainly not a woman who was mourning the loss of her upstairs neighbor.

When she strode into her building, she felt a little more on course. She would be fine. Eventually her continuous thoughts about Grant would end. In the meantime, she had a job to do. Rumor had it that senior management had been sealed up in meetings over the weekend to discuss the upcoming changes in leadership. Meaning an announcement could be made any day now.

The floor was buzzing with energy when she stepped off the elevator. Apparently she wasn't the only one who'd heard the rumors. About ten o'clock, she got a

phone call from Allen Breckinridge asking her to join
him in the conference room.

"Certainly," she said, her stomach giving an invol-
untary nervous jump. *Relax, Sophie. He could simply
want to talk about last week's figures.* Grabbing hard
copies of her reports, she headed upstairs.

She always loved meeting in the conference room.
Located on the twelfth floor, the room had large windows that let you look out at the buildings across the
street. One in particular had beautiful stonework sur-
rounding the windows. Grant would appreciate the
stonework, she thought without thinking. Just as
quickly, she pushed it away. Grant wasn't here.

Through the interior windows, she saw Allen and
two other members of the Twamley Greenwood management team seated inside. Suddenly her palms began
to sweat. She normally wouldn't meet with a group unless something important was afoot. After discreetly
wiping her hands on her skirt, she knocked on the door.
Allen waved her in. As she entered, the other two heads
turned to greet her.

"Come in, Sophie," Allen greeted. "Take a seat."

Palms sweating again, she eased into an empty seat
next to Raymond Twamley, the outgoing partner. The
senior man nodded in greeting.

"I'll get right to the point," Allen said. "You've been
a valuable member of our team for several years now,
Sophie. Personally I know I've come to appreciate your
contribution and dedication. Your hard work has helped
me more than once."

Oh, my God, this was it. She folded her hands and
squeezed them tightly. "I've enjoyed working here,
Allen," she replied.

"It shows. Which is why we've asked you here this

morning. As you know, Raymond is stepping down at the end of the year, leading us to make some managerial changes."

Sophie held her breath. In the back of her mind, Grant's memory threatened to spoil the moment. She shoved him aside.

"After careful discussion," Allen said, "we've agreed you should replace Raymond as the next managing director."

She exhaled. At last. Twenty-two years of late hours and weekends had finally paid off. The little girl from Pond Street was no more. She was now one of them. A managing director. One more box checked off on her master plan.

She always thought the moment would have more resonance.

"Thank you, Allen," she said with a professional smile. Now was not the time to worry about why she wasn't excited. "Your confidence in me means a lot."

Allen, now her peer, looked at her with cool regard. "Don't let us down."

The moment of equality faded away. "I won't."

"Good. Now, on to business. We need you to fly to Boston tonight…" He continued on, outlining a work schedule that made her current week look like a vacation.

So much for her moment of glory. She told herself she'd celebrate in Boston.

Later that afternoon she swung by her apartment to pack. The office had her booked on a seven o'clock shuttle to Logan Airport. As she walked through the front door, a brown cardboard tube propped by her door caught her eye. Sophie's stomach began to twist.

Delivery men didn't just leave packages. Not in New York. Either someone who knew her signed for it or...

Or someone from the building left it for her.

She brought the tube inside and, setting it on her dining room table, reached for the attached note. Her hands shook as she saw the male scrawl on the paper.

It was a list of contractors and phone numbers. Nothing more. No goodbye. No initial. Only a list.

Her euphoria over being promoted faded away. She let the list drop from her fingers, letting it fall to the table.

Suddenly she didn't feel like celebrating anymore.

CHAPTER TWELVE

A MONTH later, Sophie found herself alighting from a taxi, home after another week of back and forth travel to Boston. As she stepped onto the pavement, she sighed and, as she did every night, looked up to Grant's front windows. As they were every night, the windows were dark.

Far as she knew, he'd been home only a few times since leaving. On weekends. Two weeks ago, she'd heard the sound of footsteps on the stairs and pretended to get her mail as an excuse to check. Unfortunately, all she got was a view of his legs turning the corner at the top of the stairs. She'd been about to call to him when she stopped herself. He saw the lights on in her apartment; if he'd wanted to say hello, he would have knocked.

Now she paid the taxi driver, collected her receipt and slowly made her way to the front steps, her overnight bag dragging behind her, *dragging* being the operative word. The past thirty days she had traveled from New York to their Boston office a dozen times. She was bone tired.

At least she was finally home. Leaving her bag in the living room, she padded her way past the panel doors, sorting through the mail as she did. The knowledge failed to thrill her as it normally did. Oh, she still loved her apartment, but the place felt off. Not quite as perfect as it had when she first bought the place at the beginning of the summer. Longing welled up inside of her as she ran a palm across the dining room wood work.

Perhaps if she did something about the kitchen. The designs Grant did for her lay on her dining room table, the list of contractors still where she dropped it a month earlier. She should start calling them, asking for references and quotes. No doubt any of them would do excellent work. After all, Grant had recommended them.

Maybe when she wasn't so tired, she decided, staring at the crack made by the molding joints. Her stomach hurt right now. Nothing serious. Just a heavy, deadlike feeling that never seemed to go away. Hadn't since...

God, she should be past this by now. She dug her fingers into her hair, pulling the strands so tight the bangs worked loose of the clip holding them. Grant, Grant, Grant. He wouldn't leave her thoughts. Just when she thought she'd banished him from her head, something would make his memory come screeching back. A glimpse of sandy-brown hair. The contents of her coffee cup. The other day, she lost her train of thought during a presentation because one of the women in the conference room had been drinking peppermint tea.

Face it, Sophie. The guy is still under your skin. More than that. He was inside her. He had a far greater hold on her feelings than she cared to admit.

So lost in her rambling thoughts was she, she didn't think about grabbing her cell phone until the black square was in her palm. *You don't even know his cell phone number.* Talk about irony. The man owned her thoughts and she hadn't known him long enough to add him to her contacts. But then she hadn't had to. He was always right upstairs.

Not anymore, though.

Giving another long sigh, she carried her cell phone into the bedroom. If she could call him, what would she say? Miss you? Can't stop thinking about you? Please come back? The guy was finally moving forward, away from the guilt that had been holding him back. She should be focusing on her new job and her own future plans.

Besides, she thought, looking at her tired reflection, as if she had any business being involved with a man like Grant anyway. She was no glamorous cougar. She was still Sophie Messina from Pond Street. Turns out the promotion hadn't chased those demons away after all.

The lines around her mouth deepened as she frowned. Her fingers brushed along their groove, pulling the skin taut and letting it go. No, she repeated. She was no cougar. Just a tired financial executive who'd taken a brief detour from life's well-laid-out road and got momentarily distracted by the view. And right now what this tired financial executive needed was a long hot bath and a good night's sleep so she had the strength to get up and do it all again early tomorrow morning.

You only have to keep up this pace for a few years, she reminded herself when she groaned. *Then you can get that summer house like you wanted and rest there.*

For the first time, focusing on the next goal didn't help. Chasing the next rung didn't seem all that desirable anymore. She'd much rather smell the peppermint.

Next morning she got up, cleaned, paid her bills and found herself with an excess of energy. Without the continual banging from upstairs, her apartment was way too quiet. Too quiet to concentrate. Her knee kept bouncing up and down, and she had trouble focusing on the numbers. Figuring a run might help, she dug out her running shoes. They were in the back of her closet. She hadn't gone running since…

Don't go there. She was going to try and spend one day not dwelling on Grant.

Turned out, endorphins were the perfect tonic. After four weeks of road travel, her body loved being outside, and the late summer day made the run that much more pleasant. She took the path in the park and just kept going.

Before she realized, she'd reached the flea market. The sign on the front gate caused her to draw up short. Last Weekend, it read. A sense of sadness settled on her shoulders, the way it did when a season was ending. Without thinking, she retrieved the emergency money she kept in her shorts pocket, and paid the entrance fee.

The market was as crowded today as it had been her first visit, and if possible, the rows more overwhelming and hard to navigate. Then again, her other visit had been with Grant. If she remembered correctly, she'd been too dazed by him to worry about the crowd. What she wouldn't give to be wandering the booths with him now.

He'd looked so commanding that afternoon. Every inch the capable, confident man he was. She knew men twice his age that would kill for an ounce of Grant's natural abilities. No wonder she'd fallen for him, despite his age. He was a man well beyond his years.

After several meandering turns, she wound her way to the back row where Grant purchased his lighting fixtures. The old man who they visited wasn't there today.

In his place was a pair of young men in their twenties selling what looked like auto parts.

The vintage clothing booth was still in the same place, though. Sophie saw the vendor chatting up a customer near a display of jewelry.

She poked her way through a vintage hat display and looked at a couple of 1980s handbags, then turned right. The rack of coats was in the same place as before, still filled with brightly colored fashions. A big sign read Last Chance, Thirty Percent Off. Curious, Sophie picked through the garments, noting the large number of floral dresses and old fur coats. One garment, however, looked to be missing.

"Can I help you?" The vendor appeared at her shoulder.

"I was here about a month ago with a friend," Sophie said. "He was doing business with an older gentleman in the booth next door."

"Oh, yes, the tall, sandy-haired man." Of course, she'd remember Grant. "He comes here often."

The woman leaned forward and whispered conspiratorially. "Very nice."

Sophie resisted saying thank you since Grant wasn't hers anymore. "You had a coat I tried on that day. Blue with fur cuffs."

"Blue with fur cuffs. Sounds familiar." The woman thought for a moment. "Brocade right? Fur collar and matching cloth buttons."

"Exactly."

The woman waved her rings in the air. "I sold that piece weeks ago."

"Oh," Sophie replied, disappointed.

"If you'd liked it, though, I've got a cape with a fur collar. Bright red."

"No, thank you. I was only interested in the blue one."

"Sorry. Place like this, when you see something special, you gotta grab it. Otherwise you'll miss out."

Apparently so. Disappointed, Sophie thanked her and headed on her way. It was only a coat, she told herself. No big deal. And yet, in the back of her mind, she couldn't shake the thought she was missing out. It was the same unnerving feeling she'd had the first time. She really wished she knew why an old coat was causing her so much bother.

The crowd seemed bigger on the way out. Sophie swore it had not only doubled in size, but stopped moving, as well. She craned her neck to see what caused the delay, but didn't see anything. Then, out of the corner of her eye, she saw it. A flash of sand-colored hair on her right. A tingle moved down her spine. She wove her way closer to the booth where she'd spotted him. It was an antique furniture dealer a dozen booths down. His back was to her, and his head was bent as he examined a Victorian-era chaise. Didn't seem like Grant's style, but perhaps it was for his new job.

She moved a little closer, excited to surprise him. Maybe she could convince him to grab a bite to eat on the way home. As friends. To make up for all that happened between them. It would be a good first step, and lay the groundwork for later.

Three or four booths closer, she was about to call out his name. Her mouth had barely opened when suddenly a petite brunette sidled up and joined him. Sophie's heart sank as the woman wrapped her arms around his narrow waist. *No.*

The man turned his head, and to Sophie's relief, she didn't recognize the profile. Now that she looked closer, she realized the man's posture was all off, as was his build. He lacked Grant's broad shoulders and natural self-possessed carriage. Actually, the only resemblance at all was the sand-colored hair. Her mind made up the rest.

Slowly her heart rate returned to normal. The clothing vendor's advice came rushing back. *When you see something you like, you got to act fast or miss out.*

CHAPTER THIRTEEN

"PHILADELPHIA treating you well?"

"Good enough. Saw the Liberty Bell."

"What's St. Pierre like to work for?"

"Eccentric. He's the one who dragged me to the Liberty Bell."

"Okay, do you want to talk about it?"

Grant looked up from his plate. "Huh?"

"Whatever's bothering you," Mike asked. "Do you want to talk about it?

"No." He did not want to talk. He did not want to mention Sophie's name. Sophie with her perfect, kissable lips and her age-appropriate companion who had dominated his thoughts for the past month.

"Okay." His brother shrugged and reached for his imported lager, the buttons on his navy blazer reflecting the glow of recess lighting. Only Mike would wear a blazer to a sports bar on a Saturday afternoon. His idea of casual dress.

"Mom and Dad tell you they were going to France?" he asked instead.

"They are?"

"This fall. Apparently the idea's been on Mom's bucket list for years."

Terrific. Another woman with a bucket list. Grant

stabbed at the ketchup with his French fry. "What is it with people and bucket lists, anyway?" he asked aloud. "If you want to go to Paris, just go. Why do people have to make a production out of everything by making a list of 'someday items.'" He'd had his fill of goals and life plans.

Mike set down his bottle. "Okay, what's wrong?"

"Nothing's wrong. I don't like bucket lists is all." Especially when checking off the items on the list means more than the people in your life.

"Uh-huh."

"Seriously."

"Then why are you smashing the life out of your French fries?"

Grant looked down at the potato wedge, smushed and half-drowned in ketchup. Maybe he did need to talk, if for no other reason than to get the woman out of his head. Stewing alone in his hotel room certainly wasn't working.

"If you must know, it's Sophie."

"Who?"

"The downstairs neighbor. My former downstairs neighbor."

"The 'cease and desist' lady."

"Yeah, her." He'd forgotten Mike didn't know the whole sordid story. "Before I left town, we were—" he scratched the back of his head "—seeing each other."

His brother blinked over the rim of his glass. "You were? Last I knew, she'd ticked you off and you reacted very poorly."

"Let's say I repeated the pattern." Starting from the beginning, he laid out what happened, ending with the scene in Sophie's office. "So I broke things off and took the job with St. Pierre."

"Ouch." Mike swallowed his beer. "Relegated to dirty little secret. I can see how that hurt."

More than Grant thought possible. It felt as if someone sucked the heart out of his chest and stomped on it. Then stomped on it again when she called their relationship a fling and said Allen was the key to her future. He'd thought by now the ache would have subsided, but the more time passed the worse he felt. He missed her like crazy. Her and her maddening behavior.

"I can see her point, though," Mike added.

Grant stabbed another fry into the ketchup. "Why am I not surprised?"

"Hey, I didn't say I agreed with how she treated you. But there are companies out there that demand one hundred and ten percent. Personal lives come second. If her career is that important to her…"

"It's everything to her."

Tired of destroying his food, Grant sat back in his chair. Thing is, he hadn't asked her to give up her career. He'd simply wanted to be on equal footing with her career aspirations. More than anything, he wanted to know their relationship meant something to her. That she needed him in her life the way he needed her.

Instead, she picked Allen and her promotion.

"I was kidding myself," he muttered. Once again, he'd failed to see the truth right in his face.

"Kidding yourself about what?"

That she felt the same way he did. Whenever he thought about how he raced to her office, like an eager little puppy ready to share his feelings, he wanted to kick himself. "Nothing."

He could feel Mike's eyes studying him. "Wow. You've got it bad for her, don't you?" he said a few moments later.

"Worse than bad," Grant replied, washing a hand over his features. He'd never felt this intensely about a woman in his entire life. She'd gotten inside his head and under his skin. Dominated his thoughts to the point of utter distraction. He missed her smile, her warmth, her flawed interior. He must have picked up the phone a half-dozen times to call her only to come to his senses at the last minute.

"You'd think I'd know better," he said aloud. "The fact she shoved 'cease and desist' notes under my door should have been enough of a warning to stay far, far away."

"So what hooked you?"

"My own idiocy." Picking up his fork, he twirled his cocktail napkin, each turn causing the paper to bunch and tear. "Do you remember the doll Nicole used to keep on her bed? The one with the frilly blue dress?"

"You mean the one you ruined with Magic Marker?"

In spite of his bad mood, a corner of Grant's mouth twitched upward. "I prefer the word *enhance,* thank you very much. Sophie reminds me of her. On the outside, she's all pretty and polished, but underneath she's got lines and scars like everyone else." *I used to wish I could fly....*

"Maybe more," he added in a voice almost too low to be heard over the crowd. "She thinks she has to be this perfect employee. Like she's afraid if the world sees the real Sophie, she'll be some kind of failure. I wish she could see those flaws are what I love about her."

He paused. Love? Having never made such a declaration before to anyone besides family, he was shocked how easily the word slid off his tongue. Yeah, he loved Sophie. Had since that day they visited Nate. Fat lot of good it did him now.

Across the table, Mike continued studying him. Instead of his usual no-nonsense business expression, however, he wore a strange, almost contemplative expression. "Fear of failure can be a pretty strong motivator," he said after a moment. He raised his beer again. "Trust me, I know."

"I suppose." But Sophie, Grant hoped would be different. That she'd want to be different.

Why? a voice asked. Because he'd gotten her into his bed and convinced her to sleep in a few mornings? Talk about misplaced faith. No one was that good a renovator. Not even him.

He gave the fork another twist. "You want to hear ironic? When I called her on her behavior, she actually accused me of being the frightened one."

Mike looked to his pasta carbonara.

"You've got to be kidding me. Don't tell me you agree with her."

"I didn't say that."

He didn't have to. Annoyed, Grant tossed his fork down. It landed on his plate with a loud clank. "I can't believe this. You're both crazy."

Are they? a little voice in the back of his head asked, much to his irritation. *Where there's smoke there's fire.*

"If I'm so afraid," he said, challenging Mike and the voice, "why'd I take the job with St. Pierre?"

Again, Mike said nothing, apparently still fascinated by his pasta. "I don't know. Why did you?"

To avoid Sophie. The thought hit him like a ton of bricks. He'd been running away. "I thought you were glad I took the job."

"I am. I'm just wondering what made you reverse your position after two years hiding from anything remotely close to success."

This time Grant was the one staring at his food. "What can I say? I decided it was time to move on. You're the one who told me I had to stop blaming myself for what happened to Nate."

"Have you?"

No. Not really. Deep in his heart the fear he would become the man from the emergency room window still lurked. He was beginning to wonder if he would ever truly outrun him. Maybe if he had more in his life besides a job. Like Sophie.

An unreadable expression crossed Mike's face, one Grant had never seen before. "Look, I'm all for you finally letting go of your guilt. If you really are. If you aren't accepting one painful reality to avoid another."

Grant arched a brow. "No offense, but you sound like one of those afternoon television psychiatrists."

Mike shrugged. "I just want you to be happy, little brother, and you haven't been. Not in a long time. I'd blame Nate, but I'm not sure you were happy before that."

He'd been too busy to be happy, thought Grant. And then Nate had his heart attack and he'd been too guilty. Too scared.

Except for the week he spent with Sophie. If every week was like that week, he'd be over the moon.

Unfortunately, that ship had sailed and he'd helped launch it.

"You should talk to her," Mike said.

"Sophie?"

"No, the waitress. Yes, Sophie. It's obvious you're still nuts about her. Maybe she misses you, too."

Grant shook his head. "She made her choice."

"You sure? Like I said, fear makes people behave in weird ways. Some run away from work, others bury themselves with it. And some, didn't know their lives could have more than what they already have."

For the first time, Grant heard regret in his brother's voice. Perhaps the Templeton way hadn't been as kind to his older brother as he thought. Could he have misread the signs with Sophie, as well?

"You'll never know unless you try," Mike told him.

What do you know? Turns out his brother might actually have useful insight after all. "Maybe you aren't such a hard-hearted windbag after all," he teased.

If he'd underestimated his brother, had he underestimated Sophie, too?

"Besides," his brother added, signaling the waitress. "Since when did a Templeton not go after what he wanted?"

Grant sat back. Dammit if his brother wasn't right. Time he stopped running from things, and head toward them.

Gotta grab it. Otherwise you'll miss out.

The damn words were like a cadence the entire way home. *Gotta grab it. Gotta grab it.* Over and over until by the time Sophie reached her living room she wanted to scream, "I get it! The coat was Grant!"

Okay, she'd let something special slip through her fingers. She'd mistakenly believed that she had to stay a certain course and that any detour was wrong. Her psyche didn't need to beat it into her head. Besides, Grant was in Philadelphia. It wasn't as though she could do anything with the lesson except log it for next time.

If there was a next time. Grant really was like the coat. One of a kind and unlikely to be repeated.

She flopped on her sofa, not caring if she was sweaty and disheveled. Grant had liked her that way. He'd wanted the Sophie with the flaws. A person she didn't think anyone could want.

And she loved him. Of all the realizations to hit, that hit the hardest. Sure, she'd said things like loved and lost, but it dawned on her that she really loved him. Like forever, I-don't-care-if-you're-twenty-nine-or-ninety-nine love.

Oh, man, she was the biggest idiot on the face of the earth. Soon to be the loneliest idiot on the earth. As if she could be any lonelier. She already missed Grant like she missed breathing.

Somewhere in the middle of her pity party, she heard the sound of footsteps on the stairs and the sound of a door closing. Her heart stopped. It was Saturday. Grant was home.

Sophie sat up. When she was a kid, did she feel sorry for herself or did she pull herself up and get away from Pond Street? Exactly. So why was she lying around feeling sorry for herself now?

In a flash, she was on her feet and heading to Grant's door. He was going to listen to her and hear her out whether he liked it or not.

Clearing the last few steps, she ran to his door and knocked.

Her shoulders slumped. No answer. Same as the first time she knocked.

Face it. Grant wasn't home. She'd been so certain when the realization hit, she heard the footsteps but didn't think about the fact they might not be Grant's. She sank to the floor. What now? Camp out until he got home? What if he was on a date?

Oh, God, what if he showed up with some pretty young thing and saw her sitting here by his door like some lonely stalker?

Maybe this was a bad idea. The best thing would be to go downstairs and think out a plan of action.

No. Plans are what got her in trouble in the first place. She was going to sit right here and wait. Though wasn't that in itself a plan?

The sound of knocking interrupted her internal debate. Took her a moment, but she realized the pounding came from her apartment. Pushing herself back to her feet, she walked to the top of the stairway.

Grant stood at the bottom.

Sophie's breath caught. He looked as handsome as ever, his shoulders broad and strong. Shoulders Sophie knew now were perfect for leaning against. And his eyes, caramel and sparkling with surprise. How had she thought her world would be all right without those eyes?

"The coat was gone," she said, coming down a few steps.

"What?"

"The coat was gone," she repeated. As statements went, she could have done better, but her brain was too scared to think of anything but grabbing hold of what she really wanted. "I went back to the flea market and someone else had bought it. The vendor told me you have to move fast if you see something or risk losing out. Especially if you see something you really, really want."

He looked at her, confused. "What are you talking about?"

"I didn't know," she told him, risking another step closer, "because I didn't realize then what I know now.

"See, you're the coat. Took me a long time and a whole lot of wasted shuttles to Boston before I understood what I really and truly needed. And it's not being managing director. I thought when I got the job, I'd feel more secure. Safe. I don't."

"Wait, back up. You got the job?"

That's right, he didn't know. She nodded.

"Congratulations."

"Don't bother. The job is lonely. I spend all my days on the road. I haven't slept in my own bed for more than two nights since I took the job. Even when I do sleep at home, it's not the same."

"I know what you mean."

She glanced up through her lashes. Her vision was blurring. "I bought this co-op because I wanted the home I never had. Thing is, the only time it really felt like a home was that one week we were together. I want that back, Grant. I want to come home and share my day with you, have coffee in the morning and listen to you tease me about all the frozen pizza I've stored in the freezer. I want to spend my weekends procrastinating over my to-do list and soaking in your big tub while you complain about modern design."

Grant blinked. His caramel-colored eyes glistened, even though there was no sunlight. "Do you mean that?"

"Uh-huh. I was an idiot for not realizing sooner. Truth is, it doesn't matter how much younger you are than me or what you do, or what I do. Only thing that matters is being with you. I love you, Grant Templeton. I don't know how it happened or why or what it means to you, but I love you. And I'd like us to have a second chance. Please."

She took another step. "I don't want to lose you."

Unless she already had. His silence was beginning to scare her. Sophie's heart began to crumple. Too little, too late. She'd taken too long to realize what she had.

"You were right—no good ever comes out of tunnel

vision. If you're willing to give us a second chance, I swear I'll remember and never—"

That's as far as she got because Grant leaped up the last few stairs and pulled her tight, his mouth claiming hers in one swift movement. They stumbled sideways, arms wrapped around one another, until they found the wall. There they grasped and clung to one another, neither able to get close enough. It was a kiss of mutual possession, of mutual need, of mutual surrender.

Eventually Grant broke away to breathe and Sophie found herself looking into hooded eyes that glowed with an emotion she was too nervous to name. She needed to hear the words said aloud.

"I love you, too, Sophie. That's why I was banging on your door. I was so focused on not repeating my mistakes, I made the same ones again. I forgot to fight for the person I cared about."

She pressed her fingers to his lips. "Grant..."

"No, no, let me say this." He kissed her fingertips. "I should never have walked away from you that night. I should have grabbed you and told you what I was feeling then and there. You were right, it was my ego. And fear."

"We were both scared, Grant. I still am," she admitted, a shiver running down her spine.

"Me, too. But I'm not avoiding it anymore."

He smiled and Sophie warmed from the inside out. "And I'm going to take the risk," she said, sealing the promise with a long intimate kiss.

Grant brushed his nose against hers. "I really do love you, Sophie Messina. I think I have from the second you accused me of stealing your water."

"I promise I'll never accuse you of that again."

"Hope not, since I plan to be sharing that water with you."

He kissed her again. Gentler this time, with a promise of all the time in the world. Sophie lost herself in the moment, so much so she gasped when she felt her feet leave the ground.

"What are you doing?" she asked, only to realize Grant had swept her in his arms.

"Shh. I'm going for a romantic gesture. Don't ruin the moment."

"Sorry," she whispered. "Carry on." She laid her hand on his shoulder, amazed at how happy she was. Happier than she could ever remember. She really had come a long way from Pond Street after all, hadn't she? Of course, they still had a lot of issues to deal with. His job in Philadelphia. Her job in New York. Their age difference. What if he wanted kids? Not that she wouldn't mind carrying Grant's child. In fact, the thought actually made her heart jump a little.

"Sophie." Grant was looking down at her and reading her thoughts. He pressed a gentle kiss to her forehead. "We'll figure it out as we go."

Seeing the love reflected in his eyes, Sophie suddenly realized that, yes, they would. Closing her eyes, she rested her cheek against his heart, and let the man she loved carry her home.

EPILOGUE

"ARE you sure you want to do this?" Grant asked.

Sophie nodded. She sat on the kitchen counter, where Grant had dropped her following his arrival home. Her stocking feet swung shoeless against the cabinet. She'd left her shoes somewhere along the way; it was so hard to keep track when you're being carried and kissed senseless at the same time. Absence did make the heart grow fonder after all.

Although they weren't spending all that much time apart anymore, were they? "We don't have to do this," Grant continued. "You still have time to think about it."

"Nope. I have thought about it, and I love everything. Besides, I'm done with making plans, remember?"

"Really? I seem to recall a new master plan?"

Sophie rolled her eyes. He would tease her about that. A couple of weeks after their reunion, she'd decided that spending her weeknights in different hotel rooms was not satisfactory, particularly when Twamley Greenwood had an office in Philadelphia. And so, amid much teasing from Grant she embarked on creating a new master plan. This one had her marching into Allen Breckinridge's office and demanding a transfer. Turns out, Allen, king of the demands, actually responded to ones made of him, as well. Either that or Sophie really was his go-to gal because after some initial grumbling, he capitulated. Now, instead of jetting back and forth to Boston, she jetted back and forth to Philadelphia, and spent many more nights wrapped in peppermint-scented bliss.

"Just get the sledgehammer," she ordered him.

"As you wish." Opening the pantry door a little wider, he picked up the hammer and headed inside, only to poke his head out again. "You know that design-wise, we are breaking all sorts of rules."

"Stop it. This was your idea."

"Yes," he said with a sigh. "It was, wasn't it?" He disappeared into the pantry. A few moments later, Sophie heard a giant bang, followed by another, and then a loud crack.

"Did you break through?" she called out. Eager to see, she hopped down off the counter.

"Careful, there's splinters on the floor," Grant cautioned her when she peeked through the doorway. He was covered with white dust, and peeling away bits of plaster. "There you go," he said, grabbing a flashlight. "One secret passage."

Sophie followed the flashlight beam. Faintly, through the hole, she could make out the shape of the stairs. They were rickety and old, but they were intact.

"With a little bit of work, we'll have a real working staircase," Grant said, his smile glowing white in the dark space. "Our apartments will officially be connected."

Sophie smiled. "The way they should be," she told him. "The way they should be."

* * * * *

SOLDIER ON HER DOORSTEP

BY
SORAYA LANE

Writing romance for Mills & Boon is truly a dream come true for **Soraya Lane**. An avid book reader and writer since her childhood, Soraya describes becoming a published author as "the best job in the world" and hopes to be writing heart-warming, emotional romances for many years to come.

Soraya lives with her own real-life hero on a small farm in New Zealand, surrounded by animals and with an office overlooking a field where their horses graze.

Visit Soraya at www.sorayalane.com.

For my mother, Maureen.

CHAPTER ONE

ALEX DANE didn't need a doctor to tell him his pulse-rate was dangerously high. He pressed two fingers to his wrist and counted, trying to slow his breathing and take hold of the situation.

His heart thudded like a jackhammer hitting Tarmac.

If he didn't have such a strong sense of duty he'd just put the car in gear again.

But he couldn't.

He checked the address on the crumpled scrap of paper before screwing it into a ball again. He knew it by heart, had committed it to memory the day it was passed to him by a dying friend, but still he carried it with him. After all these months it was time to get rid of the paper and fulfill his promise.

Alex dropped his feet out onto the gravel and reached back into the car for the package. His fingers connected with the soft brown paper bag and curled to grasp it. He felt his heart-rate rise again and cursed ever having promised to come here.

It was everything he had expected and yet it wasn't.

The smell of fresh air—of trees, grass and all things country—hit him full force. Smells he had craved when he'd been traipsing across remote deserts in war zones. From where he stood he could only just make out the house, tucked slightly away from the drive, cream weatherboards peeking out from an umbrella of trees that waved above it. It was exactly as William Kennedy had described it.

Alex started to walk. Forced himself to mimic the soldier's beat he knew so well. He swallowed down a gulp of guilt—the same guilt that had plagued him on a daily basis ever since he'd set foot on American soil again—and clenched his hand around the package.

All he had to do was introduce himself, hand over the items, smile, then leave. He just needed to keep that sequence in his head and stick to the plan. No going in for a cup of coffee. No feeling sorry for her. And no looking at the kid.

He found himself at the foot of the porch. Paint peeled off each step, not in a derelict type of way but in a well-loved, haven't quite gotten around to it yet way. A litter of outdoor toys was scattered across the porch, along with a roughed-up rug that he guessed was for a dog.

Alex looked at the door, then down at the bag. If he held it any tighter it might rip. He counted to four, sucked in as much air as his lungs could accommodate, then banged his knuckles in fast succession against the wooden plane of the door.

A scuttle of noise inside told him someone was home. The drum of footsteps fast approaching told him it was time to put the rehearsal into practice. And his mind told him to dump the bag and run like he'd never run before. A damp line of sweat traced along his forehead as he fought to keep his feet rooted to the spot.

He never should have come.

Lisa Kennedy unlocked the door and reached for the handle. She smoothed her other hand over her hair to check her ponytail and pulled the ties on her apron before swinging it open.

A man was standing at the foot of the porch, his back turned as if she'd just caught him walking away. It didn't take a genius to figure out he was a soldier. Not with the short US Army buzz-cut, and that straight, uniformed way he stood, even when he thought no one was watching.

"Can I help you?"

Was he a friend of her late husband's? She had received

plenty of cards and phone calls from men who had been close to him. Was this another, come to pay his respects after all these months?

The man turned. A slow swivel on the spot before facing her front-on. Lisa played with the string of her apron, her interest piqued. The blond buzz-cut belonged to a man with the deepest brown eyes she'd ever seen, shoulders the breadth of a football player's, and the saddest smile a man could own. The woman in her wanted to hold him, to ask this soldier what he'd seen that had made him so sad. But the other part of her, the part that knew what it was to be a soldier's wife, knew that war was something he might not want to recall. Not with a face that haunted. Not when sadness was raining from his skin.

"Lisa Kennedy?"

She almost dropped the apron then. Hearing her name from his lips made her feel out of breath— winded, almost.

"I'm sorry, do I know you?"

He closed the gap between them, slowly walking up the two steps until he was standing only a few feet away.

"I was a friend of your husband's." His voice was strained.

She smiled. So that was why he'd been walking away. She knew how hard it was for soldiers to confront what another man had lost. She guessed this guy had been serving in the same unit as William and must have just been shipped home.

"It's kind of you to come by."

Lisa reached out to touch his arm, her fingers only just skimming his skin before he pulled away. He jumped like she'd touched him with a lick of fire. Recoiled like he'd never felt a woman's touch before.

She slowly took back her hand and folded her arms instead. He was hurting, and clearly not used to contact. Lisa decided to approach him as the stranger he was. A wave of uncertainty tickled her shoulders, but she shrugged it away. The man was nervous, but if he'd served with William she had to trust him.

Now that she'd had longer to study him, she realized how

handsome he'd be if only he knew how to smile, to laugh. Unlike her husband—who had had deep laugh lines etched into his skin, and a face so open that every thought he'd had was there for all to see—this man was a blank canvas. Strong cheekbones, thick cropped hair, and skin the color of a drizzle of gold, tanned from hours out in the open.

She put his quietness down to being shy—nervous, perhaps.

"Would you like to come in? I could do with an iced tea," she offered.

She watched as he searched to find the right words. It was sad. A man so handsome, so strong, and yet so clearly struggling to make a start again as a civilian.

"I… Ah…" he cleared his throat and shifted on the spot.

Lisa felt a tug at the leg of her jeans and instinctively reached for her daughter. Lilly hadn't spoken a word to anyone but Lisa since she'd been told that Daddy wouldn't be coming home, and clung on to her mother at times like she never wanted to let go.

The look on the man's face was transformed into something resembling fear, and Lisa had a feeling he wasn't used to children. Seeing Lilly had certainly unnerved him. Made him look even sadder, more tortured than before, if that were possible.

"Lilly, you go find Boston," she said, fluffing her daughter's long hair. "There's a bone in the fridge he might like. You can reach it."

Lisa looked over at the man again, who had clearly lost his tongue, and decided that if he was used to orders then that was what she'd give him. A firm instruction and a knowing look.

"Soldier, you sit there," she instructed, pointing toward the big old swinging chair on the porch. "I'm going to fix us something to drink and you can tell me exactly what you're doing here in Brownswood, Alaska."

Something flashed across his face, something she thought might be guilt, but she ignored it. He moved to the seat.

Lisa stifled a smile. When was it that you became your own mother? She was sounding more like hers every day.

This man meant her no harm, she was sure. He was probably suffering something like shell-shock, and nervous about turning up on her doorstep, but she could handle it.

Besides, it wasn't every day a handsome man turned up looking for her. Even if it was only sharing a glass of tea with a guy who didn't have a lot to say, she wouldn't mind the company.

And he'd obviously come with a purpose. Why else would she have found him on her doorstep?

Alex summoned every descriptive word for an idiot he could and internally yelled them. He had stood there like a fool, gaping at the poor woman, while she'd looked back and probably wondered what loony hospital he'd come from.

What had happened to the sequence? To the plan? He looked down at the paper bag on the seat beside him and cursed it. Just like he'd done when he'd first held it in his hands.

William had said a lot about his wife. About the type of person she was, about how he loved her, and about what a great mom she was. But he had sure never said how attractive she was.

He didn't know why, but it made the guilt crawl further, all over his skin. He'd had a certain profile of her in his mind. And it wasn't anything like the reality.

Maybe it was the long hair. The thick chestnut mane that curled gently into a ponytail. The deep hazel eyes framed by decadent black lashes. Or the way her jeans hugged her frame and the tank top showed more female skin than he'd seen in a long time. A very long time.

Then again, the fact that she was minus the pregnant belly he'd been expecting might have altered his mindset too. Would he have even noticed her figure if he hadn't been searching for the baby? Alex knew the answer to that question. Any man would. Lisa was beautiful, in a fresh-faced, innocent kind of way, and he'd have to be cold-blooded not to notice.

So had she lied to her husband about the baby she was expecting? Or had Alex lost track of time and the baby was already born?

Alex went through the plan in his mind and cursed ever coming here. He hadn't introduced himself. He hadn't smiled. And he hadn't passed her the bag or refused to stay.

His assessment? He was a complete dunce. And if the kid had any instincts whatsoever she'd probably be scared of him too. He'd looked at her as if she was an exotic animal destined to kill him.

When he'd been deployed it had been all about the plan. He had never strayed from it. Ever.

Here, one pretty woman and a cute kid had rendered him incapable of even uttering a single word.

Or perhaps it was glimpsing family life that had tied him in knots. The kind of life he'd done his best to avoid.

Alex looked up as he heard a soft thump of footfalls on the porch. He took a deep breath and made himself smile. It was something he was going to have to learn to do again. To just smile for the hell of it. Sounded easy, but for some reason he found it incredibly hard these days.

But he needn't have bothered. The only being watching him was of the four-legged variety, and he beat Alex in the smile stakes hands down. He found himself staring into the face of a waggy-tailed golden retriever, with a smile so big he could see every tooth the canine owned. He guessed this was Boston.

"Hey, bud," he said.

As he spoke he realized how stupid he must sound. He had been tongue-tied around Lisa, yet here he was talking to her dog.

Boston seemed to appreciate the conversation. He extended one paw and waved it, flapping it around in midair. Did he want Alex to shake it?

"Well, I'm pleased to meet you too, I guess."

A noise behind him made Alex stop, his hand less than an inch from taking Boston's paw. Lisa was walking out with a tray. He pretended not to notice the flicker of a smile she tried to hide. At least he was providing her with some afternoon entertainment.

She placed the pitcher of iced tea and a plate of cookies on the table in front of him.

If he'd felt like an idiot before, now he felt like the class clown.

"I see you've met Boston," she commented.

Alex nodded, a slow movement of his head. How long had she been standing there?

"He's well trained," he finally said.

Lisa laughed. It caught Alex by surprise. It seemed like forever since he'd heard the soft tinkle of a woman's happiness.

"Lilly likes to teach him tricks. You could say he's a very fast learner." She tossed the dog a broken piece of cookie. "Especially when there's food involved."

They sat there for a moment in silence. Alex fought for the words he wanted to say. The bag seemed to be staring at him. Pulsating as if it had a heart. He knew he could only make small talk for so long until he had to tell her. It had been eating away at him for months now. He had to get it out.

She pulled over a beaten-up-looking chair and sat down in it. He watched as she poured them each a glass of tea.

"I'm guessing you served with my husband?"

He had been expecting the question but still it hit him. Gave him an ache in his shoulders that was hard to shrug.

Alex allowed himself a moment to catch his words. Talking had never really been his thing.

"Lisa." He waited until she was sitting back in her chair, nursing the tea. "When your husband returned from leave, we were assigned to work together again."

He fought to keep his eyes on hers, but found it was easier to flit between the pitcher and her face. She was so beautiful, so heartbreakingly beautiful, in a soft, unassuming way, and it made it harder to tell her. He didn't want to see the kind features of her face crumple as he described the end. Didn't know if he could bear seeing this woman cry. Seeing those cracked hazelnut eyes fill with tears.

"We became very close during that tour, and he told me a lot about you. About Lilly too."

"Go on," she said, leaning forward.

"Lisa, I was there with him when he died." He said those words fast, racing to get them out. "He passed away very quickly, and I was there with him until the end." He eliminated the part about how the bullet should have been for him. How William had been so intent on warning Alex, on getting him out of harm's way, that he had been shot in the process. *Always putting his men first.* That was what the army had said about him. And it was a statement Alex knew first-hand to be true.

He looked back at Lisa. He had expected tears—uncontrollable sobbing, even—but she looked calm. Her smile was now sad, but the anguish he had worried about wasn't there.

Her quiet helped him to catch his breath and conjure the words he'd practiced for so long.

"Before he died, he scrawled down your address. Told me that I had to come here and see you, to check on you, and to tell you that…"

Lisa moved from her seat to the swinging chair, her body landing close to his. He could feel her weight on the cushion, feel the heat of her so close to him. This time when she reached for him he didn't pull away. Couldn't.

He turned to face her.

"He told me to tell you that he loved you and Lilly. That you were the woman he always dreamed of."

Now she did have tears in her eyes. A flood of wetness threatening to spill, overflowing against her lashes. She gave him a small, tremulous smile.

"He said that he wanted you to be happy," Alex finished.

Alex felt a weight lift as he said the words—words that had echoed in his head from the moment he had been told them— as if he had been scared that he might forget them. Words that had haunted him.

"Typical," she said, tucking one foot beneath her as she dabbed at her eyes with the back of one finger. Her other hand left his arm. He could feel the heat of where it had been. "He goes and leaves me, then tells me he wants me to be happy."

Alex looked away. He didn't know what comfort he could offer.

Then his fingers touched the bag.

"I have some things of his," he said. "Here." He passed it to her and another feeling of relief hit him. It felt so good to finally pass it on to her. The guilt would have eaten him alive had he not gone through with this. And he didn't need any more guilt to live with. He was carrying enough already.

He felt her sit up straighter.

"What's in here?"

"Some letters, a photo of Lilly, and his old tags."

"He asked you to give these to me?" she pressed.

Alex nodded.

"Have you read them?" she asked, her fingers already clasped around the cluster of papers inside.

"No, ma'am."

She slipped them back into the bag and leaned forward to place it on the table.

"My husband trusted you to come here, to visit me, and I don't even know your name," she said lightly.

Alex stood.

"Alex Dane," he said, arms hanging awkwardly at his sides.

"Alex," she repeated.

The smile she gave him made him want to run. Even more so than earlier, when she'd opened the door. This woman was supposed to be grieving—unhappy, miserable, even. Not kind and smiling. Not ponytail-swishingly beautiful.

He had been prepared for sadness and she'd thrown him.

"Thank you for the tea, but I'd better get on my way," he announced abruptly.

"Oh, no, you don't," she said.

He grimaced as she grabbed a hold of his wrist, but didn't let himself resist.

"You're staying for dinner and I won't take no for an answer."

He let himself be frog-marched toward the front door and fought not to pull away from her.

He should never have come.

A set of blue eyes peeking out from beneath a blonde fringe watched him from the end of the hallway. The smell of baking filled his nostrils. A framed photo of William smiled down at him from the wall.

He was in another man's house. With another man's wife and another man's child. He had stepped into someone else's life and it wasn't right.

But, even though he knew it was wrong, he felt strangely like he'd arrived home.

Not that he should know what a home felt like.

Lisa filled the kettle and set it to boil. Despite his odd behavior, she felt at ease with Alex in her home. It wasn't like she had a lack of visitors—ever since she'd heard the news of William's passing she'd had family and friends constantly dropping by. Not to mention her sister, acting as if she was a child needing tender care. It seemed she always had an excuse to drop past.

And she'd had plenty of soldiers visit. Just not for a while now.

She glanced over at Alex. He was sitting only a few feet from her, yet he could have been on the other side of the State. There was a closed expression on his face, and she was certain he was unaware of it. From what she'd read about returned soldiers there were many who never recovered from what they'd seen at war. Others just needed time, though, and she hoped this was the case with Alex. She could feel that he needed help.

Part of her was just plain curious about him. The other more demanding side of her wanted to interrogate him about William's death, and about what it was that troubled him. She guessed she had some time to ask questions, but how much could she ask him over one afternoon and dinner?

"Do you take sugar?"

She watched as he looked up at her, his gaze still uncertain.

"One sugar. Thank you."

She spooned coffee granules into each cup, added sugar, then poured the now boiled water. Lisa could feel him watching her, but she didn't mind. There was something oddly comforting about knowing that he'd been with William at the end.

She cleared her throat before turning around and passing him his coffee. She noticed that his eyes danced over her body, but she had the feeling he wasn't checking her out. It was more as if he was making an assessment of her, looking for something.

"I don't have a handgun on me, if that's what you're worried about." She laughed at herself, but he didn't even crack a smile. Instead his face turned a burnished red. She felt an unfamiliar flutter herself. Maybe she'd been out of the game for so long she didn't even know when a man *was* checking her out! It felt weird. Not uncomfortable, but not exactly something she was ready for. Although now she'd obviously made *him* uncomfortable. "I'm sorry, Alex. I was joking."

He looked away. "I'm just confused, that's all."

She raised an eyebrow in question.

Alex sighed and clasped the hot mug.

"William mentioned you were expecting another baby."

Uh-huh. The penny dropped. She almost felt disappointed that Alex *hadn't* been sizing her up, but then she guessed it wasn't really appropriate for a widow to get excited about another man anyway. It was just that she hadn't seen her husband for such a long time, and it had been months since his passing, and she...wanted to feel like a woman again. Not just a widow, or a mother, or a wife. Like a woman.

It didn't mean she didn't love her husband. She did. She had. So much. She blinked the confusion away and smiled reassuringly at Alex, knowing how uncomfortable he must be, saying something like that. It wasn't like she owed him an explanation, but the guy had traveled from heaven only knew where to visit her, to fulfill some dying wish of William's, and she didn't mind sharing. Not if it gave him some peace of mind before he left and went back to his own family.

"I fell pregnant when William was home on leave. I had an inkling and took an early test the day before he left."

Alex was still blushing. She guessed he wasn't used to talking pregnancy and babies with another man's wife. But he'd asked.

"I lost the baby during my first trimester, but I couldn't quite figure out how to tell William. He was so excited that we were finally having a second child, and he was unsure about being away again. I didn't want to let him down. But then he died, so he never knew." Lisa paused. "If I hadn't lost the baby it would have been born a couple of months ago."

She took a sip of coffee and then gazed into the liquid black depths of it. It was still hard talking about William, knowing he wasn't ever going to be coming back, but she was dealing with it. She felt like the deepest grieving was over, but sometimes it was still hard. Sometimes the sadness was…trying.

"Sorry. Time kind of gets away from you when you're away," he said.

Lisa nodded.

"Were you right in not telling him what had happened to the baby?" he asked.

Alex's question surprised her. He wasn't accusing her. Nor offering an opinion. It seemed he was just asking it the way he saw it.

"Yeah, I think so." Her voice sounded weak even to her own ears. "I'm glad he died thinking that I was going to have a baby to love. That Lilly would have a brother or sister."

She hadn't talked about her miscarriage to anyone, really. Not even her mother. It felt good to get it out, especially to someone who wouldn't make a fuss or make the pain of it come back to her.

Alex didn't respond. He'd wanted to know but she guessed he hadn't banked on hearing that.

"I'm sorry. I mean, I'm just…"

"Not sure what to say?" she finished for him, trying to put him at ease.

"Yeah."

She nodded. Her usual response would be to touch, to reach for the person she was talking to. But she stopped herself. Alex wasn't her usual company, and she needed to give him space.

"Would you like something to eat?"

He shook his head. "No, don't go to any trouble."

Lisa rolled her eyes at him, getting used to his short answers and lack of expression. "I write cookbooks for a living. Believe me when I say that fixing you something to eat is not going to put me in a tailspin."

She placed her hands on the bench and caught a smile on Alex's face. Not a big smile, just a gentle curling of his lips at each corner and a dance of something she hadn't seen in his eyes earlier. A lightness that had been missing before.

"You'll have to battle it out with Lilly, though. That girl eats like a horse," she said wryly.

Alex chuckled. A deep, sexy baritone kind of a chuckle that finally made Lisa feel like they were having an adult, woman-to-man kind of conversation.

"I'm hungry, but I don't think she'll be much competition."

They grinned at one another and Lisa hollered for her daughter.

"Lilly! Time for a snack."

A cacophony of feet on timber echoed down the hallway. She watched as first Lilly appeared, then Boston, his tongue hanging out the side of his mouth. They were inseparable, those two. Best friends.

She placed a glass of milk on the counter to keep her daughter busy while she dished out the goodies.

"Would you like to say hello to our guest?"

Lisa knew it was highly unlikely, but the therapist had said to act like everything was normal. To ignore her not talking and just behave as usual—as if she was still speaking to people besides her mother and the dog.

Lilly shook her head, but she wasn't as shy as she'd been. She climbed up onto the third stool, leaving the one in the middle empty, her eyes wide and fixed on Alex.

"This is Alex," Lisa told her. "He was a friend of Daddy's."

That made Lilly look harder at him. Her big eyes searched his face intently.

Lilly smiled and gave him a little wave.

"Hi," he said.

Lisa was more shocked at hearing Alex talk, albeit mono-syllabically, than if Lilly had spoken! "Alex is a soldier," she explained.

Lisa glanced at Alex and saw how uncomfortable he looked at being so thoroughly inspected by a child. Back straight, pupils dilated, body tense. She guessed if you weren't used to the curiosity of a child it might come as a surprise. Did he not have a family?

She left them both looking at one another and opened up the pantry. Lilly would guzzle that milk in no time and start wriggling for something to eat. Everything was neatly stacked before her—jars and containers filled with all sorts of goodies. She made Lilly eat plenty of fruit and vegetables at other times, but a mid-afternoon snack was their one daily indulgence and she loved it. Lisa reached for her homemade brownies and iced lemon cake, putting the containers within reach and placing an array of each on a big square white plate.

"I hope you have a sweet tooth, Alex. This will have to do for the meantime."

He still looked like a nocturnal animal caught within the web of a bright light, but she ignored it.

"Are you planning on staying in the area?" She pushed a plate of baking toward him.

"Ah…depends on what the fishing is like. I hear it's pretty good," he said awkwardly.

"You're a fisherman, then?"

She watched as he finished his mouthful, Adam's apple bobbing up and down.

"I just like to look out at a lake and fish. You know—take time out. It's more about the sitting and thinking than serious fishing," he acknowledged.

Oh, she knew. It was exactly why they'd bought this house in the first place. Was he camping out alone? After being away on tour she'd have expected he'd want to be with his family. With friends.

Lisa moved away to locate some napkins and stopped for a heartbeat to look out the big kitchen window. The water seemed to lull her, made her feel like anything was possible as she briefly stared into its depths. She'd never really liked fishing, but she loved to think, to just sit and stare at the water. When she'd heard the dreadful news that her husband had died, that was exactly what she'd done. For hours every day.

Lilly tugged at her arm. She hadn't even seen her slip off the stool. Lisa bent down so Lilly could cup her hand around her ear.

"Tell him we have lots of fish to catch."

She smiled and nodded at her daughter.

"Tell him," Lilly insisted.

The little girl hopped back on her stool and smiled at Alex. He looked confused.

"Lilly wants me to tell you we have lots of fish here."

"Fish?"

Lilly nodded while licking at her fingers, devouring what was left of the brownie. Then she reached, slowly, for Alex's hand. She gave it a tap and jumped down.

Alex looked from Lilly to her.

"I…ah…think she wants you to go with her. To the lake."

Lisa held her breath as Lilly stood, looking expectantly up at Alex. If she didn't know better, she'd have thought his hands were shaking. He didn't move, his eyes flitting between her and her daughter, but then slowly he shifted his feet and drew himself up to his full height. He towered above Lilly. Like a bear beside a bird.

"Okay," he said uncertainly.

Lilly reached for his hand and tugged him along, and all Alex could do was obey. He looked like a placid cattle beast being led off to slaughter, but Lisa wasn't going to step in and save him.

It was the first time Lilly had interacted with a stranger in a long while. Lisa didn't care how uncomfortable their guest was. This was a major turning point. Lilly hadn't spoken to him, but she'd definitely wanted to communicate.

There was no way she was going to intervene. She couldn't.

Lisa nodded at Boston to go with them, then held her breath. Alex was either going to bolt at the first chance or respond to Lilly, and for both their sakes she hoped it was the latter.

He was a stranger, so she knew how odd it was, but deep down she hoped he *would* stay for dinner. So they could talk about William. About the war. She felt a bond with him, knowing that he'd probably spent more time with William than she had in the past couple of years. It was an opportunity she didn't want to miss.

Besides, although she'd never admitted it to her family, she was kind of lonely. At nights, mainly. She always had been, but at least she'd known one day it would be a house she would share full-time with William. That one day in the future she would have him home every night for dinner.

Lisa put down her coffee with a shaky hand and decided to change her mind and follow them after all. It wasn't that she didn't trust this Alex with her daughter, she just wanted to make sure it wasn't too much for Lilly. Or for Alex.

Right now she was Lilly's chief interpreter. And besides, she was curious to see how this unlikely pair were going to get along down by the lake.

CHAPTER TWO

"Has Lilly always been quiet?"

Alex glanced at Lisa as they turned back toward the house. They'd been walking along the river, back and forth, Alex throwing a stick out into the water, Lilly clapping her hands and wrestling it back from Boston the moment he retrieved it.

It wasn't like he'd asked Lilly much when they were alone—he didn't even know what to say to a child—but she seemed very quiet for a little girl.

"She's been virtually mute with everyone but me since William died."

Alex nodded thoughtfully. "How old is she?"

"Six."

He'd wanted to know whether the little girl was able to speak or not, but he didn't want to talk about it. He knew what it was like to have a rough time as a kid, and it wasn't a place he wanted to go back to, even in talking about someone else. When he'd joined the army he'd tried to leave all those memories, those thoughts from his past behind.

"She's having a good day today, though. I thought she'd be too shy to be around you but she's not at all," Lisa said.

Alex liked that the girl wasn't afraid of him, but he didn't want to get involved. Didn't want to bond with anyone. Not even the dog.

"Boston seems pretty protective of her," he commented.

That made Lisa laugh. He wanted to jump back, to walk away from her. It all seemed too real, too normal, to just be talking like this after so long thinking, wondering how he was going to cope seeing her, and now to hear her laugh like that…

"That dog is her best friend. I don't know what we would have done without him. Worth his weight in gold," she told him.

They kept walking. Alex didn't know what to say. Part of him wanted to get in the car and drive—anywhere, fast, just to get away—but the other part of him, the part he didn't want to give in to, wanted to stay. To be part of this little family for a few hours, to see what William had lost, to know what his friend had sacrificed to let *him* live.

"Come on, Lil, let's go back inside."

She came running when her mother called, but Alex knew deep down that her being so quiet wasn't right. He hadn't exactly had much experience with children, but he knew that she should be squealing when the dog shook water on her, yelling back to her mother when she called. Instead she smiled quietly, not obviously sad or grieving, but obviously mourning her father in her own silent way.

He wished he didn't know what she was going through, but he did.

The army had been his only family for years. It had been the source of all his friendships, the place where he had a home, his support.

So he knew exactly how alone a person could feel.

Lisa rummaged in the fridge to find the ingredients she needed. It was going to be an early dinner. The only way she had been able to relieve Alex from being Lilly's sidekick was to order them both inside because it was almost dinnertime. Now she had to rustle something up. Fast.

She thought about the times William had returned from duty. He'd always been ravenous for a home-cooked meal. Hadn't often minded what it was, so long as it resembled comfort food. The type they missed out on over there in the desert.

"How long were you on tour this time, Alex?" she queried.

He was back sitting on the bar stool, casually flicking through one of her older cookbooks. He looked up. She could see a steely glint in his eye. Got the feeling it was a back-off-and-don't-talk-about-the-war kind of look emerging.

"Months. I kind of lost count," he finally admitted.

She didn't believe it for a second. Her husband had always known exactly how many days he'd spent away each time. Had probably been able to work out the hours he'd been away from home after each tour if he'd had a mind to.

"You been back awhile, or fresh off the plane?"

There he went with that look again. "About a week."

It was like a wall had closed, been built over his eyes, over his face, as soon as she'd started talking about the army. She could take a hint. There was no reason to pry.

"Well, I'll bet you're hankering for a nice home-cooked meal, then."

He nodded. Politely. She was desperate to ask him more. Why he wasn't sitting right now with his own family having a meal. What had made him come here to visit her so soon after he'd arrived home.

She wondered at how he and William had gotten on. They were so different. Alex was quiet and guarded—or maybe that was just a reaction to her questions. Her husband had been open and talkative. Forward.

But she knew from all the stories he'd told her that it was different at war. That men you might never have made friends with, men you ended up serving with, became as close to you as a brother. She hoped it had been that way with Alex and him.

She began peeling. Potatoes first, then carrots.

"I think what you need is Shepherd's Chicken Pie."

He smiled. A half-smile, but more open than before.

"Want to give me a hand?"

He nodded. "Sure."

"Would you mind slicing those potatoes for me? Knife's just in the drawer there. And then put them in the pot to boil."

Alex slipped down off the chair and moved to join her. She should have suggested it all along. Even if he wasn't sure what to do, keeping him busy and not interrogating him was probably the best way to help him relax and eventually open up a little about William.

She was desperate to hear some stories. If only the task didn't feel quite so similar to drawing blood from a stone!

"When you're finished there you can take over the dicing here, and I'll pop out back to pick some herbs," she instructed.

His arm moved slowly back and forth, his other hand holding the vegetables in place as he cut them. She'd never thought about it before, but the way a person cooked, prepared food, showed a lot. Her, she made a mess and enjoyed herself, when it came to family cooking especially, but Alex was meticulous. He sliced each ingredient with military precision. If she stepped closer, she'd bet she'd see that every piece of carrot was diced to exactly the same dimensions.

He was a soldier. The way he moved, held himself and carried out tasks, marked him as army. It comforted her.

William had been similar in many ways. Not exactly like Alex, but the soldier aspects still made her think of him.

"You all right there for a moment?" she asked him.

He stopped slicing and looked at her. She could see a softness in his gaze now, a change that showed her she'd been right to just give him a task and leave him be.

"Sure."

Lisa served the pie. The potato top was slightly browned, the gravy running out over the spoon as she manhandled it into three bowls.

"Lilly, why don't you take yours into the TV room? You can watch a DVD."

Her daughter nodded eagerly. Lisa hardly ever let her eat away from the table, but tonight she wanted the luxury of chatting openly to their guest.

Lisa passed her a smaller bowlful, and then set the other two on the table.

"I really can't thank you enough, Alex. For coming here to see me."

He quickly forked some pie into his mouth—so he didn't have to answer her, she guessed wryly.

"I've had plenty of soldiers drop by, but none for a few months. Still the odd call sometimes—to check up on me, I guess—but not many house calls." She paused, but he didn't respond. She tried again. "William didn't often tell me the names of his soldier friends. Well, he called them by their last names, so I kind of got lost."

"Yeah, that's army for you," he muttered.

She took a mouthful of dinner herself, and gave him time to finish some more of his.

"The time you spent together—did you…ah…get along well?" she pressed cautiously.

His lips formed a tight line. His face was serious, eyebrows drawn together. His entire body rigid. She'd pushed him too far, too soon.

"Ma'am, I…" He stopped and took a breath. "I'm not really one for talking about what happened over there."

She felt embarrassed. She should have known better. It was just that she felt like they only had a few hours together and she wanted to hear everything. Was curious to find out more.

"I'm sorry, Alex. Listen to me—interrogating you when you've come here out of kindness," she apologized.

He put down his fork. "I don't mean to be rude, I just…"

"I understand. My husband was a talker—he liked getting everything off his chest," she explained.

They both went back to eating. The silence that was suspended between them felt knife-edged.

* * *

He knew she wanted him to open up, but he couldn't. It just wasn't him. And what could he say? *Yeah, William and I got on real well while we knew each other. Before he took a bullet intended for me. Before he died trying to save me.*

The food was great. He did appreciate it. But she was treating him like the good guy here. What would she think if she could actually see what had happened over there? Could watch it like a movie before her eyes and see William dive into the line of fire to cover *him*?

He forced more food down. Anything to put the memories back on hold.

"Where's home, Alex? Where do your family live?" she asked.

Alex felt a shudder trawl his backbone. He fought the tic in his cheek as he clamped his jaw tightly. He didn't want to talk about his family. Or lack of. He didn't want to talk about why he didn't have a home. "I don't have a place at the moment," he bit out tersely.

"But what about your family? They must be excited to have you back?"

He shook his head.

Lisa watched him, her eyes questioning, but to his relief she didn't ask again. He didn't want to be rude, but there were some things he just didn't want to talk about.

She didn't need to know he was an orphan. He didn't need any sympathy, pity. Lisa was best not knowing.

"Well, I'm glad we were able to have you for dinner," she said after a long pause.

"I promised William I'd find you." He looked up, braved her gaze. "I set out as soon as I was debriefed."

She nodded. "Well, I certainly appreciate you coming here."

"Great food, by the way. Really good," he said stiltedly.

It didn't come easy to him. Just chatting. Making small talk. But he didn't want to get on the topic of family again, and she was making a real effort for him. It wasn't that he didn't appreciate it, he just wanted to keep certain doors firmly closed.

"I'm going to check on Lilly. Help yourself to more," she offered.

Lisa pulled the door to Lilly's room almost shut, leaving it so a trickle of light still traced into the room, and wiggled her fingers at her. She'd read her a story, kissed her good-night, then turned the light out.

She heard Alex down in the kitchen. He might have been in the army for years and be as quiet as a mouse, but he was well trained. He'd cleared the table and started the dishes all before she'd scooted Lilly upstairs to bed.

"You don't need to do that." She swallowed her words as soon as she saw the kitchen. The counter had been wiped down, the dishwasher light was on, and the sink was empty. He'd even fed the dog the leftovers.

He shrugged. "It's the least I can do."

She didn't know about that. He'd traipsed from goodness-only-knew-where to get here, brought things to her that meant the world, and started to cheer up a six-year-old who was undergoing serious counseling for trauma. Lilly had been happy and bubbling when Lisa had marched her up to bed.

"Alex—stay the night. Please. It's too late for you to find somewhere in town," she said.

He looked uncomfortable. She wished he didn't. A frown shadowed his face. Whatever it was that was troubling him was firmly locked away. She'd seen it written on his face tonight at the table.

"I really appreciate the offer, but you've already cooked me dinner and…"

"Don't be silly."

The man seemed to have no family. Or none that he wanted to talk about. No place to go nearby anyway. She wasn't exactly going to turf him out. Not after what he'd done for her. Not when he'd been the man to give William comfort as he died.

"Lisa, I didn't come here expecting accommodation," he said abruptly.

She put her hands on her hips. "No, you came from miles away to do something nice for a stranger. It's me who feels like I owe you."

He had that awkward look again. On his face, in the angles of his arms as they hung by his sides. He looked up at the clock on the wall. It was getting late. "Are you sure? I can pitch my tent out back."

Lisa laughed. "Oh, no, you won't. Come on—I'll show you the guestroom."

Alex hesitated. "I've got my camping gear…"

"Don't be silly. The bed is made. You can get a good night's sleep. Come on," she said firmly.

He didn't look entirely comfortable about the situation, but he didn't argue. She smiled.

Resigned acceptance traced across his face. "I'll…ah…just grab my things from the car."

Lisa went to flick the switch on the kettle. She reached for an oversize mug and stirred in some of her homemade chocolate.

By the time he reappeared, duffle bag slung over his shoulder, she had a steaming mug of hot chocolate waiting for him.

"This is for you," she said, passing the cup to him before walking off.

She led the way up the stairs. She didn't turn, but she could hear him following. The treads creaked and groaned under his weight, as they had done under hers. She led him to the third bedroom and stepped aside so he could enter.

His big frame seemed to fill the entire room. The spare bed looked too small for him. She stifled a laugh. He looked like a grown-up in a playhouse.

"Just call if you need anything. Bathroom's the last room down the hall."

He nodded.

"Well, good night then," she said.

"Night," he replied.

Lisa pulled the door shut behind him. And walked away.

The image of him standing forlorn, bag over one shoulder and hot chocolate in hand, stayed with her, though.

She went back down the stairs, careful to avoid the noisy steps, and flicked off the lights. She reached to switch on a lamp instead.

The paper bag Alex had given her rested on the side table. Her fingers took ownership of it. Lisa found herself wondering whether the bag had come with Alex from war or if it was something he had put the items in after he'd arrived home.

She tipped out the contents. A crinkled photo of Lilly fell on to her lap. Lisa retrieved it and held it up to the light. Lilly was maybe four years old in the shot. Her blonde hair was caught into a tiny ponytail, and she was sitting on the grass.

Lisa remembered the day well. William had been between postings. They'd had an entire summer together—probably the best summer of her life. Lilly had been entertaining them right up until that moment, when she'd gotten a bee sting.

It had been William she'd run to for comfort. It always had been when he'd been home. Like she wanted to spend as much time with her daddy before he left as possible.

Lisa put the photo back on the table. She reached for William's tags this time, and slung them around her neck. The cool hit of metal chilled her chest, but she didn't remove them. Instead she let her left hand hover over them. Feeling him. Remembering him. Loving him.

Then she took the letters out. There were three of them in total. She guessed he had been waiting for an opportunity to send them.

Her heart skipped when she unfolded the first one. Saw his neat, precise writing as it filled the page.

To my darling wife.

He'd always started his letters the same way. He hadn't been one of those soldier husbands who'd been macho and brave with his family. He'd always told her he loved her on the phone, whenever he'd been able to call, regardless of how many men surrounded him. They'd always been close.

Lisa bit the inside of her lip as a wave of tears threatened. Her bottom lip started to quiver and she pushed her teeth in harder. But every word she read, every sentence that pulled her into his letter, made more tears form, until they rained a steady beat on her cheeks.

She could taste them as the salty wetness fell, trickling into her mouth.

William had died months ago, and in the year before that she'd only seen him once—the six weeks he'd spent at home on leave.

But when she read the words he had so lovingly penned for her it made her feel as if they'd never spent any time apart at all. As if he was in the room, his warm body tucked behind her on the sofa, whispering the words in her ear.

They'd been best friends, her and William. Friends before they'd become lovers.

They were friends first—that was what they'd always said to one another. Friends because they would do anything for one another, comfort one another and support one another through anything. Friends because they didn't want to hold one another back or stop the other from doing what they wanted.

And as his friend she had a strange feeling that he wouldn't be nearly as upset about the tiny flare of attraction she had briefly—very briefly—felt for the man staying upstairs as most deceased husbands would. He was so different from William, but Alex reminded her in so many ways of him. Made her pine for her husband all over again.

William had always said to her, every time he'd left to go back offshore, that if anything ever happened to him she was to move on and be happy. That she wasn't to grieve and stay in a black hole of sadness.

It wasn't that she wanted to move on. Not yet. Not at all. She just didn't want to feel guilty for being mildly attracted to another man. A flicker of attraction, nothing more, but still something she had wanted to chastise herself for at the time.

With Alex upstairs, she didn't want to feel unfaithful to William. Because she *had* felt a stirring within herself. She couldn't lie. There was no denying it. He had made a tiny beat pound inside her chest.

He was a troubled soldier. She was a widow.

But it didn't mean she couldn't appreciate that he was an attractive man.

Was it right that she'd asked him to stay the night? She hoped so. From his lack of response earlier, it was obvious he didn't have anywhere else to go.

And she'd never turn a friend of William's away.

CHAPTER THREE

LISA watched through the window as Lilly tripped along the lakefront, looking over her shoulder every few steps to check that Alex was following. The child had dragged him outside as soon as they'd finished breakfast, and he'd been forced to accompany her. She wasn't talking to him, but her expressions said a million words. Boston trotted along behind, his nose tipped to sniff the air.

Lisa moved away to put her coffee mug in the sink, and stopped for a heartbeat to look out the other, larger kitchen window. The water twinkled at her, comforted her. Then a tree, waving, caught her eye. Made her glance at the little cottage only just visible.

She tried not to smile.

That was it!

She had always believed in destiny, and as the cottage peeked back at her an idea hit her.

It was the perfect solution.

It would give Alex time to fish, and she could get to know the man who had seen her husband gulp his last breath and try to help him.

She looked at the cottage again. When they'd first moved here they'd talked about doing all sorts of things to it. Turning it into guest accommodation…making it into a studio for her to write in. But in the end having strangers to stay for a bit of extra money had worried her more than anything, and the last thing she'd want would be to work on her recipe books away from the kitchen.

The last time William was home they'd had a poke around out there. Dumped some old boxes and wiped some cobwebs away. Then they'd decided it would be for Lilly—as a playhouse while she was young, and as a teenage retreat for when she was older.

They had called it a cottage, but it wasn't really worthy of the name. Maybe a cabin was more fitting? There was one large room that doubled as the living and sleeping quarters, plus an old bathroom and a measly kitchenette.

Alex caught her eye. He glanced into the house at her. She raised a hand in a wave. He didn't smile back, but she saw recognition in his eyes. Like he was reaching out to her.

He was afraid.

She decided to go out and rescue him.

She was no therapist, but she could tell when people needed healing, and Alex Dane needed a lot of rest and recovery.

So did Lilly.

Lisa just had to convince him to stay.

Alex felt lost. It wasn't that he didn't like it here—the place was magical. A silent lake bordered the property, and it felt as if it belonged exclusively to this parcel of land. But he could see it was huge in size. The neighboring properties would border it too. And on the other side a huge state forest or something equally large loomed.

But even though the place felt magical he still felt uncomfortable. It had been so long since he'd been around people who weren't soldiers. So long since he'd been able to just relax, act like a normal human being.

He looked back to the house again and saw that Lisa was outside now, walking toward him. She was hard not to watch. There was an openness, a kindness about her face that seemed to draw him in. But these days that kind of face was more terrifying to him than armed insurgents. It made him more nervous, more unsure, than any wartime scenario.

"You like it out here?" she asked as she approached him.

He looked back at the water. "It's pretty special."

She moved to stand right next to him. He didn't look at her.

"I've lived in Alaska all my life, and when I saw this place I knew I'd live here forever," she said wistfully.

He envied her that—having a place to call home all your life. He'd moved from town to town into different foster homes before he'd been old enough to escape that life. Having a house, a place, anything that remained the same, was something he'd always wished for.

"You mentioned you wanted to do some fishing?" she prompted.

Alex nodded. He hooked his thumb over his shoulder to point. "I've got my rod, a sleeping bag and some camping equipment in the car. Thought I'd just see where the wind took me for a while."

He could feel her eyes roving over him. It made him feel uncertain.

"But you were planning on staying in Alaska?"

He shrugged. Perhaps.

Lisa turned away and started walking. He didn't want to watch her but he couldn't help it. She had tight jeans on that hugged her legs, ballet flats covering her feet, and a T-shirt that skimmed her curves. He swallowed a lump of…what? It had been so long since he'd felt attracted to a woman that he didn't know what to think.

He ground his teeth. What he had to think of was that she had belonged to someone else—to the very man who had taken a bullet for him. And she was also someone's mommy.

He determinedly averted his gaze.

"Alex, there's something I want to show you."

His head snapped up. Maybe if he'd been better at sticking to the plan he wouldn't be torturing himself like this.

Still, it would be rude not to follow her.

He started to walk. Then stopped when he saw her standing at the foot of a hodge-podge-looking cabin perched behind a cluster of low trees. He hadn't even noticed it before. Although if you weren't looking it wasn't exactly visible for all to see.

Lisa pushed at the door, and he watched as it slowly fell open. She stood back and gestured to him with one hand. "Come have a look."

He obeyed. He had no idea what he was looking for, but he had a scout around with his eyes. The interior was dim. Light filtered in through grubby windowpanes, it smelt a touch musty, and there was an old bed lying forlorn in the corner.

He looked at her for an answer.

She smiled. "If you're looking for a place to bunk down for a while, we'd love to have you."

Alex looked from Lisa, where she stood on the grass outside still, back into the cabin. Stay? Here?

She must have seen the scared rabbit look on his face.

"I mean, just until you figure out where you want to go. A couple of weeks, perhaps?" she offered gently.

He kept staring at her incredulously. He couldn't help it.

"It's not that I wouldn't want you to stay in the house. I just thought you'd prefer some space," she went on.

He shook his head. A slow movement at first that built up to something faster. "Lisa, I…"

"No, don't refuse." She ignored his frantic head-shaking and started to walk back toward the water. It was only meters from the cabin—so close you could practically swing through the trees and land in it.

She swung back around to face him. "I need to fix the cottage up, and it's not like I'm ever going to be able to do it myself. Please. You can stay, fish, help me out, then move on once it's done."

He didn't know what to say. It wasn't that he didn't like the idea of staying here. The place was great. But how could he take up this kind of hospitality knowing that her husband wasn't coming home because he'd chosen to save Alex's life? How could he look at that little girl every day and know that he was the reason she wasn't going to see her daddy ever again?

"I can't stay." His voice was gruff but resolute.

"Alex." She moved closer to him. He saw her hand hover, as though she was about to touch him, and then she crossed her arms. Perhaps she'd already sensed he was damaged goods. "Please. It would mean a lot to me."

Until he braved telling her the truth.

He ignored the familiar trickle of guilt. It had followed him his whole life, was something he was used to living with. But he still recognized it.

"I don't..." He clenched his fists in frustration at not knowing the right thing to say.

She waited patiently.

"You don't want me here," he finally gritted out.

She looked surprised. This time she did reach for him.

He tried to ignore the flicker within him at her touch. There was something too intimate, too close, about seeing her fingers over his forearm. He didn't want to be touched by her.

"I *do* want you here," she insisted. "To be honest, I'd appreciate the company. And fixing this place up was meant to be William's task once he came home."

He fought not to grind his teeth. There was the guilt again. If William hadn't sacrificed his own life for Alex's he'd be here, home, attending to the cabin himself.

"Think on it. If you do decide to stay you'll be helping me out, and you'd have somewhere to fish," she wheedled with a smile.

Her grin was infectious. He didn't know when he'd last wanted to laugh, but she was having some sort of effect on him.

"I don't know," he muttered, but he saw a flicker of something cross her face. She knew he was cracking.

"Just say you'll think about it," she insisted.

He nodded. Just a hint of a nod, but she didn't miss it.

"You think it'll take just two or three weeks to fix this place up?" he asked warily.

She nodded, a gleam of obvious triumph in her eyes.

Alex sighed. It wasn't like he had anywhere else to go. And he owed it to her to help out. "Okay, I'll stay for a while," he said.

"Great!"

He still wasn't completely sure about it, but at least he could do something for her. He had no plans. No direction. He'd just wanted to give her William's things and then spend some time alone. Find himself. Think.

He looked around. The water twinkled at him. The trees seemed to wave. The cabin looked sturdy, albeit rundown.

There were plenty of worse places he could have ended up.

Besides, it was just a few weeks.

"It feels like the right thing, you know, having you here for a while. Makes me feel like part of William is here with you," she said softly.

"Thanks, ma'am. I really appreciate it." He did. Even if he found it hard to show. Foster care did that to you. Stripped you of emotion. Besides guilt and anger, that was. The army hadn't helped much either.

She just smiled.

"I'll make sure to stay out of your way," he added.

Lisa shook her head. "You don't need to stay out of my way. But you might want to stay in the house again tonight, until we've had a bit of a tidy up in here."

He nodded his agreement.

"Come on—I'll show you around," she offered.

Alex fell into step beside her. "You been here a long time?"

Lisa slowed so their steps matched. "We moved here before we were married. It's the kind of place you find and never want to leave."

He liked that. The idea of having a place that you knew would make you happy for life.

"You have a place that you want to settle now that you're a civilian?" she asked.

He shook his head politely, but it was hard to unclamp his jaw to find words.

She glanced at him. Made eye contact briefly. He read her face, knew that she hadn't meant to make him uncomfortable.

"I grew up here. Alaska born and bred," she continued.

Much better. He could listen to her talk all day so long as he could keep his own mouth shut about his past. Some things were better left forgotten.

Like where he was from. Family. And why he had no one in his life besides the army. Army life *was* family life for him. It was virtually all he'd ever known.

Lisa didn't know quite what to feel. Had she pushed Alex too hard? The last few hours had passed pleasantly, but she was worried about forcing him if he wasn't ready.

Maybe she had been a touch insistent. But that was beside the point. He needed a place to stay—somewhere to just be himself and work through the issues he'd brought home with him.

She could do with the company, and Lilly could do with whatever it was that Alex did to her. Her face hadn't lost the shine it had enjoyed all morning. Not a word had been said, but her actions had been more than obvious. The girl was happy and, lately, that was rare.

Alex was a mystery, though. Why did he have nowhere to go? No family? At least none that he wanted to talk about?

She hoped he'd tell her. Eventually. But she only had a few weeks to coax it out of him—unless he decided to stay on longer. But the flighty look in his eyes told her that staying put was not part of his plan.

Alex hacked at the over-hanging branches as if they'd done him some serious harm in the past. He had acquired a good pile already. A body of leaves, branches and debris littered the ground beside him.

It felt good to work up a sweat.

The morning air was coolish, but nice against his hot skin. His stomach was growling for breakfast but he ignored it. Even when it hissed and spat like a cougar.

Yesterday he'd had mixed feelings about staying. Issues about hanging around. But this morning everything seemed different. Maybe it was the good night's sleep—his first in a while—or maybe the fresh air was doing something to him, but he just felt different. And it was good to be doing something positive.

It was still unnerving. Being around William's family. Staying in another man's house. But William was gone now, and Alex had made him a promise. He might have fulfilled that promise, passing William's widow the items and telling her the words, but what kind of man would he be to come all this way and not help a woman in need? He owed it to the man. Owed him his life, in fact.

Even without this drawing them together, making him feel closer to William even though he had passed away, he and William had shared a bond. They had been in the same small unit more than once, and being posted to the places they had been sent meant they'd shared a kind of trust that was hard to explain. It was what made being here even harder—because he knew how much William had cherished what he'd left behind to serve his country.

Alex might have lost his family young, but honor and integrity were high on his list of morals. Of values. He knew how different his own life might have turned out if he'd had his family, if he hadn't lost everything as a child. Even the memories he'd clung to all these years didn't make up for what he'd lost. So he knew how important this little family was.

Lisa and Lilly only had each other now, and if she wanted the cabin fixed up he was happy to be of assistance. It was *his duty* to be there for them, to serve them.

Part of him hoped that staying, doing what he could, would help him put some demons to rest. But even if it only gave him peace of mind for a short time it would be a welcome reprieve from the guilt he had lived with of late.

He looked up at the cabin. It was shabby, there was no denying it, but it was habitable. Plus the view was incredible. Deciding to stay here might be the best decision he'd made in a long time.

He was officially discharged from the army, and he had no idea what he wanted to do. There was enough money in his savings account to keep him going for a while—a very long while—and he didn't want to start anything until his head was clear.

He just wanted to work with his hands. Fish. Chill.

And preferably not get too attached to his host family if he could help it.

"Morning."

He looked up. Lisa was watching him. She was dressed, but she still had that early morning glow. Her hair was wet, hanging down over her shoulders, leaving a damp mark on her T-shirt that he could see from here. She was nursing a cup of something hot.

"Morning," he replied. He reached for his own T-shirt, tucked into the back of his jeans, and tugged it on.

"You've been busy," she remarked.

He stepped back and looked at the mess he'd made. "Too much?"

She laughed. "I don't think any amount of work in or around that cabin could be called too much."

He wasn't used to casual chat with a woman anymore, but he was starting to warm to her. She was so easy, so relaxed. As if she expected nothing from him. Yet he knew she'd expect more. An answer. An explanation.

He swallowed the worry.

"You ready for some breakfast?"

His stomach doubled over in response. "I didn't want to go poking around in the cupboards."

She motioned with her hand for him to follow. "You're welcome to anything we've got here. Make yourself at home."

If only she knew how promising that sounded to him. Only he didn't really know how to make himself at home anywhere. Except in an army camp, perhaps.

"I hope you're hungry." She threw a glance over his shoulder.

"Yes, ma'am."

Lisa stopped and gave him one of those heart-warming smiles. "Good—because I've got eggs, bacon and sausages in the pan for you."

He'd never thought breakfast could sound so good.

"Oh, and Alex?"

He walked two beats faster to catch up with her step.

"Please don't call me ma'am again. It makes me feel like an old lady."

He sucked a lungful of air and fell back a pace or two behind her. And wished he hadn't. He had to fight not to look at the sway of her hips.

The term *old lady* hadn't crossed his mind when he'd looked at her. Ever.

Lisa patted the bacon down with a paper towel to absorb the grease and then placed it on a large plate. She saved a rasher for herself, and slipped the spatula beneath the eggs to turn them. She hoped he liked them easy-over.

"Do I take all your work out there this morning as notice that you're definitely staying?" She didn't look over her shoulder, just continued getting breakfast ready. She thought he'd feel less pressured without her watching his face.

"Ah…I guess you could say that," he answered warily.

She pursed her lips to stop from smiling. "Excellent." She spun around and just about tossed the plate and its entire contents over Alex. "Oh!"

He moved quickly, grabbing the plate and steadying her with the other hand.

"Sorry. I was just…"

She felt a sense of cool as his hand left her upper arm.

"…going to help you with the plate," he finished.

Lisa felt bad that his tanned cheeks had a hue of crimson adorning them.

"Aren't you having any?" he asked in concern, looking at how much she'd given him.

That made her smile. She couldn't cook breakfast and not partake. "Just a small version for me."

She sat down at the table with him, her own plate modestly loaded. His hands hovered over the utensils.

"Please start," she told him, wanting to put him at ease. "Eat while it's hot."

He did.

She watched as he firmly yet politely pierced meat and cut at his toast, practically inhaling the breakfast. She wondered if she'd served him enough.

"I've got work to do today, so I'm not going to be any help to you out there," she said.

Alex placed his knife and fork on the edge of the plate and reached for his coffee. She forced herself not to watch his every move. Strong fingers curled around the cup and he wiped at the corner of his mouth with the other hand.

"Where do you work?" he asked.

She was pleased he'd asked. Maybe food *was* the way to communicate with a man after all.

"I work from home," she explained, rising to collect the toast she'd left cooling in a rack on the counter. She brought it back to the table. "As I mentioned before, I write cookbooks, so I'm usually trying out new recipes, baking things."

He swallowed another mouthful of coffee. "Right."

"And today I'm under pressure, because my editor wants recipes emailed to her by the end of next week."

He looked thoughtful. She opened a jar of homemade jam and nudged it toward him. Alex dipped a knife in and spread some on a piece of toast.

"Do you have to take Lilly to school soon?"

She shook her head. "Spring break." She sighed. "But she hasn't gone back to school since William died, so I've had to start home-schooling her."

Alex looked like he was calculating how long that was.

"I do my best, but I need to get her back there." She sighed.

"Have you tried therapy?" he asked.

She blew out a deep breath. "Yup."

She couldn't tell if he approved or not. For some reason his opinion mattered to her.

"I'd better get back out there," he said.

She rose as he did, and collected the plates.

"Thanks for breakfast," he added.

He looked awkward but she ignored it. "No problem. I owe you for taking on the jungle out there."

The look he gave her made her think otherwise. That he thought *he* owed *her*. The way his eyes flickered, briefly catching hers, almost questioning.

"You need a hand with those?" he offered.

Lisa turned back to him. To those sad eyes trained her way. "I'm fine here. I'll have lunch ready for later, but help yourself to anything you need. The door's open."

She watched as Alex walked out. His shoulders were so broad, yet they looked like they were frowning. He looked so strong, yet sad—tough, yet soft. As if he could crush an enemy with his bare hands, yet provide comfort to one of his own all in the same breath.

She wished there was more she could do for him. But something told her that whatever she was doing was enough for now.

Lisa looked out the window as he appeared nearby. He

reached for the ax and dragged it upward in the air before slicing through a tree stump. She felt naughty watching him. Indulging in seeing his muscles flex and work, seeing the tension on his face drain away as he started to gather momentum.

She would be forever grateful that he'd come all this way to give her William's things. It had given her some sort of closure. Made his passing more final, somehow.

The tags Alex had given her had been William's older ones—the more current ones had come home with his body—but she had taken comfort in wearing them.

This morning she had tucked them in her jewellery box, along with the folded letters and the photo of Lilly.

She had made a decision too.

To stop grieving. To be brave and take a big step forward.

William was gone. It had taken her a long while to admit that.

He'd been a great husband and an even better father. But he'd also been a soldier. And that meant she'd always known that this day, being alone, could come, and she had to face it.

The reality of being a soldier's wife was that you had to risk losing him. That you couldn't hold him back.

Well, she'd loved William with all her heart, but she'd also accepted that his being a soldier, facing live combat, could mean he could be taken from her.

And he had.

This was the first day of her new life as a woman dealing with life, accepting what had happened to her, and being the best mother she could be. Not a widow. The word was so full of grief, so depressing, and if she stopped thinking of herself that way it might make it easier to move forward.

She had loved her husband. In her heart she knew no one could ever attempt or threaten to replace William. He had been too special, too important to her.

But she did want to keep a smile on her face and try to be happy. If Alex's company helped her do that, then she wasn't going to feel bad about it.

CHAPTER FOUR

THERE was something nice about having a man in the house again. Although Alex wasn't technically *in* the house, having him in the cabin was equally as good.

She'd never felt nervous, exactly—not out here—but there had always been a certain element of unease that she'd never been able to shake. A longing to have a man at home every night. Someone to protect the fort. Someone in the window if you came home after dark.

It was stupid, but it was true. She was a woman and she liked to feel protected and nurtured.

The phone rang. She saw the caller identification as it flashed across the little screen.

Great.

Lisa had been avoiding her sister since Alex had arrived, but Anna wasn't someone who took to being avoided very well. Her mother? Well, she wasn't so bad, but her sister could be downright painful sometimes.

"Hey, Anna." She put on her best sing-song voice as she answered the phone. If Lisa didn't talk to her now, Anna would be likely to turn up here before dark to check on her.

"Hello, stranger."

Lisa could tell her sister was worried. She had that slightly high-pitched note to her voice. "Sorry, hon, I've just been flat out trying to get these recipes in order."

"You still need a life, though, right?" Anna said.

Lisa glanced out the window and spied Alex working on a cabin window. He was trying to force it open. Did having him here constitute having a life?

"Hmm, I know. I just want this book to be good."

"They're always good," her sister replied instantly.

The vote of confidence helped.

"How about you and some of the girls come by on Saturday afternoon for a tasting?" Lisa suggested.

"Love to. Want me to organize it?"

"Sounds good," Lisa agreed.

"Just the usual gang?" Anna asked.

Five women were plenty, Lisa thought. "Yup—and Mom."

She heard Anna flicking through what she presumed was her calendar. That girl knew what everyone was up to!

"Nope. Mom has that charity fundraiser meeting going on. I'll tell her you asked, though," Anna said.

Lisa tucked the phone beneath her ear and rinsed her hands in the sink. Her eyes were still firmly locked on Alex.

"You sure you're okay?"

Lisa nodded.

"I can't hear you if you're nodding," her sister said dryly.

Damn it! It was like Anna had secret cameras installed in the house!

"I'm fine. I just need to get all this sorted," Lisa told her.

"Need me to come by?" Anna asked.

"No!" she yelled. "I mean, no. I'm fine." The silence on the other end told her she hadn't convinced her sister. "Come by with the girls on Saturday afternoon. I just need some time and we'll catch up then, okay?"

As Lisa said her goodbyes and hung up the phone she felt guilty. She usually shared everything with her sister. Everything. And yet she had a very big something hanging around out back, staying with her for the next few weeks, and she had omitted even to mention it.

Lilly was marching back and forth outside, Boston at her

heels. She had a huge stick in her hand—one that Alex had no doubt cut down before she'd claimed it.

Lisa went about fiddling with quantities and ingredients, dragging her eyes from the window.

She couldn't deny that she liked what she saw. But then what woman wouldn't?

Alex walked inside with Lilly on his hip. He'd thought the dog was going to attack when he'd first picked her up, but after a few gentle words and a futile attempt to stop the kid crying he had hoisted her up and into the house.

But his feet had stopped before they'd found her mom.

Lilly's cries had become diluted to gentle hiccups. It was awkward, holding her so close, but he'd had little choice. It had been a very long time since he'd held another human being like that.

Lisa was swaying in time to the beat of the music playing loudly in the kitchen. Her hair was caught back off her face with a spotted kerchief, and she had a splodge or two of flour on her cheek. The pink apron added to his discomfort. It had pulled her top down with it, and she was displaying more cleavage than he guessed she would usually show.

And she still hadn't noticed them above the hum of the music.

"Huh-hmm." He cleared his throat. Then again—louder.

She looked up, lips moving to the lyrics. Her mouth stopped, wide open, before she clamped it shut.

Lilly burst into much louder tears as soon as her mother noticed her, and all Alex could do was hold her out at a peculiar angle until Lisa swept her into her own arms.

"Baby, what happened?"

The lips that had been singing and smiling only moments earlier fell in a series of tiny kisses to her daughter's head. Lisa nursed her as she moved to turn off the speaker that was belting out the tunes.

"Shh, now. It's all right—you just got a fright," Lisa crooned.

She hugged her daughter tight. Alex couldn't take his eyes off them. It tugged something inside him, pushed at something that he hadn't felt in a long while.

"How about Alex tells me what happened while you catch your breath?" she murmured.

He cringed. Taking care of kids wasn't his thing. This one might have taken a shine to him, but he had no experience. No idea at all. "I'm sorry, she just…ah…she fell from a tree. I should have been watching her. I…"

Lisa drew her eyebrows together and waved at him with her free hand. "She's a child, Alex. And she's *my* child. If anyone should feel bad for not watching her it's me."

A touch of weight left his shoulders. But not all of it.

"I was…"

"Enough." She put Lilly down and crouched beside her. "If you wrap children in cotton wool they can't have any fun. Tumbles and bruises are all part of being a child."

He swallowed. Hard. She was inspecting Lilly, checking her, but she wasn't angry.

"You're fine, honey. How about you go play in your room for a while? Take it easy, okay?"

Lilly was still doing the odd snuffle, but Lisa simply gave her a pat on the head and blew her a kiss.

"I'm sorry," he muttered.

"Alex! For the last time, it was *not* your fault. Do I look angry?" she asked.

He ran his eyes over her face. He had seen her look worried before, concerned, but, no, not angry.

She obviously wasn't like most moms.

"You're just in time to try a few things," she said, changing the subject.

That sounded scary. He followed her, then sat down at the counter. Same spot he'd ended up when he'd arrived.

"I want your opinion on this slice. And this pastry."

That didn't sound too hard, he thought.

She straightened her apron and wiped at her cheek. He was almost disappointed when the smudge disappeared.

"What's your book called?" he asked curiously.

She turned around, turning her wide smile on him. "I'm thinking *Lisa's Treats*, but my editor will probably have other ideas."

Huh? "Doesn't that bother you?"

She fiddled with a tray, then scooped a tiny pastry something onto her fingers.

"What?"

"Not being able to choose the title yourself?" he explained.

She raised an eyebrow before lifting the pastry to his mouth. He opened it. How could he not? She was holding something that smelt delicious in front of it.

"They know how to sell books. I just know how to write what's inside. Good?"

He swallowed. *Very good.* "Good," he agreed.

"Just good?" she probed.

That made him nervous. Hadn't she just asked for good? "Great?" he tried.

"Hmm, I'd prefer excellent." She whisked away, and then twirled back to him. "Try this."

Once again she thrust something into his mouth.

Oh. Yes. "Incredible."

"Good." She had a triumphant look on her face.

He was still confused, but he tried to stay focused on the food. If he didn't look at the food he'd have to look at her. And the niggle in his chest was telling him that could be dangerous. Very dangerous.

"And this?"

This time when she twirled around she had a spoon covered in a gooey mixture. It looked decadent. Delicious. Just like her.

"Last up—my new chocolate icing."

She leaned across the counter toward him. Too close. He

fought the urge to lean back, to literally fall off the stool to get away from her. Lisa's eyes danced over his. The connection between them scared him rigid.

He sucked air through his nostrils and tried to stop his hands from becoming clammy.

Lisa held the spoon in the air, waiting for him to taste from it. He gathered courage and obeyed, his face ending up way too close to hers.

"Good?"

He could almost feel her breath on his skin. Or was he imagining it? He raised his eyes an inch. She didn't pull away. There was a beat where he wondered if she ever would.

"Excellent." He was learning how to play this game. Praise at least one word higher than what she'd asked for.

"Okay—that's me done for the day, then," she announced briskly.

She walked away from him fast. Like she'd been burnt. The flush over his own skin was making him feel the same. He glanced around the kitchen. At the trays littered across the bench, the dishes piled in the sink and the ingredients scattered. Maybe it would be polite to help, but he needed to get out of here. Put some distance between them.

Yet still he lingered. Good manners overrode emotion.

"Want a hand with all this?" he asked tentatively.

She gave him a cheeky grin. "Want a hand outside?"

Alex shrugged his acquiescence. Inside, his lungs screamed.

"Great, then I'll leave this till later," she told him happily.

Two hours later Alex was still working outside while she tinkered inside the cabin. She flicked a duster around all the surfaces, before giving the bed a good thump and making it with the linen she'd brought out.

She liked having him here. Every hour that passed she couldn't help but think she'd done the right thing asking him to stay. It wasn't just the effect he had on Lilly, he affected her too.

All went quiet outside, and he appeared in the doorway. His body filled the entire frame.

"How you getting on out there?" she asked. She could see a line of sweat starting to make a trickle across his forehead. It made her gulp. He was…well, very manly. And it was doing something to her, if the caged bird beating its wings with fury inside her stomach was any sort of gauge.

"Getting there."

She used her head to indicate where the water was. He followed.

"Thinking it will take longer to get this place habitable?" she asked.

He shook his head.

If she'd just spent years at war, and years before that in army bunkers, she'd probably think the cabin wasn't half bad either. Lisa fiddled with the duster and then stopped. She pinned her eyes on him. "Alex, I was thinking—did you actually see…you know…how William died?"

His shoulders hunched. He stopped guzzling water like he'd just emerged from the desert and stayed still. Deathly still.

So he *did* know.

It didn't matter if he didn't want to tell her. She already knew William had died from multiple bullet wounds. She'd just always wondered *how. Why?* What had actually happened over there? Who had fired? For what reason?

He dropped to an armchair in the corner. Dust thumped out of it but he seemed oblivious to it. Lisa knew she'd been wrong in asking so soon, but she couldn't take it back. Not yet. Not now.

The question hung between them.

"We were…" He took a long pause before continuing. "I mean, we came under fire."

She sat down too. On the bed. Despite just having made it.

"They think there was one, maybe two guys waiting for us. Snipers."

She could see the torment on his face. The emotion of pulling memories to the surface again. But she wanted to know.

"I'm sorry. I can't talk about it." Alex jumped to his feet and walked out the door. Fast.

Lisa sighed. She should never have pushed him. It was too early to be asking him things like that. Things that didn't really matter anymore. Not when nothing could be done about it.

"Alex, wait." She rushed out after him.

Emotion seeped from him. She could see it. Feel it. Smell it. He practically radiated hurt and confusion as she walked slowly up behind him. He had one hand braced against a tree. The other hung at his side. She stopped inches away from him, her body close to his. She didn't touch him.

"I'm sorry, Alex. I had no right to ask you that."

In a way she was lying. She *did* have the right to know. But not yet. Not until he was ready to tell.

She stood there for a moment. Watching him. Waiting. "We need some ground rules. If you want to talk about what happened, you can—anytime." She paused. "But I won't ask you about it again."

She sensed relief from him. He swiveled—just slightly, but their eyes met. She understood. She still struggled with telling people that William was gone sometimes. Felt all alone and lost.

"When you're ready to talk, tell me," she reiterated.

He just stared at her. His eyes acknowledged her words with a faint flicker.

"Sound okay to you?" she pressed.

"Yeah." His voice lacked punch.

Lisa turned and went back into the cabin. He needed some tender loving care. There was obviously no one to give it to him. But she wasn't going to ask him about that either.

This had to be a safe place for him. A place where there was no pressure and where nobody asked him questions they had no right to ask. At least not yet. Not before he trusted her. Not until she had made him feel comfortable enough to talk. Not until he'd had time.

And she wanted him to hang around, so the last thing she was going to do was push him away. He made her feel close to William, somehow. Comforted her.

Alex lay on the bed. It was almost too short for him, but if he kept his legs slightly bent he fit fine. Besides, it wasn't the bed that was stopping him from falling asleep.

It was Lisa.

Every time he closed his eyes he saw her. Sometimes Lilly was there as well. But he saw Lisa every time.

When they were open he saw her too.

It was a no-win situation.

Today had been tough. The hard labor had done him good, fired him up and taken the edge off his turbulent emotions. But being in such close proximity to a woman he found so darn attractive had put even more strain on him.

He was guilty. Guilty as a man who'd just committed a crime. Guilty as a bird who'd just stolen a piece of bread. And he hated it.

When he'd agreed to come here, to visit William's widow, he'd formed a picture in his mind of what it would be like. She would be plain, pleasant, standing in the doorway with a child beside her and one hand on an extended pregnant stomach. She would fall to her knees crying as he said the words he'd rehearsed. He'd pass her the things, put one hand on her shoulder as comfort, then turn and walk away.

Turning back had never been part of the plan. Neither had getting caught up in the emotion of her pain.

But then he'd also banked on the guilt falling away once he'd fulfilled his promise. Rather than wishing the woman before him was his own wife and that he'd just arrived back home. Or that he could just die, then and there, and give her her husband back.

He felt the excruciating guilt again now, like a knife through his chest. Saw everything flash beneath his eyelids as if it was happening all over again.

He turned as William called his name. So fast, so quick. He looked up, tripped as William launched himself at him and threw him to the ground.

A round of bullets echoed just before they hit the ground, then more. Punching through the air. Then the wet, warm splatter of blood hit him in the face.

He opened his eyes and found William staring at him, gasping.

The sniper was gone. Silence thrummed through the air like it was alive.

He moved William off him, gently. Placed him on the ground, on his back, propping his head up and listening hard to his rasping words. William ordered him to take the photo in his pocket, scrawled the name and address of his wife, then whispered words for her. He told him where to find the letters he had waiting for her at camp. To give them to her. To find her. Then he took his last breath.

Alex sat up, exhausted from his own thoughts. He dropped his head into his hands. How had this situation become so complicated? He could get up right now. Get up and leave. Start driving and never look back. But could he? Really? Could he just turn his back on Lisa and Lilly now?

He knew the answer to that. He'd only known them such a short time, and yet he felt something between them. He and Lilly understood one another, even though they didn't talk. He didn't get what to do around kids a lot of the time, but he knew about loss, about heartache. Especially about losing a parent. Or in his case both.

A shudder ran down his back—the same shudder that always came when he thought about his parents. About the other time he'd been splattered with blood that wasn't his own.

It was as if he'd cheated death twice. As if the grim reaper had come for him and somehow he'd managed to avoid him.

Twice. His parents had been taken, his friend had been taken, and yet he was still standing. Why?

The image in his mind turned back to Lisa, and the feeling of sadness that had just ruptured inside him was replaced by harrowing guilt once again.

If he'd ever fantasized about the kind of woman he could settle down with, he knew the picture would have looked a lot like her. Beautiful, so beautiful, and yet so much more. She had a way about her—a way of looking at a person or situation with complete understanding. He'd been so impressed with how she'd handled Lilly's fall today. Careful, methodical in checking her, yet not allowing the child to make a fuss.

And she was dealing with her daughter's inability to communicate with others well too. She must feel worried, but she stayed calm. Treated Lilly as if nothing had changed.

Alex knew first-hand what being in Lilly's shoes was like, and he wished he had the courage to tell Lisa how well she was doing. That she was doing the right thing.

Lisa. Her name consumed his mind.

He was attracted to her. More than attracted to her, he realized. But he wouldn't act on it.

Couldn't.

If it wasn't for him her husband would be coming home after his term serving overseas. If it wasn't for him her daughter wouldn't be traumatized. Grieving.

But he wasn't going to run out on them.

He lay back down and squeezed his eyes shut.

If he wasn't entertaining such intimate thoughts about another man's wife, maybe sleep would have found him by now.

CHAPTER FIVE

LISA resisted the urge to swipe her finger through the lemon icing as she arranged the cakes on a tray. It was stupid, but she was nervous.

Before she ever sent a book away to her editor she always hosted an afternoon get-together, so it wasn't like she had first-time jitters. Besides, they were her friends coming over—not a bunch of strangers. But there was something about living in a small town that jangled your nerves when it came to gossip.

When you knew it was you who was about to become the center of it.

She shrugged off the worry and rolled her shoulders. The knot at the base of her neck didn't disappear, but she felt a touch more relaxed.

Her kitchen looked ready for some sort of fairy birthday party. Pink macaroons, swirls of lemon zest atop white icing, and just about everything chocolate a girl could want. She hoped it was enough to distract her sister from the man living in her cabin.

She reached for a mini-cake and took a huge bite. The sugar rush made her feel mildly better, but she still felt as if she was doing something illicit.

A tap at the door made Lisa swallow fast, lick the icing from her teeth and throw the rest of the cake in the trash. She heard footsteps echo down the hall.

It was her sister. The other girls would wait to be let in.

"Hi!"

Yes, definitely Anna.

I am a grown woman, she chanted silently. I have nothing to be ashamed of. I still love my husband. Alex is only staying because he has nowhere else to go. Because he can help me out.

"There you are." Anna passed her a bunch of flowers and kissed her cheek.

"You're early," Lisa said.

"Hardly." Anna ran her eyes over the food. "Looks delicious."

Lisa walked the flowers into the kitchen and dropped them on the counter. She reached for a vase and filled it with water.

"So, little sis, what's been happening?"

"Nothing." Lisa took a breath and turned the water off. "I mean…you know—just working on recipes, baking up a storm, that kind of thing."

"Huh."

She didn't like that noise. It was the noise Anna always made when she knew something was up. When she didn't believe her but was happy to let it lie. Temporarily.

Lisa glanced at the cabin and prayed that Alex wouldn't emerge. Or be anywhere within sight of the kitchen or lounge for the next hour.

"Lisa, I…"

A rumble of heels on timber followed by a knock saved her.

"Anna, be a gem and get the door, would you?"

Her sister paused, gave her a look, and walked out.

Lisa leaned against the counter and tried to calm down. This was awful. She'd never been good at secrets—especially not ones like this.

She forced herself to fiddle with the flowers, set the vase on the center island and took a final look at the goodies.

This was going to be a long, long afternoon.

* * *

"Lisa, this is amazing!"

"Mmm."

She grinned as her friends licked at their lips and reached for more.

"You know you *are* allowed to say when you don't like something," she said.

"Honey, you're the best. You know you are, or people would stop buying your books," Anna defended her loyally.

She leaned into her sister and laughed. "You're family—you have to say that."

Lisa looked up as she heard a noise. Please, don't let it be Alex. Surely he wouldn't have just changed his mind and walked in? She'd told him the girls were coming over, and his joining them had seemed to be less likely than him pouring out his heart to her.

"Mom!" She jumped to her feet. What was her mother doing here?

"Hello, darling."

Lisa looked at Anna. Her sister just shrugged.

"I thought you had a meeting today?" Lisa said.

"Turns out I managed to sneak away," her mother replied with a smile.

She smelled a rat. They had a group attack planned. She could feel it.

"Where's my granddaughter?"

Lisa watched as her mother folded her sweater over a chair and placed her handbag on top of it.

"Yes, where *is* Lilly?" Now Anna was looking around.

"She's just out playing with Boston. Looking for bugs, climbing trees." Lisa took a deep lungful of air and determined to slow her voice.

Nothing got past those two, though. While her friends kept nattering and sipping coffee, her mother and sister were watching her as if she was up to something.

"Oh—my—word."

Lisa's head swiveled to lock eyes on her friend Sandra. A crawl of dread trickled sideways through her stomach.

"Who is *that*?"

Lisa squeezed her eyes shut for a moment, then looked out the window. Every woman in the room had her eyes trained on the exact same spot.

At least he had his shirt on. The other day, when she'd caught a glimpse of his bare chest, she'd realized the sight was enough to send any woman crazy.

Alex was standing next to Lilly. The pair of them were side by side as he demonstrated how to throw the fishing line into the water. Lilly had her tongue caught between her teeth, was trying hard to mimic him, but the rod was almost as big as she was.

Lisa saw him as her friends would. Big, strong man, with shoulders almost as wide as Lilly was long. Muscled forearms tensing as he cast the line back and forward.

He bent over to correct Lilly's grip and almost ended up wearing a piece of bait in his eye. She started laughing. It took a moment, but Alex started too. They both stood there, this giant and his fairy, giggling.

Lisa had never seen anything like it.

Had Lilly even laughed like that once since she'd been silent? It looked so natural. Seeing Lilly respond like that to Alex was special. Very special.

"Huh-hmm."

Lisa realized where she was again.

"Yes, Lisa. Who *is* that man cavorting with your daughter?" her sister asked pointedly.

She decided not to turn to face Anna. "I wouldn't say he was *cavorting*, exactly."

She grimaced and waited for it. Sandra spoke before her sister had a chance to reply.

"I don't care what he's doing, but I wish he was doing something to me!"

That set the whole room off laughing.

"Enough, ladies, enough." Lisa pulled herself away from the window and faced the room. "He's just an old friend of William's come to visit. The last thing he needs is us ogling him. Besides, you're all married."

The women kept their eyes on the view.

"I'll get some more coffee," she muttered.

"And I'll help," snapped Anna.

Her sister grabbed her elbow and marched her to the kitchen.

She guessed that talking about the handsome man outside the window was non-negotiable.

Lisa chanced a glance at her sister's face.

Definitely non-negotiable.

But she didn't have to tell them that he was living in the cabin.

No way.

Lisa felt as if she'd been a very naughty girl. Hell, she was thirty years old, not thirteen, and yet somehow she was still cast as the little sister. Was that something she was stuck with for life?

"Start talking," Anna ordered.

She straightened her shoulders, evaded her sister's stare and filled the jug with water. "There's nothing to tell. I don't know why you're making such a fuss."

"Such a fuss!" Anna threw her hands in the air. "Lisa, you've been avoiding me for days, then I find out you've got a man here. Are you seeing him?"

She glared. "Don't you *dare* ask me that!" Lisa growled the words at her. How could Anna accuse her of seeing another man? Every beat of her heart reminded her she still loved William. She might be attracted to Alex, but she was not doing anything inappropriate.

Anna just shrugged.

Her mother walked in. "I've heard enough, girls."

They both kept their mouths shut. They knew better than to argue with her when she spoke in that tone of voice.

"Let Lisa explain."

Huh. So she wasn't exactly off the hook.

Lisa pulled out a seat at the counter and sat down. Her neck was aching, shoulders tense, and she was exhausted. Like she'd run a marathon twice over. "His name is Alex. He served with William and he needed a place to stay."

"Stay!" Her sister nearly exploded.

A sharp look from their mother silenced her.

"Yes, stay," Lisa repeated. "And don't go jumping to any conclusions."

Anna kept her mouth shut for once.

"It's nice he felt he could come here," their mother remarked calmly.

Lisa smiled at her mother. "He's got some…well, some traumas to work through, and it just seemed like the right thing to do."

Anna still didn't look impressed, but Lisa ignored her.

"I see Lilly's taken a shine to him?"

Lisa's face was hot and flushed. The last thing she wanted was for her mother to be hurt. Seeing her granddaughter laughing with a stranger, even if she wasn't saying any actual words to him, was tough. She saw plenty of her grandmother, had done all her life, but she'd been closed off to everyone but Lisa herself up until now.

Except for this stranger. Except for Alex.

"Come on—let's get the coffee out to everyone. They're probably still drooling out the window," Lisa said.

"You still should have told us."

They both turned to look at Anna.

"I mean, how long have you even *known* this guy?"

Lisa put a hand on her mother's arm and gave her sister a narrow smile. "He's not a psychopath, if that's what you're worried about." She put on her bravest face. "And I wasn't trying to hide him. I wouldn't have had you here today if I was worried about you seeing him."

"We might need iced drinks!" A shout from the living room made them all turn. "It's getting hot in here!"

Lisa prayed that Alex hadn't taken off his shirt. Heavens, she'd have the girls here all evening if he had!

Lisa shut the door with a satisfied bang and leaned against it. The timber felt cool against her back. She'd been naïve to think her friends seeing Alex would go down without some interest, but she had been surprised by her sister's reaction.

The fact that her sister was still in her kitchen wasn't helping either.

Her mother she wasn't so worried about. But Anna?

She had as good as idolized William. The two of them had always gotten on well, right from the beginning when Lisa and he had first started dating. Once they were both married they had double-dated, hung out together whenever William was home on leave.

Anna and her husband were Lilly's godparents. They were all best friends. But it didn't mean Anna had a right to judge her.

She was judging herself enough, without needing to worry about others doing it too. Every time she felt her eyes drawn to Alex. Every time she felt a dusting of attraction. It made her feel guilty. Unfaithful.

Where William had been chatty and bright, like an energetic ball of sunshine, Alex was brooding. Lost in thought. Closed.

But she couldn't help the way she felt. The way she wanted to help him. Nurture him. Be the one to bring him slowly from his shell. It didn't mean she wanted to move on. At least she didn't think so. Confusion danced a pattern through her mind.

"Almost done, dear."

She smiled as her mother crossed the hall. "Thanks."

"Are you feeling okay?"

Lisa nodded. Her mother walked a few steps closer. "You should have told us, Lisa, just for your own safety. But this is your home, and it's your life. William's been gone now for months."

"I'm not *seeing* Alex, Mom." She felt like she was going to cry. Felt unfaithful to her darling husband just having to defend herself.

"Maybe not. But it doesn't mean you shouldn't if you want to."

Lisa swallowed away her emotion and linked arms with her mother. She dropped her head on her shoulder as they walked. Why did it have to be so hard?

"Can you tell Anna that?"

"Does that mean you *are* dating him?" her mother asked.

She flicked her mother on the arm and they both laughed.

No, but it didn't mean she hadn't thought about it. No matter how much her stomach crawled with guilt and worry, she couldn't deny thinking about Alex like that.

"So, do we get to meet this man?" Anna asked waspishly.

Lisa tried her hardest not to roll her eyes. "His name is Alex." She put up a hand before Anna had a chance to speak again. "And, yes, you can meet him right now."

Her mother smiled. Encouragingly.

"I'm just going to pour them each a glass of homemade lemonade and…"

"I'll get some cake," her mother finished.

Lisa filled the tray.

"Come on, then," she said, beckoning with her head. "And go easy on him."

It wasn't that she was worried about how he'd react to them. She'd told him plenty about her family. But he didn't like being asked about his past. His family. Or about war zones. She had picked up on that pretty fast, and she had no intention of pushing him unless he was mentally ready for it.

"Do you think it's okay to leave Lilly with him?"

Lisa ignored Anna's question. Was it okay? The kid hadn't spoken or shown interest in anyone except her and Boston for months, and yet she had taken to this guy like a bear to honey.

And he was hardly likely to hurt her. The man was more frightened of Lilly than she could ever be of him!

Plus, Alex just gave off the right vibes. Sad? Yes. Emotional wreck? Check. But dangerous? Even if *she* had judged his character wrong William wouldn't have. Not after serving with him. If he trusted him enough to send him here, knowing that she'd be alone, then that was all that mattered.

She heard Lilly laughing. If she'd been alone she would have stopped to listen. Wondered at what Alex had said, or done, that she found so funny.

"Lilly! Boston!" Lisa called out to alert them. She didn't want it to seem like she was sneaking up on them. "Anybody hungry?"

Boston appeared first, leaping from the trees and landing on the path in front of them. He sported his usual big smile, tail wagging ferociously.

"Hey, Boston."

Boston was sprinkled with water and his big feet were covered in mud.

A shadow caught Lisa's attention. It was like an umbrella had been whisked across the path. She felt rather than heard Anna go silent. Lisa looked up. And locked eyes with her guest.

"Hey, Alex."

He smiled. Less reserved than the smile he'd given her the day he arrived, but still cautious.

"I wanted to introduce you to some of my family," she told him.

He looked wary. She didn't blame him. She couldn't see the look on her sister's face but she could guess at it. As if he was the enemy. As if somehow this man was to blame for William not coming home.

Lilly suddenly burst from the trees.

"Bost…"

The name died in her mouth as she saw the others.

Lisa gave her a big smile, put down the tray and opened her arms. Lilly didn't hesitate before running to her mother.

"Say hello to Grandma and Anna."

Lilly gave them a wave and a big grin, before turning her eyes back to Alex. If she were older, Lisa would have thought she had a crush on the man.

"Alex, this is my mother, Marj, and my sister Anna." She gestured with her free hand.

"It's lovely to meet you, Alex." Her mother came forward and reached for his hand.

Alex moved slowly. Lisa found herself holding her breath.

"Marj," he said, like he was trying her name out. "I've heard a lot about you."

Lisa practically felt the silent words of her sister hovering in the air. *Wish we'd heard a lot about you.*

"And, Anna," he said, before she could say anything first. "Nice to meet you too." He held out his hand to her.

Anna clasped it. Lisa tried to ignore the tightness of her sister's smile. The way her eyes seemed to question him.

"What brings you to Brownswood?" her sister asked.

Alex looked uncomfortable. There was no way Lisa was going to let him feel bad about being here. Not when he had obviously faced a big battle just turning up here to meet her. She interrupted. "Alex was kind enough to bring some of William's things to me," she explained. Lisa started to walk, giving Alex the opportunity of some breathing space. "He was with William…ah…before his passing."

She glared back at her sister. The news had done little to change the look on her face, but she could see her mother softening.

"That was very kind of you, Alex," Marj said.

He shrugged his shoulders. Lilly squirmed and wriggled in Lisa's arms to get down. She bent and released her.

Boston took up the game and raced after Lilly as she ran, blonde hair streaming out behind her.

Lisa stifled a gasp as she watched. Lilly had caught Alex's hand, just lightly, as she moved past him. Just a touch, just a glimpse of contact, but contact nonetheless.

He didn't react. Well, hardly. But she didn't miss the slight upturn of his fingers. He had made contact back. And she guessed her sister hadn't missed the closeness between man and child either.

"Alex, are you okay taking the tray?" Lisa asked.

He turned around. Embarrassment fell upon his face like a shadow over water. Only he had nothing to be embarrassed about. Lilly was reaching out to him. There was nothing wrong with that.

"Sorry, I…"

"Don't be sorry. I just thought you could take this to the lake while I see these guys off."

He nodded.

"Come on, ladies," Lisa urged.

Her mother didn't hesitate, but Anna gave her another pointed look before saying, "It was lovely to meet you, Alex. Hopefully we'll see you again soon."

They started to walk back to the house. Alex had obviously been a touch uncomfortable, but the meet hadn't gone down too badly.

"He's awfully quiet," said Anna.

Lisa didn't need a thesaurus to figure out the meaning there. Not like William, her sister meant. William who'd worn his heart on his sleeve and been able to natter with the best of women.

"He's just come back from war—isn't that right, Lisa?" Marj said gently.

She nodded at her mother.

"You'd best remember that, Anna, and give the man a break," Marj said.

Lisa sighed. Sometimes having your mom around was the best medicine. It didn't matter what her opinion, or her own view, she was always supporter number one.

"You don't need to see us out, dear." Her mother patted her on the shoulder as they reached the house. "Go enjoy your afternoon."

* * *

Alex sat beside Lilly. He was still struggling with the whole kid thing. Not that she wasn't great, but he just wasn't used to it. Not to the enthusiasm. Not to the unpredictability. Not to the inquisitiveness. And she managed all that without saying a word.

He watched as she bit into a pink cake. He had no idea what the little bite-size sugar rush things were called, but they tasted good.

He listened to footfalls as Lisa approached. He didn't turn. He felt like he was slowly becoming desensitized, but there were things he would never shake. The quietness of the lake, or a bang that could signal danger.

"Hey, there," she said casually.

He liked that about Lisa. It was as if she knew what he was going through—understood, almost.

Alex drew one leg up so he could turn to look at her.

"Good…ah…cake." He held up what was left of the pink item.

"Macaroon," she corrected, dropping to sit beside him. "It's a rosewater macaroon."

He couldn't help the grin that stretched his face. "Rosewater? What happened to plain old strawberry?"

She laughed and reached for a tiny iced treat herself. "Went out with the nineties."

He guessed she saw the confusion cross his face when she started hiccupping with laughter. "Kidding, kidding!" She put up her hand. "I'm just doing a trial on some different things. There's still plenty of room for good old-fashioned flavors."

Lilly stood up and wriggled between them. She glanced up from under her lashes at Alex before cupping Lisa's ear. Then she dropped her hand, like an afterthought, and sat back down.

"Alex is gonna help me catch a real fish tomorrow," the little girl announced clearly.

"Really?" Lisa asked, determinedly nonchalant, but catching Alex's eye meaningfully.

He could see she was trying to stay relaxed. Lilly had spoken out loud. Not to him directly. But definitely so he could hear. She had changed her mind on whispering privately to her mother and actually spoken aloud.

He watched. He couldn't not. There was something mesmerizing about observing the pair of them together. As if Lisa wasn't enough, the girl was enchanting. Especially when she spoke.

"I'm going to do what?" he asked, trying to encourage her to talk again.

Lilly gave him one of her crooked quirks of a smile and then ran, arms stretched out wide as if she might fly.

"Catch a fish!" she called out.

"Huh." He stared at the water, feeling the quiet lull as he stared into it. "If you don't catch *me* with the hook first."

He looked sideways at Lisa. It didn't seem to matter when he looked at her, what time of the day, there was always a trace of a smile turning the edges of her mouth upward. But today there was a big one.

Lilly skipped off.

"You were great with her today, Alex." She turned to him, suddenly serious.

"You saw us?"

She nodded. "It means a lot to me."

He didn't speak as she paused. He recognized it now—she was thinking about William, or the past, or worrying about Lilly.

"And did you notice her speaking just then?" Her voice was low, but it thrummed with feeling.

He grinned. "I know."

"She always understood why Daddy was away, but since the service, since I told her, she's just been…different."

"Like with the not talking?"

Lisa closed her eyes. He wanted to reach for her. To cover her hand. Brush his fingertips over the soft smoothness of her cheek.

But he didn't. It had been a long, long time since he'd touched someone like that. Known what it was like to do something like that so naturally. So long since he'd had someone to care about him. Or vice versa. The army might have been a great substitute family, but it was all about control and order. What he'd missed out on were the casual touches and gentle love of a real family.

So instead he just watched. Absorbed her sadness and stayed still, immobile, unable to comfort her.

"I get it," he said.

She opened her eyes and looked at him.

"It's hard to talk sometimes. Just give her time," he elaborated. He knew that first-hand. Years ago he'd been Lilly. Deep down, after all he'd lost and what he'd seen, he still was that quiet child inside.

Lisa reached for his hand. Gave him the comfort that she herself needed. He almost pulled away, but the gentleness of her skin on his stopped him. Forced him to halt.

"That's why she likes you. Because you understand one another. Somehow," she added wryly.

He looked back out at the water. He guessed she was right. He did recognize what Lilly was going through. Maybe she sensed that.

When he turned back, Lisa's eyes were still tracing his face. Openly watching him. As if she was trying to figure him out.

"Are you still taking her to the therapist?" he asked.

"Next week." Lisa bent her knees up and moved to stand.

She leaned close to him, because she had to rise, and he felt it. Felt the heat of her body, smelt the faint aroma of baking on her clothes.

He turned away.

"I'll see you inside," she said.

Alex gave her a smile but stayed still.

"Come on, Lilly!" she called. "Time to come in."

But even as she called, pulling away from him, he saw the look on her face. Her eyes flickered when they settled on him. Something passed between them that he didn't want to recognize.

He dragged his eyes away. He was on dangerous territory here and he knew it. There was no room in his life for complications. His entire past had been complicated enough to last a lifetime.

She was a widow. Confused. Still in love with her husband. Definitely not the type of woman he would ever take advantage of. Ever.

He'd built a wall around himself for a reason. And he needed to remember that the gate was destined to stay firmly shut. He didn't want to love or lose again. Ever.

CHAPTER SIX

His head was pounding. Alex was fighting feelings of wanting to run, and others of wanting to stay in this cabin his entire life. Being with Lisa yesterday had affected him. Being the recipient of her warm gaze, seeing the appreciation in her eyes, had just made him feel like a traitor. So guilty. Yet he couldn't bring himself to tell her.

Then Lilly had kept talking all afternoon, forgetting her silence, and that had made him feel worried all over again.

He could see her walking down the path to him now, skipping over like she hadn't a care in the world. He knew otherwise, but it was wonderful to see such a lightness within her.

"Hey, Alex! Wanna fish?"

Alex didn't want to go fishing, but she looked at him with the biggest, most innocent gaze imaginable, and he couldn't say no. Just hearing her speak directly to him had him tied in knots.

"Aren't you sick of fishing?" he asked.

Lilly shook her head fiercely before reaching for his hand. She gave it a couple of insistent tugs. "Come on, Alex. Let's go in the boat."

He should have just said yes to fishing. Now he had to get the boat out and spend the next hour or more with the kid. He usually wouldn't have minded, but today—well, he just wasn't in the mood. But he knew what a big deal it was, her coming out and talking to him like that.

"Okay, go ask your mother and then come back out," He instructed.

She skipped off. He wished he could be more like her. Truth was, he *had* been her—in a way. He'd been the kid with no voice, the kid who'd lost a parent. Only he had lost both. Had gone from having two parents to none in a matter of minutes. So he hadn't had a mom to coach and nurture him like Lilly had.

Alex looked up as a whine hit his eardrums. Boston was sitting maybe a few meters away, his head cocked on one side, watching him. Alex let his elbows rest on his knees, staying seated on the step.

Even the dog knew he was troubled.

"You don't have to hang around with me," he said softly to the dog.

Boston changed the angle of his head.

"Seriously, you don't want to know my troubles."

The dog came closer, sitting so near he almost touched Alex's feet. But he faced away from him now. Had his back turned to Alex, his head swinging around as if to check he was okay with it.

Alex let his hand fall to Boston's soft back. His fingers kneaded through his fur. The motion felt good.

He'd always wanted a dog. From when he was a kid to when he'd dreamed of the life he'd never had while away serving. Now he knew why. There was something soothing about having an intelligent animal nearby who wasn't going to judge you. A dog who knew the comfort his fur offered and turned to let you stroke it. An animal who knew when to stay with you and when to leave you alone.

"I don't know if it's harder being here, or harder thinking about leaving," Alex mused.

Boston just leaned on him. Alex liked this kind of conversation. The dog wasn't going to think badly of him. He was just going to listen. But it was true. He'd run from this kind of life, stayed away for this very reason for so long, yet here he was starting to think about what he'd sacrificed for being scared.

Lilly appeared. Her tiny frame a blur of pink clothing against the green of the surroundings. She raised her little hand in a half-wave as she ran back toward him.

Boston wagged his tail. It thumped Alex's foot.

"What did your mom say, kiddo?" he asked.

Lilly grinned. "She said to stop bothering our guest, but if he asked me I could go."

Alex laughed. She never failed to lift his mood, even if he didn't want her to. "I won't tell if you won't."

Lilly wriggled over to him and grabbed hold of his leg.

He was getting too attached to these two beings, not to mention the third one inside the house, and it scared him. But he felt happy. Actually happy. And it wasn't an emotion he felt often, so he wasn't going to turn his back on it. Not yet.

Lilly sat in the boat as Alex hauled it. She looked like a queen sitting in residence as he labored it over to the water.

"Faster, Alex!"

He gave her his most ferocious look, but she just laughed at him. It made him laugh back—a real laugh, the belly-ache kind of stuff. Until he tripped over as Boston launched himself in beside Lilly, landing square in the middle of the boat.

Lilly's peals of laughter forced him to push up to his feet. Fast. "That dog needs to learn some manners," Alex grumbled. He looked over his shoulder quickly, but to his relief he couldn't see Lisa anywhere. It made him feel better. Not quite as embarrassed to have been felled by a dog.

"Can Boston come fishing too?" Lilly pleaded.

Alex was going to glare a refusal at her, but he knew it would do no good. The child who had once looked at him warily, with big clouds of eyes, closed off from him to a large extent, was now completely immune to his reactions.

"Does he have to?" Alex groaned.

Lilly swung an arm around Boston and hugged the dog tight to her. The dog looked like he was laughing.

Alex could see the irony of it. He was a tough soldier, a man who had fought for years on foreign soil, but here in Alaska the dog was head of the pack.

"Fine," he acquiesced.

She resumed her queen position, with Boston as her king.

Alex guessed that made him the peasant.

Alex eyed Boston as he sat, tongue lolled out, focused on the water. He didn't trust the dog not to launch himself straight out into the water if he saw something of interest, causing the boat to capsize.

"Careful with that line." He placed his hand over the end of Lilly's rod. "Hold it like I've shown you, and carefully cast it over."

"Like this?"

A surge of pride hit him in the chest. She'd finally started to listen. "Good girl."

The smile she gave him nearly split her face in half.

He grinned back. He hadn't spent much time with children, but this little girl—she was something else. Teaching her, talking to her, was so rewarding when she listened or followed his instructions.

"Now we sit back and wait," he said.

She fidgeted. Waiting probably wasn't her favorite part. For him, waiting was what he lived for. The sitting back, feeling the weather surround you, thinking, losing track of time, it meant everything to him.

For kids? It was probably the worst part.

The water lapped softly at the edge of the rowboat; the wind whispered over the surface, causing a tiny rock. Boston lay asleep, and Lilly had tucked up close to Alex, leaning against him to stay upright.

"Lilly, I want to tell you a little story about what happened to me as a boy," he said.

It almost felt wrong to make the mood heavy—especially when she'd only just stopped yapping to him—but he wanted to help her. Alex hated talking about his past, and usually never did, but this time he had to. If it meant he could do something to help Lilly overcome her fears and find her voice with others he needed to tell her this.

She looked up at him, her eyes like saucers. "Like a story?"

He nodded.

Alex kept his eyes out on the water, one hand firm on the rod. He swapped hands, putting it into his left so he could swing his right arm around her. He didn't want to scare her, or make her feel upset. He wanted to comfort her. Wanted to help her like he wished someone had helped him as a kid.

"When I was a boy—a bit older than you—my mommy and daddy both died." He gave her a wee squeeze when she didn't say anything. She felt soft, not tense, so he continued. "I was just like you, with no brothers or sisters, so when they died I didn't have anyone. You've got a mommy, but I had no parents at all."

He'd had great parents. The type who would do anything for you. But his life had gone in one fell swoop from happy families to sadness. From light to dark. That was why being here shook him so much. Because he felt responsible for ruining this little family as his had been ruined.

"So who looked after you?" Lilly whispered.

Her eyes upturned to catch his held such questions, such worry, that he didn't know what to say. He certainly wasn't going to tell her the whole thing. This story was to help her, not to get the lot off his chest. "Someone kind looked after me, but it wasn't like having my parents."

He felt bad, not telling her the whole truth, but the reality of being in care had been ugly. He'd come across decent people in the end, but foster care was no way to live life as a grieving child. It had made him hard. Steeled him against his pain. Made him feel like it was his fault he was there. Alone.

"The thing was, I was very scared. And very sad," he said.

He watched her little head nodding. "Me too."

"And, just like you, I stopped talking," he admitted.

She dropped her rod then. He scrambled to grab it. "Just like me?"

He passed her back the rod and waited for her fingers to clasp it. "Yep, just like you."

They sat there in silence, bodies touching. She felt so tiny next to him. So vulnerable. Alex's chest ached. The pain of memories that he'd long since put to rest was bubbling in his mind, but he had to help Lilly if he could.

"It was different when I wouldn't talk, though. Do you know why?" he asked.

She shook her head.

"Because you have a mommy who you can still talk to. I had no one. So when I stopped talking I didn't say a word to anyone. I had no one to talk to. You are very lucky, because your mom loves you and you can talk to her," he said quietly.

She sighed and let her head rest against his arm. "But I don't want to talk to anyone else."

"You talk to me." He whispered the words, conscious that maybe she hadn't actually thought much about the fact that she spoke to him.

"Something's different about you," she whispered back.

Alex wished her therapist could hear all this. Maybe to a professional it would make more sense. "Why? What's different about me?"

"You make me think of Daddy."

A hand seemed to clasp around Alex's throat. Squeezed it so hard he couldn't breathe. But this was Lilly. This was the child he was trying to help. He couldn't stall on her now. She was waiting for him to say something.

"Is it…ah…okay that I make you think of him?" he asked.

She gave him a solemn nod. "It's nice."

Damn it! The kid had pulled out his heart and started shredding it into tiny pieces. "So, when do you think you'll start talking again? You know—to other people?"

She shrugged. "When did you start talking?"

He didn't let his mind drift back to where it wanted to go. Couldn't. He had been *forced* to talk again. Forced to deal with the fate life had handed him.

Being picked on and bullied had been bad enough. But being the kid who didn't talk? That had made life even worse in the first foster home he'd been put in. But he'd been tougher by the time it came to the second home. Harder. He'd had to find his tongue again in order to stand up for himself, although he'd kept his voice to himself most of the time. Tough kids talked with their fists, and he'd had to learn that type of communication too.

Alex had gone all his life wondering what it would have been like if someone had genuinely tried to help him. Had talked to him and wanted to help make it right. The army had been like family to him up until now, but those men he'd served with had all had someone to go home to. They had been there for one another, and he'd known true support and compassion and camaraderie, but it wasn't the same as having a real family.

He let his arm find Lilly again and drew her close. It didn't matter how hard this was for him—he had to do it for her. "No one can tell you when it's the right time to talk again, Lilly."

She snuggled in. Alex's heart started pounding loud in his ears. Beating a rhythm at the side of his neck.

"When you see someone like your grandma do you want to talk to her? You know? When she talks to you first?"

"Yes." It was tiny noise, one little word, but it was honest.

"How about next time one of your grandmas or your Aunt Anna talks to you, you take a big breath, give them a big smile like I know you can, and think about saying something back?" he suggested. He could almost hear her brain working. Ticking. Processing what he'd said. "If you can't say anything, that's okay, but if you think hard about what you want to say back, and try really hard to say it, it might work."

"Will you help me?" she asked softly.

He put his fishing line between his feet to hold it and hugged her, tight enough to show he meant it. "I'll be here for you, Lilly. You just be strong."

"Aaaaggghhhhh!" Her squeal pierced his eardrum.

If he hadn't been so focused on Lilly, so consumed by his own dark thoughts, he probably would have seen it coming. The dog had leaped out of the boat, which now rocked precariously and tipped before he could do anything about it. Alex kept hold of Lilly, more worried about her than the fact the boat was turning over. They hit the water hard, but he still had hold of her. Had Lilly pressed tight against his chest, her forehead against his chin.

Alex instinctively started treading water. He could do it for hours if he had to. "You okay?" he asked urgently.

His eyes met laughing ones. Lilly looked like they were on some sort of adventure, not as if she could have drowned!

"Boston saw a duck!" she spluttered.

He followed her gaze. Sure enough, Boston was paddling fast towards a few ducks that were lazily swimming in the other direction.

He could have killed the dog!

"Mommy told you he liked ducks," Lilly laughed.

Hmm, so Mommy had. Alex shook the water from his eyes and swapped Lilly into his left hand, so he could use his right for swimming. He hoped for Boston's sake he wasn't feeling quite this annoyed when the dog showed up on solid ground.

What on earth…? Lisa almost turned away just to look back again. Why were they both soaking wet? She ran to get dry towels and headed out the door.

"What happened?" she called as she ran. Her heart was pounding. Talk about giving a mother a fright!

She watched as Alex gave Boston a dirty look. The dog was soaking wet too. Standing on the riverbank.

"Oh, no. Did he...?"

"Leap out of the boat and capsize us?" Alex was at least smiling, if somewhat wryly. "Yup."

Lisa laughed. She couldn't help it. She held out her arms to Lilly. "Come here, my little drowned rat."

Lilly scuttled into her arms and Lisa wrapped her in a towel. Then she passed one to Alex.

"He saved me," her daughter said proudly. "Alex grabbed me and swam me in, and then he went back for the boat."

Lisa smiled at Alex and mouthed *thank you*. He just shrugged. She turned back to her daughter. "Lilly, if I'd known you were taking Boston in the boat I would have been able to warn Alex. You know he isn't usually allowed in without a lead."

"Lilly Kennedy, did you forget to tell me that?" Alex asked incredulously.

Lilly looked sheepish.

"Off with you!" He ruffled her hair to show he wasn't cross with her. "And take that filthy mongrel with you."

"He's *not* a filthy mongirl!"

Lilly's struggle with the word had Alex and Lisa both in hysterics.

"Well, he *is* filthy, so off with both of you," Lisa finally managed to say.

They watched her run off after the dog, still wrapped in the towel.

"I think there's a hot shower with your name on it," Lisa hinted.

Alex grinned. "Good idea." He started to walk off.

"Thank you, Alex."

He turned back to her. "What for?"

She wanted to stay like this, in this moment, forever. He was so different, happy. Open.

"For saving her, for taking the time to talk to her. It means a lot to me," she elaborated.

"She's not exactly a hard kid to be around."

Lisa knew that. When Lilly was happy and talking she'd draw anyone in with her smile and chatter. These last few months it had been like having a nervous, tiny shadow of her daughter—a sliver of the fun little girl Lilly used to be. Her father had been away for a lot of her young life, but she had loved every minute with him when he'd been home, and had lived and breathed the excitement of having him return home one day for good once his term was over.

Now this stranger, this soldier, had turned up, and it was like Lilly's inner dragon had started to breathe fire within her again. Lisa couldn't thank him enough for that.

She stood and watched as Alex made his way inside. He might not say a lot, but when he did his words counted.

CHAPTER SEVEN

"ALL I'm saying is that it's hard to meet someone who'll take on a woman and a child," Marj said calmly.

"Great—thanks, Mom." Lisa scowled at the phone. "So you're likening me to used goods?" She scribbled down the final ingredient in a recipe and dropped her pen. Having her mother on speakerphone was not helping.

"Honey, you know I don't mean that," Marj protested.

Did she?

"I'm just saying that he must be a good man."

"Mom! For the last time, there is nothing—*nothing*—going on between me and Alex," Lisa said through gritted teeth.

"Well, what I'm saying is maybe you should give the guy a chance," Marj said.

Would it be so bad, moving on from William? Lisa heard a shuffle of feet and hit the hand control. She didn't want anyone else hearing this conversation. And she didn't want to discuss moving on. She still loved William. Period. What she felt for Alex was just attraction. A natural reaction for a lonely woman with a handsome man nearby.

"Honey?"

"Mom, I appreciate the support—I do. But I just need a little more time." She sighed.

She could feel his presence. Sure enough, within a handful of seconds Alex appeared in the living room.

"I've got to go. I'll come by soon." She hung up the phone. "Hi," she greeted him a little nervously.

He raised a hand in a casual wave. "Hey."

She tried not to let him see she was rattled.

"I didn't mean to interrupt you," he said, when she didn't say anything more.

"Don't be silly. It was just my mother. And I told you—the door is always open," she said in a rush.

He nodded. "She keeps a close eye on you, huh?"

"More like she's nosy. Her *and* Anna," she muttered. But she sensed he didn't really want to talk about her family. Well, that was fine. Neither did she.

"I'm about to head into town to run some errands," she told him.

Something crossed Alex's face that she couldn't put her finger on. Then his expression changed.

She waited.

"Would you…ah…like me to drive you?" he asked tentatively.

Lisa smiled. She'd love the company. "Sure—that'd be great." She watched as his face softened, like he hadn't known how she was going to react to his offer. "Let me grab a few things and we'll go."

"Am I okay like this?"

He looked down at his attire. She followed his eyes. What about him wasn't okay? Long legs clad in faded jeans. Tanned feet poking out below. Bronzed forearms hanging loosely from a fitted black T-shirt. Her gaze reached his handsome face and went down his gorgeous body again before she finally managed to wrench it away.

It was just an attraction. A natural reaction to a good-looking, fit, healthy male. It would pass, she told herself fervently.

"You look good. Add a pair of shoes and you'll be good to go," she said.

He wriggled his toes. She saw it. Which meant she was still

watching him. Darn it if her eyes weren't like magnets drawn to him!

"Let me get Lilly and my handbag and I'll see you at the car." Lisa forced herself to move. To walk away from him. She could feel him. Sense his big masculine presence. It was like when William had been home on leave, or between postings. The house had felt different. A feeling in the air. Only William had been a comfortable change. Solid, dependable. With Alex it was electric.

Lilly made the house feel alive, kept Lisa from ever feeling truly alone, but she couldn't deny that there was a sense of security, of strength, in a house when there was a man in residence. She dug her nails into her own hand. It was *William's* residence. Alex was just a visitor. Passing through.

But, wrong as it may be, there was definitely something comforting about having a man in her home. Even if it wasn't the man she was supposed to be sharing it with.

She looked at Lilly's closed bedroom door. There was a little thump and lots of giggling. Then there was a woof. Lisa guessed what was going on. Boston would be lying on the bed, on his back, legs in the air. His head would be settled on the pillows. Lilly would either have a bonnet on his head, socks on his feet, glasses on his nose, a blanket tucked around him, or all of the above. She treated the dog as if he was a living doll.

"We're going into town soon, honey," Lisa told her through the door.

"Can we take Boston?" Her voice was slightly muffled.

"Yes, we can take Boston."

Lisa let her forehead rest on the door. She owed a lot to that dog. Without him, Lilly would have been even worse. Would have been even more lost over William's death.

She heard a bout of giggles again. Lilly was definitely getting back to her old self. It was nice to have a daughter who was slowly filling up with fuel for life again.

"Get a wriggle on, girl. Two minutes!" Lisa warned.

Lilly didn't answer.

Strange as it might be, it was almost like things *were* getting back to normal again. Or as normal as life had ever been being a soldier's wife. Having Alex here felt right. In some ways. But deep down she didn't want it to be right. If she could wish for anything in the world, it would be to have William back.

So where did that leave her feelings for Alex?

Alex looked out the window as they chugged along. He didn't look at Lisa. He couldn't. Even though he'd intended driving her in, she'd laughed, told him to enjoy the scenery and jumped in on the driver's side herself.

Seeing her behind the oversize wheel of the baby blue Chevy had been bad enough when she'd waved him over before they'd left. There was something about her that just got to him. The casual ponytail slung high on her head, the way she wore her T-shirt, even the way her fingers tapped on the wheel to music.

He wound down his window and let a blast of air fill the cab. Boston straddled him and let his tongue loll out the window, nose twitching. Lilly wriggled next to him on the bench seat.

"Tell me again why Boston couldn't ride in the back?" Alex wanted to know.

Lisa laughed. Loud.

Relief hit him. Hard. Like a shock to the chest. He'd wondered if they were ever going to get that easy feeling between them back again. He'd missed it.

"Lilly won't have him in the back," Lisa explained.

He looked at the kid. She shook her head. Vigorously.

Alex pushed Boston back and wound the window up. He liked dogs, but four of them squished up-front seemed a bit—well, ridiculous. He went back to scanning the landscape. He might be biased, given the years he'd spent seeing sand and little else when he was deployed, but Alaska was beautiful. Incredible.

He'd dreamed of wilderness and trees and water every night before coming back to the US. Now he was here. In a part of the world that seemed untouched. It was the postcard-perfect back-drop he would have sketched when he was away. The idyllic spot he'd hankered for. As a child, he'd always dreamt of what his life could have been like, the kind of place he could have lived in with his family if they'd been around, and if he could have chosen anywhere Alaska would have made the list.

Even without Lisa and Lilly this place was perfect. *Although they sure did add to the appeal*, a little voice inside him whispered insidiously.

They'd only been driving maybe five, seven minutes before a stretch of shops appeared. They had an old-school type of quality—a refreshingly quaint personality. He'd driven into Brownswood this way, but he'd been so focused on following directions, on finding the Kennedy residence, that he'd hardly even blinked when he'd passed the row of stores. There was every kind of store here a person could need.

Lisa gave a toot and waved to an older woman standing on the street. She turned down the radio a touch and rolled down her window. "Hey, Mrs. Robins."

A few other people turned to wave. Small-town feel, small-town reality. The thought suddenly worried him. Was his being with her going to affect her standing? Surely she wouldn't have agreed to him coming along if she'd had hesitations? But still... He knew firsthand how small-town gossip started. And spread. When his parents had died it had been as if everyone had been talking about it. Pitying him. Whispering. But no one had stepped up to help him or take him in. They'd just watched as Social Services had taken him away.

Alex started pushing the painful memories back into the dark corners of his mind, like he always did. Just because he'd been doing better these past few days it didn't mean he was ready for this. Didn't mean he wanted to be seen or have to interact with anyone.

He did enjoy Lisa's company, he had to admit. That didn't mean he was ready to brave the world again, though. It had taken him years to learn how to force unwanted feelings down.

To push them away and lock them down. But now that he'd left the army after ten years he was struggling. Because he didn't want to be alone.

Having company again was kind of nice.

Lisa wasn't going to hide just because she had Alex with her. She had to keep mentally coaching herself, reassuring herself that she wasn't doing anything wrong, but it was hard.

These people had known her since she was a little girl. Known William since he was in diapers. Not to mention known them both together as husband and wife for a good few years. And the worry, the guilt, was eating at her from the inside. She cared about what people in her community thought about her. Plus she cared about her husband. She didn't ever want to be disloyal to him, or to his memory.

For some reason, though, it felt like she was.

But Alex was a friend. *A friend.* There was nothing wrong with having a friend who was a man. Nothing wrong at all.

Besides, she had been forced to start a new chapter in her life the day William had passed away. Like it or not, the residents of Brownswood were just going to have to accept that. She loved being part of the community, but would they expect her to be a widow forever?

Lisa focused her attention back on Alex. At her friend and nothing more. Pity about the flicker of fire that raced through her body when she looked at him. "Is there anything you need? Anywhere you want to go?"

Alex dragged his eyes back toward her. She didn't know what he had been looking at—maybe everything—but he'd seemed another world away in his own thoughts.

"Sorry?"

He *had* been another world away. He hadn't even heard what she'd said. "Is there anywhere you particularly want to go?" she repeated.

He shook his head. "Maybe a fishing shop, if there is one, but it's not really necessary."

Lisa pulled into a spare parking bay. It wasn't like they were hard to come by here, but she hated to have to walk too far. "I just need to do the grocery shopping, grab a prescription from the pharmacy, and take Lilly to her therapist appointment."

"I'll come help carry the groceries," he suggested.

She appreciated that he liked to be a gentleman but she didn't want him to feel like he owed her. Didn't want to need his help.

"Why don't you take a look around and meet me outside the store?" She pointed with her finger at the grocers. "I'll be about twenty minutes in there, and then I'll take Lilly to her appointment."

"Okay."

She watched as he gave Lilly a hand out of the cab, her petite fingers clasped in his paw. The one with the real paw whined, but stayed put.

"Won't be long, Boston." Lilly waved to her dog.

"See you soon, then," Alex said.

Lilly waved to him too.

Alex felt like a fish out of water. He hated that everyone he walked by would know he was new in town. It didn't look much like a tourist spot, so they probably looked at newbies as fresh meat on the block.

He decided to avert his eyes from the few people milling around and check out the shops instead. A hardware store, a small fashion shop, then a bookstore. He let his step quicken as he noticed a place across the road. Bill's Bait & Bullets. He crossed the road.

A stuffed moose head filled the window, along with an assortment of feathered varieties. He wasn't into hunting, but he loved to fish, and if the sign on the door was anything to go by then he was in luck.

"Howdy."

Alex nodded his head at the man behind the counter who'd just greeted him. He sported a bushy mustache and was a wearing a blue and white plaid shirt. He guessed this was Bill.

"You after anything in particular?" Bill asked.

Alex did a quick survey around the shop and eyed the rods.

"Looking to do a spot of fishing," he said, walking in the right direction. "Wouldn't mind a new rod. Or two."

The man rounded the counter and came back into view. "You've come to the right place, then." He walked over to the rods. "That what brings you here? Fishing?"

Alex didn't see the point in lying. Not when everyone around would be gossiping later. But he wasn't about to start telling this Bill all his business.

"Here to see an old friend." He left it at that. "I need a rod for me, and one for a kid. About so high." He gestured with his hands at what he estimated Lilly's height was. "Six, I think."

"Girl or boy?" Bill enquired.

He gave the man a stern look. Asking politely was one thing, getting nosy was another. It wasn't like fishing rods came in pink or blue. Bill was just trying to guess which kid in town Alex was buying it for.

"I just need a rod for a child," he reiterated firmly.

The man shuffled away, and Alex moved to look around the shop. It was at times like this he thought of William, about what he might be doing now if he'd survived. They'd spent a lot of time talking about what they liked to do, and William had always talked about his family.

When they'd kicked a ball around in the sand, sat back when there was nothing else to do, or lain side by side waiting for their orders, there had been nothing else to do but talk. And while Alex hadn't opened up much about his past, other than to tell William he had no family, his friend had reminisced about his little girl and his wife. Told him how he wanted to teach his daughter to fish and follow tracks in the forest one day.

So Alex felt good being here buying a rod. Felt right about doing something he knew William would have done, had he lived. He wasn't trying to take his friend's place—part of him still wanted to run when Lilly so much as looked up at him—but this was something he could do. In William's memory. This was the way he could help William's family through their loss.

Lisa found Alex leaning against the hood of the car when they returned for the second time. He'd long since packed the groceries into the back, after she'd met him at the vehicle with the bags, and he was now leaning with one foot against the front wheel arch and the other out front.

Lilly bounded up to him, then decided to give Boston, who was still inside the car, her attention instead. She'd coped well with the therapist. Now she was open as a spring flower, and Alex and Boston were helping to keep her like it.

"I didn't know if he was allowed out or not," Alex said, gesturing to the cooped-up canine.

"No, he isn't!" Even Lilly laughed at her mother's appalled expression. "He has a track record of stealing sausages from the butcher, snatching sandwiches—all sorts of things," Lisa explained.

Alex cracked a grin. It stopped her in her tracks. She'd seen him smile more than once now, plenty of times, but they were often sad smiles. Often haunted. This one was powerful. It showed off straight white teeth and set his eyes to crinkling.

"That the real reason he travels shotgun?" he asked.

"You've got me there." She smiled.

Alex opened the door and Lilly scrambled in. "She get on okay?" he asked.

Lisa gave him a thumbs-up. "Big progress." She crossed around the side of the car to jump behind the wheel. When she got in, it wasn't as crowded as she'd expected.

Lilly had crawled into Alex's lap.

Lisa's hand shook as she tried to put the key in the ignition. She turned on the engine. Then looked at Alex. His eyes were pleading. Torn between terror and something she couldn't identify. She was about to tell Lilly to get in her seat. About to take action. When Lilly's head fell against Alex's chest.

It nearly broke her heart.

Lilly had always sat like that with William. Lisa had always found them in the car like that, waiting for her to emerge from a shop.

And now she was sitting like that with Alex.

It was the first time since he'd come into their lives that she'd seen him fill William's boots. The idea of replacing William made her feel physically sick. But the ever-present thrum of attraction, of being drawn to Alex, quickly pushed away the nausea.

She met his eyes again. He didn't blink. Didn't pull his eyes away. The brown of his irises seemed to soften as he looked back at her. She watched as one hand circled Lilly, keeping her tucked gently against him. Lisa could see the gentle rise and fall of his chest. He still hadn't looked away.

She swallowed. Tried to. But a lump of something wouldn't pass. Lilly's doctor's words echoed in her mind, but she swept them away.

Something had changed between them. In that moment the goalposts had moved. It had been building up, simmering below the surface. But right now something had definitely changed.

She knew it and he knew it.

Alex wasn't pulling away from her daughter—but then she hadn't ever seen him truly pull away from Lilly before. They were like kindred spirits. The way they connected was—well, like nothing she had imagined, believed, could happen.

But he'd always pulled away from *her*. Always kept himself at a distance. Kept himself tucked away.

Not now.

Now Lisa could finally see with clarity that he felt it too. She'd been caught in his gaze too long.

Lisa placed her hands on the wheel. Her palms were damp. She put the car in gear, looked over her shoulder, then pulled out onto the road.

And then she saw her.

William's mother stood on the footpath. Watching them.

She raised a hand to wave to her, and cringed as guilt crawled across her skin. Swept like insects tiptoeing across every inch of her body. Brought that nausea to the surface again. Made her wish she could just stamp on the attraction she felt for Alex and go back to pining for William.

His mother raised her hand too. But Lisa could see the look on her face. It was pained and confused and upset.

Lisa thumped her foot on the accelerator to get away. She couldn't face her. Not right now.

She'd done nothing wrong, so why did she feel so guilty?

And why did she feel like nothing was ever going to be the same ever again?

She glanced over at Alex, taking her eyes from the road for a nanosecond. Lilly was still tucked against him. Boston had his head resting against his leg.

Could she really ever be with another man? William had been her one and only lover. The only man in her life. Her high-school sweetheart and best friend. The only man she'd ever wanted.

Did thinking about Alex romantically make her a bad person? She hoped not. Because there was no chance she could ignore Alex.

Not a chance.

She knew that now. And she didn't have the strength to fight it much longer.

No matter how much it was tying her in knots.

CHAPTER EIGHT

LISA couldn't look at Alex. She got the feeling he felt the same.

As soon as they'd arrived home he'd carried the groceries in for her, placed them in the kitchen, then made for the door. He hadn't even spoken to Lilly.

Lilly had fallen asleep against him on the short drive home, waking only when Lisa had taken her from his arms and carried her inside. She was still napping now.

Lisa poured herself a cup of strong, sweet tea.

She hadn't lied to Alex earlier, Lilly's therapy session had gone great. Lilly had smiled, drawn happy pictures, and nodded in answer to the questions the therapist had asked. She hadn't spoken, but she'd communicated in the way the doctor had asked her to. Through creative expression.

But at the end the doctor had called Lisa aside. She'd told her that Lilly was making a sudden burst of progress, and asked about Alex. Lilly had drawn pictures of him—a large man standing beside them. A man with a smile. Which meant he was both important to her and a current source of happiness.

The doctor had pointed out that she'd drawn a family picture. With Alex cast as the dad.

It was fine. Lisa could deal with that image in theory. But the doctor had cautioned her that Alex leaving at any stage, for whatever reason, might cause Lilly to go back, to retreat further into a state of grieving.

Lisa didn't even know if Alex had been officially discharged from the army. For all she knew he might only be back for a few months or so before he was redeployed somewhere millions of miles from Alaska. And he was only staying here for another—what?—two weeks? Would they just try to go back to normal and forget he'd ever existed once he left?

The very thought of him going back to the place that had taken William from her made her sick to her gut. But soldiers were soldiers, and they went where they were needed. She'd been a patriot all her life, and just because William had been one of the casualties of war it did not mean she had any right to want Alex not to go back. Or even to think it.

But the thought of him leaving worried Lisa, regardless of where it was he might go. She could ask him to leave now, before they became too attached to each other, but that could do Lilly as much harm as losing him in a week or more. She could explain that because he was a friend of Daddy's he had to go back to his own house, but did she really need to burst that bubble now if Lilly honestly thought he was staying for longer? Did she even understand that he wasn't here for good? Lisa was struggling with the idea herself.

She rubbed at her neck. The base of it seemed to hold all her stress these days. It was worry. She knew that. Her neck had prickled ever since… Well, she was going to stop thinking about that. About Alex. Every time she did it reminded her that she was a widow, and she didn't need a fresh wave of guilt on her conscience. Thinking about him didn't mean she was cheating. Didn't make her disloyal. Surely?

Seeing William's mother had given her a good enough dose of that.

Lisa looked around the kitchen. She could bake. That always made her feel better. But she'd already finished creating her recipes and ideas for the book. What she needed was a break. Plus that reminded her that she actually had to send her work to her editor.

The house was silent. Birds cawed in the trees outside, their noise filtering in. The sun let its rays escape in through the window, hitting the glass and sending slivers of light into the room.

What was Alex doing? She couldn't hear him, so he obviously wasn't working on the cabin.

She got up. Her feet seemed to lead her on autopilot toward the door. There was something forbidden about what she was doing. But she didn't stop. Just seeking him out felt like she was prodding a sleeping tiger.

It wasn't like she'd never gone out looking for him before, but today was different. Today she was haunted by the look in his eyes earlier in the car. Today she was a woman thinking about a man. Today she was fighting the widow who loved her husband still. Today she just wanted to be a woman who happened to like a man.

Lisa stopped before stepping outside to check her hair. She ran her hands across it, making sure her ponytail was smooth. She pressed her hands down her jeans and fiddled with her top.

She had no idea what she was doing. Why she was looking for him. But she had to see him. Had to prove to herself that there had been something between them in the car today. Something she wasn't imagining. Something that was worth feeling guilty over.

She followed the beaten path through the short grass and let her eyes wander out over the water. He was nowhere to be seen, but the lake calmed her as it always did.

Maybe that was why Alex had chosen to stay? Because he'd taken one look at that water and known he wanted to see it every morning when he woke up. She didn't dare wish that she'd been a reason factored into his decision.

Lisa gulped. Hard.

The door was ajar. Was he in there?

Her feet started walking her forward again. They didn't stop until she was at the door of the cabin, and still they itched to move.

She didn't know why, but she didn't call to him. Didn't tell him she was there. She didn't know why she was even seeking him out. She nudged the door open and took the final step inside. Her eyes found his straight away.

It was her who wanted to flee this time.

She looked into his face. Tried to ignore the fact that he was shirtless. That his tanned stomach with its tickle of hair was staring straight at her.

He remained wordless.

They just stared at one another. There was nothing to say.

They *had* both felt it in the car. It wasn't just her imagining it. She could tell from the sudden ignition of fire in his eyes that he felt the same.

He stood up. It was like a lump of words was stuck in her throat and no amount of swallowing was going to dislodge it. Or force it out.

His body sported an all-over tan. Or what she could see of it at least. His arms were firm, large. In a strong, masculine way—like he'd worked hard outside for a lot of hours. She didn't dare look down any further.

She met his eyes and wished she hadn't. She'd never seen him like this. Never.

"You need to go."

His voice had the strength of a lion's growl. She felt told off. He had demanded she leave and yet she couldn't.

"Alex." His name came out strangled.

He stopped in front of her. So close that she could feel the heat from his body.

She was immobile. Glued to the spot. She raised her hand from her side, moved it palm-first toward him. She ached to feel his skin.

He caught her wrist in a vice-like grip before she made contact.

"No." His voice was still firm, gruff, but it was losing its power.

They stared at one another, glared. His breath grazed her skin.

She wasn't going to look away. Every inch of her wanted him. She'd never felt so alive, so desperate.

"Lisa, I can't—" His voice broke off.

She could see the torment in his eyes. He looked cracked open, yet so strong. Determined.

But he was as weak as her.

When she'd been with her husband it had been warm. Soft. Comfortable. It had *never* been like this. Attraction, intensity, punched the air between them.

His grip on her wrist slackened but she kept it still. He shuffled one step closer to her, their bodies now only inches apart. His lips parted and his mouth came toward hers.

She leaned forward until their lips touched. Just. He caught her bottom lip in the softest of caresses.

Lisa let her hand fall against him. Felt the softness of his skin, just like she'd imagined, beneath her palm.

He moaned. She could only just hear it. His lips still traced softly against hers. It was the deepest, most gentle, most spine-aching kiss she'd ever experienced. And still it went on.

So soft that she almost wondered if she was dreaming it.

She opened her eyes.

The six-feet-plus of bronzed, strong male before her convinced her that it was real. That *he* was real.

It was as if he'd felt her eyes pop.

He pulled back. Hard. Then jumped away from her as though she was some sort of danger to him. Pulled away like she was poison.

"No!" He belted out the word.

She was numb. Couldn't move.

"No." Quieter this time.

She let her face ask the question. *Why not?*

"Leave, Lisa. Please, just leave."

His voice belied the emotion tearing him apart. Guilt cascaded through her. She was the cause of it. Of his pain. Why had she done it? Come looking for him?

"Alex…" she whispered.

"You're another man's wife, damn it! Leave!" he barked.

She shook her head, tears forming in her eyes. Because she wasn't a wife. Not anymore. William was gone. *Gone!* She was no man's wife. The knowledge hit her like a blow to the gut. She was going to tell him that, but he looked torn. Grief-stricken. He wouldn't listen anyway. Besides, she didn't want to talk to him.

His back was turned. So she walked out. Kept her chin high as the tears started to trickle down her cheeks.

This wasn't fair. Life wasn't fair.

She still loved William. But she wanted Alex too.

Was it wrong to wish for both?

Alex watched her leave. He couldn't drag his eyes away from her if he tried. And he had tried.

It was like he was lost in her. Powerless to pull away from her. But she wasn't his. She could *never* be his.

Hadn't he already thought all this through?

His body had rebelled. She had felt so good against him. Lips softer than a feather pillow, hands lighter than a brush of silk.

He straightened and reached for his shirt.

Yes, he had already decided that she was forbidden. But that was before. Before Lilly had tucked up on his knee like a puppy. Before their afternoon out in the boat. Before Lisa had looked at him like that.

Before he'd let himself fall in too deep.

It was reminding him too much of what he'd lost. What it had been like to be a child with happy parents. And how much it hurt losing something like that. He'd long ago decided you were better not having it in the first place than risk losing it.

The last foster-family he'd been with had put a roof over his head and food in his belly, but he'd still felt like they'd just had him in order to collect the welfare checks. They'd never treated him like they did their own son. And when the other soldiers, his family, had pinned up photos of their loved ones Alex had never been able even to look at the crumpled photos of his parents. Which was why he'd never let anyone close to him since they'd died. Because he had never wanted to feel that way ever again.

Alex looked out the window.

He had to force Lisa out of his head. Just because he liked being here, liked feeling part of this little family, it didn't mean he had a right to be attracted to her. Didn't mean she had a right to be attracted to him.

All he knew was that he wanted her. And that she was forbidden.

It would take a stronger man to pull away from her again, though. And he didn't think he could be any stronger. Alex had fought it for so long. Thought he could go without love. Without family. Forever.

But the pain in his chest, the pain that had been there suffocating him for most of his life, told him he was wrong. That no matter how hard he tried to forget, to move on and not think about the past or what could have been, he would do anything for a family to call his own. To recreate what he'd lost. And that was why he hated the fact that William had saved him and not thought about himself instead. Because family was everything in this world. It was the reason why Alex felt he had nothing.

Now he knew more than ever how much he really craved what he'd lost. How much he wanted what could have been. And it was killing him that he was yearning for the family that William had sacrificed to save Alex's life. How twisted was that?

It was time to move on. Or at least to get this cabin fixed up as soon as possible so he didn't look like he was running out on them. And then he'd leave as fast as he could.

* * *

Lisa wanted to curl into a ball and never emerge. What had happened out there?

Oh, she knew. She knew because she'd been the one to go out there searching for him. She'd known that there was something between them, and she'd gone out there hoping to find out exactly what it was.

It had certainly been an emotional day.

First she'd had to deal with the therapist, not to mention her mother on the phone. Then she'd seen her mother-in-law in town. And Lilly had curled up on Alex's lap, and then... Well, she didn't quite know what had happened with Alex in the cabin. What it was they'd shared.

She only knew that they'd both acted on it.

And it had been Alex who'd pulled away. When it should have been her.

Alex. Just thinking his name sent tickles through her veins. Made them jump beneath her skin.

He was handsome. He was strong. And yet he was also vulnerable. So unlike her husband it scared her. William had been so together. So controlled. Yet at the same time like a wide open book. Alex was mysterious. Hard to read.

Yet sexy as hell.

She was beyond confused.

There were people who'd like her to be a grieving widow forever. Her sister was one of them. William's friends fell into that category too. She had no desire to be miserable and alone for the rest of her life. No desire at all. But then she didn't exactly want to move on yet either.

She thought of William's mother. Her in-laws were possibly the only people in her life who were allowed to make judgments. She wouldn't blame *them* for wishing she stayed a widow forever. She had been married to their only son. She was the mother of their only grandchild. Of course it would hurt to see her moving on with her life.

But even though William had been dead only eight months, to Lisa it felt like an eternity some days. And like yesterday at other times. Yet she'd hardly ever seen him. She'd been a single mom in many ways for most of their marriage. It didn't mean she hadn't loved him—she still did—but she wasn't going to be made to feel like she didn't care about his memory just because she was a little attracted to Alex.

Truth be told, if Alex hadn't come into her life she might have taken years to date again, let alone think about another man the way she was thinking about him. But he was here now, and there was something between them, and she wasn't going to let what other people thought get in her way. She was the only one to make decisions about her love life. And right now she didn't know what she was thinking!

She lay on the sofa and closed her eyes. It felt good. Relief washed through her as she stayed motionless. Her eyes stung from having cried, but she felt surprisingly okay. If she could just sleep it off maybe she'd feel better. Lilly was having a power nap, so why couldn't she?

Lisa woke with a start. How long had she been asleep?

She stretched out her limbs and combed her fingers through her hair before retying her ponytail.

Lilly.

Lisa hurried up to her bedroom and pushed open the door. She was up already, but Lisa knew where she'd be.

Less than a week ago Lilly would have been tapping her on the shoulder to wake her up. Now she wouldn't have had a thought for her snoring mother as she skipped out to find their guest.

Alex. She didn't particularly feel like seeing him right now, but she didn't have much of a choice.

She rounded the corner. Sure enough, there they were, standing side by side at the lake. Boston lay nearby, but he rose to greet her. The other two didn't bother to turn. Lilly might not have heard her, but she knew that Alex had. If he'd been a dog his ears would have twitched he was so alert.

"Hey, guys," Lisa said.

Lilly swiveled. She nearly took Alex out again with her hook. "Mommy, look what Alex gave me!"

She gave Lilly a beamer of a smile and went forward to inspect it. Now she had pointed it out Lisa could see she held a pint-size rod. Perfect for her little hands. "Wow! Your own rod, huh?"

Lisa acted like everything was normal, even though hearing Lilly talk in front of someone else still stole her breath away and made her want to jump for joy. But, just as the therapist had instructed her, she ignored it. For good measure she kept her eyes away from the lure of Alex.

Lilly had excitement literally dripping from her.

And Lisa couldn't help but look.

Alex still had his eyes trained on the water, his line out. But she knew he was listening. "I hope you said thank you to Alex, sweetie?"

Lilly nodded. Smugly.

Lilly turned back to the water and put the line over her shoulder. Lisa could tell there had been some practicing going on.

"Cast it back in the water like I showed you, nice and steady," Alex said quietly.

"Watch, Mom, watch!"

Lisa couldn't not watch, although half her gaze was focused on Alex. He stood with his feet spread shoulder-width apart, arms raised slightly from his sides. He looked as if he would be comfortable standing like that all day.

"Alex! Alex! Something's pulling!"

Lisa jumped at her daughter's excited train of words.

Alex calmly put down his own rod. "Stay still. Keep your hands steady."

Lilly did as she was told.

Alex moved to stand behind her and placed his hands over hers. Lisa couldn't hear what he was saying, but he was whispering in Lilly's ear as he guided her.

A splash indicated the line had emerged from the water, followed by an excited squeal from Lilly. "It's a fish!"

Lisa knew what would come next.

Alex helped her bring it in, then placed it on the grass. He worked to unhook it as they watched.

"Don't hurt it!" Lilly exclaimed.

Lisa tried not to laugh.

Alex looked confused. Lisa watched in amusement as his eyebrows formed a knot. "Aren't we going to have the fish you caught for dinner?"

Lilly shook her head. At rapid speed.

He sighed. "Shall we throw it back in, then?"

She nodded this time. A big grin on her face.

Alex threw Lisa a wry look over his shoulder—the first time he'd looked at her since what had happened between them earlier. "Here goes."

He let the fish go. Lisa knew as well as he did that it might die anyway, but Lilly looked happy.

"Bye, Mr. Fishy."

Alex shook his head in mock dismay.

"Let's catch another one, Alex!"

Lisa thought she could listen to her daughter talk to Alex all day. Now that she was speaking to him she'd probably never stop.

Lisa knew something was wrong the moment she walked inside. The light, happy feeling bubbling inside her from hearing Lilly talk turned off like a tap.

Something was wrong. Then she heard it. A soft rasp at the front door, only just audible. She went to see who it was. Her sister or mother would have just walked in. She knew it was unlocked because she'd been too caught up in her thoughts to go and lock it earlier.

Lisa swung it open. The person standing there took her breath away. It was William's mother.

"Sally." She tried to hide her discomfort. "I…ah…it's good to see you."

The woman looked like a shell of a human. Her eyes had lost the freshness they'd once enjoyed. Lines tugged at the corners of her eyes where before her skin had been seamless.

Lisa knew how she felt. That hollow feeling, and then the desperate barrage of grief-stricken emotion. It was what she'd experienced herself when the messenger had come. It still gripped her late in the night, when the cold sweat on her skin told her that William was gone for good.

For Sally, the torment was written all over her face. She would never see her son again. Just like Lisa was never going to see her man again. But at least Lisa had Lilly to keep her going every morning when she held her in her arms.

Sally had her husband and her grandchild, but she had lost her only son.

Lisa ignored the guilt tugging within her belly. She wasn't trying to replace William—she could never do that—but today she had for the first time wondered if she could actually start over. Give herself another chance while at the same time not forgetting William. The guilt she felt now told her that maybe she wasn't ready yet. She might never be. Not entirely. But Alex had at least made her want to find out.

"Lisa, I'm sorry, I shouldn't have come," the other woman said tremulously.

Lisa stepped forward and pulled Sally into her embrace. "Yes, you should have."

They stood like that, wrapped in one another's arms, not moving.

"Sally, about before—" Lisa started.

The older woman stepped back and dabbed at her eyes with a handkerchief, a shaky smile on her face.

"You've nothing to explain," Sally insisted.

Lisa appreciated not being judged. "But I want to."

"It's just—well, people were talking. After seeing you. I wanted to know for myself," Sally said.

Lisa nodded. Oh, she knew how the town would be gossiping. They'd all have her dripping in black and a grieving widow until the end of her days if they could. But deep down she didn't care about them. Or anyone. Except her husband. And her family. And Sally was family, even if they were no longer connected by her marriage.

She linked her arm with Sally's and led her into the kitchen. "There's someone outside who I want you to see."

Sally looked confused.

"The man you saw me with." She paused as Sally's face took on a hue of uncertainty. "He is—was—a friend of William's."

She sensed relief in the other woman. Her shoulders suddenly didn't appear so hunched, so shriveled.

"He served with William. He's just returned home."

Sally's eyes looked hopeful. "Was he with William…at the end?"

"Yes."

Sally closed her eyes as Lisa held her hands even tighter.

"He's—well, he's troubled," she warned. "He doesn't like talking about what he saw over there."

Sally nodded. "Not many do." She gave Lisa a brave smile. "Not like our William did."

"I do want you to meet him,' Lisa reiterated. "But I want the time to be right."

"I understand," Sally said.

Lisa beckoned with her hands and stood up. Sally did the same and Lisa put her arm around the older woman and led her to the window.

Alex was visible. He was still with Lilly. They stood side by side at the edge of the lake.

"Are you two…ah…" Sally cleared her throat "…seeing one another?"

Lisa shook her head slowly. "No." She wasn't lying. There was nothing between them. Yet. If there was she would have said.

But she *had* thought about it. Had wondered if there was

any chance of something happening for real between them. Although after his reaction earlier…

Sally leaned into her. "Do you want there to be?"

Lisa didn't answer straight away. She'd known this woman for years. She'd been a fantastic mother-in-law. And she wasn't about to start lying to her—not when she'd never done it before.

"I think so." It felt strange saying it, but it was the truth. If there was a way to be loyal to William, keep her family happy, *and* attempt to develop something with Alex—well, she would do it. The thought made her bones rattle.

Sally started to nod, and as she did she also started to cry. Tears pooled in Lisa's eyes too, but she fought them. She didn't want to hurt this woman—or herself.

"Would William approve of you being with him, do you think?" Sally asked.

Lisa knew the answer to that. She'd wondered that in the night. This afternoon too. Hadn't wanted to think about it, but she knew the answer without even pondering on it. William had been kind, open and loving. He would have wanted her to be happy.

"Yes." She hugged Sally tighter. "In his absence, I can honestly say that, yes, he would." Tears stung her eyes once more.

Sally still had her gaze trained on Alex. Lilly was leaning against him, like she was tired. "Then you have my blessing," she said quietly.

Lisa's shoulders almost rose to the ceiling. It was as if the heaviest of weights had been removed. Not because she definitely wanted to move on, or because she was sure about her feelings for Alex yet, but because it was one less thing she had to battle with. To feel guilty about.

"You know this doesn't mean I didn't love William," Lisa said urgently.

Sally turned damp eyes on her and put both hands on her

shoulders. "You were a good wife to him, Lisa. And we'll always love you."

The Kennedys were good people. But she'd never thought they could be so understanding. Not when she wasn't even sure about her feelings or whether she forgave herself for being attracted to someone else so soon.

"Would you like to come around on Sunday night? That will give me some time to…get some things organized," Lisa suggested.

"That would be great. Why don't you come to our place, though?" Sally offered.

Lisa wasn't sure how happy Alex would be about going, but she knew he'd make the effort. Maybe it would help him. Just maybe. And maybe it would also help her to finally figure out her feelings.

CHAPTER NINE

"WHAT do you say we go for a picnic today?"

Lisa looked up at Alex as she asked the question. He was sitting eating his breakfast. There were kitchen facilities out in the cabin, but Lisa had made a habit of asking him in for meals.

She liked the company—although he was nothing like William had been in the mornings, up before her, chatting up a storm, planning their day. She enjoyed Alex's company even if he was quiet. There was something about him, about his presence, that appealed to her. And he seemed to have forgiven her for seeking him out and precipitating their kiss yesterday.

Besides, there was no fridge out there, so he wasn't exactly going to keep milk, was he?

He chewed his toast. Thoughtfully. Lilly sat beside him, slurping at a bowl of cereal.

"Okay," he said.

Lisa stifled her laugh. He didn't get a very good score in the enthusiasm stakes. "I thought it would be nice to take a walk through the National Park. Boston can come with us on a lead."

Alex nodded. This time he didn't take so long to make a decision. It was like something had changed between them yesterday. Even after what had happened, they seemed to have silently moved on. He was more open. Different. And there was even more of a closeness between him and Lilly. Lisa could sense it. Perhaps they'd been talking more than she realized?

"Do you walk the same track each time?" he wanted to know.

Lisa enjoyed a ripple of excitement as she saw she'd piqued his interest. One of the reasons this property was so special to her was its connection to nature. It was a nice feeling to think he was going to share it with her.

"I'll meet you outside the cabin in an hour. You'll find out all about it then."

Alex went back to eating his toast and Lisa rifled through the fridge for the makings of the picnic. Lilly loved going on excursions, but she knew better than to rush off empty handed.

And it helped keep her mind off Alex. There was a spark, a flame that traveled between them when they were close, but he was so hard to get to know. The barrier he'd built around himself was made of something strong.

Lisa loved being outdoors. Loved hanging out with her daughter and enjoying the weather. She hoped Alex would too. Anything to bring him a little further out of his shell. Right now it was like they went two steps back for every one forward.

She wanted to know more about the demons he fought. She wanted to know if she could help him. Yesterday, she'd never thought it would be possible. Not when she still loved William so much. Not when Alex had pushed her away.

Now she was wondering if maybe, just maybe, something real could develop between the two of them. If they both took a big leap of faith.

Lilly was dancing along the edge of the river as Lisa attempted to haul the rowboat from its makeshift house. She heaved hard, but it was only moving an inch at a time.

"Hey!"

She turned at the sound of the voice and watched as Alex crossed the yard.

"Let me get that."

She stood back. Grateful. She didn't much mind rowing it, and it usually wasn't so hard to get it out, but it had sat dormant since William's last visit home and then gone back wet the other day after it had been capsized. She should have told Alex to just leave it out.

He made it look easy, though. Alex hauled it behind him, the thick rope looped over his shoulder.

"You want to launch here?" he asked.

"Perfect."

She passed Alex two packs, which he placed in the boat. Then he reached for Lilly.

"Need me to do anything else?" he said.

"Grab the dog." That was the part she hated. Boston usually leapt and toppled them out, or she had to pick him up already wet.

Alex chased the dog and tackled him. "Come here, you filthy mongrel!"

Lilly laughed. Alex was trying his best to look stern.

Lisa decided not to point out how dirty Alex's T-shirt had become. He manhandled Boston into the boat, but the dog didn't seem to mind. He'd taken to Alex almost as quickly as Lilly had.

"Sit!" Lisa used her sternest voice.

Boston surprised her by obeying for once. She wondered if it was her command or the dirty look Alex gave him that had him sitting still.

Alex took up the paddles. "Where to?"

"I can row," she offered.

Alex looked her up and down before shaking his head. "I could do with the exercise."

That suited her just fine. She sat back with Lilly. Besides, it meant she got to admire him while he pulled the oars. Today was the first time she didn't feel quite so guilty about admitting she liked the look of him. Didn't feel quite so sinful.

"Head upstream. We go maybe ten minutes up, then get out to follow a trail," she instructed.

He started to row. She watched his arms flex back and forth. Her ten minutes might not even make it to sixty seconds, given the speed at which he was propelling them!

"Just watch out for ducks," she said slyly.

He slowed. Then gave her a pointed look.

"Boston tends to jump." She grinned.

"You think I don't know that?" he said.

Lisa laughed. "Just reminding you."

Alex shook his head and glared at the dog. "Not again."

Boston looked up at him like a sweet little lamb. Lisa knew that look well, and didn't trust him one bit.

"It's beautiful here," Alex commented, looking around.

"Take us in over there, by the outcrop," she said, pointing.

He slowed his paddling and expertly guided them in.

Lisa reached out to catch the edge and tie the little boat to it. She looked back at Alex. He was holding both packs. She took one and strapped it to her back.

"Ladies first," he said gallantly.

She climbed out carefully, and then put her hand out to take Lilly. Alex helped guide her. Boston was long gone.

"I thought we had to have him on a lead?" Alex said.

"We do. He got away from me, lead attached." Lisa grimaced. "Boston!" she called.

He emerged, flying out from between the trees, and came to a flying halt at Lilly's feet. Lisa grabbed him by the leash.

"Want me to take him?" he asked.

She threw Alex a grateful look. "Please."

They walked along in a comfortable silence that strangely made her feel closer to Alex than ever before. Lilly skipped behind them and inspected spiders' webs and bugs attached to the trees. Lisa kept up a steady pace, which had her lungs blowing after a while, but she didn't give up. Alex looked like he hadn't even walked an inch. His breathing was steady. No sweat. Just loping along. It was driving her crazy. Maybe she needed to do some army-style training to get her body up to speed.

He looked like he was chewing something over in his mind. She didn't pry. From what she'd seen of him so far, he needed to walk it off. Think. Not feel pressured. And he seemed relaxed despite it.

Lisa had already learnt the hard way not to expect too much in the conversation stakes. She was a compulsive talker, so it wasn't easy, but she could appreciate his pain. The way she felt about William wasn't exactly something she knew how to talk about. What he was feeling she guessed was on par with her pain.

"Tell me about Lilly."

Just when she thought he'd gone and lost his tongue, Alex surprised her by talking.

She slowed down. Lilly had fallen behind anyway. So much for a punishing pace! If she went any faster she'd lose her own child.

"What does her therapist think about her progress?" he asked.

She still hadn't figured out why he had bonded so well with Lilly. What it was in her that resonated with him. Why she'd chosen him to talk to after all these months. Lisa was too scared to ask either of them in case she rocked the boat. But what was it that her daughter's eyes had seen that had made her want to connect with him so strongly?

"That she's doing okay, but she's taken William's death incredibly hard," Lisa told him.

He stopped. His hand fell to Boston's head as he looked back at Lilly.

"Has she been prescribed any medication?"

Lisa thought that was an odd question for him to ask. "No. There were things offered initially, but one school of thought says time and routine is enough. I'd rather go for the non-medicated option."

"Good."

Good? What did he know about therapists and medication?

Did he go to one himself? If only she was brave enough to ask him.

"You're lucky to have a therapist in a town this size," he commented.

Yes, they were. "She travels in every other week. Does the rounds of a few small towns."

She sensed Alex had moved on. He seemed focused on the path ahead now.

"Where do you want to stop?" he asked.

"We keep following this path, not much further, then there's a small pond and a clearing. A few picnic tables."

"Mind if I run ahead?"

Boston looked ready to go too. "Go for it," Lisa said.

He surged into action. A steady rhythm that he seemed to find from his first stride.

She couldn't steal her eyes away.

His calves were bare, shorts ending just above his knees. His back stayed straight. Then he disappeared.

Alex waited for them at the clearing. The run had done him good. Boston lay sprawled out beside him, still panting.

Lilly came into view first, followed by her mother.

They were a pair, those two. Lilly had her hair tied into pigtails, but a handful of the hair from each had escaped. She gave him her usual grin and collapsed beside him. Lisa—well, he didn't even want to look at her too closely.

"Have you seen anything yet?" Lilly asked him.

He wasn't sure what she meant. Should he be keeping an eye out for something in particular?

"Mommy always says to keep your eyes peeled for moose and bear and caribou and elk and even wolves!" Lilly elaborated.

Lisa was shaking her head.

"Well, that's one very informed mom you have there," Alex teased.

Lilly smiled proudly.

"Let's have this picnic before any of the above find our stash, shall we?" Lisa said.

Alex ignored the niggle in his chest as Lilly sat beside him and Lisa fiddled with the food. Getting too close to these two would mean more pain. Emotions that he couldn't deal with again. So why did he suddenly feel prepared to risk his heart for the first time since his parents had died?

They sat on a rug beneath scarcely waving branches as sunlight filtered through to warm their skin. Lisa was conscious of Alex's leg close to her own. So conscious that if she as much as wiggled her leg her thigh could be pressed against his.

She hadn't brought up the kiss, but then neither had he. They'd skirted around the issue, and she had a feeling it wouldn't ever be spoken of if she didn't bring the subject to the table. Literally.

Right now it was like she'd been released. As if she'd realized that she could be happy again. That she could be a woman and enjoy the pleasures of another man's company without disrespecting her husband.

But she needed to understand this man. Know more about him.

"Alex, you've never mentioned anything about your family," she murmured.

Other than implying he didn't have one.

A wary look danced across his face. She recognized that look now. Knew it meant for her to back off. Fast.

"You don't have to tell me. I was just curious," she said reassuringly.

He lay back, his hands finding a spot beneath his head. Lisa held her breath. He was going to talk. She could feel it. To her it seemed like a major breakthrough. As if they were finally connecting. What they had, the bond between them, meant he could finally trust her.

"My parents are both long-dead. It's just me," he said tonelessly.

So there was a reason he'd never mentioned them. A reason he'd kept them close to his chest. "You lost them young?"

"Yup."

She drew her knees up to her chest and hugged them. Maybe if she offered him something of her own past he'd keep communicating. "My father died of a heart attack when I was pretty young. So then it was just me, Mom and my sister."

He propped himself up on one elbow. "You were close to your father?"

She gulped. It still made her feel sad, thinking about her father. "Very." She might have been eighteen when he'd died, but it had still hit her extremely hard.

Lisa watched Lilly where she sat with Boston less than a few feet away. She was sprawled out with him, stroking his fur. They often spent hours like that. "Where do you live, Alex? I mean before your term away where did you live?"

A shadow over his face told her she'd probably asked enough questions for the day. But she needed to know. Wanted to know more about him.

"California. Originally."

She nodded.

"But I haven't exactly had a place to call home for a long, long time," he admitted.

"That must be hard. Not having somewhere to go."

They sat silent for another few moments. Lisa looked up at the trees, her head snapped right back, and Alex plucked at the short shoots of grass.

"Alex, are you going to be deployed again?"

She sensed him tighten.

"No."

Lisa could have leapt to touch the highest branch! She had been fighting that question for days, hours, and to hear him say no was the best news she'd received in a long while. Relief shuddered through her. She didn't need to pine for another soldier. Not ever. Losing one was enough. She wasn't even sure if she could ever truly let another man into her life. Even Alex. She certainly could never, ever cope with losing another one.

He drew up to his full height and brushed off his shorts. "Shall we get back to the boat?"

Lisa didn't push him. There was nothing else she needed to ask. She put out a hand for him to help haul her up. He did. His hand clasped over hers and pulled her upright. His fingers felt smooth, firm against hers.

She didn't want to let go.

She was starting to read him. To understand him. To put all the pieces of the jigsaw together slowly. He might have stopped talking, but he hadn't closed himself off. His eyes were still light, open. He wasn't shutting her out. Alex's lips hinted at a smile. Hers were more than hinting, but she was trying to keep herself in check.

He's not going back. He's not going back. The words just wouldn't stop ringing in her ears. Did it mean she could let something happen between them? That if something special developed she could find room for both William and Alex in her heart?

She let go of his hand as he pulled back. Reluctantly. He started to scoop up their belongings and she helped him to pack.

What she needed was to keep him talking without pushing the wrong buttons. They'd covered enough heavy stuff for today, but it felt good to just talk openly without him being guarded.

"Do you cook?" Was that a silly question for her to ask, given the years he'd probably spent in the army?

"I do a mean lasagna, and that's it," he replied.

"One signature dish?"

He nodded before swinging a pack in her direction. A wolfish smile turned the corners of his mouth upwards in the most delicious arrow. "Just the one."

She'd bet it tasted good too. It had been a while since anyone had cooked her a meal, but she'd like to try his lasagna. Might even pick up a few tips.

"I'll do it for you one time before I go," he promised.

A drum beat a loud rhythm in her ears. She'd almost forgotten their being together was coming to an end soon.

"Come on, Lilly." She forced her voice to comply with her wishes. To not show him how upset she was.

Lilly stretched like a kitten, then stood up. She grinned at Alex. Lisa didn't miss the wink he gave her.

"Let's go."

Alex fought to keep his pace slow and steady. He liked moving fast, but he wanted to enjoy walking beside Lisa. He'd had fun with his army buddies, his makeshift family, but times like this were a rarity for him. Once he'd enlisted he'd volunteered for every deployment and opportunity he could to stay overseas rather than come back to America. Because he'd had nowhere to go, nowhere to call home.

When others had gone home for even a few days if they could, jumped at every opportunity to come back, he'd stayed away. When the army was your only family you didn't have anything else or anyone to turn to.

Which was why this felt so special. This was what he imagined all those men loved about being back home with their loved ones. Just walking side by side with another human being, with a woman who made you feel happy and light. He could only imagine what it would have been like to come home to his parents—to his own family, even. Children.

For years he'd told himself he didn't want that kind of life. That he liked being a loner and didn't want to risk losing anyone close to him again.

But maybe he just hadn't realized what being loved, being part of a real family, would be like. Just what he'd sacrificed by closing off that part of him to any possibility of finding that kind of happiness for himself.

"Why are we stop—?" Alex's sentence died in his mouth.

Lisa turned to him. She motioned him to step backward. *Bear,* she mouthed frantically.

He obeyed instantly. "Quiet, Boston," he growled, only just loud enough for the dog to hear.

Lisa watched as Alex wound the lead tight around his fist, twice, then reached down to half his height to gather Lilly up to him.

Lisa felt a tremor of fear run through her body, gather momentum, and then explode within her. She'd never experienced it before. She was usually so careful, so aware.

They were still edging away, and the bear hadn't noticed them. Not yet.

"She's fishing," Lisa whispered.

Alex nodded.

"She hasn't seen us," she added thankfully.

Alex pulled them away behind a thick cluster of trees before stopping. "But she knows we're here," he warned.

Lisa's body shook again. Did she?

He must have seen the question in her eyes. "She knows. She just doesn't see us as a threat. Yet," he clarified.

They could still see her. Only just. If Lisa hadn't been so afraid she would have found it beautiful. This huge black bear, female, flipping her paw into the water and expertly tossing fish out.

Lisa glanced at Alex. He didn't look at her, but just like the bear she knew he had seen her. He'd just chosen not to look back at her. Yet.

"We need to move. If she has young we could be in real trouble," he murmured.

Lisa agreed. But she wasn't volunteering to move. Not with the bear right there.

"Can we walk back if we have to?" he asked.

She nodded. "It would be tricky, but it's possible."

He looked uncertain.

"They feed often at this time of year," she told him. She was angry with herself for being careless and stupid. Her head had been filled with ideas of a picnic, and yet if she'd thought—really thought—she'd have known this was a real bear time of year. They were still hungry—plenty hungry—and they were always out fishing.

"I don't think she'll hurt us—not if she doesn't see us as a threat—but she might not take kindly to Boston if he starts to bark," Alex said.

They were in serious danger. And for the first time in all her years of being an Alaskan, Lisa was worried that another animal was going to sneak up on them while they sat in wait. That she was going to make headlines in the local *Herald* about a trio eaten by a bear.

Alex met her eyes as his hold on Lilly tightened. She might not have known him for long, but seeing the grip he had on her daughter made her realize that he'd risk his own life to save Lilly. That she could trust him to get her precious daughter to safety. No matter what happened, he wasn't the type to let anyone down in a moment of crisis.

Boston let out a low whine and she dropped to her knees to comfort him. She buried her fingers in his long fur.

"So we're just going to wait?" Lilly suddenly asked.

Lisa sucked in her breath. "Shh, sweetie."

"Stay quiet, Lilly." Alex pressed his lips tight together to show her. "Quiet as a mouse, okay?"

Lilly tucked her chin down to her chest. Her blue eyes looked double their usual size as she clung to him. Lisa wished she was in his embrace herself, being held safe, but she banished the thought. Now was definitely not the time to think about why she wanted to be in Alex's arms.

He gave her a nudge with his leg and indicated with his head. Lisa followed his steel-capped gaze and found herself wriggling closer to him. She stood against him, their bodies skimming, and she had no intention of moving away.

The bear fell back to the bank, on all four legs now, and looked around. She sniffed at the air.

Lisa's heart thumped.

The bear finally turned her nose down and loped off into the forest.

"Let's go—in case she heads back this way," Alex said authoritatively.

Lisa knew not to run, she knew it instinctively, but still she moved faster than she should.

"No." Alex's voice was no more than a whisper but it held as much command as a shout.

She slowed obediently.

"We need to move fast, but carefully. When we get to the boat I need all three of you in so I can push off quickly," he said.

Lisa understood. She was just glad that today wasn't one of those days when she'd elected to head out with Lilly alone. Although she never would have taken Lilly and Boston on her own this far. They only ever pottered around the lake in the boat or strolled down the bank close to home when it was just the three of them.

They reached the boat.

"In," urged Alex.

She took Lilly from him and he threw the dog in. They sat tight together as Alex pushed them out and jumped in. He took the oars from her.

"Hold that dog," he muttered.

Oh, she was holding him all right. And Lilly. There was no chance at all she was going to let go of either of them.

Alex steered the boat toward the little jetty. He had eyed it up the other day, and realized he should have tied it there all along instead of putting it back in the shed.

A shudder hit him as he finally slowed. They could have been mauled by a bear today. Actually mauled. Or worse. Thank goodness the bear had stayed put. He didn't want to think about what could have happened out there.

He didn't want to think about being responsible for losing

someone he cared for again. For allowing another person he loved to die on his watch.

His parents had died taking him somewhere he'd begged to go. William had died protecting him. And now he'd been close to losing Lilly and Lisa because he had been less than aware of his surroundings.

Alex leaned forward to catch the side of the jetty and almost collided with Lisa. "Sorry," he said quickly.

She flushed slightly, but he noticed it. Alex tied the rope and turned back to help his passengers out. Boston first, since he was moving from paw to paw, then Lilly.

He looked at Lisa, then offered her a hand.

She took it, but not before turning a smile his way that sent a *ping* straight through his skin. There was something about her, something that made him want to touch her and look at her and talk to her. But he couldn't. He was torn between want and guilt. Every bone in his body wanted her, craved her, but it was guilt, worry, responsibility that held him back.

"Thanks for what you did back there," she said.

He didn't know what answer he could give her. He'd done nothing. Just acted like any man would have. Looked out for a woman and her child. He'd just been lucky the bear hadn't turned on them.

"It was nice knowing you were there for us," she went on.

"Just doing what I had to," he answered.

She stepped out onto the timber jetty, then turned, her hand raised to shield her eyes from the sun. "Don't think so little of yourself, Alex. Not all men can trust their instincts like that."

She walked off before he could answer, with her hips swaying and hair swishing. Maybe if they'd met under different circumstances—if he hadn't caused her husband's death—then he'd have been able to act on his feelings. Maybe if he didn't feel like he'd already caused too many people close to him to lose their lives, then perhaps he could have given in to his feelings.

But he'd never have met her if he'd hadn't been the cause of

William's death, been there by his side when he'd lain there dying. He'd never have made his way to Alaska if he hadn't been fulfilling his promise to his friend.

And what a place it was. Wilderness to satisfy even the most enthusiastic of campers or nature-watchers, and water to soothe a man's soul. Or at least he hoped that would be the case. He had his pack in the car, ready to go camping, fishing—anything so long as he was with nature. When he moved on from here, getting to know the terrain was exactly what he'd thought about doing.

"Hey, Alex?"

He looked up. Lisa was walking back toward him.

"I might take you up on that dinner offer."

A grin tugged at his lips. He couldn't help it. "Yeah?"

"Yeah." She laughed and shuffled from foot to foot. "If you like you can cook up a storm in the kitchen while I send my book off to my editor."

He shook his head, torn between laughing along with her and crying out loud like a baby. This was starting to feel too real, this thing he felt for her. Far too real. Despite his inner struggle, despite knowing it was dangerous, he wanted it all. To cook for her. To be with her. To laugh with her.

He should be packing up and moving on, not coming up with reasons to stay, to be closer to them. Trouble was, Lisa and Lilly were getting to him. They were under his skin and it was starting to feel good.

CHAPTER TEN

THE smell of food hit Lisa's nostrils and made her mouth fill with hot saliva. She hadn't realized quite how hungry she was. She penned a brief message to her editor, then hit 'send'.

Relief washed through her like a welcome drizzle of sunlight on heat-starved skin. Her brain and her creativity were zapped. Energy depleted. For now.

Lisa was grateful to have Alex downstairs. Having William home had always meant a happy, relaxed household, but he'd never cooked. Not in all their years together.

She didn't exactly know what she and Alex had. She just knew that being cooked for gave her a tingle of pleasure.

Lisa went into her bedroom and changed out of her walking clothes and into a favorite pair of jeans and a soft cashmere sweater. She eyed a pair of earrings but decided against them. Alex was cooking dinner in her own home. It wasn't like it was a date.

She squirted a spray of perfume in the air and walked through it, then decided to brush out her hair before twisting and pinning it loosely on her head.

Another waft of cooking tickled her nostrils and she followed it down the stairs. This was just too tempting.

Alex could possibly be her favorite person ever—for now.

Whoever had said that the way to a *man's* heart was through his stomach obviously hadn't met her ravenous appetite.

* * *

Alex looked up as Lisa appeared. He liked the look he found on her face. Even though she was laughing at him. Part of him had put the garment on just to see if he could make her smile.

"I see you found my apron?" she said, giggling.

He looked down and shrugged. "Seemed to fit, so I thought I would wear it."

She slipped past him and sniffed at the air. "That does smell like good lasagna."

He wasn't going to deny it. It felt good. Cooking again felt good. Being in Lisa's company felt wonderful. Just talking to another human being without having to look over his shoulder. Without having to jump at every bang. It all felt fantastic.

Without wondering if he might have fallen in love with her too.

Enjoying her company was one thing, but it couldn't be anything more. Not when it was his fault her husband had died. He had to remember that.

"Anything I can do?" she asked.

He snapped out of it.

Lisa leaned against the counter, her palms pressed flat behind her on the stainless steel. Her tummy peeked at him, her top riding up to reveal it.

"No." He said it more firmly than he'd wanted, but she didn't seem fazed.

He forced his eyes back to the oven. He stared hard at the lasagna. *No* to being attracted to her. *No* to wanting her. *No* to anything that involved her in an intimate way.

He growled. A low rumble in the back of his throat.

"Sorry?"

Alex turned. "I didn't say anything." He tried not to cringe.

She looked puzzled, but she didn't press the issue. "Wine," she announced. "I can pour wine."

She reached for the glasses—he hadn't known where to find them—and he saw a glimpse of lightly tanned skin again. This time he swallowed the groan. The growl. Not wanting her was a fight his will was struggling to push back against.

"I hope you don't mind but I found a bottle. I opened it to let it breathe," he said unevenly.

She turned that supersize grin on him again. "You *are* domesticated, soldier. Who would have thought?"

He didn't know whether to be flattered or offended. He decided to go with flattered.

Lisa twirled with the glasses and set them down. Then she held the bottle in the air, looked at the label, and poured it. "So tell me—who taught you how to make this world-famous lasagna?" She smiled as she held out the wineglass to him.

He took it. But he didn't exactly want to answer. "Just something I've learnt somewhere in my years."

She didn't need to know that he'd sought to replicate his mother's signature dish as soon as he'd been old enough to cook, or try to.

"Ah," she sighed, before sniffing delicately at the wine, swilling it and then taking a sip. "Just what I needed."

He couldn't take his eyes off her. Couldn't stop staring at her no matter how hard he tried. For once desire was overpowering his guilt. The knowledge shook him. There was obviously a first time for everything.

Alex took a sip, a much larger one than she had, then forced the glass to the counter. His fingers were in danger of crushing the stem.

"I see you managed to keep Lilly entertained." Lisa took a few steps so she could look into the lounge at her daughter.

"I guessed I was being had when she told me you *always* let her watch movies before dinner," he said ruefully.

Lisa winked at him and swilled another sip. "She's already figured that you like to say yes to her."

"I guess."

Lisa looked back and watched Lilly some more. *"Lady and the Tramp?"*

Even Alex knew it was an old movie. "She likes the greats, does she?"

He leaned on the counter—close to her, but not too close. He could smell her perfume, the light, fruity spice lifting up to fill his nostrils. She smelt divine. And his willpower was so diminished it was non-existent.

"I think it's the dogs slurping spaghetti together that gets her." She looked at him. "That was what made it my favorite movie."

Alex found it hard to swallow.

"Are you sure there's nothing I can do to help here?" she asked.

He shook his head. Firmly. "Nothing at all."

Lisa shrugged gracefully, then gave in.

What he hadn't expected was for her to wiggle up on a stool and rest her elbows on the counter to watch him.

He found it awkward. Exciting. Knowing she was sitting there behind him. He also found it unnerving. He'd never cooked for a woman before—never felt so intimate with another human being.

"You sure look good in an apron," she commented as he bent over to peek in the oven at the bubbling lasagna.

He cringed again and straightened hurriedly. Did that mean she was looking at his rear end? Now he felt really uncomfortable!

Lisa watched as Alex moved about the kitchen. If he wasn't so nervous he'd look perfectly at home there. He kept himself busy, finding ingredients and chopping.

She liked to watch a man work. Make that *loved* to. And she particularly liked to see a man in the kitchen. Or she now realized she liked it. She'd never actually had a man cook in her kitchen before.

Only problem was that she was starving. Her eyes flitted over Alex's body, up his chest and to his face. If she had a few more glasses of wine she'd be tempted to admit she was starving hungry for more than just food.

Alex cleared his throat. She made her mouth shut. Any wider open and she'd have dribbled the wine right down her front. It felt naughty. But somehow so right.

"I think we're almost ready," he said.

Lisa dropped her glass to the table, then went to retrieve his. It was almost empty. She reached for it, and the bottle. Then she went back for the salad. She attempted to steal a piece of cucumber, but her hand froze mid-move.

"Huh-hmm." The rumble of his voice made it impossible to steal anything.

She looked over her shoulder. Alex was holding the spatula at a very ominous angle.

A giggle rang out. Lilly was standing by the table, watching them.

"I didn't take you to be so protective of a salad." Lisa said the words dryly, but inside she felt weak. Not witty at all.

"Out of the kitchen, woman. Out now," Alex ordered.

He hadn't moved or changed his stance. Lilly was still in hysterics.

Lisa put her hands up in the air like a criminal caught in the act. "Okay, okay. Guilty as charged."

Having a man in her kitchen felt as intimate as having one in her bedroom. It had been her private space for so long, her domain, and yet here he was, taking charge and looking so... at home.

It scared her. And excited her.

Butterflies started to tickle their wings inside her stomach. She sincerely hoped food would appease them.

"No laughing at your mother." She gave Lilly her sternest look before falling into the seat beside her at the table. Lilly ignored her, as she'd known she would.

Alex came over with the lasagna.

"Yum!"

Lisa met Alex's gaze as Lilly banged a fork on the table in

excitement. Lisa would usually tell her off for bad manners, but tonight she was less about manners and more about living in the now.

Would this feel more like a date if Lilly wasn't here? If they weren't in the house she'd shared with William?

Resolutely, she turned her mind back to the food. She needed to focus on safe thoughts. Happy thoughts. Like eating. Like her daughter. Like the weather…

Who was she kidding? It felt like the first date of her life, even though it was neither her first, nor anything resembling a date.

"I hope it's okay." Alex drew her attention back to reality. "It's been a while since I've made it."

"It smells delicious," Lisa said with honesty. She nodded at Lilly. "And this one doesn't lie."

Alex served Lilly first, but when he went to serve her salad she shook her head. He angled his. It was like they were speaking in a secret language.

Lisa wondered for the umpteenth time what it was they had between them. And she wondered exactly what had been said that day they'd been in the boat alone, before it had capsized.

It was no surprise to Lisa that Lilly won the dinner battle.

"She does usually eat greens," explained Lisa.

The look Alex gave her said *yeah, right*, but it was true. Although there was nothing usual about tonight, so she was throwing caution to the wind. For once.

Tonight she wasn't a widow. Or anybody's wife. Tonight she was just a single mother, enjoying dinner with her daughter and a friend. That was as far as she was going to let her mind go, for now.

She passed her plate to Alex and watched as he ladled it with lashings of lasagna and a pile of salad. Her perfect meal.

Lilly was already tucking in, despite how hot it was, picking around the edges. Lisa was ready to do the same. Anything to distract her from Alex.

"Bon appétit." She raised her glass in the air.

He did the same, but they didn't clink them. Instead they watched one another. Slowly. Letting their eyes drink their fill. She didn't dare hope that he was thinking the same as her. Didn't even know what *she* was really thinking.

Lisa reached for the wine. "Another?"

"Please."

He looked away then, and it took her a long time before she could brave a look back at him.

Her toes were wriggling. Her tastebuds were alight.

"You're going to have to share the recipe for this tomato sauce with me," she said.

Alex tapped at his nose. "Family secret."

She felt the pain of that comment. That made him the last person to hold that secret. But it was the first time he'd made a joke like that. It felt as if he was, in a way, finally letting her see the true him.

"I could trade you for the secret of pink macaroons?" she offered.

He grinned at her. Really grinned. "Rosewater macaroons don't sound very manly. Besides, everyone can have your recipe. Your book'll be on the shelves when?"

"Maybe a year. Maybe longer."

He laughed. "My point exactly. You can't trade something secret for something that will be public knowledge."

"I'll have you know that my recipes are not available for *public knowledge*, Alex." She stared him down. "The privilege of that will set you back at least twenty bucks."

Lilly pushed her plate in. "Finished."

There was not a lick of pasta or sauce left.

Alex reached across the table and tickled at her hand. "Did you slip that to Boston while I wasn't looking?" he teased.

She shook her head. Her just-grown top teeth bit down on her lower lip.

"Promise?"

"Promise."

She slipped away from the table and Lisa refocused on Alex.

They sat there in silence, finishing off their meal.

"What do you say I put Lilly to bed and we go for a walk outside?" The question burst from her. It felt like a big risk, blurting that out.

Alex's eyes looked hungry. Eager. She couldn't mistake it.

"I'll clean up while you put her to bed, if you like?" he suggested.

"Deal."

Lisa didn't like the cook having to clean too, but it was only once. She didn't like putting Lilly straight to bed on a full stomach either. But sometimes rules were made to be broken.

Alex wasn't sure whether to sit, stand, or just go wait outside. The two glasses of wine had started to help, but now they were just making him even more nervous.

Of what? He wasn't sure. All he knew was that there was something about being in a space alone with Lisa that made him feel in equal parts terrified and excited. Exhilarated, almost.

He stood, awkward, in the middle of the room. He could hear her upstairs, probably saying a final good-night to Lilly.

Alex decided on the sit option. He dropped to the armchair. It wasn't as comfortable as the sofa, but it did the trick.

Then he locked eyes with William.

His whole body jerked.

The photo of William in its frame just stared at him with an empty gaze. Guilt stung his body once again, with the ferocity of a blizzard of wasps.

A noise indicated that Lisa was descending the stairs.

He closed his eyes, counted to five, then opened them, looking in the other direction. William was not going to haunt him now. Alex wasn't doing anything wrong. They'd just had dinner, they were now going for a walk, then he'd wish her good-night.

His thoughts might not be pure, but his intentions were. He knew his place, what he'd come here to do. That he had to be careful.

He *knew*.

"Hey." Lisa stood there, looking like an angel descended from heaven before him. Her hair was loose about her shoulders. All reason left his mind as blood pumped through his body.

Alex noticed her legs, slender beneath her jeans, and her arms, hugged tight by the jersey. He noticed everything about her.

He was in way over his head.

"Hey." He answered her greeting softly.

Sorry, William. He sent a silent prayer skyward. He'd dealt with guilt all his life. But now…now he just felt like a man who was attracted to a woman. Drawn to a woman like he'd never been before in his lifetime.

If he could have done it without Lisa knowing he would have turned William's picture face-down to avoid those eyes. For once he didn't know if he could control his feelings, his emotions, his desires.

The cool night air snapped at their skin. Even though it was spring, the evening temperature still fell. Lisa skimmed her hands over her arms.

They walked along the bank, where grass fell down to the water. It was magical at this time of night. The water endless, the moon shining her white light down low. Lisa always wanted to walk after dinner, but it wasn't something she liked to do alone. Wasn't something she'd ever thought she'd enjoy with a man again. Not after so many years of sharing it with her husband. Not after believing she'd never fall in love again.

With Alex, right now, it was perfect.

"Let's hope we don't come across any bears."

She laughed at Alex's joke. Sometimes he was so quiet, yet other times he made light of a situation and made her feel completely at ease. She could only imagine what he'd have been like had he not been haunted by war.

"Did you miss this while you were away?" she asked cautiously.

He slowed his walk so that he was just swinging one foot in front of the other at irregular intervals. She slowed too.

"I missed the feel of earth that wasn't sand. I missed the wave of trees, the smell of the country. The comfort of being somewhere no one wanted to take your life," he replied.

She closed her eyes. She had no idea what it would be like to be in active combat, and she didn't want to know. William had always tried to skim over it, tried to make her think it wasn't that bad, but the honesty of Alex's words was precise. Real. He was saying it like it was.

"You never did say how long you were over there?"

He didn't hesitate. "I volunteered for back-to-back tours."

She looked out toward the water. It sang to her like a lullaby. Did it have the same effect on him? "How did you do it, Alex? How did you stay over there?"

There was a raw-edged honesty to his voice. "I had nothing to come back to. Nothing to want to come home for. The army was all I ever had for years." He paused. "When my parents died there was no one to take me in. So I ended up in foster care. The army was my chance to get out. Make something of myself."

She had no idea what it would be like to be an orphan. To have no family to care for you. The thought, to her, was unconscionable.

"So why have you left the army after all these years?"

He glanced at her. "Because I couldn't do it anymore. I felt like I'd seen too much, been there too long."

Alex stepped closer to the water. Closer to its silky depths.

She watched him. The breeze sent another shiver across her goosepimpled arms.

She couldn't deny it anymore. She wanted him in her life. Wanted to reach out to him, to tell him they could have a chance together. That they had nothing to feel guilty about.

Lisa walked up behind him. She stood there, so close she

was almost touching him, before placing her hands one on each arm. They settled over his forearms—strong, muscled forearms that clenched beneath her palms. Her fingers curled slightly, applying pressure to let him know she wasn't letting go.

"Alex…" She whispered his name.

He didn't react. Didn't move. He just stayed still.

Lisa started to move her fingertips, so lightly they barely made an imprint on his skin, until he made a slow half-turn toward her.

Alex met her direct gaze with his own. His eyes engaged hers with such intensity she felt a flicker of something unknown unfurl in her belly.

"Alex." She murmured his name again, but this time her fingers traced a path up his arms.

He raised a hand to her face. Touched her with his forefinger, running it down her cheek, while his thumb nestled against her chin.

Lisa felt a quiver that ran the entire length of her body. The softness, lightness of his touch sent a tremor across the edge of her skin.

"Alex." His name was the only word she could conjure. The only word she wanted to say.

He acted this time. Didn't answer her, didn't say her name, but answered her with his body.

Alex crushed her mouth hard against his. His lips met hers with ferocity, so different from that first time their mouths had touched.

Alex's free hand moved to cup the back of her head, pulling her against him as if he couldn't fit her body tightly enough against his if he tried.

Lisa felt her way to his torso, then ran her hands up the breadth of his back, up to his shoulders and down again.

"Lisa." His eyes looked tormented, wild.

She took his hand, slowly, carefully, and turned. He resisted. For a heartbeat he resisted. Before clasping her fingers tight, interlocking his own against them.

They walked back to the house in silence. This time it was not a comfortable silence. Lisa could have cut the tension with a blunt knife it was so acute.

She didn't even know if she could be with another man. But she wanted Alex so much it hurt. He was never going to be William, but she didn't want him to be. All she knew right now was that she desired Alex. Period.

Alex wasn't sure he could do it.

Lisa reached out to touch his face, just with one finger, and he resisted the urge to pull back. To turn on the spot, flee, and never look back.

But Lisa's eyes stopped him. The soulful depths of them, the honesty and trust and worry he saw there, made him reach for her hand again. She only stopped moving to lock the door.

The click of it hit him in the spine. He was inside for the night, and he'd never felt more apprehensive in his life.

Lisa turned those eyes on him again. She was so honest he couldn't bear it. So trusting.

She was waiting for him to make a move. Waiting for him to do something to say it was all right. But he didn't know if it was right. Couldn't tell her that it was.

The only light that was on was in the kitchen. He let go of her hand and went to turn it off. Darkness set its heavy blanket over them. Only a hint of the moonlight that had guided them outside let him find his way back to her.

"Lisa." This time it was him saying her name.

He could make out the tilt of her chin even in the dark. So defiant, so brave. He also saw the light quiver that made it tremble. She was scared. Not brave. As scared as he was.

He let his lips find hers, then he kissed down her neck, deep into her collarbone. Forgot everything and just focused on her.

"Upstairs." She choked out the word at him.

It felt wrong, yet at the same time it felt so right. He stomped on his inner demons and trusted her. Trusted that they were doing the right thing.

"Upstairs," he repeated.

She obeyed.

Lisa wished she could take a tablet to quell her nerves. A lamp provided some light, but she would have preferred darkness.

She'd only been with one man before, and it had never felt like this. The quiver in her stomach was back with a vengeance, her skin felt like acid was dancing along the surface of it, burning the tiny hairs on her arms. With William it had been kind, comfortable. With Alex the intensity of her own desire frightened her.

Alex shut the bedroom door behind him.

She looked at him.

He looked back at her.

Then he crossed the room like the strong, determined soldier he was. His long legs ate up the carpet before he pressed into her and walked her two steps backward until she felt the wall touch her spine.

Alex's touch was like fire. His mouth found hers. His hands seemed to search every inch of her. He bent to trace her collarbone, her neck, like before, then nibble lower, so slowly it tormented her.

Alex dropped to his knees. He ran a hand down one of her legs before slipping her foot from her ballet flat. He did the same with the other.

His hands found a trail up her legs as he stood up slowly once more, his mouth back to press hard against hers.

"Are you sure?" He mumbled the words against her skin, his lips talking into her neck.

"Yes," she whispered, her back arched with the pleasure of his touch. *"Yes."*

There was an unspoken nervousness between them. But Lisa wanted this like she'd never wanted anything in her life before. Her skin was alive. Blood was pumping with adrenalin through her body as if she was about to plunge from a cliff for the first time.

Yes, she was sure. She wanted Alex. She could no more put a stop to it now than she could stop breathing.

Lisa didn't know if he was asleep or not. His chest was rising in a steady rhythm, and she could hear the soft whistle in and out of his breath, but she didn't know if he was asleep.

She didn't think sleep was ever going to find *her*. She was exhausted, mentally and physically, but sleep wasn't searching her out.

Lisa felt incredible. She was tired, but her senses still felt ignited. In a way she felt brand-new again. Tonight had been about being brave despite her fears, pushing through her own personal barriers and Alex's too.

Tonight she had said finally goodbye to her marriage. She kept William in a part of her heart, but accepted she could be with somebody else and not taint the memory of him. It was like she'd become a woman all over again.

She moved closer to Alex. Anything to feel his body hard against hers again, to feel the planes of his skin and muscles beneath her fingers.

"Go to sleep." He spoke without moving an inch.

So he wasn't asleep.

"Alex?"

He didn't move. But she knew he was listening.

"Good night," she murmured.

His grip on her arm tightened, ever so slightly. Lisa settled her head on his chest and closed her eyes.

She hoped he had no regrets. She didn't. And she doubted she ever would. Never in her life could she have believed that another man would touch her heart the way William had for so many years. Yet here she was, with Alex, knowing that maybe—just maybe—she had enough love, enough room in her heart and soul, for both men.

She didn't ever want to forget William. But she also didn't want to push happiness and love from her life.

Love might just have come looking for her, and admitting it made her feel a whole lot better. For the first time she didn't expect nightmares. Instead she closed her eyes with a smile on her face.

CHAPTER ELEVEN

THE smile she'd given him, the closeness of her body before she'd fallen asleep, had made Alex stiffen in alarm. Even more so than when he'd first set eyes upon her that day on the porch.

It had been dark, and he'd mostly had his eyes shut, but he had seen that look. Seen the way she'd been watching him. It wasn't right. Not with Lisa. He was meant to be giving her a hand with the cottage out of loyalty to William. What he'd done was inexcusable. Weak. Wrong.

As William Kennedy's widow, she was forbidden to him. If he didn't know better he'd think he was falling in love with her. Actually falling in love with a woman who was so very much out of bounds to him.

He should be banged head-first into a tree for even thinking it, let alone admitting it to himself. Love was not something he'd ever seen in his future. The life of a soldier's wife was no life for a woman, and now here he was thinking about absurd things like love. The only people he'd ever truly loved were his parents, and he'd determined never to feel like that again in his lifetime. Never to be in a position to feel grief.

He couldn't ignore Lisa, though, or the effect she had on him. It had kept him awake nearly all night, that smile of hers. Haunting him with its power. Teasing him with its honesty. Making him question himself.

He looked up at her bedroom, at the curtains still shutting

the early-morning light out. He should have stayed with her. Should have been there for her when she woke up. Should have nurtured her like she deserved to be the morning after making love to her.

What had he done?

His mind skipped back to the night before. He couldn't not have done it—couldn't have pushed her away.

But why?

He had resisted beautiful women before. Not often, but he had. So what was it about this one? What was it about Lisa that haunted his soul more than any horror image of what had happened at war? What was it about her that made him push the boundaries, disrespect his friend's memory, and go back on his vow to keep his heart guarded forever?

He didn't need to soul-search to locate an answer.

She was different because she was a real woman. Not just some girl he'd met on a night out. Not a girl who had the same idea in mind as him, which consisted of one word. *Fun.*

Lisa was the kind of girl most men searched for. The kind that you took home to Mom because she would please even the most demanding of parents.

Lisa was the type of woman you wanted to love. To see mothering your children. Lisa was the type of woman he'd always avoided in the past. To protect himself.

But he had no family to take her home to. He had no one. He wasn't the type of guy who deserved a girl like that. Especially not her. Not when he'd taken her husband from her, ruined her chance for a family life.

Even with William's smiling face watching him from the hall and framed in the lounge he hadn't been able to resist her. He couldn't control himself, stop himself, when it came to Lisa.

And now he felt even more guilty than before. She was not the type of girl you made love to and then left in an empty bed alone. He'd been foolish last night, and had acted like an idiot this morning.

If he'd had the courage he would have crept back up those

stairs and crawled in beside her. Pretended like he'd never been gone. Pressed his body into hers and felt the warmth of her as she woke from slumber. Held her in his arms and kissed her eyelids before they opened for the day.

But he couldn't.

She hadn't been his to begin with, and there was too much keeping them apart to pretend she was. Or ever could be.

They had no future. It was impossible.

He had to tell her the truth. That if it wasn't for him William would still be alive.

He'd slept with the wife of the man who'd saved him. What kind of thanks was that? All he'd had to do was deliver William's bag of items to her. Comfort her, perhaps, if he'd really wanted to do something helpful. But take her to bed?

That was just unforgivable.

He'd taken advantage of a widow. Of a woman he should have vowed to protect. He'd taken from her, disrespected William, and there was nothing he could do to change it.

Being here with them, being part of their lives, had drawn him in. He'd run from it his entire life and he didn't want to be part of it now. Couldn't. Not after what he'd done. Not after holding William as he died, with a bullet in his chest that had been intended for Alex.

His friend. The man who'd talked about his family, told him and everyone else who'd listen how much he loved his life and what he had back home. So how was it fair that Alex was the one here and William was buried in the ground?

He heard a noise in the house.

It was now or never.

Alex kept his eyes open to avoid the memory or war, of what had happened, and focused on the porch to keep from seeing William lying in his arms. Looking up at him that day. Talking to him with such love in his eyes despite his pain.

To stop seeing scenes of his childhood that had started playing over and over in his mind. Of his family before they'd been taken from him. Of what he might have had to come home to if they were still alive.

When Lisa appeared he was going to tell her the truth. It was what he had to do.

A smile lit Lisa's face as she walked. Last night had been incredible. Even her skin felt as if it was still alive beneath Alex's touch. There was no guilt. Or remorse. She still loved her husband, but what she felt for Alex was great. Different, but wonderful all the same.

Lisa was pleased Lilly was still asleep. It wasn't often she slept in, but this morning it was welcome. She wanted to spend some time with Alex alone before they were interrupted. Talk to him, kiss him, taste him. Reassure herself.

She scanned the living room and the kitchen but there was no sign of him. He must be outside already. She hugged the blanket tighter around her and tried to dull down her smile. Just because she was happy it didn't mean she had to go around grinning like a cat who'd caught a rabbit.

Lisa pushed open the door and stepped onto the porch. Her eyes hit his. She could tell he was watching, waiting for her. So why hadn't he just waited for her in bed?

He looked every part the soldier this morning. His eyes were steady, chin tilted, stance at ease. So different from William. More serious, more like a soldier even when he was off duty.

She noticed the change in his face, though. Recognized it from the man who'd arrived here, not the man she'd been with last night.

It worried her.

She could tell before he spoke that something was wrong. That something had changed from when she'd said good-night to him. What had happened between now and then?

"Alex, what are you doing out here?" she asked.

She slipped into a pair of flip-flops that were resting on the porch and walked the three steps down to the lawn. A touch of wet hit her toes—the ground was still damp from the night—but she barely felt it.

"Alex?"

"I haven't told you the truth." His voice was filled with grit.

She reached for his arm but he stayed still. Too still. She let her hand drop. He was pulling away from her. Emotionally, she knew that she'd lost him. That wall had gone up again. Even more so than before, if that were possible.

"There was a reason I came home and William didn't. You asked me if I saw how he died, and the answer is yes."

She wasn't sure where he was going with this, but she stayed silent. He'd already said yes when she'd asked him that question before, but there was obviously more to the story. Alex looked angry, and she didn't want to interrupt him.

"We were on a mission when he died. We'd finished. Thought it was over. But it wasn't."

She kept her eyes on his. He was hurting and all she could do was listen. His jaw was clenched so tight a stranger might guess it was wired so. A vein she'd never seen before strung a line down his neck.

"I was out in the open. William saw the enemy before I did. He called my name, distracted me, then threw himself over me." He walked backward a step but didn't break his stare. "I was meant to die that day, Lisa. They were aiming for me. He didn't have to do it—save me—but he did."

She didn't know what to say. It didn't make any difference. Not now. It didn't matter what he said. Her hands started to shake.

"He had everything to live for, Lisa. And I had nothing. It should have been me who died that day, me who came home in a body bag. Not him."

His eyes were tortured, flashing. His hurt stabbed her in the chest but she didn't let him see it. Kept it hidden, tucked away, not wanting him to see her emotion.

"If it wasn't for me your husband would still be coming

home. He'd still be alive," he reiterated, as though torturing himself with that truth.

"Alex." His name came out strangled, broken. "Alex, please..."

"Don't you see, Lisa? It's all my fault. Everything that's happened to you, what's happened to Lilly, it's *my* fault."

He punched out the words with such fury she didn't know what to do.

His words stung—not because they hurt her, but because they were so raw. Emotion cut through his body, his face, visible for all to see. Every angle, every plane of him was angry. Hurting.

A sob choked in her chest.

She had woken up this morning thinking it was the start of something fresh. That she and Alex had something special between them. Now he was ranting at her like he'd deliberately taken something precious from her, like he'd done something unforgivable. When all he'd done was be a soldier at war. A man. He'd done nothing wrong. How could he not see that?

"If you'd known this you never would have let me stay. You never would have invited me into your home."

He spat the words out and she didn't want to answer him— not when he was like this.

"If William hadn't been such a hero and I hadn't been so careless he'd be here right now. Not me."

And with that Alex spun around and started to march off.

"Don't you *dare*, Alex. You *cannot* walk away!" Her voice was tearful, but she fought to keep it strong.

He turned, his eyes wild, almost glaring at her. "Damn it, Lisa! I've wanted a family all my life. Dreamed about being brave enough to recreate what I lost as a boy."

She stared at him. Unblinking. Questions in her eyes.

"And you—you and Lilly—you've shown me that it's worth fighting for. That family does mean everything."

She nodded mutely.

"I'm sorry that I ruined your family. I am, Lisa. That's two families I've mucked up now."

"No, Alex." She glared back at him, incensed at what he was saying. "You were a boy when your parents died. A *boy*. You had nothing to do with it."

"If I hadn't asked them for an ice cream—if I hadn't begged them to take me for one—they'd still be alive. If William hadn't—"

Lisa reached for him, and this time he didn't fight her. He let himself be pulled into her arms. She held him like she would comfort a child.

"You know William would have done the same for any of his men. You *know* that, right?"

He stayed ominously still.

"You can't keep blaming yourself, Alex. You're an intelligent man. You know a child cannot take responsibility for death. For fate. Lilly wanted to go for a picnic the other day, but it wasn't her fault that we came across a bear."

Alex pulled back and watched her. She saw recognition in his eyes, but he still looked angry.

"Alex?"

He took a deep, shuddering breath.

"I understand, Alex." She kept hold of his arms. "It doesn't mean you stop hurting. It just means you need to let go of the blame you feel. The guilt. Don't let your past stop you from…"

He watched her intently.

"From a second-chance family."

He looked at her long and hard. Then he carefully detached her hands from his arms and turned around.

He started walking.

And he didn't look back.

Lisa's eyes were too filled with tears to watch where he went.

She fell down onto the porch step. Her legs folded, buckled and refused to hold her up. Her hands shook like they had received an electric current that had torn every thread of her skin. Her muscles felt weak, bones liquid.

She had gone through every emotion possible when William had died, when the messengers in uniform had knocked on her door to tell her the news in person. They'd asked her if she had someone to come and be with her, watched with doom-filled eyes as she'd dialed her sister with a shaking hand and asked her to come over.

When they'd told her, as Anna held her hand, she'd sobbed with the uselessness of the situation, knowing that he'd been dead how long—maybe hours? An entire day?—and she'd just gone about her business with no idea that her husband had been gunned down. Then she'd been angry, beaten at the sofa with all her might.

Then she'd felt relief. A sickening wash of relief that there would be no more days of worrying, of hoping he was okay. Because he'd already gone.

Up until the day Alex had arrived she had still been heaving with different emotions, feelings. She still was.

But this? This was equally bad.

Because she'd finally pushed through her sadness, her grief and her anger, and she'd been ready to start over again. Comfortable with the choice she'd made last night.

How wrong she'd been.

And now Alex was going to leave for good. She could feel it.

He was going to leave and she'd never see him again.

The man she had been slowly falling in love with was going to leave her, and there was nothing she could do about it.

A few months ago she'd felt like the black widow. As if life was over and she'd never be able to claw her way back to normality. Well, she had. She'd forced her head above water, gotten on with life despite her pain, and then found Alex on her doorstep.

The man had been a stranger to her then, but now he was real. And she wanted him to be there beside her as she started this life. She'd chosen to love Alex without guilt in her heart. But instead of returning that love he was going. Blaming himself for something he had never had the power to control. Holding on to pain from the past that she wanted to help him say goodbye to.

She loved him. If she hadn't loved him she never would have invited him into her bed last night.

Alex walked. He walked like he'd never walked before. As if there was a demon after him that wanted his life and if he stopped it would grab him by the throat.

He'd grabbed his pack from the car on the way past and it thumped rhythmically against his back now as he moved. What he needed was a night out in the open to clear his head. He couldn't care less if it was illegal to camp in the National Park. The place bordered the property, and it was surrounded by thousands of miles of forest. No one was going to bother about a single man minding his own business.

His feet pounded, ignoring the tug of roots as they tripped at his boots. The aroma of pine trees that he usually found so alluring did little to appease him. To tease the thunderous mood from him.

He'd told her the truth. The whole truth. He'd never forgive himself for what had happened that day, for not being alert enough to notice the snipers, for not screaming *no* at William as he'd moved to save him. For not acting fast enough himself and preventing the situation in the first place. Just like he'd never forgive himself for asking for ice cream that day of the crash. For putting his parents in the car that day.

Alex stopped. He stopped walking and braced one hand against a tree trunk to steady his breathing. And his mind.

It had all happened so fast. Too fast for him to do anything about it. Too fast for him to realize what was going on around him. Too fast for him to stop William from sacrificing his own life. Just like he'd been powerless as a boy.

His mind flashed to Lisa. To the torment on her face. He'd hurt her.

He should have told her right at the start. Should have explained what had happened and asked for her forgiveness that first day as they'd sat on the porch. Instead of letting things get this far before admitting his guilt. Instead of taking her to bed and letting her become intimate with the man she should be blaming for the way her life had turned out.

If he could take it back he would. If he could go back in time and take the bullets that had been destined for him he wouldn't hesitate. Not when it meant giving a woman her husband back and a child her father.

Because who would miss *him*? Who would even care that he was gone? Wasn't that why he had joined the army? Why he had always been so good at his job? Because he'd had no fear.

All his adult life he'd never had anything to live for, and it had made him fearless in the field.

Until now.

He had done his time in the army and he was finally putting that chapter of his life away. He'd never thought the day would come, but after William had died something inside him had had enough. He'd finished his tour and then asked to be relieved of his duty.

He might not have any plans, no idea of what he wanted to do yet, but it didn't involve the army. Not anymore.

The only thing he *was* sure about was that he couldn't stay here. Not now. He had to leave.

Lisa would probably have his stuff packed. She'd probably already chucked his belongings in the back of his car and was waiting to bid him farewell.

A knife stabbed at the muscles of his stomach, but he ignored it as he would a hunger pang.

Then he started marching.

The demon was after him again and he wanted to lose it.

* * *

He'd crossed the spot she'd mentioned that time they'd all been out together. Close to the neighbor's boundary. Then he'd followed the river until he'd come to a trail, and then he'd walked until he was exhausted.

He should have brought his rod with him. A man could only walk so far. Even he knew that. And yet his anger, his determination and guilt, had seen him pound out miles even he hadn't known he was capable of.

If he'd brought a line with him at least he could have eaten.

Alex guessed it to be about two o'clock. He squinted up at the sun. Yes, at least two. He fell in a messy heap to the ground and dragged his pack off his back.

He'd thrown the bag together before he'd left the mainland, thinking he'd be camping his first night out, but it still didn't hold everything he needed.

There was a box of wax matches, a few snack bars, his sleeping bag, and a tall bottle of water. He pulled off the lid and sculled a few deep mouthfuls.

It was stupid, his being out here without preparing properly first, but it wasn't as if his decision to march off into a national park had been made via logical conclusions.

He knew how to survive, could fend for himself for a decent amount of time out here if he had to, but he didn't really fancy being this far from civilization. Not at this time of year, when the bears were still hungry. Not to mention the wolves he'd heard call out in the night from the cabin.

He jumped back to his feet. What he needed was enough wood to start a fire. At least that would keep predators and any four-legged foes at bay.

Alex started to work. He scouted the site for timber, and his search didn't take him far. But he still worked up a sweat. Wet heat clung to his forehead and neck. He removed his shirt and wiped his skin, before tucking it into the back of his jeans. Then he sought out stones for the fire's perimeter, which proved harder. He marked his trail, lightly, and headed back out to the river-edge. It took him at least half an hour to walk in and out with the first load of stones, but the next two trips were shorter.

By now he'd only counted one sign of wildlife. Two elk drinking greedily from the river. They'd scarpered fast when they'd seen him.

The loud twitter of birds had built to an almost deafening crescendo. He was pleased they were only just starting to sing like that. It meant he still had time to get this fire belting out heat and a steady flame glowing before darkness fell like a consuming blanket.

He pushed away the thoughts that niggled at his mind. He might have been stupid coming, but he was here now, and if anything he could punish himself by sleeping rough for the night.

He tinkered with the fire, blowing on the dried leaves he'd built up in the centre, cupping his hands to stop the wind dispelling the lick of flame that tickled the base of the leaves.

It only took him one try to get the fire breathing back at him.

Alex reached for a second snack bar and chewed each mouthful slowly. It had to last him until morning.

He had a feeling he should rest now too. When the wolves started their nightly ritual and sang to the forest, or the rustle of animal moved between the trees, he wasn't going to get any shut-eye. Plus he wanted to keep that fire stoked all night, to make sure he didn't become part of the food chain.

Alex took the waterproof sheet from his pack and strung it between the low branches of three trees that surrounded his spot. It was close enough to the fire to allow protection and a glimmer of heat, and the way the trees met with thick brush meant his back would be partly protected.

He dragged his T-shirt back over his head as the air began to cool around him, threw another few branches on the fire and slipped into his sleeping bag.

On second thought... He unzipped the end so his feet poked

out. At least he'd be able to run quickly if something did happen. The idea of being stuck helpless inside a bag was not one he wanted to entertain.

It was dark, and still he hadn't come home. Lisa was starting to worry.

The trouble was, she didn't want to call her mother or her sister. What would she tell them? That the man she'd kept insisting was just a visitor had left, as he was entitled to, and not returned? It wasn't like she was wanting to keep tabs on him, but walking out into the forest and not coming back before dark was not something she had expected him to do. Even that angry, she hadn't expected him to do that.

Alex never would have left the rental car sitting in her drive if he wasn't coming back, and his things were still in the cabin. She didn't have to check to know that.

Right now all she cared about was seeing his large frame walk back up her lawn. Seeing his shadow move behind the blind in the cabin. Or hearing his knock at the door.

She'd locked it, for safety, but she was ready to open it if he arrived home.

Home. It was a word she knew well. But she knew the same could not be said for him. It hurt her knowing that he had no one and nowhere to call on.

This was a man who had turned up on her doorstep looking for her. A man who had seemed so traumatized that there was no hope for him. But she'd seen a transformation firsthand. Seen the change in him when Lilly started to talk to him. Felt the change in him when they were together, just like she'd felt it within herself.

As Lilly had found her words, so Alex had seemed to start finding himself. Whoever that might be. She liked him whatever way he came, because she knew that deep down he was a kind, brave, honest person. He was just hurting. And she wanted to help him.

Her heart continued its steady thump against the wall of her chest. She tried to swallow but her mouth kept drying out.

She went to check on Lilly again. Her little girl was snoring, ever so lightly. Boston raised his head, then tucked back into her.

Before William's passing Boston hadn't been allowed on the bed. Now he slept with Lilly every night. If it brought her daughter comfort she was happy to turn a blind eye to the hair he left behind.

Lisa walked to the window one last time. She pressed her forehead against the glass and conjured an image of him. Of Alex.

He was a soldier, she reminded herself. That meant he could survive.

And when was the last time a human had been taken by a bear in these parts? Plenty of people camped in the National Park.

She quickly rid her mind of thoughts of camping. The average tourist stuck to the camping grounds. They didn't just take off and set up camp wherever their feet stopped walking.

Lisa pulled her eyes away. It was so dark out she couldn't see a thing anyway. The lights on her porch didn't filter light out that far.

She went downstairs and pulled her wheat bag from the bottom drawer. She put it in the microwave to heat it.

Lisa watched as the numbers counted down from four minutes. That was as long as she'd give herself. Four full minutes until the bag was hot, then she was turning in for the night.

There was nothing she could do to help Alex except try and make him see reason when he eventually turned up again.

She was no use traipsing off into the forest with a torch. She couldn't even call the local park ranger. Their trainee had left a few months back, and the ranger who had served the area for two decades had suffered a heart attack. Right now it was just a group of townsmen who'd banded together to take turns until a replacement was found.

Her brother-in-law was one of those men. She wasn't going to wake her sister up at this time of the night.

All she could do was wait it out.

William. She called him in her mind. He would never have done anything silly like this—walking off into the forest and staying out after dark. But then William hadn't been troubled like Alex. William had been a talker. Had grown up with love and without pain.

She liked that both men were so different. It helped her to know she wasn't trying to replicate what she'd had with William.

Alex had shown her she did want to love again.

If only he'd come back and give her the chance to tell him that.

CHAPTER TWELVE

THE door to the cottage was open. Alex fought against the clench of his jaw and forced his feet up the steps. His entire being felt shattered. Exhausted. More emotionally wrung out than he'd ever been.

His back ached, his mind was drained, and all he wanted to do was have a hot shower and rid himself of any memory of the hours he'd walked or the night he'd spent sleeping rough.

He had expected a mess. He had wondered if Lisa would throw all his things in a heap or politely have them waiting for him in the car. Thought she would have become angry, furious with him for what he'd done.

He was wrong on both counts.

Lilly was sitting on his bed. So was Boston. He ignored the dirty paw marks and levelled his eyes at Lilly instead. "Hi."

She gazed up at him. He could see questions in her eyes, things she wanted to ask, but he didn't push her. He didn't want to. He didn't even think he wanted to know what the questions were.

"Alex," she answered.

He hadn't got off as easily as he'd hoped. His head ached—an insistent, dull drumming of pain that banged at his forehead. He dropped to the seat across from the bed and looked at the little girl.

The last thing he'd wanted was to get close to her. In some ways he still felt nervous about how to talk to her, what to say, what to do around her. But other times it just seemed so natural to hang out with her and help her through her not speaking. Like they were connected by what had happened. But when he looked in her eyes he still saw what she'd lost. And it hurt.

"Alex, I know you're not my daddy, but sometimes I wish you were," she said in a small voice.

His eyes snapped shut. No. No, no, *no*. This was why he couldn't be here. Shouldn't be here.

He *wasn't* her father. He could never fill that role. And here she was, saying words that she didn't understand. Not knowing what had happened over there. Why her father had died and under what circumstances.

"Lilly…" He could barely whisper her name.

"I think Boston would like you as his dad too," she continued.

Alex crushed the fingers of his left hand with his right, and tried to control the tic in his cheek and the pounding of his heart. It felt like his pulse was about to rupture from his skin.

She jumped from the bed with Boston in pursuit. "Want to come fishing?"

Alex shook his head. "Not right now, Lilly."

She shrugged and ran off.

He tried to put his mind back together, like a tricky puzzle missing some of its pieces.

A knife had just been turned in his heart, giving him a fatal blow, so how was it he was still breathing? Why was it that the idea of being a daddy to that little girl had fired something within him that he hadn't even known existed?

He heard laughter, and then muffled talking from outside. Alex rose to close the door, then lay back on the bed.

He had no idea what to do.

He'd fought getting too close to anyone, being part of a family for so long. Now he felt as though he was on a precipice, dangerously close to the edge. One wrong move and he was lost.

* * *

"Alex?" Lisa tapped at the door. Her knuckles fell softly against the timber as she called.

A noise made her step back. She didn't want to be too in his face—not after how he'd acted last night. Not when she didn't know what was happening inside his mind.

But at the same time she wanted to scream. To yell at him and tell him how worried she had been, how she'd lain awake all night and prayed that he'd survive the night and then come back to her.

The door swung open. Relief hit her in the gut and stole the breath from her lungs, left her throat dry.

He looked terrible. Like a man who'd been out on the town for nights on end. Only she knew he hadn't. The darkness under his eyes was from the never-ending cycle of guilt and anger that she was determined to dispel. Even if she hated that he'd walked away, wanted to shake him and curse at him, she still wanted to throw her arms around him and hold him tight and beg him never to leave her like that ever again.

No matter what happened between them she wanted to help him. And there was one way she could do that. Without telling him anything, without letting her emotions take hold and make her say or do something she could regret, what she needed to do was *show* him something.

"Alex, I wondered if you might come somewhere with me?"

He looked wary. She understood. He'd expected her to be angry with him, to blame him, to shout back at him, but she didn't. She'd known William too well for that. If he'd decided to put himself in the line of fire to save another man—well, that had been his choice and she admired him for it. When it was your time to go, it was your time. Alex had had nothing to do with that. Just like as a boy he'd played no part in his parents' death.

She also didn't want him to know that she'd noticed his absence while he'd spent the night camping. Noticed it as if one of her vital organs had been slipped from her body for an entire night.

He just stood, watching her still, his eyes unfocused yet looking at her.

"Please?" she said.

He shifted his weight, then went back inside. She waited. He emerged maybe four minutes later with his boots on, hair damp from the quick shower he'd managed.

"Where are we going?" Even his voice sounded husky, like he was hungover.

She smiled at him. "You'll see. Go get in the truck and I'll grab Lilly."

He waited. He let his forehead rest against the butt of his hand as he leaned on the door. It was as if all his energy had drained through his feet and left them heavy with the residue of it.

He saw movement and looked up. Lilly was holding her mother's hand as they crossed down and over to the car. She jumped up beside him and sat in the middle of the bench seat before Lisa jumped behind the wheel.

"No Boston today?" he asked, trying to make normal conversation.

Lisa shook her head. "He'll be fine here for a little while. We're not going to be that long."

He looked back out the window. He had no idea where they were going and he didn't much care. When they got back he was going to leave. He couldn't stay.

They rumbled along the road in silence. Even Lilly stayed quiet.

Alex sat there and observed. That was all he could do. There was nothing he could say, nothing he wanted to say, and Lisa had turned up the radio—presumably in an effort to avoid conversation.

They pulled up outside a nice enough single-level home. It

was set back off the road and sported a rustic feel, like most of the places they'd passed on their way here.

"We'll just be a minute," Lisa said.

Lilly reached out and skimmed her fingers against his, before smiling at him and following her mom out the door.

A lump formed in his throat but he pushed it away. He didn't want to watch them but he had to. Couldn't drag his eyes away if he tried.

He saw Lisa's sister emerge from the house. They embraced and Lisa kissed her cheek. Her sister placed her arm around Lilly and led her inside.

Lisa started to walk back to the car. He was pleased her sister hadn't acknowledged him—it was, after all, what he deserved—but then maybe she hadn't even seen him.

She got into the cab and started the engine. They pulled back out onto the road. He wanted to ask her where they were going but he didn't.

She could take him wherever she liked.

The silence in the car became knife-edged. Although she hadn't really needed confirmation to guess that he wouldn't like cemeteries.

Every time she came here she thought of the funeral service. Now she wished Alex had been there to say goodbye to William too. Maybe it would have helped him find closure.

The memory of the jolt that had run through her body when the guns were raised and fired in a final salute still hit her spine every time she visited, but it was less pronounced than it had been the day of the service.

Full military honors and nothing less, and it had been very fitting for her husband. She'd taken home the flag passed to her by his commanding officer and tucked it in a special box in Lilly's wardrobe, there for her to have when she was old enough to appreciate it. Along with his uniform.

She cut the engine and turned in her seat to face Alex.

"Come with me," she instructed.

Alex wouldn't look at her.

"Alex?"

"No." He threw the word at her.

"I need you to come with me," she said firmly. She opened her door and took a punt that he'd follow her. Eventually. She traced the path to William's headstone, standing white, tall and proud amongst many older ones.

Lisa came here every week. Every Sunday she usually came with Lilly, and they ran a rag over the stone to clean it and placed fresh flowers in the grate.

It didn't hurt her coming here—at least not the sharp pain it had been to start with. Now she just wanted to make William proud by looking after him, looking out for him even in death. To show him that she loved him still.

Lisa felt a presence behind her. She didn't turn to look. She knew Alex was there.

"William was a great man," she said, forcing her voice to cooperate. "But he had many different roles."

Alex stood still behind her. She could feel the size of him, the warmth of his body, as he stood his ground. This had to be uncomfortable for him, but she hoped he wouldn't walk away.

"William was a son, a husband, a father and a soldier. He valued each role, but his life was the life of a soldier, and we all knew and accepted that. *I* accepted that."

She studied the headstone and hoped William could hear them. He *had* been a good man. She wasn't just saying it because he wasn't around to defend himself. He'd been great at everything he'd turned his hand to, but the role he'd been most destined for had been that of a soldier. He'd been a patriot, had strongly believed in serving his country, and she had never, ever resented that. Even now that he was gone she wouldn't let herself feel that way. She'd loved that he believed in serving and protecting. Apart from missing him when he was away, he had been the husband she'd always dreamed of.

"William was a soldier because he believed in fighting for

what was right. He was the type of man who would jump into a lake to save another human even if it meant he could drown himself. And that's why he saved you that day, Alex. Because that's the type of man he was."

She turned then. Let her feet swivel until she was facing Alex.

He didn't look any better than he had earlier, but she knew he'd listened. He could look her in the eye now, and that was more than he'd been able to do earlier.

"What I'm trying to say," she said, slowly reaching her arms up until her hands rested on his shoulders, "is that he couldn't *not* have saved you. It wasn't your fault that he died. He would have saved whoever was in the line of fire, and that day it just happened to be you."

Alex looked like he was going to cry.

In all her years as a married woman she had never, ever seen a man cry. William had smiled, laughed, shown anger on the odd occasion. But not even when Lilly was born had he cried.

She pulled Alex into her arms and held him as tight as she could, as if he were Lilly and needed all the comfort in her mother's heart. Alex resisted for a heartbeat, before falling against her. Clinging to her.

He buried his face in her hair and held on to her. Hard.

"William wouldn't judge us, Alex. He wouldn't. If I thought I was disrespecting him I never would have let anything happen between us. I admit that it took me a while to feel that way, but I do honestly believe it now."

His hold didn't change. She had thought he might shed some tears, but he was holding them firmly in check. She almost wished he'd let it go. She knew that holding tears back did nothing to help. That to move on sometimes you had to let go.

Alex straightened and cleared his throat.

"I'm sorry you feel like William's death was your fault, Alex. I really am. But I don't blame you, and I never will. You need to stop blaming yourself too," she said.

She didn't wait for him to respond. Instead she turned around, closed her eyes, and whispered a silent prayer. It was the same one she said every time.

Alex still stood behind her. He hadn't moved.

"I'm going to go back to the truck now," she told him.

He nodded. "Give me a minute, okay?"

She walked one step toward him, stretched to whisper a kiss on his cheek, then left him.

This was what she'd hoped for. That she could bring him here, tell it like it was, and leave him alone to make peace with William.

She got in the car and watched him.

Alex had crouched down. His long legs buckled under him as he squatted in front of the headstone, reading the words, then he sat back on the grass.

Lisa wanted to look away, to give him privacy, but she also wanted the chance to watch him while he couldn't see her.

The night before last had been incredible. Even if he had woken up troubled about what they'd done it had been amazing. Being in Alex's arms, being caught up against his skin, had been more than she'd ever experienced. Made her realize how different he was from William and how much she appreciated that.

His touch had filled every vein within her body with fiery light, made her want to keep him in her bed and never let him out. But it had been more than just physical. For the second time in her life she had fallen in love. Truly fallen in love.

She almost felt guilty. How was it that she'd had the privilege to fall in love twice? To have two amazing men come into her life and be able to love them both? She felt incredibly lucky, so special. She'd thought it would feel wrong, that it would trouble her, but it didn't at all.

Alex fought the urge to sink to his knees. He wished the ground would open up and swallow him in William's place, but he pushed the thought away.

He needed this. He needed this so badly—to say goodbye and ask William for forgiveness.

While they had been friends in real life, after leaving the army their paths might never have crossed again. Yet now their lives had intertwined in a way that neither of them could ever have imagined.

I'm sorry, William. He closed his eyes and reached one hand out to the tombstone, the cold hitting his palm. *I wish I could make things different, but I think I've fallen for your wife.*

Alex's heart twisted at the silent confession. He still didn't want to admit it, but whenever he thought of Lisa, whenever he acknowledged what had happened between them, he knew something inside of him had changed irrevocably.

And it terrified him.

But William had loved his wife. And he'd also valued their friendship and what they'd shared throughout the years.

Deep down Alex knew what William would say in response to his confession. He'd heard the words himself as he'd listened to him gasp his final breath.

Tell Lisa I want her to be happy.

Alex knew he'd meant it, had seen it in the openness of his friend's eyes despite the pain.

If Alex truly believed he could make Lisa and Lilly happy, then William would give him his blessing.

He sighed and dropped into a crouch, sitting low to the earth once more.

Goodbye, my friend.

Alex caught Lisa's eye as he stretched to his feet.

She met his eyes through the windscreen and saw what she'd hoped to see. He smiled at her.

A tickle traced her skin like a feather. Had she finally managed to put a sledgehammer through that wall? That fierce, impenetrable depth of solid concrete that had kept his heart tucked away?

The dread that had traipsed through her like a spiky stiletto was replaced with a nerve-edged flutter of calm.

Maybe they did have a chance. Just maybe they did.

The cottage was almost finished, and the thought of him leaving early made her want to convulse in pain. Maybe getting through to him like this would make him hang around longer. Every pore in her skin longed for him to stay.

CHAPTER THIRTEEN

"COME in with me to get Lilly."

Alex didn't particularly want to go in to Anna's house, but he did.

They walked up to the front door together, side by side.

"Anna's husband is called Sam. You'll like him," she promised.

"Was he a friend of William's?" Alex asked dryly.

"His best friend."

Alex stopped. He couldn't help it.

Lisa grabbed him by the arm and tugged him. Firmly. "Come on. You've got that look about you that you had that first day on my porch. Sam's not going to bite, and neither is Anna."

He let himself be led.

He wasn't so sure she was right about her sister, though.

But Lisa had been there for him today when he'd needed her. When all he'd wanted was to run, to be alone, she had guided him from the darkness into the light.

For the first time since his parents' death he had finally let someone in.

The house was exactly as he'd expected. The hallway was slightly dim, but it led into a large living room that was filled with Alaskan sun.

"Yoo-hoo! Hello?"

No one had answered when Lisa had knocked at the front door, so they had just walked on in.

He saw Lilly first. She was sitting outside in the sun with her aunt, painting. They had a huge sheet of something, and Lilly had a paintbrush in one hand and a tube in the other.

A man he guessed was Sam sat slightly in the shade, with a bottle of beer resting on his knee.

"Want a drink?"

Alex looked over at Lisa. She had the door to the fridge open.

"Sure."

"Beer?"

He nodded.

She popped the top on two bottles and passed him one. He took a long sip before following her outside.

He had a feeling he was going to need the infusion of alcohol to make it through this afternoon.

Earlier, he had thought Lisa would be on the verge of kicking him to the curb. Now he was at her sister's place. With her. As if they'd moved on and were taking a giant step forward together.

He took another swig. Lisa had bent down to talk to Lilly, and Sam was looking at him.

He smiled. Sam smiled back before rising to his feet.

It appeared not to be a hostile situation.

The air had a faint tinge of night to it. Lisa could smell the hint of rain leaving a dampness in the air before it even fell.

"We might have to relocate inside for dinner."

Lisa watched Alex as he helped gather up some plates with Sam. It had gone down pretty well, having him here with her, even if Anna *was* a touch on the sulky side.

"Lilly." She called her daughter over. "I think it's time to go wash your hands."

Lilly bolted into the house and headed for the washroom.

Alex walked beside Lisa, juggling plates. She took some

of the load. Their eyes met, flashed at one another before she looked away.

Lisa was pleased he was enjoying himself. There had been a tension between them that she hated, and she had wanted to dispel it as fast as possible. Last night, which he'd spent goodness only knew where, had been one of the most painful, the most worrisome of her life. She liked him, had fallen for him, and she didn't want to see him hurt, alone, so lost ever again. She also didn't want him to leave. Not yet. Not until they'd figured out what was happening between them.

Anna called out to her from the kitchen. She went to investigate as Alex joined Sam back outside.

Her sister was tossing a salad.

"Want me to take care of the potatoes?" Lisa asked.

Anna nodded in their direction. "Dish—top right-hand corner."

Lisa reached into the cupboard for it and gently brought it down.

"So, you guys are out of the closet now, huh?" Anna sniped.

Lisa put the bowl down. That type of question didn't warrant an answer.

"Come on, Lisa. I can see the way you look at one another."

Her face flushed hot. She wasn't embarrassed. It was just...

"Lisa?"

She spun around and waved a spoon with all the fury she could muster. "Enough, Anna—*enough*," she snapped. "We are *not* in a relationship, but if we decide to be it won't be based on whether or not we have *your* permission. I'm sick of trying to please everyone."

Anna glared at her. Her eyes were angry, wild. Lisa had hardly ever seen her sister looking like that. Not since they'd been kids and she'd broken the head off of her Barbie doll.

"It's too soon, Lisa. William's only been—"

"I said *enough*! Don't ruin a perfectly nice evening by sticking your nose where it shouldn't be," Lisa said.

Both their heads snapped up when a deep noise rang out.

Lisa felt guilty when she saw Alex standing there. He'd cleared his throat—loudly—to alert them, but how long had he been there? How much had he heard?

She glared at Anna. Her sister just shrugged. Lisa knew what it was about. Her sister wanted her to be miserable, to stay a widow and never emerge. Well, she wasn't going to, and no one was going to tell her when it was okay to come out of mourning. No one. She wasn't trying to replace her husband. Never! But she also wasn't about to be guilted into not moving on.

"Alex, could you help me carry this out?" Lisa asked.

"Sure." He jumped to attention.

She grabbed him before he reached her, stopped him with a hand to his chest, and stood on her tiptoes to plant a smacker of a kiss on his lips.

He didn't move. The stunned look on his face was priceless.

"Thanks," she said. "Here." She passed him the dish.

Alex walked out, still in a daze.

"You'll catch a fly if you keep your mouth open like that," Lisa commented to Anna.

Her sister clamped her mouth shut and stared at her in disbelief.

Lisa just shrugged. Two could play at this game. It wasn't her style, but she was sick and tired of being the serious one, of trying to please others.

Lilly adored Alex, and so did she. Right now that was all that mattered.

Alex still couldn't quite shake off the memory of that quick kiss. Even now, after dinner.

He sat with Sam while the girls nattered. He hadn't missed the tension between the sisters earlier, but they'd obviously pushed past it. Or they were just ignoring it for now and leaving the arguing until later. In private.

"Did you serve with William for long?"

Alex turned back to Sam. He had completely lost the focus of their conversation. He angled himself so he couldn't look at Lisa in order to give Sam his full attention.

Not that he particularly wanted to talk about William right now, but it would be rude not to reply.

He thought about the cemetery again, and calm passed over him. If Lisa could forgive him, then he owed it to himself to do the same.

For some reason hearing Lisa say William's name held less punch. Perhaps because she talked about him fondly, but with finality. Everyone else seemed to talk about him like he was still going to walk back in the door.

"We served together a few times, but this last time we were in the same unit permanently for around two months—maybe longer." He didn't say it, but it would have been much longer than that if they'd both served out the full tour.

Their friendship had been the kind that could only be formed by trusting another person so much it was as if they were a part of you. Knowing how they reacted, how they moved. He and William had been like that.

Sam nodded and held up another beer. Alex shook his head and motioned toward Lisa. "I think I'll drive. She's had a couple."

Sam opened one for himself and sat back. "William and I went way back. We both started dating the girls our last year of senior high."

Alex had guessed they'd been friends a long time.

"I can see why William liked you," Sam added.

"Yeah?"

Sam grinned at him. "Lisa obviously doesn't mind you either."

Alex felt uncomfortable. Was he joking for real, trying to hint at something, or saying it was okay?

"Sam, I—"

The other guy held up the hand that gripped his beer. "What you and Lisa do is your own business. I'm not part of the gossip brigade."

"Your wife sure doesn't seem happy about it," Alex pointed out.

He watched as Sam smiled over at his wife. Lisa looked their way too. It was as if the girls knew they were being talked about.

"Lisa's her little sister. Anna's just looking out for her."

"What about the rest of Brownswood?" Alex said ruefully.

Sam shrugged. "Small-town life is what it is. It's whether you care about the talk that matters." He looked hard at Alex. "And I don't take you for the type to care what strangers think."

"Guess you're right."

His attention was back on Lisa. She had risen, and was rubbing at her arms like she was cold. He ached to go to her and warm her, put his arms around her, but he didn't want to do anything that might upset her sister. Not if it would upset Lisa too. He didn't know if she would be okay with it.

He had expected tonight, this afternoon, to be dreadful. Expected to be judged, to find Sam hostile, but it had been half good. Better than. It had been nice to have a beer with another guy—one who didn't want to interrogate him about war—and just behave like a regular citizen.

But then if the guy had been one of William's best buddies he probably knew enough about war to have already satisfied any curiosity he might have had.

It just felt good to feel normal. Something he hadn't felt in a long time.

Alex drove home. Lisa and Lilly were tucked up close to one another across from him, and he navigated through the steady path of rain that was falling on the road. He was pleased he'd refused a third beer. The road was slippery and he wouldn't have liked Lisa to be driving.

"You were right about the rain."

Lisa just smiled.

"Your sister was—"

"Wrong." She cut him off. "My sister was wrong."

He smiled. Was she just being stubborn because she didn't like her sister telling her what to do?

"We don't often argue, but tonight she was most definitely wrong."

"Who was wrong, Mommy?" Lilly asked sleepily.

Alex shook his head at Lisa. He wasn't going to tell if she wasn't.

"No one, honey. Alex and I are just being silly."

He pulled up outside the house and scooped Lilly up to ferry her inside. The rain was coming down hard now, trickling down his neck and wetting his hair. He managed to keep Lilly mostly dry.

Whining echoed on the other side of the door and Lilly called out. "Boston! We're home!"

Lisa emerged next to them. Wet.

She thrust the key into the lock and turned the handle. Lilly disappeared with her dog.

"To bed, young lady!" Lisa called after her. Then she turned to face Alex, pulling the door shut behind her.

The look on her face was…open.

"Do you mind telling me what that stunt in the kitchen was about?" he asked.

She grinned. "Proving to my sister that she was wrong."

"And that's all it was?" he wanted to know.

Her eyes glinted at him. "Maybe."

He shuffled forward so he was only a foot away from her. He absorbed the sight of her wet hair, just damp enough to cling to her head, the lashes that were coated with a light sting of rain. Then his eyes dropped to her lips.

She parted them. Her eyes lifted to look into his.

"We have everything stacked against us, Lisa. Everything," he warned. Then he bent slightly, so their lips could touch. Just.

Lisa let her body fall against his.

"Not everything, Alex." She sighed into his mouth as she said the words.

He tried to pull back, but couldn't. She rubbed her lips over his, teasing him, pulling him in deeper than he had intended going.

"I just don't want you to feel guilty about this later. About *me*," he insisted.

She disagreed. "We are both grown, consenting adults."

"It's not enough," he argued. He wanted to resist. He really, badly, desperately wanted to resist. But this was Lisa. This was the woman who had already forgiven him his sins and still wanted him.

It was Lisa who pulled back this time. "It's enough because there is no one judging us—no one that matters." She looked up at him. "Lilly is the most important thing in my life, and she accepts you. William would have accepted you. And in my heart I know we're not doing anything wrong."

He nodded. He knew it was the truth, but he had needed to hear it from her.

"And your family?" he asked.

"My family only want to protect me. Don't want to see me hurt. It's not that they don't like you," she insisted.

They looked at one another.

"You're not going to leave, are you, Alex? Not yet?"

He shook his head. "No."

"You're not just staying because of Lilly, though, are you? You don't have to worry about hurting my feelings, and I can comfort her—honestly. You shouldn't feel like you're trapped here," she said.

What? He traced a tender finger from the edge of her mouth down to the top of her collarbone. *Never.*

"I'm not just staying because of Lilly," he said gruffly.

"But…"

He shook his head. He felt the sadness of his smile and forced it to lift. "I shouldn't be here at all, Lisa. But I'm here because of you."

She leaned heavily against him. He felt her relief.

His mind started to play tricks on him again. A cloud of doubt hovered over his brain. "Do you only want me here because of Lilly? Because I helped her?"

She shook her head. Vigorously. "No."

Relief emptied his clouds of worry.

"I trust you, so trust me," he said.

"We're going to the Kennedys' place for dinner tomorrow night," she mumbled into his chest, not looking at him.

He gulped. Please, no… That was too much.

She looked back up at him and gave him the sweetest of smiles.

"Time for bed, Alex." She gave him a brief kiss on the lips—nothing like before.

He still stood there, stunned at hearing they were going to William's parents' house.

"Do it for me, Alex. It's just dinner."

He kept his eyes on her as she swept inside and closed the door on him. He heard the lock twist. She was punishing him still, he realized. She'd forgiven him—she'd shown him that today—but was still punishing him for running out on her after making love to her, and then spending the night in the forest by himself.

He was just coming to terms with what he'd done, and now he had to face William's parents. Great. His boots felt like they were filled with the heaviest of cement. Eating a meal with the parents of the man who'd died saving him wasn't exactly his idea of fun. But if he was going to try to move on, to open himself up, then maybe it was something he had to do.

The cottage loomed in front of him. He wished he was up in Lisa's bed with her, instead of trudging in the rain to the cabin.

Lying there in her bed, stretched out on her soft sheets, waiting for her to join him.

But he wasn't going there. Not yet anyway. He needed time to think.

Especially about tomorrow night's dinner.

Besides, Lisa had already locked the door on him.

Seeing William's gravestone today had helped him. But seeing William's parents and answering any questions they might have? Well, that was something else entirely.

He hoped he was up for it.

CHAPTER FOURTEEN

"I UNDERSTAND your loss."

He watched the looks cross George and Sally's faces and knew what they were thinking. It was what he'd thought every time someone had said those words to him.

"My parents died when I was eleven years old. We were driving home from an ice cream parlour and a car went through an intersection. They were killed instantly," he told them.

He didn't look at Lisa while he said it. Couldn't.

Almost worse than the sadness of losing his parents had been the pity. That was why he usually kept it to himself. But somehow tonight, sitting with these people, he needed to say it.

Alex looked at William's parents. He didn't see pity there. Instead he saw understanding.

Lisa reached for his hand beneath the table. He was relieved to feel her touch, but he knew he was strong enough to continue. He knew Lisa accepted him for who he was, understood that now, but being here meant a lot to him. It was the final missing piece of the puzzle to allow him to move on and stop looking back to his past.

"Do you have any other family?"

He shook his head at Sally's question.

"I went into foster care, then I joined the army as soon as I was of age."

* * *

Lisa couldn't believe he'd opened up like that.

The connection he had with Lilly was very real, and hearing his story, the full version of it, made her realize why.

Alex knew pain and loss more than anyone.

All of her own life she had felt so loved, so nurtured. As a married woman she had again known love, of a different kind, and then with Lilly she'd known she'd never be alone again.

But Alex—he was trying to start over, to put past demons behind him, and she wanted so badly to be there for him.

Lilly burst into the room then. The smile lighting her face was infectious.

"Hello, darling." Sally smiled at her granddaughter.

Lisa held her breath. The expression on her daughter's face had taken her by surprise.

Lilly looked at Alex. He moved his head, only just, but Lisa didn't miss it. Lilly smiled up at him.

"May I have dessert, Grandma?"

Lisa suppressed a squeal of delight. Sally had tears in her eyes, but—bless her soul—she just got up as if nothing was out of the ordinary.

"How does ice cream with chocolate sauce sound?" Sally asked.

Lilly giggled and sidled up to her, before winking at Alex.

Sally stopped as she passed Alex and let her hand rest on his shoulder. "Thank you, Alex. You've done her the world of good."

Alex smiled back.

He had brought light back into their lives like only William had done in the past. He had filled Lisa's world with hope for the future, had helped Lilly to find her voice again, and brought comfort to William's parents. Sharing stories. Telling them how highly their son had been respected by his men.

"Lisa, do you mind if I steal Alex away for a single malt Scotch?" George asked.

She emerged from her daydream and nodded. William had

always joined his father for a Scotch after dinner, so it was nice that Alex could share in that for one night.

"I'll join the girls in the kitchen," she said.

She rounded the corner and found her mother-in-law and daughter curled in front of the fire in the lounge. She stopped to listen to them talk.

It was like Lilly had never lost her voice.

The therapist had said this might happen. That one day she could just start talking again to everyone around her.

She'd seen the look Alex had given her daughter, though. Seen Lilly looking to him for guidance. Whatever he'd said, whatever they'd talked about earlier, it had obviously worked.

There was nothing about this situation that seemed entirely comfortable to Alex.

He didn't think he'd ever pass the buck on the guilt that still kept him awake at night sometimes, but at least this family had found comfort in his being here.

"Son, it doesn't take a genius to figure out you're troubled," George said.

Alex took the just-warm Scotch thrown over a handful of ice. He raised his glass, a brief advance in the air, as George did the same. It tore a fiery path down his throat that didn't disappear until it reached his stomach.

"Lisa and Lilly are the only family we have," the other man went on.

Alex understood how protective George must feel over them, but he'd made peace with Lisa, been accepted, and that was what he had to hold true to.

"I'm sorry that I couldn't help bring your son back alive. As God is my witness, I'd have traded places with him in an instant. But if Lisa wants me here I'm not going to turn my back on her," he said.

George sat back in his chair. "I'm not here to lecture you, Alex. You've brought happiness with you that some of us thought was lost forever. I want to thank you."

Alex sipped at his drink. He didn't know what to say.

"If you want to be in Lisa's life, in Lilly's life, we say welcome to the family."

Alex's palm was filled with George's. With the hand of William's father. He'd thought it would seem wrong, would fly in the face of the guilt that had tormented him these past few months, but it didn't.

Warmth spread through his fingers, and it didn't stop there. It traveled up his arm. Shook his shoulders. Hit him in the head.

For the first time since the night his parents had died Alex felt a burning ball form in his throat. Tears bristled behind his eyes.

He couldn't have answered if he'd wanted to.

Not without letting another grown man see him cry.

"I'd like to hear some stories when you're ready. Hear more about William. About what you went through over there."

Alex jumped to his feet, glass snatched firmly between his fingers. He swallowed the lump and turned his head at an angle.

He couldn't see anything out the window except blackness. Nothingness. It suited him just fine.

Tears stung his skin as they hit. He sniffed. Hard. Then wiped at his face. He swilled the last of his Scotch, then slung it back.

It burnt, but not as badly as his tears.

Alex wiped at his face once more and forced them back.

He felt lighter. The guilt that had sucked him dry was now turning to liquid and hydrating him once more. He was powerless to stop feeling as if everything had been lifted from his chest, the pressure finally gone.

"William took a bullet for me, George. I'll forever be grateful for that."

Alex closed his eyes as memories played back through his mind. For the first time in a long while he wanted to talk about the friend he'd lost. About how much those wartime friendships had meant to him, and how he'd never give up those memories even if he could. It was time.

Lisa pulled the covers tight up to her chin and tried to shut her mind off.

Tonight had gone better than she'd thought it would. Much better.

Sally and George's blessing meant a lot to her, but it went deeper than that. The change in Lilly was extraordinary. Exciting. But it worried her. The therapist's words kept echoing in her head. What if Alex *did* leave and she became worse than before? The thought sent a crawl of dread through her body. They'd only agreed on a few weeks. But now he had said he'd stay longer.

Something in Alex had changed tonight too. And it wasn't just meeting William's parents that had affected him. She didn't know what. Couldn't pinpoint what it was. But there was a change deep in his soul even more than the difference she'd seen in him after they'd visited the grave.

It wasn't that she only wanted him around for Lilly's sake. Far from it. What she wanted was a chance to make a relationship work with him. A chance to see if they could be together, without William or anything else hanging above them and ruining it before they even started. Without second-guessing themselves.

But it wasn't going to happen. She wouldn't be surprised to wake up in the morning and find him gone.

And it wouldn't just be Lilly hurting if he upped and left. Lisa cared for him. Deeply.

She didn't let her thoughts go any further. Couldn't. Because if she did she'd start wondering if she was in love with him again.

Lisa heard a noise. A creak. She sat bolt upright in bed. Her back so straight it could have snapped.

There was someone in the house.

She crept with stealth from her bed and grabbed the baseball bat tucked in the wardrobe. She glanced out the window. Alex still had his light on. He was awake. She could call to him for help if she needed to.

Lisa moved on tiptoes out into the hall. Her ears strained in the stark silence. The noise below cut a just audible snap through the air.

She moved quietly down the stairs, conscious of the treads to avoid from years of not wanting to wake Lilly when she was young.

A shadow loomed.

"Lisa?"

Her heart fell in a liquid heap to the floor.

"Alex!" She dropped the bat, relieved beyond all measure. "What are you doing in here?"

He didn't answer her.

She could just make him out in the half-light. He had pajama bottoms on. They were slung low, the drawstring tied in a knot.

He walked toward her. His big frame purposeful, determined. Angry?

"Alex?"

He didn't stop. But he did act.

His hand cupped behind her head. His palm filled with her hair. She heard the gasp as it fell from her mouth, but she was powerless to stop it.

Alex's lips found hers before she could even catch her breath. He took her mouth, crushed it into his own, and pulled her hard against his chest.

Her hands found his shoulders, his back, clawed at him to get her body closer to his.

"Alex…" She whispered his name against his skin as he pulled away.

He took one hand from her head and tucked it under her chin. Made her eyes meet his. The other hand was pressed into her lower back, keeping her immobile, forcing her to stay still.

But she didn't need any chains. There was no way her body would move even if her mind told it to.

"I'm sorry."

She opened her mouth to answer, but he pressed his index finger across it to silence her.

"I'm sorry, Lisa. I know now there's nothing I could have done to stop William saving me."

She nodded. His fingers still fell like a clamp across her mouth. He had finally stopped blaming himself. Had released himself. That was the change she'd noticed. His battle with himself over taking this huge step forward was finally done.

"Can we start over?" he asked.

She shook her head.

Confusion made his face crease and gave her the chance to escape him. Just.

"I don't want to start over."

He frowned. His eyes lost the glow they had been casting. His hand fell from her back.

She reached for it and put it in place again. Pulled him against her and let her mouth hover back over his.

"I don't want to start over, Alex. I like you just the way you are."

A smile spread across his face, but she didn't wait to receive it. She caught his bottom lip between both of hers and kissed him, her skin skimming his. She wrapped her arms around him, feeling his muscles, loving the masculinity of his big frame.

Alex scooped her up into his arms, and only then did she let her lips fall from his. She tucked her head against his chest and let herself be carried upstairs to the bedroom.

She had loved William. Wholeheartedly. As much as a wife could love her husband. And now she felt a different but just as powerful surge of love deep within her for Alex. Like her heart had been refilled and she had been given the chance to love all over again. Given the privilege to bask in the glow of another man's feelings toward her without having to give up loving her husband.

Alex looked down at her. He stopped halfway up the stairs.

He kissed her nose, her mouth, then her eyelids as they fluttered shut.

"I love you, Lisa. I love you. *I love you.*"

She tucked tight in against him as he started to walk back up the stairs.

"I love you too," she whispered.

From the thudding of his heart against her ear she could tell he'd heard her.

Lisa woke to light heating her face. She let her eyes pop open, then threw her hand over her eyes. Had she forgotten to close the curtains last night?

She sat up. Last night.

She didn't need to look beside her to know she was in bed alone. There was no weight causing a sag in the mattress. No one's arm had been slung across her when she'd woken. She was alone.

Nausea beat like a drum in her stomach. She reached for her nightdress, discarded on the floor, and wriggled into it before standing. She forced herself to walk to the window.

Had he gone?

She wished upon wishing that he hadn't. But for what other reason would he have disappeared before she woke?

Lisa closed her eyes and felt for the windowframe. She held on to the timber, counted to three, then looked. She didn't know what to expect, but she didn't expect to see Alex.

She placed a hand on the window, the glass cooling her palm and calming her mind.

He was there. With Lilly.

They sat cross-legged on the lawn. They were talking. It looked serious.

Please. *Please.* Don't be telling her that you're going.

She forced herself away from the window and fumbled for

her dressing gown in the wardrobe. She tugged it on and ran fast down the stairs. Her toe caught, but she fought the pain.

He couldn't be leaving.

"Al…" His name died on her lips.

Lilly had run off to chase Boston. She had bare feet and her hair was sticking out around her head, fresh from bed.

"Is she okay?" she gasped.

"She's fine." He got up. A smile tickled the corners of his mouth.

Lisa's own mouth went dry. He was smiling. That was a good thing, right? He walked toward her. She had a flashback to the night before. When he'd stalked her in the same way.

He caught her in his arms and tugged her forward. She resisted. Or tried to.

"Lilly…?"

"Is fine," he said, dropping a kiss to her nose before moving down to her mouth.

Lisa wriggled in protest.

Alex sighed. "I was just telling her something. Something I wanted her to know first."

Lisa tried to pull away from him again, but he held her tight. She was powerless. As good as an insect caught into a spider's web.

"Don't you want to know what I told her?" Alex asked.

She stopped wriggling.

He leaned back, his upper body giving her room but his lower body holding her in place.

She nodded. She wanted to know. Badly.

"You do?" he pressed.

"Yes." She wished her voice wouldn't give out on her in times of need. It sounded no better than a frog's croak.

"I told her," he said, brushing the hair from her cheek, "that I was going to ask her mommy to marry me. I had to check she was okay with that first, before I did it."

Lisa stared at him. *Marry her?* So he *wasn't* leaving?

"I thought you were going. That you were leaving. That you were telling her…"

Alex stopped her. Covered her mouth with his and kissed the words from her.

"Did you not hear what I told you last night?" he said, when he'd kissed her into stunned silence.

She stared at him. She remembered plenty about last night.

He caught her in his arms, lifting her from her feet and tucking him against her just like he had the night before. "I love you, Lisa." He dropped a kiss on her forehead. "If you'll have me, I want to stay. I'm not going to run. Not now. Not ever. You've taught me that. Made me realize I need to believe in family, in love, in myself again."

She closed her eyes and burrowed into him. Smelt the tangy aftershave that had taunted her from day one. Touched the biceps that had called to her from the first time she'd seen him shirtless. Pulled at the base of his neck to steal a kiss from pillowy lips that had begged to be touching hers from the moment she'd started falling for him.

"So you want to marry me?" She breathed the words against his cheek.

"I thought I was the one who was supposed to ask the question?"

She laughed. A head thrown back, deep in the belly laugh.

"Well, hurry up and ask me so I can say yes," she teased.

He didn't put her down. Just kept her folded in his arms, holding her like he'd never let her go.

A little voice squeaked from behind them.

"Mommy?"

Lisa let Alex swing her around to her daughter. She couldn't wipe the smile off her face if she'd tried.

"Did you say yes?"

Lisa didn't say anything.

He hadn't officially asked her, but of course she would say

yes. How could she not? She loved Alex. As much as she'd loved Lilly's father. So much.

Alex dropped to one knee. He took Lisa's hand.

"I think it's time to make this official. Lisa, will you please put me out of my misery and say you'll marry me?"

"Yes, Mommy. Say yes!" Lilly squealed.

"Yes," whispered Lisa.

Alex stood to wipe away her tears.

"I love you girls, you know?"

"We know," chirped Lilly.

Yes, we know, thought Lisa. And we love you too.

Earlier this year—weeks ago, even—she'd thought her heart would never open to another human being. Hadn't ever wanted it to.

But now she knew otherwise. She loved Alex now, and she'd loved William then—and still did. But her love for William was in the past: a loving, vivid memory to hold on to.

Alex was now.

Alex was her future.

EPILOGUE

ALEX ran his fingers over the emblem lying flat over his chest. The khaki shirt felt nice against his skin. Felt right.

Two months ago he'd been lost. A man without a path. Without a destiny.

Now he was happy. He had a future, and he no longer lay awake at night in a sweat with the world at play on his shoulders.

He tugged on his boots and grabbed the paper bag resting on the counter. He took a peek inside. And smiled. Neatly wrapped sandwiches, a token piece of fruit, and two big slices of cake.

It didn't matter how hard he tried to suppress it, the grin tugging at the corners of his mouth couldn't be stopped.

Alex walked out onto the porch. The lake's water shone in the early-morning light; the trees were waving shadows around the far perimeter. He stood there and looked.

When he was serving, even before that in foster care, he'd never dared to imagine a life like this. A life where everything was possible. Where he had a chance to make his own family, where a woman loved him, and where he could be part of nature every single day.

He walked across the front yard, jingling his keys.

A tap made him look up.

Lisa stood in the window, her hair like a halo framing her face. Lilly was standing in front of her.

His two girls. His two beautiful girls.

He raised a hand and then blew them a slow kiss. His lips brushed his hand before he released it to wave softly up to them.

Lisa pretended to catch it while Lilly giggled. That infectious bubble of laughter that she was so prone to throwing his way.

Alex turned, his hand going up behind him in the air as a final goodbye for the day. He heard the flutter of the flag as it waved proudly in the wind. He didn't have to turn to know it was looking down on him. The same flag that he'd tucked in his bag when he'd first joined the army. It had seen him safely through plenty of hard times, and now it was flying high in the air as a tribute to the friend he'd lost during wartime. A symbol, an ode to William and to how they'd fought over there in the desert. He wanted to show William that he'd take care of Lisa and Lilly until the day he died—just like William had looked out for him at the end.

Alex unlocked the truck and jumped in the cab. Something gave him a feeling that the other National Park ranger would give him a rough time about driving a baby-blue Chevy, but he didn't care.

The rumble of the engine signaled he was on his way.

National Park ranger by day, husband and daddy by night.

Somehow life had finally given him a hand of cards he wanted to play.

He turned up the radio and sang along to the country and western channel Lisa had it permanently dialed to.

He would have preferred rock and roll, but if Lisa wanted country he didn't mind one bit.

MILLS & BOON®

Why shop at millsandboon.co.uk?

Each year, thousands of romance readers find their perfect read at millsandboon.co.uk. That's because we're passionate about bringing you the very best romantic fiction. Here are some of the advantages of shopping at www.millsandboon.co.uk:

* **Get new books first**—you'll be able to buy your favourite books one month before they hit the shops

* **Get exclusive discounts**—you'll also be able to buy our specially created monthly collections, with up to 50% off the RRP

* **Find your favourite authors**—latest news, interviews and new releases for all your favourite authors and series on our website, plus ideas for what to try next

* **Join in**—once you've bought your favourite books, don't forget to register with us to rate, review and join in the discussions

Visit **www.millsandboon.co.uk**
for all this and more today!

MILLS & BOON®
By Request

RELIVE THE ROMANCE WITH THE BEST OF THE BEST

A sneak peek at next month's titles...

In stores from 7th April 2016:

- **His Most Exquisite Conquest** – Elizabeth Power, Cathy Williams & Robyn Donald

- **Stop The Wedding!** – Lori Wilde

In stores from 21st April 2016:

- **Bedded by the Boss** – Jennifer Lewis, Yvonne Lindsay & Joan Hohl

- **Love Story Next Door!** – Rebecca Winters, Barbara Wallace & Soraya Lane

---

Available at WHSmith, Tesco, Asda, Eason, Amazon and Apple

Just can't wait?
Buy our books online a month before they hit the shops!
visit www.millsandboon.co.uk

These books are also available in eBook format!